THE
DESIGNER

ALSO BY MARIUS GABRIEL

Wish Me Luck As You Wave Me Goodbye
Take Me To Your Heart Again
The Original Sin
The Mask of Time
A House of Many Rooms
The Seventh Moon

THE
DESIGNER

MARIUS
GABRIEL

LAKE UNION
PUBLISHING

Text copyright © 2017 by Marius Gabriel
All rights reserved.

Published by Lake Union Publishing, Seattle

www.apub.com

Amazon, the Amazon logo, and Lake Union Publishing are trademarks of Amazon.com, Inc., or its affiliates.

ISBN-13: 9781612185811
ISBN-10: 1612185819

Cover design by Debbie Clement

Cover photography by Barnaby Newton

Printed in the United States of America

For Mervat

One

Copper had only been married for eighteen months and did not consider herself an expert on marital relationships. But she fancied she knew when a marriage was in trouble. And she was pretty sure her own was.

As she listened to her husband interview the French partisan, she reflected on the advice she'd gleaned from the women's magazines that were, in the absence of a mother or available friends, her source of wisdom. She didn't 'nag, pester or complain'. She certainly didn't 'constantly demand new dresses', yet she successfully avoided 'looking slovenly and unkempt'. As for not dishing up 'unappetising meals, served on unclean crockery and stained linen', she did her best, given the constraints of wartime Paris.

But refraining from all those sins didn't mean she knew where her husband had been until two a.m. that morning, or whose lipstick was smeared on his uniform collar, or why he had taken to treating her like part of the furniture.

'Is there anything to eat?' Amory Heathcote asked, tossing her a sheet of scribbles. As his assistant, it was her job to type up his shorthand notes so they could be sent back to the States by the news service. As his wife, she also provided a moveable household, surrounding Amory with comforts, catering to his needs and insulating him from life's discomforts as far as possible.

'There's wine, bread and cheese.'

Her husband looked displeased. 'Nothing else?'

'I'll ask the landlady.' The citizens of newly liberated Paris were touchingly generous with gifts to Americans, but since the French themselves were half-starved, provisions were not easy to come by.

She went to see the landlady and returned with a prize of half a French sausage and four boiled eggs. Amory and Francois Giroux were smoking on the tiny terrace overlooking the rue de Rivoli, which still bore scars from the street battles of the recent Paris uprising. They were watching an American patrol of four soldiers flirting with a group of French girls, whose laughter floated up from the street.

'You know what we call your GIs?' Giroux said. 'We call them chewing-gum soldiers.'

'That doesn't sound very grateful,' Copper said.

Giroux scowled at the scene below. 'They swagger around Paris, handing out candy bars. We're not children.'

'They're just trying to be kind.'

'I am a Frenchman and a communist, Madame. I prefer to be under nobody's boot, German or American.'

'I wonder if you'll ever forgive us for liberating you?' Copper said. French pride, after years of humiliation and misery under the Nazi Occupation, was like a hedgehog: prickly on the outside and sensitive underneath.

'Our streets used to be full of field grey. Now they are full of khaki.' Giroux had been regaling them for the past hour with stories – some taller than others – of the heroic part he had played in the Liberation of Paris. Sensing that their interest in him was waning, he said, 'Maybe you would like to see something remarkable this afternoon?'

'Remarkable in what way?' Amory asked.

Giroux pinched out the Camel he'd been smoking. 'The collaborators think they can hide from us, but we know where they are. We find the traitors, one by one, and we deliver justice.'

'The *épuration sauvage*?'

'That's what we call it. We will punish someone today.'

Amory pricked up his ears. 'Sure,' he said. 'I'd like to see that. We'll wait for Fritchley-Bound. He'll want to come along.' He turned to Copper. 'Where is he?'

'Where do you think?' she replied.

With the Liberation of the city from the Germans, an almighty party had started, and George Fritchley-Bound, otherwise known as the Frightful Bounder, had never been able to resist a party. He was a British journalist who had attached himself to them some weeks earlier. An Old Etonian, he was more or less constantly drunk, but they had grown fond of him.

The Frightful Bounder had yet to return by the time the meal was laid out, so they started without him. The bread was stonier than the saucisson, and the wine was stonier than that, but they were all hungry.

'Who is this traitor?' Amory asked Giroux.

Giroux sawed at the saucisson with his clasp knife. 'Someone who did great harm to France,' he replied grimly. 'You will see.'

'Will they kill him?'

'Maybe.'

Copper winced. They had already seen so many horrors left by the Allied invasion – a vast wave of men and machinery rolling across Europe towards Berlin. Paris was still bobbing in its wake.

Amory was seemingly unmoved by the horribly maimed, the newly dead. But then, Amory was a war correspondent, hardened to such things. And, though she loved him, he was the coldest man she knew.

Five minutes later, the Frightful Bounder arrived. However, his reappearance was more in body than in spirit, as he was carried in, dead drunk, by two GIs.

'Nice guy for a Limey,' one of them panted (Fritchley-Bound was a large man, and there were several flights of stairs up to the apartment). 'But he doesn't know when to quit. Where d'you want him?'

They took Fritchley-Bound from his drinking companions and dumped him on his bed. From past experience, Copper turned him on his side and put a chamber pot where he could reach it. Unexpectedly, Fritchley-Bound opened one bloodshot eye and peered at them. 'Have I disgraced myself?'

'No more than usual,' Amory replied. 'But you're missing an opportunity. Giroux's taking us to see the Resistance dish out frontier justice.'

'Bugger. The rag would love that.' He tried to sit up, then clutched at his chest. His face, a crimson leather mask, turned white. They had to grab him to stop him from sliding to the floor. He looked up pleadingly at Copper. 'Copper, old thing.'

'No, George. I don't want to see anybody killed.'

'Please. Do it for me.'

'I won't.'

'Could be the making of old George. Double spread. Happy editor. Save career.' He clutched at her arm. 'Camera in the wardrobe over there. Should be few shots left on roll.'

'Damn it, George,' she said angrily. 'You can't keep doing this.'

He waved a large, limp hand – either to concede that she was right, or to brush away her protest, she couldn't tell which – and slumped back, his face corpse-like.

Amory raised an eyebrow at her. 'The dying man's last wish. Are you going to refuse?'

'For two cents, I would.' Copper stamped to the wardrobe. 'I'm not reloading the camera. If the film's all used up, that's it.' She examined the back of the battered Rolleiflex (ironically, Fritchley-Bound insisted on sticking to his pre-war German camera). There were half a dozen frames left. 'Damn!'

'You can stay home if you want,' Amory said.

Fritchley-Bound snorted into wakefulness. 'No, don't. Brave girl. Salvation of old Frightful Bounder. Eternally grateful.'

'How many times does this make?' she demanded, shouldering the camera. 'You all make a convenience of me. I'm sick of it. Come on. Let's go.'

She couldn't count the times she'd stood in for Fritchley-Bound because he'd been too drunk to work. She'd taken his pictures, and even written his articles for him. All he'd done was make a few corrections with a trembling pencil and sent off her work as his own. She'd got nothing out of it except Fritchley-Bound's gratitude and the knowledge that she was literally saving his career. Fritchley-Bound was a catastrophe waiting to happen. One of these days his newspaper was going to find out what he really was, and that would be that.

Bouncing on the hard seat of the jeep, she watched Paris sweep past her. The air smelled richly of horses and their dung. Deprived of gasoline, the city had returned to the nineteenth century, with horse traps and carriages clattering down the boulevards. The only automobiles were a few taxis, or jeeps like their own, full of soldiers, journalists and war-tourists.

Buildings were pockmarked here and there from the uprising, and they passed some burned-out trucks and a shattered German tank in the Tuileries Garden; but by and large Paris looked magnificent. Certainly compared to London, where they'd been earlier in the year, Paris was gay, tipped with gold and lined with green, the proud sweep of the Eiffel Tower rising above trees and rooftops against a cerulean sky. The Tricolour flew everywhere, and the streets were full of girls on bicycles.

'You wouldn't think there had been a war,' Copper said.

'There wasn't,' Amory replied ironically. 'Giving up is a lot easier than fighting back.'

Giroux gave him a dirty look. 'And you, Monsieur,' he enquired pointedly. 'May one ask why you are not fighting?'

Amory laughed, unfazed by the challenge, as always – he wasn't fazed by many things – but Copper rose to his defence. 'My husband is exempt from military service. He has a weak heart.'

'A weak heart?' Giroux commented, staring at Amory's lanky, six-foot frame.

'He had rheumatic fever as a boy.'

Giroux smiled. Copper had seen that disbelieving smile many times.

Having a father in banking had done more to keep Amory out of the army than the boyhood rheumatic fever, if the truth were known. Amory was the scion of a well-off New England family, and a Cornell graduate. He took his own superiority for granted. Copper, whose background was different, and who'd only been to typing college, was more sensitive to slights.

She'd allowed him to seduce her one summer afternoon on Long Island, her first lover, and somewhat to her surprise, he had married her six months later.

Neither family had been happy with the match. On the Heathcote side, there had been dismay that Amory hadn't chosen one of the eligible young butterflies who made their début each year. Copper's father, a widowed Irish millhand, had felt that Amory was the wastrel offspring of the very people who had their boot on the neck of the workers. And as one of her brothers had brutally put it, Amory was also probably a bastard with women.

However, Amory had professed to admire her family's struggles against the evils of capitalism. Like many upper-class intellectuals, he liked the idea of being rather on the left. Perhaps it had simply been the attraction of opposites. And possibly the fact that she had been open to sex in a way that girls from the gentry weren't.

She had been drawn to his film-star good looks. He had thick blonde hair and eyes of an electric, almost violet blue; a colour she'd never seen in anyone else. He also had a born-to-it sophistication and an easy familiarity with a world she didn't know but secretly aspired to.

He had come to Europe as a war correspondent. She'd refused to be left behind, so he'd brought her with him, using his family's connections to get accreditation for them both. It was to be their great adventure. He said that everyone had the right to get something back out of the war. In his case, a Pulitzer Prize. He was writing a novel that was going to be the biggest thing since Hemingway (whom he'd sought out as soon as they'd arrived in Paris). His brilliance was unquestioned, in Copper's mind, whatever his faults.

His brilliance was the main reason she was still holding on, eighteen months into the marriage, when most of her illusions about Amory had worn thin; in particular her expectation that he would be faithful. He *was* a bastard where women were concerned. Her brothers had been right about that.

One night, very drunk, he'd revealed that his father had been unfaithful to his mother all through their marriage, and that his mother had 'learned to accept it'. The implication was that she should do the same.

Copper put her head back and let the wind take her hair. Long, abundant and golden-red, it was the source of her nickname, and at twenty-six, she was now more used to Copper than Oona. Her hair went with her pale skin and grey-green eyes, proclaiming her Celtic bloodline. She relished the breeze tugging at her hair.

The women she saw on the street were so well-dressed compared to Americans. They strutted on wedge heels, had square, mannish shoulders and extravagant hats, and they mounted their bicycles with immense aplomb. Their skirts were short, showing off their calves. How did they manage? Rationing at home and in Britain had meant plain, drab clothes for the past four years. How did these Frenchwomen, under much stricter privations, look so chic? There was some Gallic secret and she was suddenly determined to discover it. To hell with 'not asking for new dresses'.

Copper leaned forward, shouting against the wind. 'I want a Paris frock.'

Amory half-turned his head, showing his Grecian profile to advantage. 'What?'

'A Paris dress. I want a Paris dress.'

He was scornful. 'I never thought of you as a clothes horse.'

'Well, I want some new clothes,' Copper insisted. 'I'm sick of khaki.' And indeed, she was weary of the olive-green dungarees and ugly uniforms that made up her entire wardrobe. She felt she was an affront to this beautiful city; a laughing stock to these haughty Parisiennes.

'What do you say, Giroux?' Amory asked.

Giroux glanced at Copper over his shoulder with a particularly sour expression. 'Women. Always the same. I have someone for you. But business first, Madame. Then pleasure.'

'Pull up here,' Giroux ordered. Amory parked the jeep where the Frenchman directed, next to a knot of young men who were loitering on a street corner in Montmartre. They were wearing shabby clothes too light for the weather.

'Are they Resistance?' Copper asked Amory.

'They look like it.'

Copper focused through the viewfinder of the camera. The men posed happily for the photo, puffing out thin chests and waving their caps and whistling.

There was a call from down the street. With a shout, the men set off round the corner, their espadrilles slapping on the cobbles. Giroux jerked his head at Copper and Amory to follow. 'Now you will see what happens to collaborators,' he said.

They ran after the little gang into the next street – a row of ordinary houses. The group of men had cornered their quarry, a young mother who had emerged from one of the houses pushing a pram. She was trying desperately to open the door and get back inside, but the men dragged her and her perambulator down the stairs.

'It's a woman,' Copper exclaimed. The scuffling intensified. She was horrified for the baby, whose wails could now be heard over the shouts and screams. Amory held her arm to stop her from going forward.

'Don't interfere.'

The woman had been wearing a coat and a beret. These were torn off her and thrown into the gutter. Her curly blonde hair broke free around her face, which was stark with terror. She was, Copper saw, no more than nineteen or twenty years old. Someone yanked the baby out of the perambulator. The mother tried to plead with the men, holding out her arms to the child, but someone struck her across the mouth and she crumpled. They pulled her back to her feet and started to rip her clothing off.

Copper's heart was in her throat. 'What has she done?' she asked.

'She was the lover of a Gestapo man,' Giroux said. He didn't take part in the attack, but watched shrewdly, a cigarette in his mouth again, eyes squinting against the smoke. 'The child is his.'

'What are they going to do to her?'

'Look how fat she is. The sow,' Giroux said bitterly. 'She fed on butter while we starved.' The woman was almost naked now, clutching her breasts and trying to hide her face. Her body was pale and soft, already marked with red handprints.

The street, which had been almost deserted at the start of the incident, was suddenly crowded. People were coming out of the houses to join the mob, or yelling from their windows. The wave of hatred was like a hot wind. A man was holding the screaming infant aloft, as though about to dash it on to the cobbles. The mother desperately tried to reach her child, but she was pushed from person to person, each assailant striking her or pulling her hair as they chose. There were streaks of blood at her nose and mouth.

The shouting rose to a sudden roar. Someone had produced an old kitchen chair and a noose.

'Oh no,' Copper gasped. She jerked her arm out of Amory's grasp and ran forward.

'Copper, come back!' Amory yelled.

Somehow Copper crossed the few tumultuous yards to the scream-ing woman, fighting through the mob like a halfback. Copper put her arms around her and tried to shield her. But dozens of hands stopped her. She was manhandled away from the victim and thrown roughly on to the ground.

'Are you crazy?' Amory demanded, catching hold of his wife and pulling her to her feet. 'You could have been killed.'

'They're going to lynch her. Do something!'

'There's nothing to be done.'

Bruised and breathless, Copper turned to Giroux. 'Stop them!'

Giroux sucked on the stub of his cigarette. 'You are brave but stu-pid, Madame.'

The mob hauled the weeping woman over to a lamp post. She held her arms out to her baby in a last, despairing gesture. Copper was unable to close her eyes to shut it out.

They pushed the victim on to the kitchen chair, where she cow-ered with tears streaming down her cheeks, the noose around her neck. A little old man was now brought through the crowd. He wore a white apron and held a pair of kitchen scissors. His wizened face was expressionless.

'That is le Blanc, the pastry chef,' Giroux said. 'He lost two sons to the Gestapo.'

The old man grasped a handful of the woman's fair hair and began to hack at it methodically with the scissors. The crowd were chanting, '*Collaboratrice! Putain!*' The woman cried out at the scything strokes at first, then fell silent, as though accepting her fate. Her head jerked to and fro as the old man chopped.

He worked briskly. A cheer went up as the last golden snake slithered to the pavement. Not content, the old man chopped at the remaining tufts until the doll-like skull was almost completely nude. Then he spat deliberately in her face and made his way back through the throng to his shop. Hands reached out to pat his back as he passed. Copper was praying it would end there and nothing worse would be done. 'Give her back her baby,' she shouted to the knot of men.

Amid laughter, the baby was passed back to the victim, who clutched it to her throat. The infant seemed to be unharmed, but it was screaming in terror, its face crumpled and scarlet. The mother put it to her breast and it sucked urgently, its little body convulsing with intermittent sobs. Giroux pushed Copper towards the woman. 'Go on, Joan of Arc. Take your photograph.'

Copper went forward. She held the camera at her waist and focused on the woman, who seemed to be stupefied with shock. All her prettiness was gone.

'I'm sorry,' Copper said. The woman stared at her with bloodshot eyes, her expression unreadable. Copper took two photographs.

The crowd began to drift away now that the spectacle was over. A few hung around to watch the half-naked woman suckle her infant, like a degraded Madonna. The door of her house remained closed, and Copper saw that the curtains were drawn at all the windows. The woman would sit there, an object of loathing, until her family finally plucked up the courage to let her back in. Her clothes had been strewn around the street, and the smart pram had been smashed.

'The end of the promenade,' Giroux said laconically.

Copper picked up the woman's torn blouse and draped it over her as best she could, to cover her nakedness. Amory pulled her away angrily. 'You were a goddamned fool,' he said. 'What the hell were you thinking?'

'How could you stand there and do nothing?'

'I wasn't doing nothing. I was reporting. And you were here to get Fritchley-Bound his shots – not run defence on a lynch mob.'

'I got the shots,' she said sullenly. 'And if he's too hungover to write the article, I'll do that as well, I guess.'

'You're too damned impulsive. You always act without thinking. You were just supposed to tag along. How many times must I tell you not to get involved?'

'That was a disgusting scene.'

'She's lucky they didn't butcher the little bastard,' Giroux said calmly. 'Do you know what the Gestapo did to their prisoners?'

'All she did was fall in love and have a baby.'

He sneered. 'Woman's logic, eh?'

'I was brought up to hate fascism,' she shot back. 'My father and my brothers were beaten up and thrown into jail by thugs like that. Your so-called partisans are no better than Hitler's bully boys.'

Giroux stared at her speculatively. Then he tossed his cigarette stub away. 'Okay. We go get your Paris frock.'

'I don't want a Paris frock anymore,' Copper said as Giroux led them back to the jeep.

'Why not? Because a whore had her head shaved? She deserved worse.'

'I don't believe that man has anything to do with the Resistance at all,' Copper muttered to Amory. 'I hate him.'

'It's perfectly possible to love Paris while detesting the French,' Amory replied equably.

They set off towards the city centre. Copper used Fritchley-Bound's remaining shots on odd details that caught her eye: bouquets left where people had died in the street, coffee drinkers enjoying the sunshine in front of restaurants where windows were starred with bullet holes, men on a ladder taking down a German sign for a soldiers' cinema. She was starting to recover her calm.

After twenty minutes, they arrived at a sober storefront on a smart street close to the Champs-Élysées. Copper saw the name Lelong, and her spirits rose. Lucien Lelong was the very breath of what she had been longing for: powder and perfume and gowns, things that rustled and smelled sweet.

'You've heard of Lelong?' Giroux asked, seeing her expression.

'Oh yes, I've heard of Lelong,' Copper said. She was almost prepared to forgive Giroux for that repulsive episode with the *collaboratrice*. To have anything, anything at all bearing the Lelong label, symbol of the most classical French fashion, would be a dream. Then her hopes fell. 'But I can't afford a dress from here.'

'Don't worry about that. I am a practitioner of jiu-jitsu.'

'Jiu-jitsu?'

He tapped his nose. 'I know how to apply pressure in the right places.'

The salon was everything Copper had expected: painted in pearl tones and hung with grey silk; lit with sparkling chandeliers.

'It's so beautiful,' she sighed. It was as though the war, with its dreary utility clothes, was already over. Here were understated gowns and sophisticated outfits displayed with matching hats and accessories. The very air was scented and soft music flowed from some unseen loudspeaker. A few *vendeuses* stood quietly behind counters. There was nobody else. Copper fingered an exquisite jacket. The *vendeuse* nearby gave her a glassy smile.

'May I be of assistance, Mademoiselle?'

'We're here to see Monsieur Christian,' Giroux said curtly, and led them up the staircase at the back of the salon.

They climbed to the second floor and reached the atelier, a long room, well-lit by a row of windows. It was silent and deserted. A dozen half-finished outfits hung, pinned together, on wooden mannequins, but there were no seamstresses and their tools were scattered on the work benches as though they'd fled halfway through their work.

Giroux pushed open a door and they entered a little salon. It was curtained in grey crêpe de chine, panelled in pearl white and lit with bronze wall brackets. There were several large mirrors for clients to admire themselves in, but this room, too, was empty – except for a man who stood looking out of the window. He was half-obscured by the curtains and wearing a pin-striped suit. He turned a pale face to them with an expression of apprehension.

'This is Monsieur Christian,' Giroux announced. 'I've brought you a customer, *mon vieux*.'

Monsieur Christian, who was balding and evidently in early middle age, came out from behind the drapes with the air of some timid creature flushed from its refuge. 'Enchanted.' He took Copper's hand in his own soft, warm one, and bent over it politely.

'How do you do?' Copper said, feeling awkward. 'So sorry to intrude into your private sanctum.'

He waved that away. 'You are most welcome, Madame . . . ?'

'Heathcote.'

He struggled with the Anglo-Saxon syllables. 'Madame Eat-Cot.' He looked her up and down with his head on one side. 'And what was it you were thinking of?'

Before she could reply, Giroux cut in. 'An outfit. Complete with hat. And accessories.'

'Oh, I don't think I could afford all that,' Copper said with a nervous laugh. 'All I wanted was a frock, perhaps—'

'It will be Lucien Lelong's pleasure to present you with the outfit as a gift,' Giroux said. 'Won't it?'

Monsieur Christian flinched. 'A gift?'

Copper was mortified. 'I couldn't possibly accept.'

Giroux ignored her. 'Where are all your customers?' he asked the couturier contemptuously, showing his sharp teeth. 'Your shop is deserted. Perhaps that is because your customers were all Nazis, collaborators and black-market queens. And perhaps it is healthier for those sorts of persons to remain at home these days.'

Monsieur Christian's cheeks went pink and he sucked his lower lip like an embarrassed child. Copper turned to Giroux. 'This isn't what I wanted, Monsieur Giroux. I don't expect anything for free. Just tell me how much it will cost.'

'It will cost nothing,' Giroux insisted. 'The House of Lelong collaborated with the Nazis for four years. Now there is atonement to be made.'

'The House of Lelong kept the Germans at bay for four years,' Monsieur Christian said in a low voice, his face redder than ever. 'It is thanks to Lelong that we have any couture remaining in Paris at all.'

'Who cares about couture?' Giroux demanded. 'You and Chanel, and the other bourgeois parasites, you pander to the rich and the decadent whatever language they speak. You're all traitors.'

'You will permit me to disagree with you, Monsieur,' the dressmaker said, his voice sinking even lower. He was clearly not a man who relished confrontation, but he had a quiet dignity. 'We have our own opinion on the matter. But it's of no account and it will be a pleasure to accommodate Madame.'

'I can't accept that,' Copper said, glaring at Giroux.

'I assure you, Mademoiselle, it will make a welcome change from standing here all day without clients,' Monsieur Christian said with the lightest irony. 'If the gentlemen will leave the room, I will take measurements.'

'Why should I leave the room?' Giroux growled.

Monsieur Christian rolled his eyes. 'It is quite impossible for measurements to be taken with gentlemen present.'

'What – not even the husband?' Amory demanded.

'Especially not the husband.'

'She's my wife, damn it.'

By way of an answer, Monsieur Christian indicated the door, his eyes closed. He was clearly not going to move – or open his eyes – until the men had departed. There was something commanding about this immobility, and to Copper's amusement, Amory and Giroux both stamped out of the room, slamming the door behind them. Monsieur Christian opened his eyes with a sigh. 'Now, then,' he said. 'If Madame will remove the camera? And the outer clothing?'

Deciding that she would discuss the issue of proper payment later, Copper took off the Rolleiflex, which was dangling heavily around her neck, and got out of her dungarees. Monsieur Christian folded her drab garments as carefully as if they were a queen's robes, and then considered the spectacle of Copper in her underwear, pinching his fleshy chin between finger and thumb.

'A pity,' he said.

'What's a pity?' Copper asked. Oddly, she felt no embarrassment at being appraised by the couturier in a state of semi-nudity.

'Your proportions.' He looped a tape measure around her bust and sucked his lip. 'But this can easily be remedied.' He produced a cardboard box and lifted the lid to reveal two generously rounded objects. 'I always recommend these to those of my clients whom nature has neglected.'

'Falsies?'

'Foam rubber. Pre-war. Very hard to obtain nowadays.'

'No, thank you. I'll stick with what I have.'

He put them away. 'Perhaps you are right. But you do not look like a Frenchwoman, Madame.'

'Is that good or bad?'

'The lack of curves would normally be a drawback which we would try to remedy with some padding.'

'Please, no padding.'

'But in your case – with these long legs, the high waist, the height, the vigour . . .' He stood back and studied her, holding one elbow and stroking his cheek with his free hand. 'You are obviously athletic.'

'I hate sports. But American girls are quite active, you know.'

'Indeed. There is a certain *garçon* air – not a bad thing in itself, you understand. In fact . . .' He seemed to be growing excited as he prowled around her. 'In fact, stimulating. A challenge. The hair is passable. And the face, of course. The legs – flawless.'

'I'm glad something meets with your approval.'

'I recall a time when showing the ankles was considered the height of obscenity. Now we require the whole leg. Well, let's begin.'

He set to work. As she allowed herself to be measured, Copper surveyed him in return. He had a long, beaky nose and a sensitive, soft mouth. She noted his gleaming black shoes and starched cuffs, the whiff of cologne.

The door opened, and one of the *vendeuses* stuck her head round it anxiously. 'Pardon, Monsieur Christian, but the man Giroux is stealing everything he can lay his hands on. He's stuffing his pockets.'

'Let him take what he wants,' the couturier said impatiently. 'Go away.'

The door closed again. Monsieur Christian jotted down a great many figures in a notebook. 'May I ask how an American woman comes to be in Paris in wartime?'

'My husband is a war correspondent. He pulled strings to get me accredited so I could tag along.'

'Not many women would be eager for such accreditation.'

'Oh, I'm always ready for an adventure. I tagged along with my dad and brothers from the time I could walk. They even gave me my own placard to carry.'

'A placard?'

'It said, "A Fair Wage for a Fair Day's Work".'

'A good sentiment.'

'I guess it was formative.'

'And your husband is a beautiful young man,' Monsieur Christian pointed out. 'Really, one of the handsomest men I have ever seen.'

'Oh, he's easy on the eye. But I can stand to tear my gaze away from him now and then. What I couldn't stand was staying at home while he got all the fun. Besides, he's pretty much helpless without me.'

'"Fun"?' He raised his eyebrows. 'I have to tell you that you are my first American client, Madame Eat-Cot. But if they are all like you, the world is in for a shock.'

'You bet it is,' she agreed.

'Hold yourself upright, if you please. Hand on hip, head to one side. Good. You have the carriage. It helps one so much. European women stay slim by starving themselves. It gives them what one might call a pinched look and they often remain flabby. This is something else. This slimness comes from musculature. And yet it's not at all masculine. It's really a very new idea.'

'There are plenty more like me in New York,' Copper replied wryly. 'Women run around there all day long, trust me on that.'

'And what, may I ask, will happen when you grow tired of "tagging along"?'

'You mean, if I get cold feet?'

'I mean, when you want something for yourself.'

'Well, there's always housework and the kitchen. There's a lot to learn about vacuum-cleaning, you know. Perfecting the American apple pie has been a dream of mine since girlhood. And having six little rosy babies, just like Mom did.'

'You're making fun of me.'

'Yes, I am,' she admitted. 'Sorry. I'm enjoying the ride so far, Monsieur Christian. I don't think too far ahead.'

'Remarkable,' he said. 'I will make some drawings and perhaps you can return in a day or so?'

'Thank you.'

'Not at all. You may dress yourself now.'

As they said goodbye, he bent gallantly over her hand so she could almost see her reflection in his balding pate. He was obviously amused by her and she was glad to have amused him. The impression she got from him was of gentleness and reserve rather than the haughty arrogance she would have expected from a Paris couturier. He saw her to the top of the stairs and watched as she walked down. She got a last glimpse of his hazel eyes following her.

'You embarrassed me,' she told Giroux roundly at the bottom of the stairs. 'Asking that sweet little man to make me a wardrobe!'

'That "sweet little man" dressed the wives of Nazis.'

'I don't suppose he had much choice.'

'Everyone has a choice, Mam'selle. Dior made his.'

'Dior?'

'That is his name. Christian Dior. He's one of Lelong's best men. The other is Pierre Balmain, but they say Dior is better.'

She noticed that Giroux's pockets were bulging with loot. A large pair of pinking shears protruded from one of them and silk ribbons spilled from another. He was giving a new meaning, she thought dryly, to the Liberation of Paris.

Two

As Copper had anticipated, the Frightful Bounder was too ill to write the article, so she did it; pounding away at his portable Underwood until her fingers were numb. George had once been a good journalist and she knew how to mimic his laconic style, so it came out well. The developed photographs were dramatic, too. The whole piece was good, if biting in tone, and an antidote to the usual gushing stuff that filled the pages of the newspapers. No sooner had George managed to raise himself from his bed than he began drinking again, so Copper even had to package up the story and the photos to be sent off to his editor. His total contribution to the article was to add his shaky signature to the covering letter. She left the package on the table for him to send. He could at least manage that much.

He was, however, pathetically grateful to Copper, and returned from his next drinking session with a gift for her – something wrapped in an oily parcel of brown paper tied with butcher's string.

'What's this?' she asked suspiciously.

'Foie gras. Goose liver. Great delicacy among the French.' He patted her shoulder. 'Very grateful to you, old thing. Can't say it enough times.'

She hadn't ever tried foie gras and didn't much like the look of the stuff; but struck by a thought, she took it with her as a gift when she went back to Lucien Lelong a day later.

She went alone this time, leaving Amory working at his typewriter in their flat. She found the salon in the same quiet state as before. The *vendeuses* were in little groups, whispering to each other. They followed Copper with kohl-rimmed eyes as she made her way between the displays and up the stairs, like gazelles watching a leopard.

There was more activity in the atelier, however: three young women were working together, bent over what was evidently a wedding dress. Their coarse hair and strong arms made a contrast to the white satin on to which they were swiftly sewing sequins. They glanced at her, unsmiling. The whole place, she thought, was like something out of a surrealist film. She found Christian Dior in the little salon in the same attitude, gazing out of the window. He turned his long-nosed face to her apprehensively. 'Yes?'

'Good morning, Monsieur Christian.'

He brightened at the sight of her. 'Ah, Madame Eat-Cot. I have a design for you.'

'Please, everyone calls me Copper.'

'Copper?' he repeated in surprise.

'I have my brothers to thank for that.' She gestured at her hair. 'Because of this. My real name is Oona, but nobody ever calls me that.'

'I much prefer Oona. Copper is an ugly name for such a striking woman,' he said frankly.

She proffered the parcel. 'I brought you this. I hope it's acceptable.' She felt embarrassed at delivering such a greasy package in such a spotless setting. But as he unfolded the paper, his eyes widened.

'A whole foie gras,' he gasped.

'Is it all right? I was told it was good.'

'This is for me?'

'If you'll accept it.'

She was dismayed to see that his eyes were suddenly moist. 'Excuse me.' He hurried from the salon with the package. In his absence, she went to the window where he had been standing. The smart street below was quiet. Why did he stand here all day, looking out, waiting – for what?

He came back into the room without the foie gras. His cheeks were flushed and his eyes were puffy. 'I hope I didn't upset you?' she said anxiously.

'I was a little overcome. You are very kind. The cards foretold a gift for me today, but I had no idea it would be from you. It has been a long time since I tasted foie gras – my favourite dish of all.'

'Oh, I'm so happy.'

'Where is your husband?'

'He didn't come this time.'

'Perhaps that's better. Between couturier and client, it's like in the confessional. The souls are bared and each brings the other closer to God.' He giggled.

'Before we go any further, I want to clear something up – there's no question of you working for nothing. That was Giroux's idea, not mine. I am happy to pay.'

He spread his hands. 'And I am happy to make you a gift.'

'Absolutely not. I'm mortified by the way Giroux spoke to you.'

His gentle brown eyes were suddenly sad. 'My dear, if you wish to find those who did *not* collaborate with the Germans, I invite you to visit the cemeteries of Paris. Those who still have legs to walk with and air in their lungs – you may be sure that they all collaborated with the Germans. My employer, Lucien Lelong, stood up to the Nazis when they wanted to move all the designers and all our workers to Berlin. He refused. He could have been shot for that.'

'I didn't know that.'

'One could be shot for almost anything. Can you imagine how it infuriated the Germans to see the Parisiennes well-dressed and smiling? They would say, "You lost the war, why are you so gay?" And we would reply, "You won the war, why are you so sad?" That was *our* Resistance.

Even to make the wives of Nazi officers stylish – that, too, was resistance. It proved how superior French taste is to theirs.'

'Then you are certainly a hero of the Resistance,' Copper said, smiling.

'Giroux is a bully boy, and so are his men.'

'Are they picketing you?'

'Effectively, yes. They admire Stalin and hate everything beautiful. Don't worry, we'll get back to work. Back to the life we once had.'

'How much would the dress . . . umm . . . ?' she asked, more delicately.

He sucked his lower lip. 'In the ordinary course of events . . . let us say about five thousand francs. But let's leave that for now.' He showed her the drawing he had made. 'What do you think?'

She studied the sketch, trying to work out how much five thousand francs was in dollars. It was an awful lot, even with the devalued franc. But the dress! She caught her breath. He drew effortlessly. The lines were flowing and graceful, outlining a ravishing costume. 'It's absolutely lovely.'

'You think so? The problem is locating enough silk. The Germans confiscated it all for parachutes. We have taffeta for the underskirt.'

'I really don't need silk.'

'You must permit me, my dear, to have my own vision of you.' He spoke with great seriousness. 'I mean, the woman inside' – he waved his expressive fingers at her khaki trousers and dingy blouse – '*this*.'

'But it will be expensive.'

He was poring over his own drawing as though he hadn't heard her. 'I love full skirts. Nothing is more romantic. The waist is drawn in. And you see the curves at the bust and shoulders?'

'I see why you wanted me to wear falsies.'

'The bust is the most beautiful attribute of a woman's body,' he pronounced. He eyed Copper's slight breasts regretfully. 'Within the scope of whatever nature supplies to each individual, of course.'

'Monsieur Christian, I suspect you have a mother complex,' she said gravely.

He blinked and then smiled. When he smiled, the corners of his mouth turned up, but his eyes seemed to remain sad. 'My mother loved fine clothes, of course. But I remember her perfume most of all.' He closed his eyes. 'Everywhere she went, the scent of flowers went with her.'

'She must have been lovely.'

'I would like to clothe all women with flowers. You remember the Bible? The lilies of the field? Solomon in all his glory was not arrayed like one of these.'

'That's an interesting ambition.'

He raised a forefinger. 'I go beyond that. My ambition is to save women from themselves.'

'Good heavens. Are we in such peril, then?'

'Between Chanel and her little black jerseys, and the beasts who design military uniforms, yes. Not to mention the *zazous* and their manias. Or the diktats of Utility, with its two pockets, five buttons and six seams. Your position is extremely perilous.'

'It's all in the cause of efficiency.'

He gave a shudder. 'That word. Please never mention it again in my presence.'

Copper laughed. 'I won't.'

'So. I will go ahead with this model.'

'If that's what you really want to do.' She had been thinking of something simple that she could show off in New York. But if Monsieur Dior wanted to turn her into a magazine fashion plate, it was ill-mannered to argue. And although five thousand francs was an astronomical price for an outfit when five American dollars would purchase a Sears frock, she might never get another chance to own a Paris gown.

'It is my decision,' he affirmed. Despite the gentleness, there was a certain steely strength in the man. 'Obtaining the fabric presents a certain challenge. I will need six metres of silk, at least. But I think I know where to find it.'

As he showed her out, he said, 'You are a captivating woman. Your husband is a lucky man.'

Copper smiled. 'I think he is, too. I'm going to go home and tell him that right now.'

Copper returned to the flat to find it smelling strongly of Chanel No. 5. It was the perfume of the season. Gallons of it had been given away to GIs by Coco Chanel in an effort to erase her wartime record as a Nazi collaborator. The GIs had, in turn, bartered the perfume for sex; and the stuff was now being worn by every *pute* in Paris.

'Have you had a visitor?' she asked Amory, who was hammering at his typewriter, working on his novel.

'No. Why?'

'The place stinks of Chanel.'

'Oh. Yes. A grubby little man came round, trying to sell a few bottles. He splashed it all over to show it was genuine.'

'You've certainly got it all over *you*.' She evaded his attempt to embrace her and went to the bedroom. Their bed was carelessly made – not the way she'd left it – the pillows dented and smeared with face powder. She stood staring at the bed, trying not to cry. Amory came in behind her.

'It doesn't mean anything, you know,' he said.

'Doesn't it?'

'You're the only one who matters to me, Copper.'

She turned to face him. 'But apparently I'm not enough.'

'Well, it's not as though we have a sparkling sex life these days. You never seem to want to make love anymore.'

She grimaced at that painful accusation. 'Can you blame me?'

He rubbed his chin. 'I suppose I've been behaving badly lately. Too much booze, too much sex, too many parties, too much of everything, really. I've been working on my novel a lot, and that makes me promiscuous.'

'You're always promiscuous.'

'Well, that's how I am. You know that.'

She started to cry. 'Oh, Amory. In our bed.'

'I could swear that I'm going to reform. But I might as well swear to change the colour of my eyes. It's no good. And you know how they throw themselves at me.' He spoke with the casual self-confidence of a man who knew he was beautiful.

The stinging tears slid down her cheeks and she dashed them away. 'I don't think I can stand this much longer.'

'It was only a little kiss and cuddle, as it happens. We didn't go any further than that.'

'I don't believe you; not that it matters.'

He shrugged, and went back to his typewriter. Copper stripped the bed, trying to stop crying. This wasn't the first time, or the second, or even the third. She'd fooled herself about Amory's infidelities, accepting his casual lies, telling herself that it didn't matter, or she didn't care, so long as he loved her. But it did matter. And this was the first time he'd taken another woman to their bed. That hurt very much indeed. It showed that he was now completely indifferent to her feelings.

She'd once been so feisty. She'd been the littlest one who'd grown up motherless with five siblings in a crowded apartment. She'd been the ginger kid who had marched with her father and brothers on the freezing picket lines.

She'd been appointed by the small fry to deal with the schoolyard bullies. She'd been the hoyden who'd been expelled from St Columba's for slugging Sister Bridget (nobody had ever hit back before). Amory had fallen in love with her, so he'd said, for her fieriness.

But life with Amory had slowly and steadily put the dampers on her fire. He'd systematically frozen it out in that cool, calm way he had. She wanted to rage and scream, but she couldn't. The scream stayed locked up inside her. She could tackle a lynch mob, but not her husband.

Screaming at Amory didn't just come under the 'nagging, pestering or complaining' that the good wife was supposed to eschew. It would make him retreat into an icy fortress. He did not tolerate displays of emotion. And the fear that he would grow tired of her was always there. If a marriage was in trouble, you were supposed to fix it, not walk away. That's what the experts said.

She went to the kitchen. 'Do you want coffee?' she asked Amory, in as near to a normal tone as she could manage. She saw his face relax as he realised that she wasn't going to make a scene or demand further discussion.

'Sure. How was Dior?'

'He's designed an outfit for me,' she said, putting the percolator together blindly. Her voice was strained as she reached for a façade of normality. 'I insisted on paying. He wants five thousand francs.'

'I'll give you the money.'

She was not going to be bought off that easily. 'No, thank you,' she said in a brittle voice. 'I've got the money.'

'If that's what you want to spend it on. Fashion is dead. Everyone knows that.'

'What would you know about it?'

'Don't snap at me.'

'Then don't talk nonsense to me.'

He rattled out another sentence on his typewriter, his long fingers deft. 'Let's go out tonight.'

'Where to?'

'La Vie Parisienne. Said to be the most decadent bar in Paris.'

'I think I've had enough decadence for one day.'

'Oh, come on, kid. We're in Paris. It won't do either of us any good to sit at home moping.'

If she didn't go with him, she'd have no idea what he was up to. But the idea of having to keep tabs on her husband was repugnant. It wasn't much of a choice. Sitting home wondering what shade of lipstick he would get on his collar was marginally worse.

'Okay,' she said emptily. 'I'll come.'

La Vie Parisienne turned out to be just the sort of place that Amory liked. In every city they'd been together, he'd found such haunts where he seemed able to relax and enjoy himself, observing, taking notes and getting drunk.

The place was located in a narrow street close to their apartment. The entrance was grotto-like, and a number of raucous women in garish clothes were standing outside, apparently squabbling over money. They ogled Amory as he made his way between them.

Inside, the impression was even more cavern-like. The rooms were crowded, dark and smoky. The walls were hung with hundreds of portraits. At the far end was a piano where a fat woman in a man's suit and bowler hat was playing jazz. A few couples were dancing. All the tables seemed full. Copper was put off by the atmosphere of the place, but Amory cheered up immediately. 'This is more like it. Let's get a drink.' The bar was crowded and people were staring at them with apparent hostility. Suddenly, a sleek form floated out to meet them. It was Christian Dior in evening dress, his smooth cheeks flushed. 'What a surprise to see you here.'

Copper was happy to see a familiar and friendly face. 'Monsieur Dior!'

He took their arms. 'Come to our table. It's in the corner where we can watch everyone. It's our favourite occupation.' Edging their way to the far corner of the bar, they passed a table where a shock-haired man with a thin face was holding forth to a circle of devoted listeners. 'Cocteau,' Dior told them. 'He never stops talking. I want you to meet my dear friend Francis Poulenc, the composer. Francis, this is the American beauty I told you about, and this is her husband.'

Poulenc was a pleasantly ugly man with hair cut *en brosse*, who greeted them courteously as they squeezed around the cramped table. Copper, who was not musical, had never heard of him, but Amory obviously had.

'Monsieur Poulenc, I'd be glad of the chance to interview you. I'm a war correspondent.'

'Well, I'm not General de Gaulle, though I have been a humble infantryman.'

'You were in the army?'

'Poulenc and I were called up together. We performed the only glorious part of an inglorious campaign,' Dior said. 'We dug onions. Wearing hideous wooden *sabots*. Each foot weighed two kilos, I assure you.'

'Three, at least,' Poulenc said. 'If you wish to understand the term *saboteur*, you need only consider the French *sabot* in all its massive, indestructible majesty – a shoe to derail a train or crack even a German cranium.'

'The soul of France,' Dior agreed. 'Unyielding to the last. What will you drink?'

'Something French,' Copper said. Her spirits were lifting for the first time since that morning. 'No – something Parisian.'

'Leave it to me,' Dior said, and disappeared into the crowd again.

'He's been describing you to me,' Poulenc told Copper.

'Really?'

'He's impressed with you. He says you are a new breed of woman and the world is in for a shock.'

'I'm not sure if that's exactly a good thing.'

'It's rare for him to make new friends. He's very shy.'

'But he likes to get his own way.'

'Ah, so you've learned that about him already,' Poulenc said solemnly. 'You began well with the gift of a whole foie gras, I might add. That was a good start to the friendship.'

'I only took it to him because I had nothing else to give.'

'You couldn't have chosen better. He's as greedy as a child. You may be sure that he has eaten the whole thing already.'

'He's too fat,' Amory said from behind his notebook.

'Yes, don't you think he looks like a penguin in his dinner jacket? And I, a seal?'

'He seems to have done well under the Germans,' Amory commented.

'His sister, Catherine, was arrested by the Gestapo,' Poulenc said mildly. 'Just a few weeks before the invasion began. She was in the Resistance. They've sent her to Ravensbrück, a concentration camp in Germany.'

'Oh, how terrible,' Copper exclaimed. 'Is there any news of her?'

'Only from the clairvoyants Dior consults every day. He's very superstitious, you know. They assure him that she's alive, but—' He shrugged.

Dior had returned with a waiter who was bearing a tray of drinks. 'Kir Royale,' he announced. 'Made with Dom Pérignon, of course. I adore Dom Pérignon.' They raised their glasses. 'Do you like this place?' Dior asked her, his head on one side. He was subtly different out of the atelier, Copper thought – more relaxed and less inhibited.

'It's interesting,' she replied diplomatically. 'But tell me – are those strange-looking women outside prostitutes?' she asked.

Dior's eyebrows rose in surprise and he seemed at a loss for words. Amory grinned at her. 'I'm sure you're half-right, anyway, honeybun.'

'What do you mean?'

Nobody answered her. The champagne cocktails were followed by another round. The bar was becoming even noisier and more crowded. To a burst of applause, a handsome and statuesque blonde woman went up to the piano and began to sing in a rich contralto.

'That's Suzy Solidor,' Poulenc said to Copper. 'She owns the bar. Cocteau put up the money. He's very shrewd – they're making a fortune. You see all these paintings on the walls? They're all of Suzy.'

Looking closely, Copper saw that Poulenc was right. 'There are so many. Some are better than others, though.'

He pointed. 'That's the best one. De Lempicka. Over there is a Picasso. And next to it, Braque. She's determined to become the most painted woman in history. It's colossal vanity or genius; nobody can tell which.'

'I think she's wonderful,' Copper said, rapt by the singer's striking face, platinum bob and throbbing voice.

'You think so?' Poulenc said, watching her. 'I can introduce you, if you want. At your own risk.'

'Oh, I'd like that.'

'Of course,' he replied with a half-smile. But again, she had the impression of not quite getting something that was obvious to others. The pianist now struck up 'Lili Marlène'. Though the song was popular with Allied soldiers and being sung in French tonight, it was a German song, and Copper was surprised to hear it here and now. And indeed, there were catcalls and boos from some of the audience – and something defiant in the way Miss Solidor delivered it.

'It's her signature song,' Poulenc put in. 'She sang it to Nazi officers every night. The Resistance hate her. She sings it to show she's not afraid of them now.'

'Suzy is brave, but not wise,' Dior said.

Copper smiled wryly. 'Funny. Someone said that about me recently.'

Poulenc leaned over to her and murmured, 'She and Cocteau dined with Coco Chanel at the Ritz every week during the Occupation. Only the close friends of the Germans were allowed to stay there. Chanel had a suite. There was a certain sector sympathetic to the Nazis – you understand?'

A group of three young women now took the table next to theirs; young, beautiful and beautifully dressed. 'Schiaparelli's mannequins,' Dior said. 'The envy of every couturier in Paris. Aren't they marvellous?'

Copper stared at the women, resplendent in their satin gowns. They were so ravishing that she didn't even feel embarrassed at her own scruffy outfit. Their clothes were astonishing. No matter how she dressed, she could never be as brilliant as one of these women.

The gossip round the table was wild, punctuated with bursts of frenzied laughter. The Allies had reached the Marne. Coco Chanel had been exposed as a Nazi spy and had fled to Switzerland with her German lover. The communists were poised to take over Paris. The Maquis had shot Maurice Chevalier as a collaborator and were hunting Mistinguett. They had killed Marshal Pétain and stuck his head on a spike. It was dizzying how many rumours were sweeping to and fro.

And the champagne was dizzying, too. She hadn't drunk like this for a long time, and after a while her head was spinning. But not enough to prevent her seeing that Amory was now talking to a young, curly-haired woman whose low-cut dress displayed a spectacular cleavage, to which he was giving his full attention. Copper saw the woman throw back her head to laugh gaily at something he said.

She turned away from him to Poulenc and Dior, who were sitting together like shy children at a grown-up party. 'Everyone is entitled to be loved,' she said, her words slurring.

'Francis and I are too plain to have lovers,' Dior said, draining his glass. 'I think we need more drinks.'

'He has a very low opinion of himself,' she said to Poulenc when Dior had gone.

'Very low and very high.'

'He stands at the window all day, looking out as though he is waiting for something.'

'Ah, yes. We're all wondering what will come next for our little Monsieur Dior. He's quite the genius, you know. He had a terrible disappointment. His father went bankrupt, and Christian was forced to close his art gallery and sell all his paintings – masterpieces by Dufy, Miró, Dalí and the rest – for a song. Now he designs dresses for ladies.'

'Amory says fashion is dead.'

'They told me music was dead. That every possible combination of notes had been exhausted and that there were no new melodies to be written. And yet, I flatter myself that I have managed to compose some new tunes that nobody has heard before. Perhaps simple, but pleasing, easily remembered and fresh. I should be surprised if Dior is not capable of the same feat.'

'Then perhaps that will make him rich and famous.'

'He has friends who love him anyway. And he has luck. With Dior, there are three things you can count on: his luck, his talent and his friendship.'

The talented Monsieur Dior returned with another round of drinks. Amory's companion was still squealing with laughter, her bright blue eyes sparkling, her brown curls dancing around her face as she flirted. Copper noted that she was English with a saucy cockney accent.

'Who is that woman?' she asked Dior.

'A Londoner. She calls herself a model.'

'She's making up to my husband.'

Poulenc shook his cropped head. 'That one makes up to every man in sight.'

Chairs were being pushed together to accommodate new arrivals: Jean Cocteau, Suzy Solidor and some others had joined them. Poulenc beckoned the blonde singer to the chair next to Copper.

'This is Copper, Suzy. She wants to meet you. She is Christian's latest muse.'

Suzy was not as young as Copper had first thought; perhaps in her mid-forties. But she was a beautiful woman, with a face that was somehow mask-like. She examined Copper with hooded brown eyes to her platinum hair. 'Christian always has excellent taste,' she said in her husky voice.

'Oh, I'm sure I'm not Monsieur Dior's muse in any way at all,' Copper said, embarrassed.

The singer's hand covered Copper's smoothly. 'You are a breath of cool air,' she purred. 'Youth, energy, freshness. That's what we crave. We have become so tired of the greyness. Tell me all about yourself.'

'There's nothing to tell, Madame.'

'Suzy, please. You will make a perfect muse for Christian. When American women are beautiful, they are more beautiful than any others. Now, tell me everything.' She smiled, showing teeth that were – like the rest of her – healthy and handsome.

This rather steamy attention, flattering as it was, made Copper feel hot all over. She found herself gabbling, her tongue loosened by the cocktails, about her childhood, the death of her mother, her whirlwind romance with Amory. The *chanteuse* listened, her chin resting on her cupped hand, her eyes dreamily fixed on Copper and her nostrils arched, as though inhaling some rare incense. As Copper's recitation tailed off, Suzy leaned over to Dior.

'What a discovery, Christian. This child is exquisite.'

Dior nodded. 'But of course she is.'

'I intend to steal her from you.'

'I will not permit that.'

Though she knew she was just being teased, Copper felt uncomfortable, and tried to squirm away from the limelight. Miss Solidor kept hold of her hand, a gesture that was probably meant to be reassuring, but made her feel somewhat trapped. Luckily, Jean Cocteau was now holding forth, his hypnotic eyes sweeping over them all. Copper's rusty

French – and the Dom Pérignon – made it hard for her to follow his words.

'What's *Le Théâtre de la Mode*?' she asked, catching a phrase that Cocteau was repeating.

'It's an idea of Lelong's,' Poulenc said.

'It's not Lelong's idea, it's Nina Ricci's,' one of the mannequins said.

The others chimed in. 'Not Nina Ricci's, either; it came from her son, Robert.'

'I thought it was Cocteau's idea.'

'Not mine,' Cocteau said. 'Fashion bores me.'

'Wherever it came from, it's sheer genius.'

Dior explained. 'We must show the world that, despite the war, Paris is still the capital of haute couture,' he said. 'Not New York. We must have a spring fashion show, of course. But there are eighty or ninety fashion houses in Paris. That means thousands of new models to be made. And we don't have enough fabric. We have hardly any silk. The Germans took it all. We don't have buttons, thread, leather, fur, anything we need. So the idea is—'

'To have a fashion show with dolls,' one of the Schiaparelli models interrupted excitedly.

'Dolls?'

'Little figurines, two feet high, wearing miniature outfits.'

'On miniature sets.'

'Yes. Each fashion house would make a little stage with a theme. A fairy tale, a Paris scene. And the new models would be on display.'

'It's a ridiculous idea,' someone said, laughing.

'I think it's a wonderful idea,' Copper exclaimed, beguiled by the vision. 'It's enchanting.' She looked for Amory to share her enthusiasm with him, but he had slipped away, together with the English 'model', and was nowhere to be seen. Her heart fell sickeningly. Where had they gone? Perhaps they were in the lobby?

She got up. 'I need some air.'

'What's the matter?' Suzy Solidor asked her.

Without answering, Copper left the table and pushed through the crowd and into the lobby. They weren't there, either. She hurried out into the street. The jeep was gone. Amory and the 'model' had departed.

Dior appeared beside her. 'What's the matter?'

'My husband has disappeared.' She tried to laugh, but it came out more like a sob. 'He's gone where the grass is greener.'

Suzy Solidor had followed her, too. 'Let him go,' she advised. 'Men are all the same.' She took Copper's arm. 'Come back to the bar.'

Copper disengaged herself. 'Thank you, but I think I've had enough. I'm going home.'

'Then let me call you a taxi,' Dior offered.

'I'll walk. It's just a few streets. Besides, I don't want to arrive too soon. That mightn't be very delicate.'

'I'll walk with you,' Dior said. 'Let me get our coats.' He went back inside.

The blonde singer was studying Copper. 'I know the type,' she said. 'He's not worth your tears.'

Copper, who did not want to hear this, turned away. 'You don't know anything about him.'

'*Au contraire*,' the other woman replied, not without compassion. She patted Copper's arm. 'I do. They give a little pleasure and a lot of pain.'

'Well, he's my husband.'

'That can be changed, *chérie*.'

Dior shortly reappeared wearing a felt hat and a stylish gabardine overcoat and carrying her much shabbier one. He helped her on with it. The singer stood outside her club, watching them walk down the street. 'Come back tomorrow,' she called after Copper.

The danger of air raids had not passed. None of the street lamps were lit. But the blackout was starting to be relaxed here and there. Curtains were being left open in the mansions, like gold sequins

36

scattered on black velvet, and the boats that purred up and down the river carried sparks of red and green that were reflected in the water. There were couples everywhere, walking, laughing, kissing under cover of the darkness.

'This is kind of you,' Copper said to Dior.

'Not at all. I like to walk. One wartime privation that it's hard to mourn is the lack of gasoline. It has compelled us to rediscover our city on foot.'

'At least the Germans are gone.'

'The Germans are gone. But we're still not ourselves. We have exchanged with you Americans, to your advantage. You have the *mode*, we have *zazou*.'

She'd heard him use the word before. '*Zazou?*'

He shrugged. 'These hideous jazz women with square shoulders and heavy shoes, the hair piled up on the head like a haystack, the huge sunglasses and the crimson lipstick. It was a way of spitting in the Nazi's faces. But it's time to return to true elegance.'

'And what defines true elegance?' she asked wryly as they crossed the wide, empty, cobbled streets.

'Dressing with care.'

'Is that all?'

'Far from it. But that is the essence.'

They reached the apartment on the rue de Rivoli. To Copper's relief, the jeep was not parked outside. At least Amory hadn't taken the woman to their bed.

As if following her train of thought, Dior asked, 'How long have you been married?'

'A year and a half. We've come a long way together.'

He nodded. 'You deserve to be happy.'

'It's elusive, though, isn't it?' she replied.

'Yes, it's elusive.'

'Thank you so much, Monsieur Christian. You're most kind.'

'Not at all. We will see each other in the atelier, I hope, tomorrow.'

He saw her to her door. She unlocked it, knowing she would burst into tears as soon as she was alone. Then she took a step back. A scene of horror greeted her in the hallway. George Fritchley-Bound was lying face down on the floor in a wide, dark pool of blood.

She rushed to his side and heaved him over to look into his face. He had been lying like that for so long that the blood had jellified on his face. His eyes were rolled back in his head. He was cold and dead.

Three

'There are no external factors,' the police captain said. He was flipping through the pathologist's report. In wartime, autopsies were done almost immediately and took no more than a brutal half hour. 'The cause of death was blood loss due to a ruptured stomach ulcer.' He looked up at Copper and Amory, who were sitting on the other side of his desk. 'The liver showed signs of advanced alcoholism.'

'He was a heavy drinker,' Amory said, shrugging.

'The drinking caused the ulcer and the ulcer killed him. He emptied many a bottle and was himself, in the end, emptied.' The captain tossed the report down. 'We have no interest in the case. There will be no inquest. There is nothing further. You may collect your friend's body.'

In the street outside the police station, Amory put his arm around Copper. 'Are you okay?'

She pushed him away furiously. 'Don't you dare touch me.'

'Take it easy.'

'You left me to deal with that all on my own. How could you?'

'Well, how was I to know the old bugger had died?' he asked practically.

'Of course you didn't know. You were in that woman's bed until dawn.'

'As a matter of fact—'

'Do you have any idea what I've been through?' she demanded, shaky with exhaustion and rage. 'Finding poor George dead on the floor. Dealing with the police. The blood.' Copper covered her face. 'Oh my God, the blood. It's everywhere. It's soaked into the floorboards.'

'We'll clear out of there today. We've got to leave Paris, anyway, and get as close to Dijon as we can. We may as well set off, now that the police are finished with us.'

She shuddered. 'Thank God for Dior. If he hadn't been there, I don't know what I would have done. He was wonderful. He got me over my hysterics, dealt with the police, was an absolute shining knight.' She turned to Amory. 'I'll never forgive you for this, Amory.'

His calm was unshakeable. 'Be reasonable. I went out for a breath of fresh air. You were gone when I got back to the club. I had no idea where you were.'

'Oh, what a load. You got your claws into that woman and eloped with her in the jeep.'

'Well, you seemed happy as a clam with the lesbian.'

'What lesbian?'

'The blonde bombshell. Solidor.'

'Suzy? She's not a lesbian.'

'My dear Oona, you're surely not *that* innocent.'

She hated it when he used her Christian name in arguments. 'What are you talking about?'

'Come on. Don't you know what that club is? Didn't you notice that the women were all men and the men were all women?'

'What?'

'It's a queer hang-out. Solidor's a notorious dyke. Cocteau's a queer, Poulenc's a queer, and your Christian Dior is the biggest queer of all.'

She was taken aback. 'I suppose you'll tell me your little cockney was a lesbian, too?'

'No. She was the only normal woman in the place. That's why we went out for that breath of fresh air.'

Copper reflected on last night's company, the people at the tables, the pressure of Suzy's hand on hers, the strange, hoarse 'women' hanging around the doorway. Was Christian Dior what Amory dismissively called 'a queer'? If so, he was the first she had met. At least, knowingly met. She'd only ever heard such a condition mentioned as a term of abuse, something wicked. Christian was anything but wicked. Yet there were the feminine touches, the perfect understanding of a woman's point of view. The gentleness that was hardly masculine. 'I don't care,' she said at last, shaking her head. 'Christian behaved impeccably. He's a better man than you are, any day.'

His face closed. 'You're being a bitch.'

She felt she was seeing him as he really was for the first time and it horrified her. Her response was anger at him, at herself. 'I'm not going to be silenced by you, Amory. Last night was the end. You can't imagine how terrible it was. You're not even sorry that poor George is dead.'

He made an impatient gesture. 'Of course I'm sorry he's dead. But you heard the autopsy report. He brought it on himself. There was nothing anybody could have done. And I'm sorry you had a bad time.'

'You don't care about anything,' she said. 'I've never faced that until now. The only important thing to you is your own pleasure.'

He stood, thinking for a while, as though seriously considering her words, while jeeps and trucks trundled past. 'It's not simply pleasure,' he said at last. 'It's more than that. It's life. I'm a writer. I need experiences, Oona. If nothing goes into me, nothing will come out. I can't say no to life.'

'Are you blaming me for coming between you and life?'

'You'll never understand.'

'No, it looks like I never will. Does it ever occur to you that you might catch something? And give it to me?'

'I don't sleep with that sort of woman.'

His brazenness appalled her. 'I don't think you bother to find out what sort of women they are.' Copper took a deep breath. 'I'm not going with you to Dijon. I'm staying here in Paris.'

He blinked. 'You can't just jump the boat. You're my wife.'

'I want a divorce.'

He rolled his eyes wearily. 'Don't be absurd.'

Copper clenched her fists. 'Whatever you do,' she said through gritted teeth, 'don't patronise me, Amory.'

He shook his head in bewilderment. 'You've changed, Copper. What's got into you?'

'I mean it. I want a divorce.'

'Think what you're saying. A divorce is a serious matter.'

'It's a few words mumbled over you by a judge,' she retorted. 'Just like marriage.'

'You know you don't really think that.'

'I didn't used to. You've changed my mind.'

'I've never known you so cynical.'

'I had a good teacher.'

'If that's what you want, okay, goddamn it. But wait until we're back in New York.'

'It'll be just as good here.'

'I'm not going to leave you on your own.'

'I'm not a child. And I'm leaving you, not the other way around.'

'You seem to forget that I'm responsible for you.'

That made her lose her temper completely. '*Responsible?* I wait on you hand and foot. And you treat me like a convenience. I'd like to know who's responsible for whom.'

'I can't talk to you in this mood, Copper.'

'I feel exactly the same way,' she snapped. She turned and walked off, leaving him staring.

After a moment, he came after her and grasped her arm, turning her to face him. 'What do you imagine you're going to do here, all on your own?'

She shook her arm free. 'What I've been doing – writing articles and taking photographs for the British papers.'

Amory's lip curled. 'Honey, covering for George now and then doesn't make you a journalist.'

'As a matter of fact, I think it does. George's editor can't tell the difference between my work and his. They've printed a dozen of my pieces without question. He never got around to posting my last article. It's still on the hall table.'

'That's George's last story!'

'It's *my* story,' she retorted angrily. '*I* covered it. *I* took the pictures. *I* wrote it. George had nothing to do with it. He was in a drunken stupor the whole time. And you know what? It's a damned good story.'

'So that makes you a journalist?'

'Don't try to put me down, Amory. George is dead. I've got his camera and his typewriter. I'll get accreditation from the Brits and I'll speak to his editor. If they don't want to pay me a salary, I'll go freelance.'

'You've thought it all through, I see.'

'As I mopped up George's blood, yes. I thought it all through.'

She walked away again, and this time he didn't follow her.

Dior popped into the apartment at noon; a dapper figure with cheeks made ruddy by the autumn wind.

'I have one hour for my lunch,' he greeted her. 'I came to see how you are after such a terrible shock.'

'You're so kind, Monsieur Dior. I don't know how I would have coped last night without you.'

'Not at all. I hear it was an ulcer?'

'Yes.' They both stared at the huge stain on the wooden floor that she was trying to mop. 'I've tried bleach, but it hasn't helped much.'

'I'll get you some baking soda. We have no flour in Paris,' he added wryly, 'but plenty of baking soda.'

'Is that good for bloodstains?'

'Well, I remember the butcher telling me so as a little boy.'

'It's like something out of Agatha Christie,' Copper said. 'Except not in the slightest bit amusing.'

'You can't stay here,' Dior replied. 'It's more Grand Guignol than Agatha Christie. You'll have terrible nightmares.'

'I'm going to have to find alternative digs anyway. I've split up with Amory. I've asked him for a divorce.'

'*Ah, mon Dieu.* Was that necessary?'

'Yes,' she said shortly. 'It was.'

'Well, I know you Americans think nothing of divorce—'

'That's not true,' she snapped. 'This American takes divorce extremely seriously. The same way I take marriage.'

'All right, my dear,' he said gently. 'But you look most unwell.'

'The longer I stay with him, the sicker I'll get.'

Dior's eyes could be very sad. 'Sometimes, my dear, we have to put up with the infidelities of the beautiful in order not to lose them.'

'That's the way I've thought, up until now. But I think I'd rather be alone than be hurt all the time.'

'Loneliness hurts, too,' he said quietly.

'One gets used to it.'

'Yes,' he agreed. 'One does.'

'He says he has to be unfaithful to me otherwise his inspiration will dry up. How can I live with that?'

'It sounds like something Cocteau would say. Speaking for myself, I don't draw my inspiration from infidelities. I would give anything to have someone to love.'

She sighed. 'You're missing your lunch. I could make you something.'

'No, thank you.' He patted his waistcoat. 'It's good for me to practise a little abstinence.'

'I've got some real coffee.'

'Ah. That's different.'

'I should never have married him,' she said, half to herself, as she was preparing the cafetière. 'It was a terrible mistake.'

Despite the cold wind, they sat on the balcony overlooking the rue de Rivoli so they would be as far away from the stain as possible. 'Life is a tightrope,' Dior said. 'You set off along the wire and no matter how much it wobbles, there is no stopping or turning back.'

'There is falling.'

'Yes. I have fallen many times. And had my heart broken each time.'

She recalled what Amory had said about Dior. The affairs he was referring to had presumably been with other men? It was odd, but that didn't disturb her. In fact, she felt a kind of solidarity with him. 'Well, I guess this is my first – and last.'

'Heaven forbid.' He dug in the pocket of his trousers, producing a string of silver trinkets. 'I'm going to give you one of my good-luck charms. For protection.' He detached one of them and gave it to her. 'Two hearts entwined. That means you will find true love one day. Keep it safe.'

'I will,' she promised. 'What are the others?'

'This is a lily of the valley, so that I can always find work. This is a lucky horseshoe. This is a rabbit's foot. This is an initial "C".'

She was amused and touched by the solemn recital. 'And the star?'

'Ah. That's the most important of all. My mother gave me that before she died. It's *my* star. You know – my dream, my hope, my ambition, which I must always follow.'

'And what is your dream, Monsieur Dior?'

'Fame and fortune; what else?'

Copper smiled, thinking that it would be somewhat capricious of fame and fortune to favour this retiring, bashful man.

'Thank you for the coffee. The best I've had in many weeks. Where will you spend the night?'

'I don't know.'

'You can't stay here in this atmosphere.' He gave her a little pasteboard card. 'My address. You must come to me for the night.'

'Oh, I couldn't impose, but thank you.'

'Do you intend to reconcile with your husband?'

'I don't think so,' Copper said slowly. 'I don't think that's going to be possible.'

'Then you must come to me while you work things out. As a single woman, you will not be given a hotel room in Paris.' His voice changed subtly. 'You know that you have nothing to fear from me?'

'I know that.'

'Good. Dinner is at nine. I will expect you.'

She saw him to the door. The prospect of having a welcoming place to sleep was a great relief. An hour after he left, a boy arrived with a large package of baking soda and a note from Dior telling her to spread the powder over the stain and let it work for an hour. He had signed it whimsically, '+tian'. As she shook the powder over the floor, Copper had the feeling that she had at least one friend in Paris.

Amory returned to the apartment in the late afternoon. His expression was wary as he looked into the bedroom. 'I've taken care of George.'

'How have you taken care of him?' she asked in a grim voice.

'I've got him a niche in Père Lachaise Cemetery. He'd have liked that. The funeral's tomorrow at noon.'

'That was efficient of you.'

'I have my uses.' He eyed her suitcase, which she was packing on the bed. 'You're not really going through with this, are you?'

'If you mean, am I really leaving you? Yes, I am. You had me fooled for a while, Amory. But not anymore. I've wised up.'

'Jesus, Copper. What's got into you? This is not like you at all.'

'Matter of fact, it's very like me. It's the me you prefer to ignore.'

'This is a ridiculous overreaction. You're blaming me for George's death.'

'No, I'm not.' She folded a sweater briskly. 'I'm blaming you for destroying our marriage. And now I'm doing what I have to do.'

'And what's that?'

She thought of Dior's good-luck charm. 'Following my star.'

He sighed. 'Okay, you may have a gift for writing. But there's one thing you can't change: you're a woman. They'll never let you near the fighting.'

'I'm not going to cover the fighting,' she retorted. 'There are a dozen fascinating stories waiting to be covered right here in Paris. The story I've just written, for a start – about that poor woman with her baby. I can sell that article to one of the women's magazines. Maybe even *Harper's*. Text and photos.'

'If you're lucky. So you have one story to your credit. You'll never get another one.'

'Oh yes, I will. Paris is bursting with stories. Human stories. The recovery of French haute couture, for a start. Paris re-establishing herself as a centre of culture and fashion.'

'Women's journalism,' he said with a grimace.

'You can laugh if you want. Paris is the first great city to be liberated from the Nazis. It's a hell of a story and people are going to want to read it – men *and* women. I'm going to find magazines who'll take my stuff.'

He nodded slowly. 'So this is more than just being mad at me.'

The question surprised her for a moment. 'Yes, of course,' she said, as though considering that for the first time. 'It's much more than that.'

'At least that's something. I suppose I've been intolerable.'

'I couldn't have chosen a better word.'

'But I don't know how I'm going to get along without you.'

'You'll manage.'

'I suppose I will.' He went to look out of the window at the sky. 'Do you have to leave right now?' he asked without turning round.

'I can't spend the night here.'

'I don't mind. If George's ghost comes to visit, it will be a merry one.'

'You didn't have to scrub George's blood out of the planking with baking soda,' she pointed out. 'It's not an experience I'm going to forget.'

'We can go to a hotel.'

'No, thank you. I've got an invitation.'

Amory turned in surprise. 'Who from?'

'Monsieur Dior.'

'You're barking up the wrong tree there, Oona,' he said dryly. 'Monsieur Dior is not a ladies' man.'

'I think he's every inch a ladies' man,' she replied evenly. 'But not in the way you mean. And I think it's disgusting of you to suggest anything like that. He's kind and courteous, and a perfect gentleman.'

'Well, I suppose I am none of those things.'

'No, you're not.'

'He looks like a Kewpie doll.'

'I don't care what he looks like. He's my friend.'

He turned back to the sunset. 'I'm setting off for Dijon after the funeral tomorrow. And I'm taking the jeep. You won't have transport.'

'I'll get a bicycle.'

He let out a sigh of exasperation. 'Give it some thought, goddamn it.'

'I've given it all the thought I need,' she replied. She pushed the lid of her suitcase down and fastened the latches with a decisive click.

Of course, it wasn't as easy as that. She wept bitterly for two hours on the banks of the Seine, clutching her suitcase, ignored by the crowds that flowed around her. Amory had been the centre of her existence for the past year and a half, her mate, the star she had followed. Being without him filled her with a grief that felt – at this moment – infinite. She had no idea how she was going to get through the next hour, let alone the rest of her life.

Enveloped in the darkness and trembling with the cold that rose from the inky river, she had never felt lonelier or more abandoned. More than once, she was on the verge of lugging her suitcase back to the rue de Rivoli.

At last, as nine o'clock approached, she got up and trudged, stiff with the cold, towards Christian Dior's address on the rue Royale. The street was wide and grand, running from the place de la Concorde up to the Church of the Madeleine. On the way, she came across two boys selling mistletoe. A few francs bought her a wreath with plenty of pearly berries. Dior's apartment was in a large block, up several very dark and draughty flights of stairs. She clambered up to the fourth floor, hauling her worldly goods, until she reached his door and knocked. Dior let her in, taking her coat and suitcase.

After the gloomy autumn chill, Dior's rooms were a haven of softly lit elegance. He disappeared with her coat and case while she looked around. There were some old prints and some unusual modern paintings, a few pieces of sculpture and some fine-china pieces. The wallpaper was lush, red and gold flock, and the curtains, as she might have expected, were exquisitely done. The dining table was laid for two. A small, enamelled stove was providing some heat, but the apartment, like all of Paris, was ice cold. Nevertheless, she could have wept at the prettiness and light.

Dior reappeared, rubbing his hands together. 'Now. An aperitif. I have Dubonnet or Noilly Prat.'

'Oh, I think Dubonnet, thank you. I don't like dry drinks.' She presented him with the mistletoe she'd bought in the street. 'I know it's early, but I couldn't resist. The berries are so fresh and pretty. I don't know if it will last until Christmas. Don't worry,' she added. 'I don't expect you to kiss me under it, but I'm sure there will be someone you'll want to kiss.'

'In France, we wait until New Year to kiss under the mistletoe,' he said, taking the wreath. 'This is not the common mistletoe, you know, but the oak mistletoe. That's much rarer and very good luck.'

He hung it over a doorway. He was wearing a dark red jacket and a cravat and looked quite dashing. She realised that he was not as middle-aged as she had supposed; the pinstripes he wore at Lucien Lelong, and his general air of conservatism, made him seem older, but he was probably no more than forty. In his own home, with his receding chin and sensitive mouth, there was something almost childlike about him.

'You're being so kind to me,' she said. 'I don't know how I would have coped without you.'

'I'm happy to have been able to help. One feels so helpless sometimes. To express things, I mean. To show gratitude for being liberated.' He poured the drinks carefully. 'The years of the Occupation were hideous. You cannot imagine how bleak they were. Pétain had allied us with Hitler. The Germans were sacking France – indeed, sacking Europe. We were crushed. People died of cold and hunger in Paris. In Paris! That was the *Pax Germanica*.' He raised his glass to Copper. 'It is an honour to show a little hospitality to the representative of our liberators.'

'I am delighted to accept it on behalf of Franklin D. Roosevelt.'

They drank. 'Besides' – he raised a finger – 'you really are an innocent abroad, you know. It is my duty to protect you. And now,' he said, smacking his lips, 'you must excuse me for a moment while I attend to affairs of the kitchen.'

Copper wandered around the flat while he busied himself with the supper.

She picked up a photograph of a young woman whose face was sufficiently like Dior's for Copper to be certain this was his sister, Catherine. 'Your friend Monsieur Poulenc told me about your sister. I'm very sorry.'

He peered round the kitchen door. 'She will come back to me. Look at the back of the frame.' He'd tucked two tarot cards behind the photograph. 'The Six of Wands and The Chariot,' he said. 'They come up every time in Madame Delahaye's readings. Signifying a safe return.'

'She looks a lot like you.'

'I wish the Gestapo had taken me instead of her. But, of course, it was her they wanted. I didn't have the courage to do what she did: running around Paris on her bicycle, carrying messages for the Resistance. I wanted only to bury myself in my atelier and never face this world again.'

Copper was stricken by the look on his face. 'You must have hope.'

'But we hear terrible things. They told us that Ravensbrück was clean and healthy. Now we hear about disease, starvation, torture. And there is more. They say that the Nazis are systematically killing prisoners. A policy of extermination. Thousands – millions – gassed, and the bodies thrown into incinerators.'

She didn't know how to comfort him. 'We've heard the same thing. At first we couldn't believe it.'

'I believe anything of the Nazis. One will never forget their unique flavour.'

She continued her exploration while he cooked. He'd done up the apartment tastefully, but – she guessed – on a shoestring, using ingenuity rather than spending money. He'd created an impression of richness that was rococo without being exactly feminine. She noticed a delicate, yellow-silk Chinese screen, behind which was hidden an erotic bronze male nude. That made her think of Amory. Where was he spending the night? With the cockney? Or with someone even newer? She didn't want to dwell on that.

'Is this your mother?' she asked, picking up a silver-framed photograph of a woman in Edwardian dress.

'Yes, indeed. Don't you love the hat? Look at the ostrich feathers.'

'You must miss her greatly.'

'I do. It's been twelve years.'

'My mother died young, too. My father never remarried. He was a factory worker born in Ireland. He worked his way up to foreman, but we never seemed to have enough money. And he was passionate about working conditions. When he started, people worked a sixty-hour week for pitiful wages. The factories were so dangerous that machine operators often lost limbs or were burned to death. He led the fight against all that. But it cost him. He died of a heart attack a few weeks after Amory and I were married.'

'My father was the opposite of yours,' Dior told her. 'He was a rich man. He had a big factory. He wanted me to follow him into the family business. He was furious when I chose a career in art. Then he went bankrupt. Now I'm the one who supports him and my two brothers with my art.'

'How ironic.'

'Perhaps. But it's partly my fault that he lost everything.'

'How?'

'When he saw that neither I nor my brothers were going to take over the company, he took money out of the business and invested heavily in the stock market. The Great Depression wiped him out. I managed to buy a little farmhouse and he lives quietly there in the *zone nono*.'

'*Nono?*'

'*Non occupée*, you understand. They called us *ja-ja* France; they accused us of living under the Germans because we liked it. But I don't think it's an exaggeration to say that without the work I have here, my father and my brothers would have starved.'

'You're a good man, Monsieur Dior.'

'I am so-so. Neither *ja-ja* nor *nono*.' He emerged smiling from the kitchen in a fragrant cloud of steam. He was carrying a platter, on which was a large, crimson lobster.

'Holy Toledo,' she exclaimed.

'Sent to me from Granville, my home town,' he beamed. 'Don't you think it's most appropriate? A denizen of the sea that links your country and mine. And look what a magnificent ensemble she's wearing. What colours! What frills and bows! And look at her skirts. Not even Schiaparelli could dream up a costume like that.'

'How do you know it's a female?'

'My dear, I grew up next to the sea. I know my lobsters.'

The lobster was a gourmet feast. There was even a bottle of Pouilly-Fumé to go with it. She hadn't eaten so well since leaving the States. But halfway through, she started crying again.

'What's the matter?' Dior asked in alarm.

She put her knife and fork down and grabbed her napkin to blot her eyes. 'Everyone tried to talk me out of marrying him, but I just wouldn't listen.'

Dior patted her hand. 'But then, you know, there is the next one to look forward to.'

She laughed painfully through her tears. 'I'm not planning any others, Monsieur Dior. I think Amory was my first and last.'

'That is how you feel now. But you're young. Love will come along soon enough.'

'Is that the way it is with you?' she ventured. 'One ends and another begins?'

The corners of his mouth drooped. 'Well, I don't think you should take me as an example. I am not exactly – typical.'

'Nor am I. So what do you do – when you set off along the tight-rope and you find it's wobbling like mad, and you can't stop or turn back?'

'As you said earlier. One falls.'

She looked up at him with solemn grey eyes. 'Then behold a falling woman, Monsieur Dior. It remains only to be seen how far, and how many bones will be left intact.'

His fingertips stroked her wrist gently. 'You'll see, *ma petite*. A parachute will pop open like a white cotton ball and you will drift safely to earth.'

'That's consoling,' she said, unconvinced.

'You shall stay here for as long as you like,' he said, with a little pressure of his fingertips.

'You'll get sick of the sight of me.'

'I doubt it. You are very ornamental.'

He had made a compote of winter berries for pudding, apologising for the absence of cream, sugar and butter. There was also a tiny cup of coffee each, made from what she guessed was a long-hoarded store. She determined to get some fresh coffee for him as soon as she could.

Shortly after they had finished their drinks, there was a knock at the door. 'I hope you don't mind a few of my friends,' Dior said. 'They always drop in after dinner.'

An apparition came through the door in the form of Suzy Solidor in a lustrous, full-length sable coat. The sable was unfolded to reveal that the singer was sheathed in a shimmering, silver lamé dress. She looked like an art deco sculpture in gleaming platinum. Almost ignoring Dior, she made for Copper with both hands outstretched. 'My little Copper. They tell me you have been bathed in blood.' Her strong, icy fingers grasped Copper's, and her chilled lips kissed her cheeks. She drew back to inspect her like a bird of prey judging a dove. 'It has made you immortal. How charming you look.'

Close behind her, and no less alarmingly, appeared a fat man with wild hair and a huge, tangled beard surmounted by two cheeks like cooking apples, and a pair of protuberant blue eyes that fixed on her brightly. 'So, this is Christian's little pet,' he boomed, a lighted cigarette bobbing between his lips. 'My God! What a wolf he is. Does he keep you locked in the attic, my dear? And the key on a chain around his neck?'

Dior seemed undisturbed by these extravagant salutations. 'You know Suzy, of course,' he said to Copper. 'And this is my dear friend and namesake, Monsieur Christian Bérard.'

'No "Monsieur", please,' Bérard said. He carried a small white dog under his arm. He extracted the cigarette, stooped over Copper's hand and snuffled it like a boar rooting for truffles. 'They call me Bébé. Like Mimì. I don't know why. And this,' he added, presenting the dog, 'is Jacinthe.' He peered into Copper's face. 'How charming, that youthful complexion.' He showed stained teeth in a carnivorous smile. 'And you have left your husband, they tell me?'

'Bébé!' Dior hissed. He had obviously instructed everyone to avoid the subject of Copper's marriage.

'I can't stay long,' Suzy announced, smoothing her silver scales like a mermaid. 'I must be at the club in an hour.'

'Are you going to throw "Lili Marlène" in their faces again?' Bérard asked.

'Tonight and every night.'

'Until they string you from your lamp post?'

'Let them try,' Suzy replied. 'I'm not afraid of that rabble.'

'You should be. They've got it in for you.'

'You want me to run to Switzerland like Chanel?' Suzy Solidor made a contemptuous face. 'I never knew she was such a timid old bitch.'

'Chanel is a genius,' Dior said. 'I won't hear a word against her.'

'Nevertheless, something of an old bitch, I agree,' Bérard put in. 'I should know, I worked for her long enough.'

'She adored you.'

'Oh, everyone adores me,' Bébé replied loftily. He sniffed the air. 'I smell lobster. That means a little package from Granville has arrived. Was there, by any chance, also a bottle of Calvados, my dear boy? It's as cold as hell out there.'

Smiling, Dior produced an unlabelled bottle. The spirit was fiery enough to make Copper's head spin, but Bérard swilled it down without wincing. They huddled around the stove, into which Dior carefully fed a couple of small logs.

'I don't know why everyone is so anti-Chanel,' he said. 'She did exactly what the rest of us did.'

'Not exactly,' Bérard replied, lighting a second cigarette from the stub of the first. 'She spent the war cosily tucked up in the Ritz with her Nazi lover, toasting the German victory in confiscated champagne, and now she vanishes in a cloud of Number Five. You, of all people, should resent her, my darling.'

'Chanel did not arrest my sister,' Dior said simply.

'No, her boyfriends did. And Coco didn't lift a finger to help.'

'Why should she help me? I am nobody.'

'Nonsense. She's jealous of you. Jealous of all the young designers. Besides, she looks like a superannuated monkey these days, and *that* is unforgivable, even if nothing else is.'

While the men wrangled, Suzy Solidor put a tanned arm around Copper's neck and drew her close. 'Come to the club with me tonight,' she said in a thrilling whisper, close to Copper's ear. 'I have some divine hashish from Morocco. We'll have such fun, you and I.'

'I really couldn't,' Copper replied faintly.

The open mouth caressed her neck, sending shivers down her back. 'Why not? Your husband isn't here.'

'Well, you know I – I'm actually in mourning,' Copper stammered, aware of sounding idiotic. 'My friend died only last night. The – the funeral is tomorrow.'

'Did I hear the word "funeral"?' Bérard said, turning.

'Yes.'

'Whose?'

'George Fritchley-Bound's. He was a journalist. A friend.'

Bérard brightened. 'But I simply *adore* funerals. You must allow me to attend.'

'Well, I'm sure George wouldn't mind,' Copper replied, nonplussed. 'There's certainly not likely to be a crowd. It's at Père Lachaise Cemetery, tomorrow at noon.'

'You'll come too, my love?' Bérard demanded of Dior.

'Of course.'

'I shall sing at the graveside,' Suzy announced.

'But not "Lili Marlène", if you please.'

'No, no. Something simple, but dignified. Perhaps "Chant des adieux".'

Copper's heart was sinking at the prospect. It wasn't clear whether they were joking or serious.

There was another knock at the door and a dark, serious-faced young man in a beautiful camel-hair overcoat came in cursing the cold. 'It's like Moscow out there, damn it.'

Dior introduced him to Copper. 'My colleague at Lucien Lelong, Pierre Balmain. Far more talented than I, of course.'

'That's not true,' Balmain replied, shaking Copper's hand. 'Don't listen to a word he says.'

'We're all going to Copper's friend's funeral tomorrow,' Bérard announced. 'Suzy will sing and I will make an oration. You must come, Pierre. It's going to be quite an occasion.'

'A funeral is hardly the place for your antics, Bébé,' Balmain rejoined, raising his eyebrows. 'My condolences on your loss, Mademoiselle.'

'Thank you,' she murmured. Two more young men arrived, both gazelle-like and soigné. They were introduced as dancers from the Ballets des Champs-Élysées, and were evidently on excellent terms with Bérard and Dior, though she forgot their names a moment after she heard them. The room was warming up as it filled. The heat, the Calvados, the wine she had already drunk and Christian Bérard's endless cigarettes were making her feel quite dizzy. Nor did it help that Suzy Solidor was now pressed up tightly beside her and caressing the nape of her neck with her fingertips. It had been a dreadful day and all she wanted to do now was get into her bed and sink into oblivion, but that was impossible.

'Are you unwell, *chérie*?' Suzy murmured.

'I don't feel too good,' Copper admitted.

'You are pale. But it suits you.' Her eyes were a rich, luminous brown, set under strongly marked eyebrows. Her face was handsome rather than conventionally pretty. Her figure, too, was striking, with the athletic arms and shoulders of a swimmer or tennis player, yet with a rounded bosom and full, mobile hips. She wore a watch set with emeralds, and a single bright diamond on a platinum chain around her throat.

Dior had a gramophone and wound it up to put on a recording of Chopin nocturnes. These were dismissed by the others as too melancholy, but the Strauss waltzes he chose instead were decried as being too Germanic. He threw his hands up and invited them to choose for themselves. An argument arose around the golden trumpet of the gramophone as records were plucked from their sleeves and stuffed back in. Eventually, they settled on Milhaud's *Le Bœuf sur le toit*. She felt a little daunted at finding herself in such exotic and opinionated company.

Bérard was still wrangling with someone over Coco Chanel's behaviour, but Dior and Balmain had entered into a quiet conversation about work.

'I don't want to let Lelong down,' she heard Dior say in a low voice. 'He's been very good to me.'

'And to me,' Balmain replied. 'But we've given him five years apiece, Christian. Ten good years between us. And the war is coming to an end. Now's the time to strike out on our own.'

'All very well to say that, but where's the money to come from? You, at least, have an obliging *maman*. I have nobody.'

'You have genius. You could raise the money in a month if you wanted. Aren't you tired of being told what to do and what not to do?'

'It would be nice to be allowed to design what I liked,' Dior sighed. 'But I feel I'm still learning.'

'You've learned all that Lucien Lelong has to teach you,' Balmain replied. He had a forceful, emphatic manner. 'You simply have to make up your mind to break free.'

'The truth is that I'm too lazy to break free,' Dior said with a slight shrug. 'I don't mind obscurity at all. I don't have your commanding personality. I can't see myself at the head of a business. I would feel dreadfully awkward impersonating an entrepreneur. Besides, freedom has a price, you know. If we were entrepreneurs, we wouldn't be having this congenial evening with friends. We'd be brewing ulcers over the accounts.'

'Well, I'm going ahead,' Balmain said decisively. 'The old guard have had their day – Worth, Lelong, Molyneux and the rest. The fashion business needs new blood.'

'I shall miss you terribly when you leave,' Dior said, and Copper saw that there were tears in his eyes.

Balmain gave his friend a kiss on the cheek. 'You won't be long behind me. You'll see.' He produced a notebook from his pocket, and the two friends were soon engaged in sketching and discussing designs.

'When Dior went into couture, do you know what they said?' Suzy murmured in Copper's ear. 'They said, "Christian has thrown himself away. He's taken the easy way out. He could have been anything he wanted." He's one of the cleverest men in Paris and one of the most cultured. *And* one of the most popular. But look at him – as sensitive as a snail, drawing in his horns at every knock. He would rather grow old in Lelong's back rooms than show his face in the street.'

Copper glanced at Dior. With his rosy cheeks, epicene shape and manicured hands, he resembled a parish priest more than a great couturier. It struck her as odd that such a conservative man should have such colourful friends, inhabiting a world where, as Amory had put it, the women were all men and the men were all women.

'Doesn't he have a – a friend?' she asked delicately.

'You mean a lover? From time to time. He doesn't have the gift of keeping them. Even in love he's too reticent. The insecure make bad lovers, you know.'

'He's so kind.'

'He and his circle are all of a type, I'm sure you see that. But they don't find love with one another. They fall in love with a different class of man altogether – men who are not like them and often don't respond.'

'That's sad.'

'He thinks you bring him luck,' Suzy replied obliquely. 'Apparently, your coming was foretold by that old gypsy soothsayer of his. Even down to the red hair and the gift. The foie gras, you know. Which, by the way, is the last thing he should be eating; he's far too fat.'

'Oh dear. I hope I do bring him luck. I've never thought of myself as a lucky person.'

Suzy brushed the hair away from Copper's brow. 'Do you think of yourself as a beautiful person?'

'Oh, no. Not at all.'

'Yes. One can see that. The day that you realise how beautiful you are, the world will get a surprise.'

Copper was discomfited. 'I've never been pretty.'

'With those eyes, that mouth? My dear, some women flower late. Some early, some not at all. The late flower is usually the finest.' Her mouth, which could be tightly compressed, broke into a brief, fresh smile. She glanced at the little emerald-set watch on her wrist. 'I must go. We'll see each other tomorrow.' She kissed Copper on the cheek, leaving a perfect lipstick impression, and went to get her sable.

After Suzy Solidor had left, Copper lapsed into a drowsy state while visitors came and went and the conversation flowed around her. Poulenc arrived and gave her his condolences in a rather formal way, but she barely heard his voice. No doubt she was missing sparkling repartee, but she was simply exhausted, her French was running out, and it was a relief when the last guests departed and Dior showed her to her tiny room.

She fell instantly asleep, but not for long. An hour later, she was awake again, shivering violently. For a moment she was confused, not knowing whether she was hot or cold. It was not that she was cold; Dior had piled bedclothes on to her and she was hot, rather than otherwise. It was an intense, nervous tremor that shook her like a rat in the jaws of a terrier. She couldn't control it, no matter how she tried. Perhaps she had contracted a fever? She began to be afraid of the spasms that convulsed her and wouldn't die away, no matter what she did. At last, she realised that it was an emotional reaction to her break-up with Amory. In fact, what she was facing was nothing less than a crisis in her life. She'd never felt so alone and so panic-stricken.

Twining her life around Amory's had given her support. If that support were taken away – if she allowed Amory to leave Paris without her – would she not simply collapse, like an ivy plant stripped off a wall?

Her bold plans to continue alone, to launch her career as a journalist, seemed absurd as her teeth chattered and her legs twitched in this dark, alien room. What did she really know about journalism or photography? Let alone about life? Who was she trying to kid? She should jump up now, seek out Amory, beg him to forgive her and take her back. The alternative was to risk falling into an abyss: a black void, out of which she would never be able to crawl.

Disconnected impressions of the past few days flashed through her mind. The mother clutching her baby as the pastry cook hacked off her hair. George's milky, half-open eyes, his face caked in congealed blood. Amory's expression when she'd told him she wasn't going to Dijon with him. The erotic touch of Suzy Solidor's mouth on her throat. Bérard's staring blue eyes, impersonating a desire he did not feel. The images now all seemed so sinister to her that her shuddering intensified and her skin crawled with horror. What was she doing here? Had she destroyed her life? Had she been too harsh with Amory? She missed him dreadfully. Why had she sent him away? It had been madness.

She peered at her watch. It was three in the morning. Despite that, she couldn't stay in bed a moment longer. She emerged from the mountain of bedclothes into the icy darkness, wrapping her dressing gown around her shivering body, and tiptoed out of her room. There was a light burning in the little salon. Dior was awake, huddled by the stove with a drawing pad on his knees. He looked up in surprise.

'Are you unwell?'

'I – I can't stop trembling,' Copper said through chattering teeth. 'I think it's nerves.' She suddenly saw the figure of Christian Bérard slumped on the sofa behind Dior. 'Oh, I'm sorry. I didn't mean to intrude.'

'Don't worry about Bébé. He has smoked two pipes of opium and he won't wake up.'

'Opium?'

'He's an addict. It will kill him one day. I think I am doomed to lose all those whom I love. Come and sit with me.' He put another precious log into the stove and a dim glow flickered behind the murky glass of the door. 'It's natural to have nerves. You have been through a great deal.' He was bundled into a red paisley robe with a woollen scarf wound around his throat. He took off the scarf and transferred it to her in a fatherly way. She'd somehow imagined his body to be pink and smooth, but she glimpsed a triangle of surprisingly hairy chest. 'I always dream of dresses, you see.'

'Do you really?'

'Yes, but then I have to get up in the night. I must make sketches before I forget them.' He showed her the fluid lines in his sketchbook. 'These are cocktail gowns in satin. I saw the cut of the neckline in my dreams.'

'Then you must really have fashion in your blood.'

He glanced at her from under his heavy lids. 'Oh, I know what they say about me. Dior is a dilettante; Dior is an amateur, wasting what little talent he has on silly frocks for silly women. But there is more to it than that. Fashion is art, my dear. High art. Dior, in his way, strives to be a high artist, just like his friends.'

'I can see that.'

'It has taken me ten years to learn what little I know, first with Piguet, then with Lelong. It fascinates me more and more. Finding the right material to express my ideas. Knowing the easy fabrics, the difficult fabrics. Foreseeing the way each material falls, the way it drapes, the way it changes shape, like liquid, on a woman's body.' His hands caressed imaginary curves in the air. 'Learning what one can achieve with a shantung, with a handsome tweed, with a heavy wool or a fine linen. How to cut on the bias so that every fold moves with the woman inside. How to disguise what is ugly and enhance what is beautiful. How to pleat, fold, gather, trim. *Enfin*, the mysteries of the trade.'

She gave a little laugh that was half a sigh. His light, gentle voice was soothing and Copper felt her shivering begin to subside. 'You're a very sweet man, Monsieur Dior. No wonder your friends all dote on you.'

He glanced at Bérard who had started to snore loudly. 'They're distinctly bohemian for the most part, aren't they? And I, by contrast, am distinctly bourgeois. That has become something of an insult lately. In the mouth of Monsieur Giroux, for example, "bourgeois" is the vilest of epithets. But I know what I am and I am proud of it. I come from solid, Norman stock. What else can I be, but solid and Norman?'

'Your friends say you're a genius,' she replied.

He hesitated. 'Clothing comes between our own nakedness and the world. It can be a disguise, a fancy-dress costume, a fantasy. Or it can express one's true self more accurately than any words. For men like me . . .' He didn't finish the sentence. 'Are you really going to divorce your husband?'

'Yes. But I'm not sure where to begin. Perhaps we'll have to go the American embassy.'

'Since you are both resident in France, and are divorcing *par consentement mutuel,* all you need to do is draw up an agreement and present it to a French judge. You could be free in as little as a month.'

'A month!'

'Thanks to the Emperor Napoleon, French divorce laws are very sensible.'

Copper felt a little breathless. 'I didn't know it could be so quick.'

'Are you having second thoughts?'

'No. My marriage is over. It was over a long time ago.'

'If you like, I will help you with the agreement.'

'Thank you.'

She found herself dozing, half-hearing the scribble of his pencil and the occasional rustle of logs slumping inside the stove. When she awoke again, she found that Dior must have led her, or perhaps even carried her, back to bed. The shivering had subsided, leaving her weak and limp. She rolled over and went back to sleep.

Four

George's funeral was an unusual occasion for various reasons. For one thing, an unexpected number and variety of mourners arrived at Père Lachaise Cemetery to see him off. Several foreign correspondents and photographers turned up, many of whom were the Frightful Bounder's drinking companions and were already, by noon, in various states of drunkenness.

In addition, all those of Dior's circle who had promised to come arrived, and they brought with them a number of friends. Christian Bérard came wrapped in a billowing black coat, underneath which he was clearly still in his pyjamas, which were covered in cigarette ash and burn holes. His little white bichon frise, Jacinthe, was tucked under his arm.

Suzy Solidor was dressed as a man in a frock coat and top hat, carrying an ebony cane, her embroidered waistcoat hung with a gold chain. The two ballet dancers had come as Harlequin and Columbine and looked quite eerie flitting among the graves. There was also a person of indeterminate sex who had come in a crimson cloak. Though others were not actually in fancy dress, their hats and clothes were extravagant enough to draw attention. Some had brought flowers, or less conventional objects such as a hobby horse and a blue bicycle. The whole effect struck Copper as dreamlike, as if the occasion were not surreal enough.

The day was grey and windy. A pale sickle moon was suspended behind the trees, which were showering leaves on to the rows of monumental masonry. A marble angel nearby, streaked with green, stared at the odd gathering with blank eyes.

Amory met her at the vault where George's coffin was to be interred. He was wearing his overcoat, his fair hair blowing in the wind. He was accompanied by Ernest Hemingway, the writer, who, it seemed, had become his friend. They were both drunk. 'You're not really serious about this damned divorce business, are you?' he greeted her.

'Yes.' Copper spoke bravely, as though her terrors of the night hadn't happened. 'I'm serious. You'll get the papers. All you have to do is sign them.'

He belched. 'And you're determined on staying here?' He gazed around at the fantastical collection of mourners. 'With this crazy bunch?'

She felt that she was bleeding from somewhere inside. 'Yes. I'm running away with the circus.'

'Who the hell are all these people, anyway?' Hemingway demanded. He was wearing a khaki shirt, sleeves rolled up in defiance of the cold, a cigarette clamped in his teeth.

'Friends of Monsieur Dior's. They all insisted on coming.'

Hemingway swigged from a hip flask and passed it to Amory. 'In Paris, nobody wants to be a spectator. Everybody's an actor.'

'It hasn't taken you long to get yourself mixed up with the lunatic fringe,' Amory said. 'Every freak in Paris is here. Is this your idea of a decent funeral?'

'Considering that George drank himself to death,' she replied tartly, 'I'd say it was rather appropriate.'

Amory turned to look at the vault that was being prepared for George by two elderly bricklayers with trowels and hammers. A damp-looking tunnel had been opened in the wall. The bricklayers were scraping out moss and other debris. 'This belongs to a Protestant family who've agreed to let George be buried with their nearest and dearest. There's going to be a problem, though,' Amory slurred.

'What sort of problem?'

'You'll see,' he replied gloomily. Her determination to separate from him had made him sulky, if not shattered by grief. Perhaps he still thought she was only pretending and would change her mind at the last minute. Dior joined them, immaculate in a dark suit and bowler hat, proffering conventional condolences. She was again struck by the contrast between his middle-class conservatism and the weirdness of his friends. She was glad to have him there, standing beside her in his diffident and fatherly way.

A brisk US Army chaplain, arranged by Amory, now arrived and announced that he was prepared to begin the ceremony. The three dozen or so mourners gathered around expectantly. From behind a mausoleum, the pall-bearers emerged, rather unsteadily carrying George's coffin. Copper immediately saw what the problem was going to be. The Frightful Bounder had been a large man and the coffin had been made to fit him; but the recess was narrow, intended for a smaller recipient.

'I don't think it's going to fit,' Dior murmured in her ear.

'I can see that.'

The chaplain had started the service. The coffin was lifted, with a great deal of grunting and gasping, to the recess, which was rather high up; but it soon got stuck and would not slide in any further.

'Perhaps if the handles were removed?' Dior suggested.

The coffin was lowered again. One of the bricklayers produced a screwdriver and the handles were unscrewed, disappearing into a coat pocket. The chaplain waited rather impatiently, glancing at his watch.

Without handles, the coffin was even more difficult to manoeuvre. And once again, it got stuck. Amory cursed under his breath. The coffin was lowered to the ground. The masons began to pry off the wooden rails using their trowels. These produced a loud groaning sound

as they came away, as though amplified by the box they were attached to. Everyone winced, except Bérard, who burst out laughing.

'My God,' Hemingway snorted. 'The old bastard really doesn't want to go.'

Shorn of handles and cornices, the coffin was once again heaved up to the niche. By now the pall-bearers and the masons were all red-faced and sweating, despite the cold. This time, the coffin scraped all the way into the hole. But a new difficulty arose: the box was too long and protruded by several inches. There were sniggers and groans of dismay.

Tight-lipped, one of the masons stepped forward, unasked, and simply knocked off the end of the coffin with his hammer. It fell to the ground, revealing the worn soles of Fritchley-Bound's shoes. The masons swiftly cemented a concrete slab over the awful hole. The pall-bearers, exhausted, passed around a bottle, swigging deeply.

The army chaplain finished the service, closed his prayer book and departed swiftly, looking glad to be finished. But the bizarre mourning party was in no mood to break up. As she had promised, Suzy began to sing 'Chant des adieux', which turned out to be 'Auld Lang Syne' with French words. Her voice was strong and resonant. Amory stepped forward and chalked George's name and dates on the slab. 'The marble won't be ready for a few weeks,' he said. There was appreciative applause when Suzy finished, and the pop of a bottle being opened.

'I'm leaving for Dijon now,' Amory told Copper, turning his back on the motley crowd. He led her out of the cold wind into the shelter at the back of the mausoleum. 'You can have your divorce. Just send me the papers, okay?'

'Okay.'

'What are you going to do about money?'

'I've got some put by.'

'It's not going to last.' He drew an envelope from the recesses of his greatcoat. 'Here. Take this.'

'I don't want it.'

'Take it,' he growled. 'If you insist on being a little fool, you're going to need it.'

'Don't call me a fool.' She was so angry that she almost threw the money back in his face. But sense prevailed, and her annoyance at least helped her to dry her tears. She put the envelope in her bag. He looked wretched.

'This is cockeyed.'

'I guess so.'

'I don't want anyone to blame me if things go wrong for you,' he said. 'I promised your family that I'd take care of you. I don't like leaving you.'

'Don't worry. I won't blame you for anything that happens, Amory.'

He rubbed his face roughly, almost as though he were about to cry. 'I love you. I don't know what I'm going to do without you.'

'I would have thought you'd be glad to get rid of me. Now you won't need to feel guilty about all your affairs.'

'I never did feel guilty. Perhaps that was the problem.'

'I guess so. You've never once said that you were sorry.'

'Would it have made any difference if I had?'

'No.'

'Very well, then. I suppose this is goodbye.'

He kissed her on the cheek. His lips felt cold. 'Good luck, Copper.'

'You, too. Don't take any wooden nickels.'

And that was that. She watched him walk down the avenue between the vaults, his duffel bag hoisted on one shoulder, Hemingway at his side. There was no longer even any anger against him left. Only the loss of him – and with him, a large part of herself. How was she going to manage without him? Her bravado had long since evaporated. She felt desolate.

A comforting hand touched her shoulder. 'You should come home and rest now,' Dior said gently. She nodded her assent. He took her arm and they left the strange funeral party in full swing, almost unnoticed by the others.

Dior's apartment was permeated by an ancient, very Parisian cold and damp. The little enamelled stove had to be cleaned out and relit every morning. Facing this task, Copper found herself short of paper to light the kindling. All she had was the sheaf of women's magazines that she had been carrying around in her case, with their advice on 'How to keep a husband'.

She opened one now and read a few lines: 'Flattery is the food of men. The women who can show appreciation of their company, judgment and tastes, and be serenely oblivious of their peccadilloes, will succeed in managing their husbands.'

Yes, *that* had worked well. She ripped out the page in disgust, crumpled it and thrust it into the stove.

She tried another: 'Don't sit up till he comes home; better to be in bed and pretend to be asleep. If you must be awake, seem to be glad he came home early. He'll probably think you an idiot; but that's inevitable anyway.'

An idiot? She had certainly been *that*. This page, too, went into the stove.

A third presented itself to her eye: 'Don't mope and cry because you are ill – women should never be ill. It will only disgust your husband.'

Was this really the wisdom she had tried to follow? No wonder Amory had walked all over her. She crumpled the pages furiously and stuffed them under the wood. The rest of the magazines went into the log basket to be usefully burned. She wouldn't read them again. From now on she would write her own damned stories.

The bright flames licked up and heat began to radiate from the stove. Dior was awake now. He had the rare knack of being comforting without being obvious about it. He said nothing about Amory's departure, or her obvious misery. Instead, he made a pot of tea and sat with her, looking at her thoughtfully with his head to one side.

She cupped her hands around the warm teacup. 'Why are you looking at me like that, Monsieur Dior?'

'I am thinking that your dressing gown will never do.'

Copper had bundled herself into her woollen dressing gown. 'I know it's rather old,' she admitted.

'A dressing gown is one of the most important garments in your wardrobe.'

'Really?'

'It's the first thing you put on every day, and how your husband sees you every morning.'

'I don't have a husband, in case you haven't noticed,' she pointed out.

'You certainly won't encourage any new applicants,' he said tartly, 'if you start every day looking dowdy.'

'I don't want another husband,' she said. 'And I've just decided that I don't care about pleasing any more men, thank you.'

'Being independent doesn't mean being a frump, Copper. In my experience, the unmarried women are the smartest. Now, if you will permit me, I'm going to take your dressing gown to my seamstresses tomorrow and ask them to put on a little frilling. And perhaps some pretty velvet trim.'

They were interrupted by the telephone. After a brief conversation, he came back, rubbing his hands together.

'Excellent news. There is someone who has the silk we need for your outfit,' he told her. 'We shall go tomorrow to pick it up.'

'Monsieur Dior, you don't have to do this for me. It was just a whim, you know. I don't know what I was thinking of, in the middle of a war. I feel ashamed of myself.'

'But it was not a whim,' he said seriously. 'Everything has a meaning. And why should you be ashamed? Those who want to destroy beauty should feel shame – not those of us who want only to create it. But I haven't finished telling you – we even have a motorcar to use tomorrow. And it's the weekend. Can you imagine? We shall pay a visit to Madame Delahaye on the way.'

The 'motorcar' that Dior had promised turned out to be a most extraordinary vehicle – an antediluvian, black Simca that had been adapted to run on firewood; petrol having been unobtainable since the start of the Occupation. It had a huge, stove-like apparatus bolted on to the rear from which pipes ran all over the bodywork, culminating in a tank mounted on to the front. Copper had seen the things all around Paris, but she was aghast at the idea of travelling in such a dangerous-looking contraption herself. Dior was enraptured.

'Our own car! I haven't been in a car for four years.' He spoke as though it were a Rolls Royce.

Copper had brought the Frightful Bounder's camera along and took a photograph of the vehicle. 'It looks like one of the flying bombs the Germans are using on London. Are you sure it's safe?'

'Of course. It belongs to a good friend and she has kept it in immaculate condition.'

The Simca was rusted and dented in every panel, and the outlandish wood-burning apparatus seemed to have been fixed on in a distinctly amateur fashion. It hardly bore the hallmark of a well-maintained vehicle. Copper thought longingly of the army jeep that Amory had taken away. 'If you say so.'

'I'm so excited,' Dior said, beaming. 'Let's be off.' He was wearing an old tweed jacket with corduroys and a jersey, and he looked like a country schoolmaster. She saw that he was holding the driver's door open for her.

'Aren't you driving?' she demanded.

'Me? Of course not. I never learned. I hate mechanical things. I can't even ride a bicycle.' He frowned. 'Surely you know how to drive?'

She bit her thumb nervously. 'Well, I got a licence in the States. But I've hardly driven at all. Only the jeep a bit. And I wouldn't even know how to start this thing.' She peered inside. The back seat had been removed and the space was piled with wood.

'Extra fuel,' Dior said proudly. 'We can travel a hundred and fifty kilometres.'

A passer-by, scornful of their lack of mechanical knowledge but willing to help, showed them how to start the Simca. This involved lighting the stove on the back with a bit of rag soaked in cooking oil and waiting for the fumes to build up with a lot of hissing and roaring. Eventually, the engine chugged into life, the whole vehicle lurching to and fro on its ancient springs.

'You see?' Dior said triumphantly. 'She is magnificent.'

Copper's heart was in her mouth as they set off, the stove fuming and rumbling on their tail. She clutched the steering wheel in a death grip, fighting the machine's apparent desire to veer in any direction except straight ahead. What would happen if the whole thing exploded? The Simca jolted along at thirty miles an hour or so, with an occasional loud bang from the exhaust.

Their first stop was the house of Madame Delahaye, the fortune teller Dior set so much store by. She lived in a smart little apartment in the 16th arrondissement that did not look in the least supernatural. The woman herself was impeccably middle-class, with shrewd eyes, her hair oiled back into a bun and pearls at her throat. However, Dior behaved towards her with great respect. He evidently took her completely seriously.

Copper was presented to the clairvoyant, who stared into her face, then nodded slowly, as though confirmed in something she had long suspected.

'This is the young woman who brought you the gift – as I predicted?'

'Yes, Madame.'

'Show me your palms, Mademoiselle.'

Copper held out her hands, which were shamefully sooty from the Simca. Madame Delahaye inspected them carefully, tracing the lines and occasionally wiping off smut. 'I see much money, much love – but also much trouble. There is a golden-haired woman who casts her shadow over you. We must read your cards, my dear.'

The cards came out and were carefully shuffled and laid out on the gleaming table. Madame Delahaye pored over them.

'This young lady will bring you luck,' she announced to Dior. 'Keep her close to you.'

'I intend to. Will she get her husband back?'

Madame Delahaye pushed forward a card showing a man riding a horse. 'He travels far away,' she replied enigmatically. 'He thinks of her, but the road back to her is long and he is set in a thicket of thorns. He cannot see the way. And she' – Madam Delahaye pointed at a card showing a woman in a garden – 'she turns her back on him.'

Copper winced.

'But there is a hand coming from the east,' Madame Delahaye went on, 'which places a crown on her head.'

'How wonderful,' Dior sighed. 'And my Catherine?' he asked.

Again, the clairvoyant shuffled the deck and laid out the cards. Dior watched anxiously as she studied them. 'It's clear,' she announced briskly. 'Your sister is alive, she is well and she will soon return to you.'

'You are sure?'

'Look.' Madame Delahaye pushed a group of cards forward. 'It's as clear as day, Monsieur Dior. There she is. The cards never lie.'

Dior put his hand over his mouth, overcome. His eyes were shining with tears. 'Thank you, my dear friend,' he said, when he'd got himself under control. 'Thank you a thousand times!'

Copper was touched by Dior's emotion, but also somewhat suspicious of the clairvoyant's certainty. She was holding out a hope that she could not possibly guarantee. Catherine, she knew, was his favourite sibling. With his mother dead, one brother in a lunatic asylum and the other a suicidal eccentric, Dior's family was shrinking. That was, of course, why he clung to foolish tokens like Madame Delahaye's prophecies. What a lot of strange fancies and ideas knocked around in that supposedly solid Norman head of his.

There was a discreet episode in the little hallway after the reading, with Madame Delahaye murmuring that she simply couldn't accept the offering that Dior pressed on her, and Dior insisting that she must. It was evidently a well-practised ritual between them, and it ended with Madame Delahaye pocketing her fee with downcast eyes and a demure simper.

They continued their journey eastwards out of Paris towards Meaux. Dior was in good spirits.

'I've never known her to be wrong,' he said brightly. 'Not even in the smallest detail. If she says Catherine will come back to me, then I believe it. And I won't listen to all those cynics who tell me I'm a fool.' There was a particularly loud explosion from the Simca's exhaust that made Copper jump, and he giggled. 'Isn't this fun?'

'It might be, if I didn't have to drive.' The roads were potholed by the convoys of heavy tanks that had passed over them, though there was hardly any traffic now. The skinny wheels of the Simca were barely able to cope with the broken surface. The old car lurched wildly to left and right. German signposts still stood in places at the roadside, efficient pointers in ugly black script. Dior wound down the window, inhaling deeply.

'Smell that country air.'

A wave of cold air, redolent of cow dung, filled the car. She glanced at him. There was a smudge of soot on his nose. She couldn't help smiling. His sense of fun was infectious. 'It's nice to see you happy.'

'I want to be happy. And to make others happy. It's one of my chief desires in life – to be a merchant of happiness. That's not such a bad thing, is it?'

'It's a very good thing. Is that why you chose couture – to make people happy?'

'Well, you know, I think couture chose me, rather than the other way around.' He crossed his legs, visibly relaxing. 'From my little corner, I see what pleases people. And I learn how to give it to them. New ideas are so important. The art of pleasing is to know what people want even before they want it. Lelong has been doing the same thing for decades: changing a line here, a shade there. Every collection is more or less the same as the last collection. If you show him something new, he sends it back to the drawing board to be changed, again and again, until it's exactly like every other design he's ever sold. That's what drives Pierre Balmain crazy. The art of fashion is to make a collection look new each time; even though you have to rack your brains to do it.'

'Why don't you leave with Pierre? Set up a new fashion house together?'

'I prefer the back rooms,' Dior said firmly. 'I'm not ambitious like Pierre. I saw my father go bankrupt and I lost everything in my turn. To go through that again – no, thank you. I prefer my pencils and my tranquillity.'

They reached a small, stone village buried in the countryside. Past the straggling street of houses was a nineteenth-century warehouse, now abandoned, its rows of windows broken or shuttered.

'This must be the place,' Dior said.

The grim old mill was surrounded by formidable nettles and almost unapproachable. 'This is like a castle in a fairy tale,' Copper commented.

'And we need to find the dragon.' He beat a path to the entrance with his umbrella and knocked on the door imperiously. Eventually, it opened a little, revealing part of a female face.

'Who are you?'

'Customers,' Dior said brightly. 'May we come in?'

'The mill is closed. My father is sick in bed. What do you want?'

'Shantung,' Dior said succinctly.

'We have nothing,' the woman replied, starting to close the door.

With surprising determination, Dior pushed it open again. 'Wait. Let me just take a look,' he said persuasively, insinuating his long nose into the gap and peering inside. 'Come along, Mademoiselle. There's nothing to be afraid of – we're friends.'

Reluctantly, the woman opened the door to let them in. She was in her twenties. Copper could see why she was so cautious. The scarf she wore couldn't hide the fact that she'd had her head shaved recently – or the bruised eye and cut lip that had no doubt been administered at the same time.

'Did the Resistance do this to you?' Copper asked.

The woman nodded, looking grim. 'And they beat my father.'

'What's your name?'

'Claudette.'

'Very sorry indeed, Mademoiselle Claudette,' Dior said. 'We don't want to hurt you. The silk, now. Is it true you have some?'

'The Germans confiscated it all,' the woman replied, looking even more sullen.

'I'll pay well,' Dior said. 'Cash. And not a word to anyone. You won't get into any trouble.' The cry of a baby could be heard somewhere in the building. Dior cocked his head to one side. 'Boy or girl?'

'Boy,' she said.

'What's his name?'

'Hans,' she replied shortly.

'I am sure you will change that to Jean by and by. And I'm sure you need things for him, don't you?' He crackled notes suggestively in his jacket pocket.

Claudette hesitated for a moment, looking from one to the other. Dior's mild face seemed to reassure her. She led them through the dusty corridors to a storeroom. The rows of shelves were almost empty except for three rolls of fabric wrapped in brown paper. 'This is all that's left. There's nothing more.'

Greedily, Dior unwrapped the rolls. They contained several yards of Chinese silk – a lime green, a pale mauve and a light rose. In this grim setting, and after the khaki years, the colours were strange, almost painful reminders of a world gone by. Dior's eyes gleamed.

'How much do you want for them?'

'A thousand francs the metre.'

Dior laughed indulgently. 'Who do you think I'm making dresses for? Marie Antoinette? A hundred the metre.'

An hour later, they were heading back to Paris, the car overflowing with silk. Dior was gleefully clutching the rustling folds to his bosom to keep them from being smudged. They had settled, after a prolonged negotiation with Claudette, on 250 francs per metre. 'This is probably the only shantung left in France today,' he chortled. 'And you're going to be wearing it.' He buried his long nose in the silk, as though it were an armful of roses, and inhaled luxuriously. 'My God, how good it smells.'

'What does it smell like?' she asked, interested.

'You've never smelled silk?'

'Not that I recall,' she confessed. 'Good old American cotton is what I wear.'

'Here. Smell!' He thrust the silk into her face, almost making her veer off the road. 'What do you think of that?'

'It smells animal,' she said, wrinkling her nose. 'Kind of like children's sweaty hair.'

'That's the sericin. It's the natural glue the silkworms produce. It's miraculous stuff. Do you know that it stops bleeding? And heals wounds? And keeps skin young?'

'You're making this up.'

'Not at all. I know my trade, young lady. Silk is the best fabric to have next to your skin. It's antiseptic and it keeps away wrinkles.'

'Well then, I'll only wear silk from now on,' she said solemnly.

'Which colour do you like?'

'Green or lilac, I think. I somehow never saw myself in pink.'

'Ah, my dear Copper. How little you understand yourself.' He beamed at her. 'The time of leaves and buds is over. You are a rose. It's your time to bloom.'

'Redheads can't wear pink.'

'Absolute nonsense. As I intend to prove to you.'

'You're such a tyrant,' she said irritably. 'You keep asking my opinion and then deciding on the exact opposite.'

He laughed happily. 'It's the Socratic method, my dear. Think of it as an education.'

He didn't stop chuckling even when one of the ancient tyres burst, bringing them to a shuddering halt.

'Now what are we going to do?' she exclaimed.

'You know I'm not mechanical,' he said blithely. 'There must be some way of fixing it, if you just look.'

Copper got out, sighing. She prowled around the Simca, looking for the spare tyre and the tools with which to put it on. They were fixed under the wood burner. Dior peered out at her over his armful of shantung and waved encouragingly. She set to work, hoping her Paris frock was going to be worth it. She manhandled the spare wheel out of its cradle. Dior watched her with benevolent interest as she wrestled with the jack, which hardly seemed strong enough to lift the car with its heavy load of extra plumbing and firewood.

'I'm going to have to find somewhere to stay,' she panted, heaving on the rusty tools.

'My dear, you're most welcome to stay with me as long as you like.'

'That's so kind, but I can't trespass on your hospitality forever.'

'You're proving yourself invaluable so far. I would have no idea how to do what you're doing now.'

'Well, I have to find somewhere. I can't go back to rue de Rivoli.'

He nodded. 'That is certain.'

'And I need to get down to work. I have to earn my crust.'

'Leave it to me,' he said when she got back into the car half an hour later, very much the worse for wear after changing the wheel. 'I'll find you somewhere to stay. I have an idea.'

The next day, she took her story and photographs to the postal centre and had them airmailed to *Harper's Bazaar* in New York. She filed the story under her maiden name, Oona Reilly. If she was to make a fresh start, that seemed to be appropriate.

Applying to *Harper's*, Copper realised, might have seemed ambitious, even presumptuous, to some people. But she reasoned that if she was going into the journalism business, she would start at the top and work her way down. Besides, as she'd said to Amory, she knew it was a damn good story.

Harper's was primarily a fashion magazine, but had also been allocating space to the subject of women in wartime. There was an outside chance they might be interested. She had made the point in her article that the punishment of 'collaborators' very often turned out to be an attack by a mob of men on a defenceless woman, involving stripping her naked and shaving her hair – or worse. There was a very ugly dimension to it that had nothing to do with justice.

Now she had to wait for a reaction. In the meantime, there was her accommodation to sort out.

As it turned out, Dior had found her a rather grand apartment in a rococo block on the place Victor Hugo. The trees outside were leafless and the weather was cold, but the flat had some minimal heating, and even lukewarm water for part of the day. It had belonged to a German sympathiser, one of Christian's clients, who had fled Paris after the Liberation, leaving two months' rent paid.

'So you've got two months to find your feet,' Dior said with his usual optimism. 'Plenty of time.'

The rent was a great deal higher than she thought she could ever afford, and she quailed at the prospect of having to pay it in two months' time. There were three bedrooms and it was a lot bigger than she needed. But it was a refuge for the time being. And it was undeniably convenient. In addition, the place was still furnished with the collaborator's excellent furniture and his fine collection of Lalique glassware. Dior had even found a kindly *bonne* named Madame Chantal, who would help with the cleaning twice a week. He had paid her wages two months in advance.

However, Copper was not permitted to luxuriate in these indulgences. As soon as she had unpacked her suitcase, Dior dragged her out to see the project he was so excited about, making sure that she brought the camera she had 'inherited' from George Fritchley-Bound. Somewhat to her surprise, Dior took her to the Louvre.

The great museum had been emptied, plundered by the Nazis, and some of its most legendary works, including the *Mona Lisa*, were still in Germany. But in the Pavillon de Marsan, devoted to the decorative arts, all was hustle and bustle. Dior led Copper into a large room, where several dozen people, wrapped in overcoats and scarves against the cold, were working on an exhibition. There were several sets being constructed and painted, all in small scale. They depicted the famous parks and boulevards of Paris – or in some cases, imaginary scenes.

Dotted around these dream-like backdrops were mannequins made out of wire, about a third the size of real women. All had the same calm ceramic face; but these were not dolls. Each was being clothed in a diminutive couture outfit: dresses, coats, hats, tiny high-heeled shoes, belts and handbags.

'Some of them even have underwear,' Dior told her solemnly as they made their way around the crowded hall. 'All hand-sewn. The couturiers are rounding up all the scraps of fabric that they've been hoarding, the stuff that would have been thrown away once upon a time, and making outfits.'

'It's extraordinary,' Copper said.

'The fashion houses are joining forces to put on this show – in miniature. They're all here: Nina Ricci, Balenciaga, Schiaparelli, Rochas, Hermès. Isn't it magical?'

Copper stared at the activity all around her. 'Only the French would think up something like this. "Magical" is exactly the word.'

'Don't you think this would make an interesting story?' he said slyly. 'Nobody knows that this is happening. The press are interested in nothing except the war. You're the only fashion journalist in Paris right now.'

'I'm not even a journalist, let alone a fashion journalist.'

'Well,' he said, indicating the camera slung around her slender neck, 'now might be a good time to begin, *n'est-ce pas?*'

It was as though a light bulb had gone on over Copper's head. She raised the camera and focused on a group of young people erecting a pocket-sized Arc de Triomphe. 'Monsieur Dior, you are a genius.'

'I know,' he said modestly.

She took the shot and wound the film on, feeling excited. 'If *Harper's* don't like my last story, they might go for this.'

'Exactly. Tell the world what we're doing, Copper. Tell them it's not just death and destruction, and doom and gloom. People need something to be happy about.'

A young man bustled past them carrying a cardboard Eiffel Tower and called a cheerful greeting to Dior. 'That's Marcel Rochas,' Dior told her. 'I'll introduce you to him later.'

The hubbub of argument, hammering, sawing, and bustling workmen echoed off the severe palace walls. The illusion of a miniature city being built was heightened by the clouds of cigarette smoke and condensation that rose to the lofty ceiling, hovering above the scene like a storm in a teacup. Dior took her around the outskirts to a set representing an ornate salon that had already been completed. Two dressmakers in black were kneeling on the floor fitting exquisite outfits on to the delicately poised dolls.

'This is Maison Lucien Lelong's display,' Dior told her. 'And this is my employer, Monsieur Lelong himself.'

The famous couturier was a small, brisk man in a double-breasted, pinstriped suit. He had sharp eyes and a neat little moustache, and he bowed over Copper's hand with old-school gallantry when Dior presented her to him. 'Welcome to Paris, dear lady,' he said. His expert glance summed her up swiftly. 'You are a journalist? With which publication, if I may ask?'

'I'm with *Harper's Bazaar*,' she declared boldly.

'Excellent. I hope to see you in my salon very soon,' he purred, adjusting the trim of his moustache. He presented Copper with his card. 'I think we can show your readers that fashion is not, after all, dead in Paris.'

'What you're doing here is just astonishing.' She crouched to look at the dolls. 'And what adorable little gowns!'

'Monsieur Dior is the great talent of our house,' Lelong said, putting a hand on Dior's shoulder.

Copper saw Dior blush. 'You are kind to say so, Maître,' he murmured. Quietly, he explained the designs he'd made to Copper. There were evening dresses in glossy silk and some charming day frocks in polka dots. With his plump yet delicate fingers, he unfolded the Lilliputian creations to show the pains that had been taken: shoes that had been hand-stitched, buttons that really buttoned and zips that really zipped; belts with buckles that fastened; handbags and purses that contained tiny powder compacts and lace-edged hankies. Beneath the dresses were tiny camisoles and slips, embroidered as though by fairies.

He drew her attention to the earrings in the tiny ceramic ears and the bangle on the ceramic wrist. 'Gold and diamond,' he murmured. 'Made for us by Cartier.'

For all his shyness, Dior took on a quiet confidence when talking about his designs. Whereas Lelong's authority came from the status of ownership, Dior's came from an artist's inner certainty that his work was good.

Lelong himself stood by proprietorially, one hand in his jacket pocket, the other holding a cigarette. He had been an officer in the Great War, and years of leading Parisian fashion had not erased his military bearing. There could hardly be a greater contrast, Copper thought, between this vigorous martinet and the gentle Dior; but Lelong evidently knew the value of his employee.

She listened carefully to what Dior told her, and made abundant notes. She also took several photographs, trying hard to make sure they were going to come out well. She had to be serious about this new career of hers – and she, too, had to take on the poise of someone doing a job confidently and well.

Back home on the place Victor Hugo, and seated in front of George's typewriter, she had something else to consider – the awkward task of explaining to her family, not to mention Amory's, that she had left him. Or he had left her. In any case, that they had parted company in the middle of a war, thus fulfilling all the dire predictions both families had made about the marriage. After some thought, she wrote two letters: a short one to Amory's father, which explained very little; and a long one to her eldest brother, which explained a great deal.

She read through both letters when she'd finished. Sending them was yet another grave step on the path to separation from her husband. Once mailed, they could not be recalled. The stark state of her marriage would be revealed to all at home. Everyone would know. Patching up the marriage (not that she had any intention of doing that) would be much more difficult, if not impossible.

But if she was serious about any of this, it had to be faced.

She sealed both letters in the US Army Priority envelopes that they'd been given, and put them on the hall table to be mailed. Then she went back to George's typewriter – *her* typewriter now – to work on her article.

Five

She started writing straight away. She was inspired by the subject. Her experience doing George's articles for him also came in useful; she knew enough to keep her sentences short and lively, and to give vivid impressions of the weird and wonderful characters of the Paris fashion world. Human interest was the key to successful journalism. The result, after a day or two of work, was not unpleasing. Even better, it was certainly not unprofessional.

The fly in the ointment was the photographs she had taken. The contact prints the laboratory sent back to her showed that all the interior shots were much too dark. If she was going to be taking lots of indoor photographs, she was going to have to invest in a flash lamp; something George had never bothered with since all his photographs were taken in daylight. And that meant yet more expense.

There was one good shot of Christian Dior, but all the shots of the dolls were useless. She would have to get more on succeeding visits, once she'd equipped herself with a flash.

A visit to the bric-a-brac markets that flourished along the banks of the Seine every afternoon proved fortuitous. Photographic equipment was scarce, the Nazis having confiscated everything they could during the Occupation. But now that they'd left, various oddments were coming out of hiding. She found an old man with a collection of pre-war cameras and accessories laid out on a rickety table. Among them was a battered aluminium flash lamp that could be synchronized with a camera – or so it appeared from the faded instruction manual that had been printed in some strange language, perhaps Czech. At least there were diagrams. The old man assured her that the thing worked. Better still, he had a box of the magnesium bulbs the lamp used. She haggled fiercely for the lot, and eventually got them at what she thought was an exorbitant price.

'Be careful of the bulbs, pretty lady,' the old man warned her as he packed all the bulky equipment into a cardboard box for her. 'They sometimes set things on fire.' That sobering news was offset by the pleasure of being called pretty lady. She had posted her letters to America that morning and it seemed like a good omen.

She took her treasure back to the apartment and set about working out how to attach the apparatus to the Rolleiflex. It proved something of a puzzle and the Czech instructions didn't help. Whatever she did, she couldn't get any of the bulbs to go off. Perhaps the old man had swindled her and they were all duds.

While she was scratching her head over the problem, there was a knock at her door. She opened it to find a young woman on her doorstep. Copper recognised her instantly. It was the busty brunette Amory had absconded with on the night George had died. They stared at one another for a moment.

'He's gone,' Copper snapped and slammed the door in the other woman's face. Or tried to, but she had stuck a foot in the way. The shoe was not very stout, and the resulting thump was painfully loud.

'Ow!' the brunette yelped, hopping on one leg as she clutched her injured toes. 'Bloody hell. What did you have to go and do that for?'

'You shouldn't have stuck your foot in the door,' Copper retorted. 'He's not here, so you can take a hike, sister.'

'I'm not looking for him,' the brunette said, gingerly putting her foot back on the ground to try it out. 'Good riddance, if you ask me.'

'I'm *not* asking you,' Copper said angrily.

'He was a bad lot. You're well shot of him.'

'I'm certainly not going to thank you for getting rid of my husband.'

'*I* didn't get rid of him,' the other said back in her cockney accent. 'I think you've broken my foot.'

'I hope so,' Copper said with relish. 'What do you want?'

'I need somewhere to stay,' she replied. And now Copper saw that a suitcase stood in the hallway. She was flabbergasted.

'Are you seriously asking me to take you in?' she gasped. 'You must be crazy.'

To her disgust, the other woman started to cry, pressing a handkerchief to her face. 'I got thrown out,' she sobbed. 'I got nowhere to go.'

'Well, you can't stay here,' Copper said shortly.

'I wouldn't have come if I wasn't desperate,' she sniffed, wiping a reddened nose. 'I've been walking for hours.' She gulped. 'Can't I just come in for a glass of water? And rest for a moment?'

Copper was annoyed. 'You can have a glass of water and then be on your merry way. I don't even want to look at you.'

She'd barely finished speaking before the little brunette had hobbled swiftly into the apartment, hauling her suitcase, which was covered with luggage stickers from smart hotels. She flopped on a chair, stretching out her shapely legs. 'You couldn't stretch to a cup of tea, could you?'

'You've got some neck.'

'It's just like a glass of water,' the other woman wheedled, 'except hot, and with tea leaves in it.'

'I know what a cup of tea is. And I don't drink it. I'm American. We drink coffee.' Copper marched to the kitchen and filled a glass at the tap. 'I'm not running a restaurant.'

'Oh, bless you.' The new arrival gulped the whole glassful down without stopping for breath. 'I needed that.' She was, on closer inspection, a rounded, pretty bonbon of a woman with a rosebud mouth, a pink-and-white English complexion, and bright blue eyes that were now suspiciously free of tears, though the dark lashes were still becomingly wet. She was not quite as young as she had at first appeared. Aware of being scrutinised, the woman drew herself up in the chair, puffing out her ample bosom like a pigeon. 'They call you Copper, don't they? Which is funny, really, because they call me Pearl.'

'What's funny about it?' Copper growled.

Pearl showed pretty teeth in a cheerful smile. 'You know. Copper and Pearl.'

'I have no idea what you're talking about.'

'Well, it sort of sounds like jewellery, doesn't it?'

'No, it doesn't. How did you know where to find me?'

'I heard people saying at La Vie Parisienne that your Monsieur Dior found you this place. Look, there's something I need to say.' She took a breath. 'I'm sorry I went off with your husband that night. Really sorry. I was wrong. I could say I didn't know you were married to him, but that wouldn't wash, would it? I mean, you were sitting right there, weren't you?'

'Yes,' Copper said stonily. 'I was sitting right there.'

'But he's a very attractive man, isn't he? And oh-so-charming. I mean, how many men do you know who can make you really laugh?'

'Just the one.'

Copper's grim expression wiped the smile off Pearl's face. 'Look, sweetheart—'

'Do *not* call me sweetheart.'

'He made it perfectly obvious that it had happened before. Lots of times. And that you didn't care.'

'But I did care.'

'I know that now, don't I? All right.' Giving up attempts to explain her way out of it, Pearl pulled up the sleeves of her jacket. 'This is what I got out of it.' Livid on the plump white flesh were the purple marks of a man's violent fingers.

'Who did that to you?' Copper asked, taken aback.

'My old man. And there's more. Elsewhere.'

'Your *father* did that to you?'

'No, sweetheart. Where I come from, your old man is your husband. Well, he's not exactly my husband, Petrus, is he? More of a business manager. Cum boyfriend.'

'I'm sorry about all this, but it's your affair, and—'

'And if I'm there when he gets back tonight, he'll give me more. In fact, he'll probably cut my throat.'

Copper recoiled. 'You're kidding.'

'No, sweetheart. He's got a knife about this long.' Pearl held her hands apart. 'I know he's killed two men. He'd think nothing of killing me and dumping me in the river.'

'Then you should go to the police.'

'Yeah, and get myself in trouble. No, thanks. It's nice here, isn't it?' Pearl said, looking around. 'You've got it lovely. Such nice taste.'

'It came furnished,' Copper said, reluctant to take credit for the apartment.

'Did it? My word! You've struck it lucky with your Mr Dior. Funny, I always thought he was a pansy.'

'There's nothing like that.'

The china-blue eyes widened. 'You mean he's not paying the rent, so to speak?'

'It's time you left,' Copper said stiffly.

Pearl pulled down her neckline to show more cleavage, clearly a gesture she used when she wanted to be more appealing. 'This place is far too big for one woman. I've got money.' She dug in her brassiere and came up with a thick roll of banknotes. 'See?'

'Please put your bosom away.'

'I've been saving up for simply ages. I knew I'd need to get away from Petrus before he killed me.' She waved the bankroll to and fro. 'Unless your old man has left you a pile of money, you're going to need this.'

Copper opened her mouth to retort, but the words didn't come. She now had less than two months before she had to start paying the rent; and after today's expenses, her little supply of ready cash was even further reduced. The financial aspect certainly made sense.

'From ear to ear,' Pearl said in a chilling voice. 'He says you have to completely sever the jugular vein and the windpipe to be sure. He's done it before.'

'Stop it.'

'He says their heads almost come off. And the blood shoots out like a fountain.'

'Don't be crass. I'm not going to be blackmailed like this.'

'I'm not looking for charity,' the brunette replied. 'It's strictly a business arrangement. And we've got things in common. We'll be great chums.'

'What could we possibly have in common?'

'We both wound up with bastards,' Pearl said succinctly.

'Except you got your bastard *and* my bastard.'

'You're welcome to mine, but I wouldn't recommend it.' Pearl got up to examine the camera equipment spread out on the table. 'You're a reporter, aren't you? Got all the gear, I see.'

'Don't touch anything,' Copper ordered.

'I'll model for you, if you like,' Pearl volunteered. 'That's what I am, you know. A photographic model. Artistic, of course. Nothing vulgar.'

'I'll bet.'

'It's how I met Petrus. Artistic photography. He's a publisher.'

'Oh, really? I suppose the men he killed were rival publishers.'

Pearl looked surprised. 'Yeah, how did you know?'

'Just a lucky guess.'

Pearl patted her glossy curls. 'I'm his top model.'

Copper snorted, and then had a thought. 'Do you know anything about cameras?'

'Of course. And how to develop film. Nothing to it.'

'Would you know how to make this flash lamp work?'

Pearl inspected the equipment. 'You'll need to put the batteries in. And then you need to plug this bit in to this socket. And you need to screw this bracket on to the bottom of the camera.' With surprising deftness, Pearl assembled all the pieces. The dented aluminium dome of the flash looked rather imposing, attached to the side of the camera. The whole thing, in fact, had taken on a professional appearance. 'Go on,' Pearl said, handing her the camera. 'Try it out.' She pushed up her bosom even further and struck an enticing pose. That small mouth could stretch into a smile wide enough to show every one of her white teeth, and the blue eyes could widen like a child's looking at a birthday cake.

Copper focused the Rolleiflex. She was remembering the old man's warning that the bulbs 'sometimes set fire to things'. With any luck, pressing the shutter now would set fire to this annoying Limey and burn her to a cinder, thus eliminating her unwelcome presence. She pressed the shutter.

There was loud pop and a brilliant flash that illuminated Pearl and the entire room behind her. A cloud of metallic-smelling smoke swirled up to the ceiling.

'There,' Pearl said, returning to normal and pulling her dress straight. 'Works perfectly. You're in business. Wait! Don't touch it.'

It was too late. Wanting to inspect the burned-out bulb, the exhilarated Copper had tried to remove it. It was hot enough to blister her fingers, making her yelp. She ran to the kitchen to run them under cold water. While she was dancing with the pain, she heard Pearl call out, 'Blimey. This place is huge.' The cockney had taken advantage of her absence to explore the apartment.

'What are you doing? Get out of there.'

'Oh, I love this room. Small, but perfectly formed. Just like me. I'll take it.'

'No, you won't, damn it.' Copper hurried out of the kitchen. Pearl had already heaved her suitcase on to the bed in the room next to her own, and was popping the latches open. 'Out you go.'

Pearl sighed. 'Be reasonable, sweetheart.'

'Don't call me sweetheart. And don't make me throw you out physically.'

'You wouldn't.'

'I'm bigger than you,' Copper pointed out meaningfully. 'And I grew up with four brothers. Three of them turned into firefighters and the little one turned into a union leader.'

'What more do you want from me?' Pearl asked plaintively. 'I've said I'm sorry about your old man, haven't I? I fixed your camera. I'm taking the smallest room, and I'm still paying half the rent. What more do you want?' She started to sob, blotting her eyes with her handkerchief.

'Turning on the waterworks won't cut it. Out!'

Pearl's tears dried up, as though on tap. 'Tell you what I'll do for you.' She dug out the roll of banknotes and offered it to Copper. 'Here. Take it.'

'I don't want it.'

'There's three months' rent in advance there. Plus enough to get in some groceries. And you can look after the rest for me. Hang on to it. I'll only blow it. Don't tell me you don't need the money,' she added shrewdly. 'He's left you with nothing, hasn't he?'

Copper stared at the money in frustration. This woman was as difficult to get rid of as a stray cat. But the bankroll felt so good in her hand. Real money. Her fingers tightened around it. 'You better behave,' she said through clenched teeth. 'No monkeyshines or I swear I will throw you out. And I'll use the window, not the door.'

'Oh, bless you.' For a moment, it seemed as though Pearl were going to hug her, but the expression on Copper's face forestalled that. 'We're going to be great chums.'

'We are not going to be *chums*,' Copper retorted. 'This is *my* apartment, and you're my tenant. So let's get that straight. What I say goes.'

'Absolutely, sweetheart.'

'I'm not sweetheart, or ducky, or darling, or any other British endearment you can think of.'

'Right you are, I'll call you Copper Pot.' Pearl popped the suitcase open and started pulling out what looked like very frilly and brightly coloured underwear. 'What about that cup of tea, now?'

Copper did not dignify that with an answer. She went back to the kitchen to attend to her wounds, hoping that she hadn't just burned her fingers in more than one sense.

Armed with the flashgun, Copper returned to the Pavillon de Marsan, where activity was even more feverish. This time, she took greater care over her photographs, knowing that each shot would use up one of her precious flashbulbs – and God knew if she would ever be able to get any more.

The surrealist Jean Cocteau, seated on a film director's high chair, was easily recognisable by his mass of frizzy, salt-and-pepper hair. On a similar chair beside him was his friend, Suzy Solidor, wearing a pale-amethyst trouser suit.

Seeing Copper, Suzy slipped off the chair and came swiftly towards her. Copper was reminded of an otter, or some other sinuous animal, sliding off the bank to pursue a tasty fish.

'*Chérie*,' she said, giving Copper a lingering kiss on each cheek. 'How enchanting to see you. I have thought about you so much. Are you all right?'

'I'm fine,' Copper said, trying to back away from her. But a lissom arm had wrapped around her waist, trapping her.

'I am preparing a room for you to stay at my place. The sweetest, daintiest little room you can imagine. You'll simply adore it.'

'Oh, thank you. But I've just—'

'You can't possibly stay with dreary old Christian, my darling. You will die of boredom.' The rich brown eyes seemed to want to drown Copper in their depths. 'You will have much more fun with me, I promise.'

'You're so kind,' Copper said faintly. 'But I was just about to tell you that I'm not with Monsieur Dior anymore. He's found me a lovely apartment on the place Victor Hugo.'

Suzy's strongly marked eyebrows descended. 'Cancel it.'

'But I can't. I've moved in already.'

'Move out.'

'And I've even got a tenant.'

'*Quel dommage*,' Suzy said, severely displeased. 'A waste of money. You would be far better off with me. I wish that foolish Dior had consulted me first.'

Copper had other ideas on the subject. Moving in with Suzy would have been rather like a mouse taking up lodgings in a cat's ear. But she didn't say that, of course. 'He's the kindest man in the world. If you only knew how he's helped me over the past weeks.'

'He's kind enough, I grant you that. But entirely lacking in charisma.'

'Oh, I think he's wonderful. So kind; such a gentleman.'

That surprisingly strong arm was still preventing Copper from escaping. The *chanteuse* studied her face with alarming intentness. '*Mon Dieu*. How exquisite you are. That hair. That skin. The Irish strain, of course. You are a princess from a Celtic legend. I am a Celt too; did you know that?'

'Er – no.'

'Yes. I was born in Saint-Servan in Brittany. You could practically swim to Ireland from my doorstep. We are of the same blood, you and me.' She smiled, showing a line of perfect teeth. There was something charming about Suzy Solidor, and the over-the-top seductress routine was certainly effective. She probably got exactly what she wanted from women who were so inclined. 'Come to my club tonight. I will expect you.'

'Well, I'll try to come, but I've got my article to write—'

'*Écoute-moi, chérie*,' Suzy cut in. 'There's a lot I can do for you. I can introduce you to the right people, tell you the right places to be, the right things to wear. I can teach you. If you are willing to learn. Come tonight. You won't regret it.'

'Okay,' Copper said, yielding to these blandishments. 'I'll drop by.'

Suzy warmed. 'Excellent. Come and meet Cocteau.' She led Copper to the high chair where the famous film director was perched. 'Jean, you must meet Copper. She's a journalist.'

'A journalist?' Cocteau repeated. 'I thought you were the wife of that handsome young American.'

'I'm covering the exhibition for *Harper's Bazaar*,' Copper said boldly.

Cocteau's thin, haunted-looking face lit up. '*Vraiment?*' He hopped off the chair to shake her hand. '*Harper's Bazaar* is interested in our exhibition?'

'Very,' Copper said, barefaced. 'Would you consent to a photograph, Monsieur Cocteau?'

'I think I can spare the time,' he replied smoothly. He pulled his woolly hair away from his face. The name of the great fashion magazine had exerted a magical effect already. She hoped devoutly that there was going to be some response from that quarter. Cocteau staggered a bit when the Czechoslovakian flashgun went off. It was really very powerful.

Copper gave a cry of happiness when she spotted Christian arriving, dapper and rosy in a smart overcoat. 'Monsieur Dior!'

'I think,' he said solemnly, accepting her kiss, 'that it's time you started using my first name. My friends call me Tian. What on earth is that dreadful apparatus you keep discharging?'

'It's bright, I'm afraid,' she said apologetically.

'I suspect your subjects are all going to look rather startled,' he said. 'But perhaps there is a way of harnessing your lightning to good effect. Come.'

He led her up the stairs to the gantry that overlooked the hall. As he had predicted, the flashbulbs were capable of illuminating almost the whole gallery, enabling her to take some crowd shots of the busy scene below.

'These will give a much better idea of the scale,' she said. 'Thank you, Tian. You're so clever.'

'How are your new quarters?' he enquired. 'Have you settled in?'

'Well, I've somehow got a tenant.' She told him about the arrival of Pearl and her suitcase covered with hotel stickers.

Dior raised his eyebrows. 'You took her in? After what happened? My dear Copper, was that wise?'

'Probably not,' Copper admitted.

'I've never heard of a wronged wife offering shelter to her husband's lover.'

'Nor have I,' Copper admitted. 'I'm still not exactly sure how she got around me. Do you know anything about her? She said her boyfriend was a publisher.'

'Did she? Well he is a publisher, I suppose. He publishes those collections of photographs that are sold in sealed yellow envelopes on street corners by young men who take to their heels when the gendarmes approach.'

'You're kidding. Don't tell me Pearl features in those photos.'

'I have never examined any of them,' Dior said delicately. 'But I think that may well be the case.'

'Oh, for the love of Mike.'

'Who is Mike?' Dior asked, interested.

'He's Pete's friend.'

'*Comment?*'

'At the convent school I went to in Brooklyn, profanity would get you expelled. So we learned to curse in other ways. "For Pete's sake" and "for the love of Mike". They expelled me anyway. Never mind all that – you're telling me I'm living with a woman who stars in obscene postcards?'

'Everybody has to earn their living somehow. And it could be an education.'

'I've been married. I don't need to be educated about sex.'

'Perhaps not. But you do need the money.'

'I don't need the money that badly,' Copper said with a resolute expression.

She returned to the apartment determined to have it out with Pearl. As if it wasn't bad enough that Pearl had been the final straw that broke the back of her marriage. The last thing she needed was to be entangled with someone with a reputation of that sort. And if Pearl posed for dirty photographs, who knew what else she did? And what sort of people she would bring to the apartment?

She found Pearl huddled under a pile of blankets with her eyes and nose streaming. 'What's up with you?' she asked suspiciously.

'Just getting a bit of a cold,' Pearl said thickly. 'I'll be better by tomorrow.'

'I want to talk to you,' Copper said grimly.

'I could do with a good natter,' Pearl said, struggling to come up with a bright smile.

Copper went to the bathroom and found that it had been turned into what her brothers would have called a whore's laundry. The brilliantly coloured underwear had been washed and was hanging on improvised lines everywhere. A pair of green stockings dripped over the basin, and she had to duck under wet, frilly unmentionables to get to the toilet.

When she emerged, Pearl had sunk even deeper into her nest of blankets. She was shivering violently. Copper suspected strongly that this was a piece of cunning theatre to deflect a confrontation.

'I want to know exactly what it is you do for a living,' Copper said.

Pearl's teeth were chattering. 'What does it matter?' she asked wearily.

'Of course it matters. I have to know that you're going to be able to pay your way.'

'Well, I could say the same about you, couldn't I?'

'Look,' Copper said, deciding to be direct. 'I've been hearing things about you. About what you do.'

'And you want to know if they're true.' Pearl dabbed the perspiration on her face. 'All right. I suppose you'd better see.' She emerged from the blankets, went to her bedroom and came back with a sheaf of photographs in a leather portfolio. 'There you go.'

The portfolio was entitled, in a very curly script, *Pearl, The Queen of The Cannibals*. The photographs were set in a mock-jungle and showed Pearl with a large black man.

Copper had told Christian Dior that she didn't need to be educated about sex, but these photographs were startling. Pearl's rounded, luminous body was shown in every sexual act that could be imagined.

Pearl burrowed back into her cocoon. Her face was bathed in sweat. 'I've had to do things to get by. If I hadn't done them, I wouldn't have survived.'

'You could have scrubbed toilets before you did this.'

'I've scrubbed toilets. I've scrubbed a lot of toilets, as it happens. But I decided I'd rather do naughty postcards than scrub toilets. I'm that sort of girl. I'm not a toilet-scrubbing sort of girl. But I am a three-square-meals sort of girl, and I did that to get my three square meals. Otherwise I would have starved.'

Copper tossed the portfolio aside. 'I don't think we're going to get along.'

'I'm not proud of what I've done,' Pearl said, her voice growing even quieter. 'Maybe you're right and I should have kept on scrubbing toilets. But it seemed a good idea at the time. Petrus made me feel it was glamorous and fun. And to tell you the truth, he made sure I was out of my head for those photos.'

'What do you mean?'

'Gin, hashish, cocaine, morphine – you name it.'

'You didn't have to do that, either.'

'You don't know Petrus. He's not an easy man to say no to. I had to get away from him, Copper. He was getting me on the needle.'

'The needle?'

'Cocaine. Once you start injecting it, you're hooked for life. It's a good job it's cold because I can't wear open-toed shoes for a while.' She poked a foot out of the blankets and showed Copper. 'He used the veins there because he didn't want the needle marks showing in the photos.'

Copper sat down heavily on the arm of a chair. 'Mother of God.'

Pearl contemplated her own dainty foot with its line of angry red marks around the toes. 'I'll be sick for a week, getting myself clean from this. But I'm going to face it. That's him in the photos. You can't see his face, but you can see his strategic bits. It didn't seem so wrong. It was just photographing us having a good time. But after he started me on the needle, he wanted me to go with other men. You know what I mean? So-called friends of his. You know where that ends up, don't you?'

'I need a drink.' Copper went to the drinks cabinet where the collaborator had left a few half-bottles of alcohol. She poured them both a stiff cognac.

'And while I'm telling you my life story,' Pearl went on, 'I'd better tell you that I need a job. That money I gave you? That's everything I've got in the world. I'm not going to scrub any more toilets, either. I'm going to find a proper job. Soon as I'm better. I'm going to finish teaching myself bookkeeping. I started once, and like a fool, I gave it up.' She gulped down the cognac. 'When I heard you walked out on that creep of a husband of yours, I said to myself, "That's the girl for me." You've been my inspiration, Copper. I knew you would take me in. Copper and Pearl. Like I said, we're like jewellery.'

'I've never heard of any jewellery made out of pearl and copper,' Copper said heavily. 'They don't go together.' She looked up to see that Pearl was crying; not the pretty, noisy waterworks she'd turned on during their first meeting, but silent tears that poured down her cheeks unchecked.

'You think I'm dirty. That you're going to catch something from me.'

'I just think we're not suited to each other. You say we're the same, but we're not. I've always been respectable.'

'Oh, I know I'm a bad girl,' Pearl said with a touch of bitterness. 'I've never been *respectable*. But I've never been given a chance, neither. Not since I was a little kid.'

Copper felt ashamed of having said the word. 'I understand that—'

'No, you don't. You don't know nothing about me. Or the life I've had. You're so quick to judge, like all the other women. Women are the worst, you know. Worse than men. I think it's because, secretly, they all know in their hearts they could be me.'

'I'm not judging you. We're just different.'

Pearl wiped away her tears wearily. 'Give it a couple of years, sweetheart. You'll see that we're not.'

'Maybe so. But in the meantime, we don't belong together. And every time I look at you, I remember what happened that night with Amory. I can do without that.'

'So you're throwing me out after all?'

'You need to find somewhere else to live – and as soon as you're on your feet again, I want you out. No hard feelings. Just the way it is.'

Pearl nodded. 'I'll look for somewhere else, then. Ta-ra, Copper Pot.'

Copper heard Pearl being sick in the bathroom and tried to shake off the shamefaced feeling that she'd been unnecessarily harsh. She went off to her typewriter and her article, trying to put Pearl and her troubles out of her mind.

She worked until late in the evening and then went out to La Vie Parisienne as she had promised Suzy she would.

The nightclub was buzzing. As she pushed her way through the noisy crowd at the door, a very handsome blonde man holding a cigar and wearing an impeccable evening suit came up to her. It wasn't until she was suddenly kissed full on the lips that she realised the 'man' was Suzy Solidor.

'You came! Welcome to my little establishment. Michel, take care of Miss Copper.' Suzy handed her over to the head waiter, who smilingly led Copper to a table near the stage and put a bottle of champagne in an ice bucket on her table. This was five-star service, indeed.

Dior was there in the company of a melting young man named Maurice, and there was the usual crowd of artists and writers, including a sombre-looking couple who Dior told her were Jean-Paul Sartre and Simone de Beauvoir. And she realised with a start that the simian man with the dark, staring eyes who was sitting beside a strikingly handsome woman at the next table was undoubtedly Pablo Picasso. As if wanting to confirm his identity, he was scrawling idly on a napkin with a stub of crayon, listening to the chattering people around him. He had no sooner finished the scribble than a waiter adroitly snatched up the napkin and made off with it triumphantly, no doubt to sell it for a fistful of dollars to some collector.

As though she had been waiting only for Copper's arrival, Suzy now stepped into the spotlight, graciously acknowledging the applause.

She kicked off with 'Lili Marlène', sung defiantly in her throbbing tenor. Copper watched the *chanteuse* intently throughout the performance, her chin cupped in her hand, oblivious to anything else. Even in this sunless winter, she appeared to have stepped straight off a beach on the Côte d'Azur.

'She's rather spectacular, isn't she?' Copper asked Dior. She was literally starry-eyed; she'd had a few glasses of champagne, and her green eyes reflected the lights brilliantly.

'Oh, she's colossal,' Dior said.

'It's awful what they're doing to her,' Dior's companion, Maurice, put in. Dior's fingers were clasped fondly in Maurice's. Copper noticed that Maurice's fingernails were varnished pink. 'So cruel.'

'What are you talking about?' Copper asked curiously.

'The *épuration légale* are going to charge her with collaborating and giving support to the enemy.'

'Just because she sang "Lili Marlène"?'

'Well, perhaps it was rather more than that,' Dior said diplomatically. 'She said some unwise things.'

'At least she can't be accused of having slept with any German officers,' Maurice said with a titter.

Copper frowned. 'Now that the Germans have gone, I think everybody should forgive and forget whatever happened.'

'No chance of that,' Dior replied. 'Nowadays, everyone wants to point the finger at his neighbour and say, "*He* collaborated, but *I* was a hero."'

'Human nature, I suppose.' Copper sighed.

'*Exactement*,' Dior said. 'We all rewrite our own histories.' He leaned over to her confidentially. 'Your gown is almost ready,' he murmured.

'Oh, how exciting!'

'Come for the fitting whenever you're free.'

'I will,' she promised.

The rest of Suzy Solidor's act was hardly less provocative. She did several more numbers dressed as a man, another in a sailor suit with a chorus of matelots, and another almost in the nude, her glorious body covered only by scraps of gold in what Pearl would have called the strategic areas. Her voice descended to guttural notes and erotic growls. It was sometimes hard to tell whether she was a man or a woman; and it seemed to Copper that some of the songs were directed at her. As she took in her surroundings, Copper felt that few of the people around her were definable as men or women; most were somewhere on a spectrum between the two sexes.

After her performance, the singer draped an ermine stole around her magnificent shoulders and toured the room, moving from table to table like a queen.

The burly figure of Ernest Hemingway loomed over their table. He was wearing his usual stained and faded khaki shirt.

'They tell me you're hanging out your shingle as a journalist?' he boomed at Copper.

'Yes.'

'It's a whore's trade.' He hauled out the chair next to her, almost knocking poor Maurice on to the floor, and sat down heavily beside Copper. 'Honey, I can teach you how to whore.' He leaned forward, blasting her with absinthe-laden breath. 'No better teacher.'

'You're drunk, Mr Hemingway.'

'I hope so. I'm drunk and I'm available. Room 117 at the Ritz. Come up and see me later tonight.'

'No, thank you.'

'Scared?'

'Not in the slightest.'

Suzy Solidor now arrived at their table, along with a fresh tray of champagne bottles and glasses. Also on the tray was a package wrapped in tissue paper with a satin ribbon. Suzy handed it to Copper. 'A gift for you, *chérie.*'

Surprised by the gift, she unwrapped it. It turned out to be an ornately bound copy of Verlaine's poetry. 'Thank you, Suzy,' Copper said, admiring the sumptuous, gilded leather cover.

Hemingway let out a belly laugh. 'Is that the way things are? I wondered what went wrong between you and Amory. You'll be better off in my room at the Ritz, honey,' he said to Copper. 'Just knock three times. I'll corrupt you, but not in the way this dyke intends.'

'I don't want to be corrupted by anybody,' Copper said angrily.

'She'll have you cutting that flaming red hair short and wearing boys' clothes. What a damned shame that would be.'

'There are worse fates,' Suzy said.

'Tell you what, Suzy,' Hemingway said. 'I'll take her first tonight. You can have her tomorrow night. And on Monday morning, we'll ask her to judge between us.'

Copper could bear no more of this. She got to her feet. 'I'm going home.'

'Don't go,' Suzy said, but she was already hurrying away.

'The Ritz, room 117,' Hemingway boomed after her. 'Don't forget.'

Copper got back home feeling miserable. Between them, Suzy and Hemingway had ruined her evening. She had separated from her husband, but that didn't mean she was fair game for anybody to insult. Being fought over by those two giant egos had been intolerable. Paradoxically, it made her long for the respectable state of being married.

'You're home early,' Pearl commented. She was sitting huddled in her dressing gown with a teach-yourself-bookkeeping manual. She was still shivering and pale, but she'd made an attempt to clean herself up. Her hair was in curlers (which explained where those bouncy ringlets came from). 'Had fun?'

'Not exactly.' Pearl was not someone she wanted to let into her confidence, but there was nobody else. She gave Pearl a brief account of the evening. Pearl had got hold of the Verlaine poems and was reading them, bleary-eyed.

'Here,' she exclaimed. 'You think *I'm* a bad lot? This stuff is just nasty.'

'I haven't read any of it.'

'Well, if you think a couple of naughty photos are wicked, you'd best stay away from this. It's corrupting.'

'You're a fine one to talk about corruption.'

'Whatever I've done,' Pearl said with dignity, 'was at least normal. Sex between two women isn't normal. It's unnatural.'

'You're the expert on sex, I guess,' Copper said dryly.

'In a way.' She mopped her streaming nose and eyes. 'Besides, I know Suzy Solidor. She's dangerous.'

Copper snorted. 'In what way is Suzy dangerous?'

'Once she gets her hooks into you, she won't let go. If you fall into her clutches, no man will ever look at you again. It'll follow you for the rest of your life.' —

'Isn't that a bit rich, coming from you?'

'I'm talking to you from experience,' Pearl replied. 'I know what it's like to have done things you regret.'

'Well, before you give me any more lectures, let me assure you that I am not in Suzy's clutches, as you put it. I'm not in anybody's clutches. I'm still getting over Amory.'

She took herself – and Verlaine – to bed. Reading through the poems, she was startled by their explicit descriptions of lesbian sex. She'd thought herself quite worldly-wise, but she must have been a lot more innocent than she supposed.

She laid the book aside and switched off the light. In her mind, the golden image of Suzy Solidor floated seductively, neither fully male nor fully female. Despite the coldness of the evening, she grew so hot that she had to kick off her blankets. She tried to compose herself for sleep, despite the distraction of Pearl coughing wretchedly in her room next door.

She was awoken with a start. Someone was pounding on the door of the apartment. Thinking that the apartment block must be burning down, Copper leaped out of bed, belting on her dressing gown.

She ran to the door, but before she could open it, Pearl appeared beside her and grabbed her arm.

'It's Petrus. Don't open it.'

'Petrus?'

'My boyfriend.' Pearl's face was white. 'I don't know how he found out where I am.'

Copper stared at the door, which was shaking under the hammering fists of the furious Petrus. 'I'll call the police.'

'No! They'll arrest me.'

'Well, what are we going to do?'

The hammering paused for a moment. They heard a hoarse voice shout, in bad French, 'Eh, I hear you. I hear you in there. Open!'

Pearl laid a finger on her lips, her eyes so wide that Copper could see the whites all around the blue. 'Don't say anything,' she breathed.

'Don't be silly,' Copper retorted. 'He knows we're in here.'

The pounding resumed, as if to underline the obviousness of that statement. 'Open! Open, you thieves.'

'I'm going to open the door,' Copper said.

Pearl clung to her arms to stop her. 'Please, no. He'll kill me.'

'I don't care if he kills you,' Copper said grimly, 'but I don't want him to break down my front door.' She shook Pearl off and unlocked the door.

The man who burst in was large and very angry. 'Where my money?' he snarled at Pearl. But Pearl had retreated behind Copper's back, whimpering; and Copper found herself facing the full wrath of Petrus. The photographs Copper had seen hadn't shown his face, which was remarkably ugly and suffused with rage. 'Give me my money!'

'She doesn't have your money,' Copper said.

'Yes! She steal my money.' He made to dive around her so that he could grab Pearl, but Pearl dodged to the other side. 'I kill you, *putain*.'

Copper suddenly remembered the fat bankroll Pearl had given her. There was probably some truth in Petrus's accusation. Almost in the same moment, however, she decided that she was damned if she was going to give the money back to him. 'She doesn't have your money,' she repeated. 'I've got it.'

Petrus paused, staring at her warily with yellow eyes like a lion's. '*You* got it?'

'Yes. And I'm not giving it back to you. She's paid her rent with it and it's mine now.'

'You crazy,' he spat. 'Give me.'

'I don't think so. You're going to leave right now – and if you show your face here again, I'm calling the police.'

He made another grab at Pearl. 'Call the police. She is a thief.'

Copper, getting angry now, pushed Pearl behind her again. 'You are worse. You forced her to inject cocaine.'

'*I* force her? That *putain* on her knees every day, begging me for coca. Eh, *p'tite*? Look what I bring you.' He held out a little fold of paper. 'You want this, eh? Come, I give it to you.'

Copper felt Pearl's hands clutching at her convulsively. 'Pearl doesn't want it.'

'Oh, yes, she want it.' He grinned. 'Eh, *p'tite*?' He unfolded the paper, showing the white powder it contained. Pearl whimpered. 'By now you want it very much, eh? Come and get it.'

'I'll tell the police everything,' Copper said, holding tight on to Pearl to stop her from moving. 'How you got her hooked. The photographs, the beatings – everything.'

'You think you brave, Mam'selle? You don't know who I am.'

'I know you're a drug dealer and a bully. I've faced bigger bullies than you, Monsieur. Now get out.'

He spat at her feet. '*Va te faire enculer.*'

'Get out of here.' She knocked the paper envelope out of his hand, scattering the cocaine.

He reached into his pocket and pulled something out. There was a snick and a long, sharp blade was suddenly protruding from his fist. 'Now you see that I am a serious man. Understand? She come back with me now. She belong to me.'

'She's not going anywhere.' Copper watched the flick knife intently, her heart racing. She had been brought up in Brooklyn and she'd seen the scarred faces – and occasionally, the funerals – that resulted from angry men wielding knives. But she was not going to give Pearl back to this man. 'She's staying with me. Put the knife away.'

'*Oui*, I put the knife away. In your throat.' He took a step forward, his eyes narrowing. 'Get out of my way.'

Copper held her ground, her face set. 'You don't scare me. Scram, buster. Or I'm calling the cops right now.'

'You give me the money. And you give me that *p'tite putain.*'

She was about to retort again when he suddenly struck out at her – not with the knife, but with his other hand. His fist slammed into her forehead, knocking her backwards, stars exploding in front of her eyes. Dazed and hurt, she was aware of Pearl screaming in terror. She struggled to focus on what was happening. As though in a nightmare, she saw that Petrus had seized Pearl by her hair and was dragging her out of the door. In a moment, he would be gone, and so would Pearl. Gone to an ugly fate.

Until that moment, Copper hadn't allowed any of it to seem real. Pearl's bruises, her needle-scars, her shivering and vomiting, all of it had been something she preferred not to recognise. She hadn't quite believed any of it. But now, with her head splitting from the impact of Petrus's fist, it was real. Without thought, she picked a heavy Lalique ashtray off the table and swung it at the back of Petrus's head.

She was still stunned and the blow was clumsy. The ashtray glanced off his shaven skull, making him lurch, but not knocking him down. He turned to her with a roar of pain and fury, teeth showing in a snarl. He raised the knife, ready to slash at her face.

But her head was clearing fast. She lifted the ashtray again and with an accuracy honed in a thousand baseball games in the park with her brothers, slammed the glass ashtray between Petrus's blazing amber eyes. This time there was a solid thud, and this time he went down, blood spouting from his nostrils.

'Oh Jesus, you've killed him,' Pearl gasped, looking down at the inert figure.

'Nope, he's just lights out. Nobody socks me and gets away with it,' Copper said grimly, bending over Petrus and retrieving the knife from his nerveless fingers. 'Mother of God, will you look at that thing.' She found the catch and carefully folded it closed. Petrus was by now groaning and stirring into life. He clutched at his streaming nose and tried to sit up. 'Uh-uh,' Copper said, poising the ashtray over his face again. 'Want some more?'

'No,' he said, sputtering blood. He shrank away from Copper's forbidding expression, holding up a shaking hand. 'No more.'

'Listen to me, tough guy. Next time you show your ugly face around here, I'll bust it open. *And* I'll call the cops to haul your sorry carcass to the pen. Understand me?'

'*Oui*,' he said thickly, bloodshot eyes fixed on the ashtray.

'Stay away from Pearl from now on. She's out of your life and you're out of hers. Got that?'

'*Oui*,' he grunted. 'I understand.'

'Okay.' Copper backed away. 'You can go now.'

By now, a curious crowd of neighbours had gathered in the lobby. They watched as Petrus stumbled out, clutching his injured nose. 'Bravo, Madame,' someone called. There was laughter. Copper bade them all goodnight and locked her door.

'He would have done me in,' Pearl said. 'That's the bravest thing I ever saw.'

'I grew up in a tough neighbourhood. Now, let's get you to bed.'

Six

Over the next few days, Copper helped Pearl through her withdrawal symptoms. She shivered constantly and cried from pains all over her body. All she wanted was milky tea and Copper soon became an expert in making this English concoction, which was oddly comforting in its peculiar way.

She learned a bit more about Pearl's background. Like Copper herself, she'd grown up in a poor neighbourhood – the East End of London.

'My real name's not Pearl at all. It's Winifred Treadgold. But I'm still waiting to tread on any gold,' she added wryly. She'd been a pretty child, which hadn't gone unnoticed. An older man named Uncle Alf had started 'messing about' with her before her twelfth birthday. By thirteen, she'd had a backstreet abortion and her childhood – such as it had been – was over.

Work had been an escape. She'd started out in a laundry, putting in ten-hour days and sleeping huddled next to the washtubs with the other girls, enduring the choking fumes of lye in exchange for warmth. Other men had followed Uncle Alf. She'd learned that she could use them, as they used her.

Hitler's Luftwaffe had pounded the East End relentlessly during the Blitz, killing thousands and leaving much of the city a wasteland. She'd come to Paris as soon as it was liberated, lured by the bright lights that no longer shone in battered old London, hoping for a career in modelling or a chorus line, and had fallen into the clutches of Petrus. It had taken only a few weeks before she was a slave to his needle and descending into the degradation that he had planned for her.

'He has others,' Pearl told Copper. 'I didn't want to believe it at first. I'm not very good at reading men, am I?'

'Me neither,' Copper said ruefully.

As yet, she had heard nothing from Amory. It was as though he had never existed. Eighteen months of marriage had vanished overnight, leaving her in limbo. No doubt Amory had already forgotten her. He hadn't even bothered to send a postcard.

She did, however, receive two letters from America. The first, from Amory's father, was very long and urged her to halt the divorce and patch things up with Amory as soon as possible for a variety of reasons, which he listed in great detail. She was surprised, since she'd never felt particularly valued by the Heathcote family.

The other letter, from Michael, her oldest brother, was much shorter and to the point:

> You did the right thing, divorcing him. Don't take
> him back whatever you do. Come home. I'll send you
> a ticket if you're broke.

There were no I-told-you-so's, for which she was grateful. There weren't any expressions of sympathy, either. She knew that Michael spoke for the whole family; none of them had liked Amory, and none of them had approved of the marriage. She and Michael were particularly close, but he had never been one for many words. She appreciated his support, but she had no intention of heading for home just yet. She put off answering either letter for the time being.

Her divorce papers came back. She signed her section and, in due course, Amory's part arrived through the military mail, duly signed by him. She was free. She felt only a sense of regret for the years that had been wasted.

And at last, she heard back from *Harper's Bazaar*.

The reply came in the form of a somewhat cryptic telegram, delivered to her door, which read simply: CALL HENRY VELIKOVSKY ELY-2038. It was signed, SNOW HARPERS.

She stared at the telegram, her heart thumping. 'Snow Harpers' could only be the redoubtable Carmel Snow, editor-in-chief of the magazine. But who was Henry Velikovsky? Was this it? Could this be her breakthrough at last?

Copper ran to the telephone and dialled the number. ELY was the prefix for the Champs-Élysées exchange. The male voice that answered was deep and cultured with a hint of a foreign accent.

'Hello,' Copper said breathlessly. 'I've just got a telegram from Mrs Snow – at least I think it's from Mrs Snow – to call you. At least, I think it's you.'

'It quite possibly is me,' the voice replied urbanely. 'And quite possibly it was Mrs Snow. The only unknown in the equation is you. Might I ask for your name?'

'Oh, I beg your pardon. I'm Oona Reilly.'

'Of course you are. Will you be free to join me for dinner tomorrow night at the Ritz?'

'The Ritz?'

'Yes. I'm staying there, for my sins. Shall we say eight tomorrow evening?'

'I'll be there,' Copper said breathlessly. She replaced the receiver. Pearl came into the room looking somewhat better than she had done over the past few days.

'What was that all about?'

'Someone from *Harper's Bazaar* wants to see me,' she said, still half-dazed. 'Dinner tomorrow, at the Ritz.'

'What are you going to wear?' Pearl asked practically.

'Dior.' Copper exclaimed, her eyes widening. 'I've got to see Christian Dior.'

Walking through the lobby of the Ritz in her rose silk gown, Copper felt like one of those women in magazine advertisements who assured you that Product X had changed her life. She had never worn a garment like this in all her twenty-six years. The bodice clung to her slim torso while the skirt flared around her knees. It wasn't just that it was beautiful; it fitted her perfectly, immaculately, as though it had been made for her –which of course it had. Christian Dior had seen exactly what would set her figure off best and had structured the dress around her, like a sculptor creating a second skin. He'd even forgiven her lack of bust, and had plunged the neckline between her slight breasts, showing off her delicate throat and shoulders with a chocolate-box bow over her heart. She was aware of the eyes that followed her as she swept along, her chin held high, as though she were not Oona Reilly from Brooklyn, but a visiting queen.

'I'm meeting Mr Velikovsky,' she told the head waiter at the restaurant reception desk.

'*Count* Velikovsky is waiting for you,' the man replied haughtily. He examined her dress and obviously decided to forgive her solecism. 'Follow me, Mademoiselle,' he said with an indulgent bow.

Copper followed him into a different world of rococo swirls and golden drapes, snowy linen, quiet lighting and quieter music. The ceiling above her had been painted with clouds, and she walked on peacocks woven into the soft carpet under her feet. And flowers – a profusion of flowers everywhere, whose scent hung elusively on the air.

The restaurant was crowded and the waiter led her on a circuitous path through the tables, clearly wanting to show her off to the other diners.

Her date was seated at a table in one of the alcoves reading a magazine. A tall man in a close-fitting tuxedo and black tie, he rose as she approached. He extended a hand. 'How do you do, Miss Reilly?'

'I've been instructed that you're a count,' she said, somewhat breathlessly. 'How do I address you?'

'All that nonsense went out in the October Revolution,' he said, bowing over her fingers graciously. 'But you know what snobs waiters are. I am plain "Monsieur" now.' He ushered her into her seat. 'Or indeed, plain "Henry", if you prefer.'

'But I was really looking forward to saying "Your Grace" or whatever the correct title is. Forgive my ignorance. We don't have counts in America.'

'You have Count Basie and Duke Ellington,' he pointed out. 'Much more impressive.'

Copper examined him as she settled down. He was in his early forties, she guessed, and striking, if not conventionally handsome. His dark eyes turned up at the corners, hinting at a Tartar ancestor. His nose was broad, his smiling lips full. He had the tan of a man who enjoyed the outdoors. His hair was combed back in a distinctly foreign way that was neither French nor American. 'You're Russian?' she asked.

'Yes. Does that present difficulties?'

'Only if you eat babies and burn churches.'

'Very seldom. I am a *White* Russian. My father and I fought the Bolsheviks with sabres in 1917. Unfortunately, they had machine guns so we got the worst of it.'

'I'm glad to hear it. I'm a bit of a Bolshevik myself.'

His dark eyes sparkled. 'You don't look like any of the Bolsheviks I encountered.'

'Well, we're cunning at disguising ourselves, you know.'

'So I see. Shall we have a cocktail? I have a weakness for vodka, of course, but I won't insist if you prefer something more civilised.'

'I don't think I've ever had vodka. Go ahead and order for me.'

'Two greyhounds, then,' he commanded the waiter, who melted away obediently. Velikovsky examined her with interest. 'Your disguise is one of the best I've seen. Rochas?'

'As a matter of fact, it was made by a friend. Christian Dior at Maison Lelong.'

'Dior? Now where have I heard that name? Ah yes. He's the coming man, so they tell me.'

'Oh, I'm so glad people are talking about him. We're all trying to persuade him to start his own fashion house.'

'Indeed?'

'He's afraid of letting down Monsieur Lelong, but he would make a fortune if he would just take the plunge.'

'We'll see what we can do to encourage him,' he replied. 'You seem very well-connected in the world of Parisian fashion.'

'I find it a fascinating topic.' She couldn't restrain the question any longer. 'Are you on the staff of *Harper's*?'

'I'm afraid my occupation is far less clearly defined than that. I keep myself busy moving small sums of money around.'

She was disappointed. 'You don't sell oil wells in Brazil, do you? Or valuable rings you just happened to have found in the street?'

He was amused. 'No, I'm not a con artist.'

'That's a relief.'

'Carmel Snow and her husband George are friends of mine. I've made some investments with them in New York real estate. Mrs Snow was intrigued by the article you sent her and she asked me to meet you.'

'She liked it?' Copper asked, bright-eyed.

'Very much. She's going to print it in next month's edition. In fact, one reason for our meeting here tonight is so that I can pass you payment for your work. Not a fortune, I'm afraid, but it is in US dollars. My dear, what on earth is the matter?'

Copper hadn't been able to hold back her tears. 'Sorry,' she gulped. 'This means so much to me.'

A snowy handkerchief, proffered by Henry Velikovsky, swam into her blurry vision. 'Please, my dear. Dry your eyes. People will think I'm being cruel to you. My reputation for benevolence will be quite destroyed.'

Copper blew her nose on the handkerchief, which was mono-grammed and probably very expensive. 'Thank you. That's the best news I've had in weeks!'

He leaned back. 'Well, you're good news for Carmel. *Harper's* won't be sending any journalists to France until the war is over. That puts you in an interesting position. You're the only American woman journalist in Paris right now. Carmel has asked me to find out whether you have any other material.'

'Yes,' she said eagerly. 'I do. I'm covering the most fascinating story right now.' She started to tell him about the *Théâtre de la Mode*, the words almost stumbling over each other in her eagerness to get them out. She told him that she'd already interviewed Jean Cocteau and oth-ers, and had a portfolio of photographs. 'I told them I was working for *Harper's*,' she confessed. 'I guess I got a little ahead of myself there.'

'Just a little.' His exotically slanted eyes were watching her face and hands carefully, but with a hint of amusement. He made her feel somewhat gauche, and very American.

'You're laughing at me,' she accused him.

'Not at all. It's just such a pleasure to see somebody so full of enthu-siasm. After so many years of war, you know, the world is tired. It needs freshness, youth, *joie de vivre*. And you have these qualities in abundance.'

'I do?'

'You do.'

Their cocktails arrived – a mixture of vodka and grapefruit that she found intriguing. 'I guess these are called greyhounds because they're supposed to keep you lean and mean?'

'Exactly. I gave the idea to Harry Craddock at the Savoy in London before the war. My chief contribution to Western civilisation.'

'These sums of money you move around must be pretty hefty if they enable you to hang out at the Savoy and the Ritz,' she commented.

'I prefer pleasant surroundings. I assure you, I have been poor – very poor indeed – and I never take life's little luxuries for granted.'

'You don't have Ernest Hemingway as a neighbour, do you?'

His face lit up with amusement. 'As a matter of fact, he has the room above mine. I hear him target-shooting with his pistol occasionally. He says there are mice, but I suspect pink toads. You are a married woman?' he asked casually.

'I've just divorced from my husband.'

'I'm sorry to hear that.'

'Don't be. It's turning into the best decision I ever made.' Perhaps it was the greyhound, or perhaps it was those wise, warm eyes; either way, she found herself telling Velikovsky all about the trials of her marriage, her divorce from Amory, and her ambitions for the future. He listened carefully, putting down the menu to give her his full attention.

'Your future is certainly a bright one,' he said. 'They thought highly of your article at *Harper's*. You're seen as a promising new talent.'

'Really?'

'Carmel was particularly impressed with the photograph. She's seen plenty of photos of women having their heads shaved, but yours was special. The mother and child, like a tragic nativity. She said it was hard-hitting and poignant.'

'Let me write that down,' Copper said, basking.

'And your proposed piece about the *Théâtre de la Mode* is just the sort of thing Carmel is looking for.' He paused. 'How would you feel about being assigned as a staff reporter for *Harper's*, based in Paris for the next year?'

Copper's heart jumped into her throat. She felt her cheeks and throat flushing. She tried to control her excitement. 'That's a wonderful offer.'

'I feel there's a "but" coming.'

'But I don't think I should accept for the time being.'

He raised his eyebrows. 'You don't want be a journalist?'

'Oh, I do. You have no idea how much I want to be a journalist. I've thought about nothing else. But I'd rather be a stringer for the time being.'

Velikovsky tugged at his ear, as though troubled and searching for the right words. 'May I ask how old you are?'

'I'm twenty-six.'

'You realise that not many twenty-six-year-olds get an offer like this?'

'I realise that. And maybe I sound arrogant or crazy. But I've just gotten myself out of a marriage. I'm not in a hurry to tie any more knots. I don't want to be bound to any single publication, even one as prestigious as *Harper's Bazaar*. Being freelance will let me keep my freedom.'

'Is your freedom so important to you?'

'Yes. It is.'

'Even if a staff job puts bread on your table?'

'Even if it puts caviar on my table,' she said decisively. 'I love journalism and I intend to follow it. But on my own terms. I'm so happy that Mrs Snow liked my article – and I really, *really* hope she likes my next one even more. I just want to be free to steer in my own direction and not be told what to write about.'

Velikovsky nodded slowly. 'How did you come to write that article?'

'It's kind of awkward to explain, but I stepped into a dead man's shoes.' She told him about the Frightful Bounder and the story of how he had unwittingly taught her the basics of her trade, culminating in his grisly death and the extraordinary funeral at Père Lachaise with the surrealists. He was highly amused by her description, leaning back in his chair and laughing until his eyes watered.

'It's a serious matter,' he apologised. 'I shouldn't laugh.'

'Why not?' she said, pleased to have amused this sophisticated, older man. 'Even George would have laughed.' She hesitated, remembering. 'As a matter of fact, that was the last time I saw my husband. So we buried our marriage that day, as well as poor George.' The waiter, perhaps impatient with waiting for them to finish talking, arrived to take their order, but Copper had found the menu daunting. 'Please order for me,' she said. 'You know much more than I do.'

'You flatter me. My tastes in food are simple, however. How long has it been since you had a really good steak?'

'A long time,' Copper said wistfully.

'With French fried potatoes? And a good Cabernet Sauvignon?'

'Sounds like heaven.' She watched him as he gave the order. He was trim and fit for his age, she observed. His waistcoat lay flat against his stomach and his hands were strong and neat. He was a dandy, she suspected: his tuxedo fitted him snugly, the points of his collar were immaculately starched, and his bow tie expertly arranged. Either he paid a good deal of attention to his appearance, or there was a devoted woman at home. 'Are you married?' she heard herself asking.

'Like you, I was once.'

'And you didn't like it?'

'Well, my wife left me, but in a more permanent way than your husband left you.'

'You mean she died? Oh, I'm so sorry.'

He made a brief gesture. 'It was a long time ago. We met very young. God gave us some happy years before he took her away.'

'You married young.'

'We did everything young,' he said. 'I ran away from school in St Petersburg to fight the Germans during the Great War. I was fifteen. I wanted to be like my father, who was a general. I spent a few weeks at the front before my father found me and had me sent back home. A year or two after that, the Bolshevik revolution started. By then I was seventeen and my father and I fought side by side. Unfortunately, as you probably know, the world allowed the communists to take our country from us. Winter came and that was that. I buried my father on a snowy mountainside in the Caucasus and joined what was left of our army on the retreat to Constantinople. It was during that march that I met Katia. Like me, she was from a noble family. They had lost everything in the revolution. She was nursing our wounded. We married as soon as we reached Paris.'

'That's the most romantic story I ever heard,' Copper said.

'She developed leukaemia, which was less romantic,' he replied. 'There is no treatment, even if I could have afforded any.'

'I'm so sorry.'

'Yes. The twenties were hard. But I discovered that I had remembered some mathematics, despite running away from school to kill the Kaiser. I managed to build up a little capital and became, in my small way, something of a financier. I worked night and day so as to recover from my grief. But we are not here to discuss me, my dear. We are here to learn about you.'

'My story isn't so romantic. My husband developed other women.'

'None the less a tragedy. But it seems you lost him and found yourself?'

'Something like that,' she agreed.

'And now you're on your own?'

Copper nodded. 'I guess you think I'm crazy for not jumping at Mrs Snow's offer?'

'Crazy? No. Carmel is keen to sign you up, and I admit that I will have to face her wrath if I don't convince you to put your signature on a contract. But I sympathise with your desire to remain free. I am the same. The situation is fluid and you're in a good position to jump on any story that turns up suddenly. You can write about what you like. And you can sell your work to whom you like. You are also free to accept assignments from anyone.' He tugged his ear, which she had noticed was his habit when searching for words. 'Naturally, there is the danger of starving to death. Paris is the only city on earth where starving to death is still considered an art. But I don't think you will starve to death. You write well, which is rare, and you have a unique slant on things, which is even rarer. You're not one of the herd.'

'That's a relief.'

'You have character, spirit and intelligence.'

Their steaks arrived and were as succulent as he had promised. Copper's diet had been frugal since splitting up with Amory, and she ate like a starving lioness. 'You're very understanding, Monsieur Velikovsky.'

'Henry, please. And may I call you Oona?'

'You're welcome to, but I get "Copper" from most people.'

'Copper? I like that. I made my first big trade in copper futures.'

'Really? You must have had a crystal ball.'

'It required only a little insight to see that the world was rearming for an even bigger and better war than the last one. Copper is used for making bullets.'

'You're a real Daddy Warbucks.'

'Who, pray, is Daddy Warbucks?'

'You haven't read *Little Orphan Annie*? It's an American comic. Daddy Warbucks is the rich old war profiteer who protects Annie.'

'That sounds like me.'

'And how have you spent this bigger and better war?' she asked.

'In some strange places, not so comfortable as the Ritz. It's good to be back in Paris.'

'You're being mysterious.'

'Not deliberately. The war isn't over, and nor is my work.'

'I don't see your sabre.'

He smiled. 'Wars are won with brains as well as sabres. My job is to make sure the sabres arrive in the right place at the right time.'

'And how do you arrange that?'

'I climb up trees and watch who passes by.'

'That sounds risky.'

'It has its moments,' he said lightly.

'So you're a secret agent?'

'If I were, would I tell you?'

'I'm just interested.'

'If you're thinking of including me in one of your articles, forget it. My work is off-limits.'

'And what happens if you get caught?'

'That depends on whether I'm caught by Herr Hitler or by Comrade Stalin. Things would be difficult either way.'

'Can't you retire now? The war is almost won.'

'When it is won, I will retire,' he agreed. 'Though there may be no ending, merely a change of enemies.'

'You mean the Russians?'

'I mean the communists.'

'That's a depressing thought.'

'Not for me. I don't know quite what I would do to fill my time if I wasn't at war. I've made enough money for my needs and I get bored easily. As, I imagine, you do, too.' He refilled her glass. 'May I ask why you described yourself as a Bolshevik?'

She smiled. 'Oh, I'm not really. But we got called that plenty of times.'

'We?'

'My father was what you plutocrats would call a union agitator. He led strikes against bad working conditions in the 1930s.'

'I see it now, in my mind's eye. Little Copper, shivering outside the grey walls of the prison.'

'That's pretty much how it was.'

'So you have more background in baby-eating and church-burning than I do.'

'I've developed my own ideas since then. But I'll always hate injustice.'

'Good for you. I only ask one thing, Copper. That you will keep in touch with me from now on. Agreed? I suggest we make this a regular meeting – for as long as I'm in Paris, dinner at the Ritz once a week.'

'Every week? Here?'

'Well, I have a dusty little bureau on the Champs-Élysées, but this is more congenial, don't you think? And although I travel, I try to be back in Paris every weekend.'

'I can eat an awful lot of steak,' she warned.

'That would be one of the reasons to develop our friendship – to make sure you don't starve to death.'

'And what would be the other reasons?'

'I will be able to keep an eye on your progress. When you sell an article to *Harper's*, I will arrange the payment. More than that, if you run out of money between assignments, I'll see you through.'

She looked at him warily over the crystal rim of her wineglass. 'This sounds awfully like a spider coaxing a reluctant fly into the web. If I take your money whenever I'm broke, wouldn't that automatically make me an employee?'

'Not at all. It would merely make you sensible.'

'And what will you ask in exchange for "seeing me through"?'

'The satisfaction of having fostered a rising talent,' he replied smoothly.

'That's an interesting way of putting it,' she replied briskly.

'Do you suspect my motives?'

'I'm inclined to, yes.'

'You wound me deeply,' he said, laying one tanned hand on the silk-faced lapel of his tuxedo. 'I'm here to help.'

'Oh, I can hear the milk of human kindness sloshing around inside you.'

He broke into laughter for the second time that evening. 'Very well, I admit it. I'm interested in you. I would like to see more of you.'

'I'm interested in you, too,' Copper replied. 'You're a very interesting man. But I'm not in the market.'

'What market would that be?'

'Any kind of market. I don't want any more complications in my life. I don't want any more contracts of any kind. So if you're making a pass at me—'

'I'm offering my friendship.'

She paused for a moment, then reached her slim hand across the table and gave him a brisk, American handshake. 'Your friendship is most acceptable. So long as it stays just friendship.'

'Excellent. So we'll see each other again next Saturday night, at the same time?'

'I look forward to it greatly.'

And in fact, by the time they parted, with her stomach full of good things, Copper felt that she had made a friend in Henry Velikovsky. He was just old enough to be regarded as protective, and just attractive enough to make her sit up with interest. There was, moreover, that aura of the dangerous and the exotic about him, which would infallibly intrigue any woman.

Before they left the table, he passed her a plump white envelope. The flap was monogrammed with his initials, and it turned out to be filled with crisp dollar bills. Copper was delighted. 'I can't believe this is real.'

'Absolutely real. I printed them myself.'

'Don't tease me. This is the first money I've earned from my writing.'

'But not the last.' He walked her to the street outside and called a cab for her. 'You can always reach me at the Champs-Élysées number if there is any emergency. And if I'm not in Paris, my secretary will pass on any messages.'

'Thank you so much, Henry. And thank you for listening to me all night. It's been a long time since I've had someone intelligent to talk to.'

'I hope you'll regard me as a confidant, my dear Copper. I can be useful.'

They shook hands and she got into her cab. She headed for place Victor Hugo, happier than she had been in weeks.

Pearl was awake when she got back. However, when Copper, still starry-eyed, had told her tale, Pearl exclaimed in disgust.

'You've turned down a job with *Harper's Bazaar* and a handsome millionaire – all in the same night – and you're pleased with yourself?'

Copper laughed gaily. 'I haven't turned either one down. I'm just giving myself some room for manoeuvre.'

'Room for manoeuvre? What are you, the *Queen Mary*?'

'No. But I can sell my work and have steak at the Ritz every week on their tab. And I'm free.' She threw her arms in the air and danced around Pearl. 'I'm free!'

But Pearl was morose. 'You're so lucky,' she said. 'I'll never have a man like that interested in me. Not as long as I live.'

Something in Pearl's voice struck Copper. She stopped dancing to examine her flatmate more carefully. Pearl's skin was sallow, her eyes dull with pinpoint pupils. 'Pearl!' she exclaimed in dismay. 'What have you done?'

'I haven't done anything,' Pearl said defensively.

Copper snatched up the book that had been lying at Pearl's side. Out of the pages fell a glass syringe with a little cloudy liquid still in the barrel. Copper took a step back, appalled. 'Oh, Pearl.'

'It's not so easy,' Pearl said in a dull voice, picking up the syringe and replacing it carefully between the pages of her book.

'You promised!'

'Promises were made to be broken.'

'Where did you get it?'

'Where do you think?' Pearl retorted bitterly.

Copper had to sit down. 'You didn't go back to him? You couldn't have!'

'Well, I did.'

'What about the bookkeeping?'

'Bugger the bookkeeping. I can't add up.'

'This will kill you,' Copper said, trying to hold back the lump that was rising in her throat.

'It was just the one shot. Just to get me right again.'

'I'm going to smash that needle.'

Pearl snatched up the book and clutched it to her breasts protectively. 'Don't you hear me? It's just the one shot.'

'And when that wears off, you'll want another, and then another.'

'You don't know what it's like.'

'We can take you to a doctor—'

'I don't want a doctor. I don't want anybody sticking their nose into my life.'

'Pearl—'

'Leave me be, Copper.' She went to her room and locked the door.

Seven

Copper slipped away from the table while everyone was talking and drinking champagne, and made her way through the noisy crowd that filled La Vie Parisienne every night. She'd got into the habit of coming to the club two or three times a week. It was a way of keeping up with the gossip in the fashion world, since Suzy's club was the meeting place for the designers and couturiers. But there was more to it than that.

The weeks had passed swiftly. Nineteen forty-five had arrived, and the Allies were already on German soil. Since Amory had left, it was as though the sullen laws of gravity had been suspended, letting her float free among bright clouds. Gaining the friendship of Christian Dior and his set had been the start. It had given her an entrée into the fashion world. She knew all the gossip, heard all the scandals. She was starting to understand what constituted haute couture, what was new and what was now hopelessly *démodé*. A future as a journalist who could write authoritatively about women's affairs and fashion had opened up.

Having her work accepted by *Harper's* on her first attempt had been a huge step up. Seeing herself in print – and her name in the byline for the first time – had been thrilling. Her spare, grim prose had been powerful among the articles about dresses and shoes.

Her dinners at the Ritz with Henry Velikovsky had turned into the highlight of her week. She loved the ritual of meeting him there, and hearing the stories of his adventures, his childhood in Russia, and the romantic world of sleigh rides and winter palaces he had once inhabited. For his part, he made her feel glamorous and special – feelings she hadn't had for a long time. Their friendship was slowly and almost imperceptibly turning into something deeper, though she didn't want to admit that yet. After all, she'd specifically told him that she was off-limits. But life had a way of shifting the pieces around the board.

Through him, she had sold two more short pieces to *Harper's Bazaar*. Carmel Snow was still interested in stories about Paris, especially those with a fashion angle. And they were eagerly awaiting her *Théâtre de la Mode* story, which she would file when the exhibition took place.

And then there was her third great friend, Suzy Solidor. She found Suzy sitting at her little dressing table, studying her own face in the mirror.

'I'm worried about you,' she said, sitting beside Suzy.

'*Pourquoi?*'

'The *épuration*. Everyone in the club is talking about it.'

'Don't be afraid,' Suzy replied. 'I've done nothing wrong. Those dogs can't do anything to me.'

'But they can. They can put you in jail or in an internment camp.'

'*Chérie*, the worst they can do is fine me a few francs.'

'I hope you're right.'

'I am right. Don't worry.' Their eyes met in the mirror. 'I am not an angel. But you are, *ma chérie*. You are a perfect angel.' She patted Copper's cheek, her eyes searching Copper's face. 'Do you find me disgusting?'

'Of course not.'

At first, to tell the truth, Suzy's intensity had intimidated her. The older woman's company was like absinthe, intoxicating yet dangerous. Suzy didn't conform to anyone's rules, which was partly why Copper found her so interesting. Suzy had swiftly become an integral part of her life. She had taken charge of Copper's education, improving her

French, her dress sense, her taste in food and much else. She'd introduced Copper to her favourite writers – Baudelaire, Villon, Rimbaud – and a world of new possibilities.

As with Henry – but in a different way – she had felt herself awakening. Sensuality had crept into her life like a warm breeze stealing into the windows of a room that had been shut up for a long time. Amory had been everything to her, especially at the beginning of their marriage, but his infidelities had wounded her so often and so deeply that she'd stopped having any faith in him. And when faith had died, so had desire. She'd found that she needed closeness and trust more than sex. Desire grew out of trust, not the other way round. So something in her had closed up, like the petals of a delicate flower. And had remained closed until new people had entered her life – Henry and Suzy.

'And that Russian brute,' Suzy went on. Copper shivered as Suzy caressed her neck, her fingertips light as butterfly wings. 'If you don't sleep with me, do you sleep with him?'

'Of course not.'

'*Of course not*,' Suzy echoed mockingly. 'You are a monument to chastity and your marble thighs never part. Really, *chérie*, you enjoy driving the world crazy.'

'I don't at all.'

'Liar.' Suzy pressed her lips to Copper's, clinging and moist. Refined as she was in her dress, Suzy never used perfume or deodorant. The milky smell of her skin and the darker tang of her armpits rose into Copper's nostrils, intoxicating and erotic. She pulled back quickly.

'Why will you never kiss me properly?' Suzy demanded, touching the bright waves of Copper's hair.

'I don't want to kiss you in that way.'

'Why not?'

'It's not—' Copper couldn't find the right word.

'Not decent? Not proper? Not genteel?'

'Not me.'

'But you want me, just as I want you. I can feel it.'

'You mean you think you can.'

Suzy took a fistful of Copper's hair threateningly. 'Sometimes I would like to hurt you.'

'Sometimes I wish you would,' Copper replied in a low voice.

Pearl was in the sitting room when Copper returned from La Vie Parisienne in the early hours of the morning. She was crouched on the sofa, spreading the toes of one bare foot, the needle poised.

'For God's sake,' Copper exclaimed in disgust. 'Can't you do that in the bathroom?'

'It's freezing in there.' Pearl injected herself carefully and then lay back on the cushions with a sigh. Copper watched the effect of the drug iron all the lines out of Pearl's young face, leaving it smooth and dull as dough. Pearl's relapse into drug-taking had been a bitter disappointment, but she was forced to accept that if Pearl ever escaped from her addiction, it would be on her own terms, not on anyone else's.

'You've been back to Petrus.'

Pearl's mouth twitched in the faintest of smiles. 'Yes, I've been back to my big, black devil.'

'And what do you have to do in return for the cocaine?'

'The same as you do.'

'I don't know what you're talking about,' Copper replied indignantly.

'I'm talking about the lipstick on your face. It isn't your shade, kiddo.'

Copper wiped her mouth irritably. 'Could be anybody's.'

'Not that particular virgin's-blood red. It's definitely hers.'

'She's a friend.'

'I'm older than you, sweetheart. And a bit wiser in the ways of the world.'

'Not so I've noticed,' Copper said dryly.

Pearl stretched out, her eyes already glassy. 'Are you having an affair with Suzy?'

'Not that it's any of your business,' Copper said evenly, 'but no, I am not having an affair with Suzy.'

'Well, if you're not having an affair with her now, you soon will be, because that's what she's aiming at. She's grooming you. You're her next conquest.'

Copper snorted. 'Pearl, really. I draw the line at being lectured by someone who's just stuck a needle between her toes.'

'She's abnormal.'

'If by "abnormal" you mean she's not as dull as a drugstore novel, then I agree.'

'La Vie Parisienne is fun for a while. You go to look at the freaks, have a few drinks—'

'Pick up other women's husbands,' Copper put in.

'But you're going there every night of the week. You're infatuated with her.'

'And you're an addict.'

'So are you. You look at her the way a rabbit looks at a boa constrictor.'

'I've never seen a rabbit look at a boa constrictor so I can't comment. I'll check next time I'm in Brooklyn Zoo. In the meantime, I like Suzy a lot. She's been kind to me, and I guess I look at her accordingly.'

'It's obvious what she wants from you – she's all over you in front of everybody. They're all talking about you.'

'Let them talk.'

'I know what it's like to go crooked,' Pearl said. She began to put away her 'fixings', as she called them – her collection of syringes and little ampoules – folding them in a washbag with lethargic care. 'I don't want you to end up the same way I did. It's hard to straighten yourself out.'

'I know it is,' Copper said more gently. Pearl was disappearing for hours each day, no doubt working for Petrus as she had done before, returning with her supply of cocaine or other drugs. At least she was also bringing her share of the rent money. Copper couldn't complain on that score. 'We could put you in a clinic.'

'No, thanks. Go cold turkey? Sod that for a game of soldiers. What does Henry say about Suzy?'

'Unlike you, Henry lets me live my own life.'

Pearl yawned. 'You're going to lose him.'

'How can I? I don't have him.'

Pearl's eyes were disturbingly like George's when Copper had found him dead on the floor: milky and blank. 'You've got him in the palm of your hand. He's mad about you.'

Copper wasn't going to try to explain something as private, sensitive and complex as her feelings for Henry and Suzy, especially when she hardly understood them herself. 'Henry's a lot older than I am.'

'What's that got to do with anything? Henry's handsome, rich and he adores you. What more do you want?'

'I don't want anybody. I like being free.'

'Copper Pot, when are you going to grow up and see what life's really like?' asked Pearl, who liked to have the last word. She made her way to her bedroom with the slow gait of a sleepwalker.

Copper met Dior at the Pavillon de Marsan the next day. It was a bright but sharply cold morning. They went outside into the courtyard where a kiosk with a charcoal-burner was doing a roaring trade in roasted chestnuts.

'It's freezing,' she complained.

'It's Paris. You don't come here for the weather. You look tired, my dear,' Dior commented, buying a newspaper cone of chestnuts.

'I didn't sleep awfully well last night,' she confessed. 'Pearl's hooked on cocaine again.'

Dior concentrated on peeling a chestnut and picking all the shell off the hot, sweet kernel. 'That was to be expected. There is nothing you can do. I have the same problem with Bébé.'

'And then there's Suzy.'

'What about Suzy?'

'She's been awfully kind to me. But she wants something more than friendship. She's impatient with me because I don't respond the way she wants. I don't want to hurt her, or disappoint her. What should I do?'

'You are asking the wrong person, my dear.'

'But you must understand my dilemma – you, of all people.'

'You mean because I am the way I am? But I was born the way I am. I knew what I was from a very young age. It was never strange to me to long for love with persons of my own sex.' He studied his chestnut, looking for any stray fibres. 'And I may tell you, *ma petite*, that relationships are never easy. For my own part, I have never found happiness in love.'

'Oh, Tian, what a sad thing to say.'

'Sad but true. Simply put, it does not matter whether one likes the opposite sex or one's own. The problems are identical. You see from the circle I live in that there is no single solution to the problem of desire. Look at Cocteau. He falls in love with women or men indiscriminately.'

'The only person Cocteau really loves is himself,' she replied dryly.

Dior laughed. 'Perhaps you are right. Those who are beautiful are desired; those who are not, are not. I have never been beautiful, not even when I was young, when most people have some brief flowering. I never had such a flowering. I was always dull and plain. I remain dull and plain.'

'You aren't plain.'

'But I am. And I have the congenital defect of being ineluctably drawn to the beautiful. With the result that, more often than not, I am rebuffed. Even derided for my presumptuousness. Or, if I manage to be accepted, I am soon discarded in favour of more appealing types.'

She laid her hand on his arm compassionately. 'Even if it were true that you're a plain man – and I think you have a lovely face – you have brilliance that goes well beyond mere surface beauty.'

'In this world,' he said with a wry shrug, 'it is the appearance that matters far more than the content. If I've learned anything from my trade, I've learned that.'

'I thought Amory would be my Mr Right,' she said mournfully. 'It was a long, slow process of disillusionment. I know what it's like to be discarded in favour of more appealing types.'

He laid his hand over her own. 'I have had my heart broken many times. At the age of forty, I no longer expect to find my Mr Right. I put everything into my work. But there's no reason why you should live like that. Your Mr Right may be closer than you think.'

'What do you mean?'

'Well . . .' He turned back to his chestnuts. 'There is Henry.'

'Everyone has got the wrong idea about Henry,' she said.

'And what is the right idea about Henry?'

'He's a friend. That's all.'

'Are you sure that's all?'

'He's interested in me.'

'Aren't you interested in him?'

'He's very attractive. But . . .'

'But?'

'Well, I'm a lot younger. I love my life. I love being a bohemian and having adventures. I'm not ready to give it all up for anyone. Besides, we think very differently. He's with the big battalions and I rather sympathise with the oppressed.'

'Shall we consult Madame Delahaye?'

'I don't think I need a fortune teller. I need a psychiatrist.'

'Madame Delahaye is terribly reliable, you know. Each reading is exactly the same: Catherine is alive and well and will come back to me.'

'I'm happy for you,' she replied gently, thinking how naïve he could be at times.

He nodded. 'My dear, one should be able to try new things, especially at your age, without feeling one is condemning oneself to eating the same dish for evermore. Obey your instincts.' He offered her a perfectly peeled chestnut. 'The only advice I can give you is to do nothing you don't feel is right.'

She accepted the warm little offering. 'You're lucky to have your work, Tian.'

'Lucky in work, unlucky in love. I sometimes wish I were not the way I am. There are drawbacks. It is illegal, for one thing, and that means living in fear. For another, one constantly encounters the contempt, even hatred, of a certain class of person. Sometimes it is no more than a look, a particular kind of smile, or a carefully chosen word. The wounds can be deep.' For a moment his expression was bitter. 'It becomes easier to sublimate one's desires. A gorgeous dress, a new fabric, an elegant line, can distract one from unhappiness.' He folded the paper cone and put it into his pocket. 'Speaking of which, I must get back to my dolls. Your session with Professor von Dior is at an end.'

Perhaps, she thought, as she entered the glittering portals of the Ritz, she *should* see a psychiatrist. Of the two possible romantic interests in her life, one was a man eighteen years older than she, and the other was a woman. What would Freud say? She had come a long way since the wide-eyed Brooklyn girl who had arrived in Paris a year ago.

Henry was waiting for her at their table, immaculate as always. Her heart always lifted at the sight of him. In a world of uncertainties, he was a dependable constant: always there, always supporting her. Perhaps that was the problem. Where Henry was dependable, Suzy was challenging. Where Henry was a constant, Suzy was as changeable as the moon. Where Henry made her feel safe, Suzy made her feel distinctly unsafe. It was not an easy choice – if it was a choice.

Henry kissed her three times, Russian-style, as she arrived. There was an orchestra tonight playing jazz, and elegant couples were dancing between courses.

'Would you like to dance before we look at the menu?' he invited her.

'If you don't tread on my feet.'

'I'll do my best.' He took her in his arms and they drifted between the tables cheek to cheek. He danced well. His arms were strong, but he was light on his feet.

'I tried to contact you at your office,' Copper said. 'Your secretary told me you were away from Paris this week.'

'I had some things to attend to.'

'What sort of things?'

'Boring things.'

'You expect me to tell you every detail of my life,' Copper complained. 'But you won't tell me a thing about yours.'

'Very well,' he replied. 'What is it you want to know?'

'Where you went this week and what you did there.'

He was silent for a moment, swaying her in his arms. 'The battle with the Germans is in its final phase,' he said at last. 'But a new battle is already being prepared for. The communists would like to swallow France as they are swallowing Eastern Europe.'

Copper snorted. 'That old chestnut. The bosses were selling the same scare story in the thirties and using it to keep their employees slaving for pennies in dangerous, freezing factories.'

'This isn't a question of working conditions in a few factories,' he said patiently. 'They're gearing up for civil war.'

'Okay, Daddy Warbucks.' She laughed. 'You can ease off the propaganda now. I don't want to fight you.'

They danced for a while and then sat at the table to drink what had become 'their' cocktail – greyhounds made with vodka. He was smiling at her with those turned-up, mysterious eyes of his, and his tone remained light.

'You must be careful, my dear Copper.'

'Of the bloodthirsty communist hordes?'

'Of scandal. People are talking about you.'

'Are they?'

'Paris is a small world. I hear tongues wagging about a friendship between a certain French *chanteuse* and a certain young American reporter.'

'I see,' Copper said thoughtfully, looking into the pink grapefruit juice. 'I had no idea I was so famous.'

'You are new. And you are striking. Of course you are noticed, and people want to know who you are, where you come from.'

'And where I'm going – which I guess is to hell in a handcart.'

'Parisians are very tolerant. I don't think anyone has consigned you to the infernal regions yet. But your friend is not exactly discreet.'

'At least she's not ashamed of what she is.'

Henry shrugged. 'Lesbianism has been a public spectacle in Paris since the 1850s. It's practically a profession. One of the performing arts.'

'In Paris, being a woman is in itself a profession,' Copper said ironically.

'Suzy came to Paris as a ragamuffin. She's the illegitimate child of a charlady from Saint-Malo. Her name was Suzanne Rocher. It was Yvonne de Bremond who turned her into Suzy Solidor.'

'Who is Yvonne de Bremond?'

'Yvonne is a lesbian aristocrat who was one of the great beauties of the twenties and thirties. A little older than Suzy. In fact, she and Suzy look like sisters. She took Suzy in, made her a pet project. It took her years to sculpt the raw material into a work of art.'

'How did she achieve that?' Copper asked, interested.

'Yvonne knew everything that Suzy didn't: the right books to read, the right clothes to wear, the right wines to drink, the right way to talk. She paraded Suzy in all the fashionable resorts. One saw them, in the pre-war years in Biarritz or Cannes, bowling along in Yvonne's Rolls Royce convertible with a huge dog in the back seat. Quite a sight, I assure you.'

'Sounds familiar,' Copper said thoughtfully. It sounded rather like what Suzy was doing with her. 'And then?'

'Suzy dumped her. It was quite sudden and it broke Yvonne's heart. But Suzy was tired of being the protégée. She wanted to spread her wings – and *voilà. Adieu,* Yvonne.'

'I didn't know any of this.'

Henry picked up the huge, leather-bound wine list. 'It was almost as though she had hated Yvonne all along and allowed herself to be petted until the time was right. Then she took her revenge.'

'Revenge? For what?'

'No good deed goes unpunished.' He perused the list. 'Yvonne has a smart shop on the Faubourg Saint-Honoré. She's awfully fashionable; an antiquarian, an expert on eighteenth-century furniture. Her Christmas window displays are legendary. But she doesn't see Suzy anymore. Hmm, they have some of the 1922 Château Latour. Should we order a bottle?'

She put one fingertip on the top of the wine list and pushed it down so she could look into his face. 'Is this a warning, dear Henry, dear Henry, dear Henry?'

'It's just a suggestion' – he smiled – 'that perhaps you shouldn't let Suzy make a spectacle out of you.'

'I'll bear it in mind.'

'You think I'm interfering.'

'Oh, I get this all the time from Pearl.'

He put down the menu. 'It never ceases to amaze me that you took in your husband's paramour. You really are an extraordinary woman, Copper.'

'Poor Pearl wasn't exactly Amory's paramour. More what we Americans call a one-night stand.'

'Still, you showed great forgiveness. Few women would have been so kind.'

'Pearl has her own problems.'

'You mean she's a drug addict.'

Copper shook her head. 'Is there nothing you don't know?'

'I keep my ear to the ground. I heard what you did to her – ah – manager.'

'You hear a lot of things, dear Henry.'

'And is it true that he had a knife?'

Copper's large grey eyes sparkled. 'I hit him with a Lalique ashtray. He never stood a chance.'

'You could have been killed.'

'But I wasn't. And at least he doesn't come around to the apartment anymore. He's Pearl's *bête noir*.'

He put his hand over hers. 'My dear, I know you're having fun, but it's a dangerous world.'

'You're right,' she said thoughtfully.

'That it's a dangerous world?'

'No, I don't care about *that*. But I am having fun. I was too busy feeling sorry for myself to realise it until now.'

His expression was a little sad. 'Too much fun to settle down?'

It took her a moment to get what he was implying. 'Oh, Henry.'

'I know it's very soon. And I know I'm twenty years older than you—'

'Eighteen,' she put in automatically.

'But I can offer you a great deal as a husband.'

'Henry—'

'I would never stand in the way of your career or want you to change who you are.' For a moment, his strong fingers pressed hers, hard. Then he released her hand. 'You don't have to answer now, or even soon. Just consider it.'

'I will,' she promised. She leaned forward and kissed his cheek. 'And I'm deeply honoured. Whatever happens.'

A proposal from Henry Velikovsky was not something to be dismissed lightly. And yet she felt she couldn't accept. Not now and perhaps not ever. Even if, as he said, he would not stand in the way of her career, there would be a loss of freedom; the very freedom that she so cherished.

Becoming his wife – the Countess Velikovsky, if one cared about such things – would bring with it obligations. Inevitably, her energies would be diverted, even if only in part, from her work, and would be directed towards the man she was married to. She knew that from her first marriage. And then, if children came . . .

She did love Henry already. She loved him for his kindness and his charm, for the security he offered. The fact that he was older was part of what attracted her to him.

Whether that warmth could ignite into the enduring heat required to drive a marriage was another question. Perhaps it could. But only if she added fuel to the flames. So far, they had danced together, laughed together and inhabited a sparkling world that was too like a fairy tale to be trusted. They had never gone to bed together, and until that happened they would remain in the antechamber of passion, so to speak. And she didn't know whether she wanted to open that door.

After they'd parted, Copper felt an odd mixture of elation and sadness. It was an undeniable boost to her confidence to have a man like Henry on her arm. But also, it was frustrating to see her newfound freedom jeopardised already, just when she'd attained it.

Sorting out her feelings towards Henry wasn't easy. There was a substantial age gap between them, and a substantial difference in their political instincts. She didn't like the way he made her feel like the wide-eyed orphan – childish, naïve, needing to be rescued from the difficulties she got herself into.

The fact that he was very attractive made her feelings all the more complicated. Having got rid of one overbearing, manipulative husband, she was in no hurry to acquire another.

And that was as far as she got.

Eight

In the Pavillon de Marsan, activity was feverish. The opening of the show was close now. The designers were adding the final touches to the dioramas. Most of the dolls had been completed: enigmatic mannequins wearing perfect little outfits, poised in inscrutable groups. Dior himself was using some of the silk they had gone to fetch in the Simca. Copper left him fussing over his own designs and walked around the hall with her camera, picking details out of the confusion of whirring sewing machines and banging tools.

They were all here, the great couturiers of Paris. She had learned to recognise them and identify their styles. Here was the young, frail Jacques Fath, in his thirties and already regarded with awe by the fashion world. Here, too, was Elsa Schiaparelli, aristocratic and mystical, all in black and hovering over her display with dark, intense eyes. Not far from her, the Basque, Balenciaga, similarly dark and haunted, worked with equal concentration. And behind him stooped Jeanne Lanvin, shattered by the war and said by Suzy, who was her friend and wore her designs, to be dying.

As Copper gazed around her, a voice called her name cheerily. It was Christian Bérard, spattered all over with sky-blue paint, including blobs in his huge, tangled beard. His bright eyes, which were almost the same colour as the paint, were wicked. He carried his little white bichon frise under one arm, as always, and with the other he held the large paintbrush he had been using. 'Copper! Where is your Anactoria?'

'Hello, Bébé. Who is my Anactoria?' she asked cautiously, for Bérard's mind was a strange one and his jokes sophisticated.

'Why, Suzy Solidor, of course.'

'I don't get it.'

'Ah, I forget you were raised by wolves,' he said merrily. 'If you'd had an education, you'd know that Anactoria was the friend of Sappho of Lesbos. The very *special* friend.' He rolled his protuberant eyes to make sure she didn't miss the insinuation. 'It's my little Jacinthe's birthday.' He ruffled the dog's curly fur. 'I'm having a party at my studio on Saturday night. You'll come, of course.'

'Well – I already have a date for Saturday night.'

'With your Russian? Ah, yes. I hear he is very jolly,' he said with a droll expression. 'I absolutely insist that you bring him along.'

The idea seemed a bad one to Copper. She didn't want to mix Henry with the bohemian crowd. But she did not want to refuse, either; Bérard was Christian Dior's closest friend. 'I'll ask him, I promise.'

'And bring your pornographic little cockney friend, too. She is enchanting.'

'All right.'

'Bless you, my child.' He made the sign of the cross over her with the brush, like a cardinal sprinkling holy water. She was not quick enough to avoid the shower of sky-blue paint.

'Bébé, you're impossible,' she exclaimed angrily. His squeals of laughter followed her as she ran to wash it off.

Copper had warned Henry that Bérard's parties started late, so they did not arrive until eleven on Saturday night. Henry was formally dressed, as always, in a tuxedo with a silk scarf. She was more than a little anxious about the imminent intersection of her two worlds. What Henry would think of Bérard's crowd, and what they would think of him, were imponderables.

Pearl had come with them and was in the irritable, twitchy state that meant she hadn't had her 'fix'.

The studio was a cavernous place in an old block in Montparnasse and was already filled with people. Bérard had heated it to suffocation point with his stove. Most of his guests were wearing the extraordinary garments that were customary on such occasions, but Bérard himself was in his pyjamas and cigarette-ash-daubed dressing gown. Copper had seldom seen him in anything else. He bustled through the crowd to greet them, with Jacinthe, as ever, beneath one arm.

'Welcome, welcome,' he cried out. 'And here is Pearl. Such a mouth. Such embonpoint. My dear, one could positively eat you. And *this*—' His blue eyes popping, he dropped a mock curtsey to Henry. 'This is surely the god Apollo descended from Olympus. Greetings, Phoebus Apollo! Here is Jacinthe, in whose honour you have come down to earth. It is her birthday. You may kiss her.' He held the woolly little dog out to Henry.

Copper wondered how Henry was going to take to this fat, dirty artist with his extravagant manner and wild beard, who was obviously already completely drunk. She needn't have worried. Henry appeared amused by him and kissed Jacinthe solemnly.

Bébé pulled them into the throng and began introducing them to his strange collection of friends. Most of the couturiers were in attendance, even Balenciaga – tall, darkly handsome and almost impossibly well-dressed – who seemed to be dazed by the noise and chaos around him.

The solemn Poulenc was there, as was a large, square man who turned out to be Darius Milhaud. Bérard introduced Henry to his brooding Russian lover, the ballet dancer Boris Kochno. Copper left them talking Russian together and wandered around.

A workbench was crowded with bottles of alcohol of all kinds and colours. Somebody poured her a glass of crème de menthe, which she liked, and she drifted among the crowd, half-listening to the hubbub of conversations surrounding her. Around the walls of the studio was piled an assortment of Bérard's works, finished and in progress. There were dozens of fashion drawings, which he effortlessly produced for the couturiers and magazines. He was a favourite of Coco Chanel, as well as Elsa Schiaparelli and Nina Ricci, all of whom tolerated his notorious unreliability and frequent binges because his work had an indefinable glamour that no other artist could achieve.

Towering over the party were also some huge props for the Ballets des Champs-Élysées, which he had helped to found together with Boris Kochno, and various pieces that he was doing for the *Théâtre de la Mode*. Almost hidden among all this work were the oil paintings that he did for himself. Copper paused in front of a portrait of Boris, a brilliant work. Bérard was truly a prodigious artist who poured out his talent unstintingly. She wondered how long he would be able to survive this work pace with his addictions to opium and alcohol. She'd seen George Fritchley-Bound kill himself in the same way.

Well after midnight, when the party was at its loudest and most crowded, Suzy Solidor finally arrived. She was wearing a red-and-gold Chinese jacket with a high collar. She was breathtaking, Copper thought. She made her way through the crowd towards Suzy as though pulled by a magnet. Her head was swimming with the glasses of crème de menthe she had drunk.

'*Chérie!*' Suzy greeted her eagerly. They had not seen one another for some days. 'I have missed you so much.'

'Come, I want to introduce you to Henry.'

Suzy's face changed. 'I don't want to meet that man. He's a spy, you know that?'

'He's a good man.'

'No men are good. Why have you brought him here?'

'Bébé invited him. Don't be jealous.'

'But of course I am jealous. I was looking forward to being with you alone.'

Copper laughed. 'It's a party, Suzy.'

Suzy peered through the crowd to where Henry was talking to Boris. 'You like these handsome brutes. Don't you understand they just want to dominate you? Perhaps you like that. A thick pair of lips to kiss you with and a thick pair of boots to kick you with.'

'Come and talk to him, at least. You'll see how charming he is.'

'I don't wish to be charmed by him.'

Copper gave up. 'Do you want a drink? There's a collection of weird and wonderful bottles over there.'

'No. I have something better. Come.' Suzy took her hand and pulled her out of the studio and up a flight of stairs to the rooms above. There was an empty, unlit bedroom in the silent apartment. 'Don't turn on the lights,' Suzy said. She locked the door and opened the curtains. A panoramic view of Paris was spread out below Montparnasse. The sky was bright with an icy full moon.

'It's magical.'

'It's midnight,' Suzy said. 'One half of Paris is making love to the other half.' She produced a gold cigarette case. In it was a single ciga-rette. 'Moroccan hashish. The very best.'

Copper put her hands behind her back. 'Umm . . . I'm not sure I want to. I've never tried hashish before. But you go ahead.'

'It is divine, I assure you. Why do you hesitate?'

'Well, I'm here with Henry . . .'

'What does that have to do with it? Does he rule your life?'

'No, he never tells me what to do.'

'He will start soon enough. Don't trust him. These people – they are so arrogant, so high-handed.'

That struck a chord with Copper. 'He is a little domineering.'

'I hate them. They think they own one. Has he asked you to be his mistress yet?'

'He's asked me to be his wife,' Copper said. She regretted the words as soon as they were out of her mouth. Suzy was furious.

'How dare he!'

'I'm very flattered, to tell you the truth.'

Suzy rounded on her. 'You're not thinking of accepting?'

'Not yet.'

'"Yet?" What is this "yet"? Are you saying it is a possibility?'

'Anything is possible,' Copper said, smiling.

'You have atrocious taste in men,' Suzy said shortly.

'Well, let's not discuss that tonight.'

'Then smoke hashish with me.'

'I'd rather not.'

'Nonsense.' Suzy lit the cigarette and sucked the smoke deep into her lungs. She blew the plume out over the prospect of Paris. 'Come, my beloved. Smoke with me.'

Reluctantly, Copper accepted the cigarette, hoping it would soothe Suzy, and inhaled. At once, she began to gag on the thick, acrid smoke. Suzy clamped a strong hand over Copper's mouth to stop her from exhaling. She struggled free, coughing.

'I'm going to be sick.'

'No, you're not. Again.' She offered the cigarette to Copper and made her take several more drags.

'I can't take any more,' Copper choked. 'That's enough.'

Suzy smiled at her enigmatically as she took the cigarette back. 'Is that not divine?'

Copper explored the strange feeling that was growing in her head, as though her brain were expanding in her skull. 'I feel very strange.'

'I got it from a German officer who used to come to my club. I've kept it for a special occasion.'

'What if the *épuration* find out?' Copper giggled. She was starting to feel disturbingly light-headed. 'A gift from a Nazi.'

'I didn't say it was a gift. It had to be paid for.'

'How?' Copper couldn't help asking.

'I rendered a service.'

'Don't be so mysterious. What kind of service?'

'I will show you – if you smoke it with me.'

Against her better judgment, Copper accepted the proffered cigarette and tried again. She was getting more expert at keeping the greasy smoke down. Her lungs no longer hurt. They smoked the thing between them, the room filling with the pungent, incense-like fumes. Copper felt all her anxieties and inhibitions floating away. For a while, her senses seemed heightened: every sound from the party below throbbing through her body; the air in the room like a cool caress on her skin. Then, all reality faded away. She danced silently around the room as though she had wings, her arms floating.

'How do you feel?' Suzy asked, dark eyes following her as she danced.

'Like a character in a fairy tale. Or a bird. Or an angel.'

'Now shall I show you what service I rendered the Nazi officer?'

'If you please.'

Suzy began to slowly unfasten the cheongsam she wore. Her eyes stayed on Copper's, and Copper felt her heart begin to pound heavily. One side of the red-and-gold garment fell aside, revealing half of Suzy's body. She was naked beneath the silk. The moonlight silvered the curve of her breast, the firm contours of her belly and abdomen, casting into shadow her navel and loins. Suzy's face was half-pearl, half-shadow. 'Come,' she said quietly. Copper felt herself drawn forward, as though she no longer had any control over her limbs. 'I made him kneel before me. In his uniform and his shiny boots. *Comme ça.*' She pressed down on Copper's shoulders. Copper knelt submissively before Suzy, looking up. The red-and-gold dragons on the cheongsam spat fire at her, seeming to have become sinuously alive, writhing slowly and voluptuously. Suzy opened the cheongsam fully and drew Copper's face to her loins, until the curls were brushing Copper's lips. '*Cet officier allemand – voici ce qu'il voulait, tu comprends?*'

'*Oui*,' Copper whispered.

'I laughed at him. But I don't laugh at you.' She was pressing herself more urgently against Copper's mouth, opening her thighs. 'For you, I feel something completely different. I want you. I give myself to you.' She, too, knelt, and pressed her naked body against Copper's. 'Are you disgusted with me?'

'No.'

'Even when I tell you I enjoyed playing the *putain*?'

'I'm not disgusted.'

'Truly? Sometimes I am disgusted with myself.' She kissed Copper lingeringly on the lips. This time, when Suzy's tongue pushed between her teeth, Copper could not resist. She felt it explore her mouth, firm and strong, like everything about Suzy, filling her. Suzy's hands moulded her breasts, slipped under her clothes, seeking her thighs. Her touch sent a thrill shuddering through Copper. She was in the coils of a dragon far stronger than she was, overwhelmed by its desire and its greed. Her own weakness was delicious to her, her body melting into honey.

Distantly, she heard her name being called. It was Pearl's voice, on the stairs. Somehow, Copper found the strength to draw back. 'They're looking for me,' she said in a shaky voice.

'Let them look,' Suzy hissed.

'I have to go.'

'No. Stay with me.'

'I can't.' She rose on unsteady legs, rearranging her clothes. 'I'm sorry.'

Tight-lipped, Suzy got up, fastening her cheongsam. 'You are a coward.'

'Please don't.'

Suzy seized Copper's face in her hands and kissed her passionately on the lips, hard enough to hurt. 'You are mine, *mine.*'

But Copper could hear Pearl calling her name. She broke away, shaking her head. 'I can't stay. I'll go first, you follow.'

'There you are, Copper Pot,' Pearl said, meeting Copper coming down the stairs. They went back into the deafening noise of the studio. 'Where have you been?' she demanded. 'I've been looking for you everywhere.'

'I went out for a breath of fresh air.'

'In this freezing weather?' Pearl demanded. 'You'll catch your death. Look, I've got to get back to the flat. I need a fix.' She took Copper's hand, which was indeed as cold as ice. 'What's wrong with you?'

'Nothing,' Copper replied dully. But she felt frightened and dazed. The drug was so overpowering and she was trying to hide its effects.

'Are you sick?'

'I'm fine,' Copper muttered. The party was in full swing now, a carnival of music and colour. Bérard had put on one of the ballet costumes that hung around the walls – an extravagant clown's outfit in vivid oranges and yellows – and was dancing to loud applause. His face was suffused with blood, his eyes almost closed. He was lost in his own world.

Henry pushed through the crowd to reach them. He looked into Copper's face. 'Copper? Are you all right?'

'I'm fine,' Copper repeated.

'You are very pale.'

'Just tired.'

'She was with that woman,' Pearl said. She pointed to Suzy Solidor across the room, a spectacular figure with her platinum hair and her red-and-gold Chinese dress. Her eyes locked with Copper's for a moment. Then she turned back to her conversation, her aquiline profile indifferent.

Copper swayed. Henry put his arm around her shoulders. 'Maybe you should go home, my dear.'

Copper's voice was dull. 'You're right. I'm ready to go home now.'

Copper stumbled as the three of them went out into the street. Henry had to steady her. His face was troubled. The night was bitterly cold, a sparkle of ice starting to form on metal surfaces. They had to walk down the steep, cobbled street to find a wider road where there was a chance of getting a cab. Though Henry held on tight to Copper, her shoes skidded on the ice and she almost fell twice. She said nothing. The hubbub of Bérard's party faded away behind them and the city was silent.

'I wish we'd never come,' Pearl muttered angrily. Henry said nothing, concentrating on supporting Copper.

By good fortune, they found a cabbie who had started work early and set off for home.

Copper lay back in the seat, her eyes closed, her face white. She made no responses to questions. Pearl was furious.

'She's done something to her.'

'Who's done something to her?' Henry asked.

'That dyke.'

'You mean Miss Solidor? What has she done to Copper?'

'Given her something. Drugged her. I know the signs, trust me.'

By the time they got back to place Victor Hugo, Copper was feeling awful. She ran to the sink in the corner of her bedroom that sat under dangling ribbons of developed negatives, and retched violently, her knuckles white as she clutched the ceramic. Her skin was clammy and cold and her face was the colour of ivory. Henry held her forehead, his other arm around her waist. Pearl got a towel and mopped her face.

When Copper had finished being sick, Henry and Pearl helped her into bed. The weird feelings in her head were starting to fade and she felt less panicky. Henry kissed her and left, looking troubled.

Pearl was angry. 'She doesn't give *that* for you,' she said, snapping her fingers. 'Do you really think she cares for you? She doesn't. Can't you see what she is – a heartless actress, making an exhibition of her perversions for money. While Henry—'

'Don't talk to me about Henry.'

'He's a good man, Copper.'

'What would you know about him?'

'I know a diamond when I see one. You're going to lose him if you don't give Suzy up.'

'I won't give Suzy up. I'd sooner give Henry up.'

'Oh, for God's sake.'

Copper rolled on to her side. 'Go away. I'm going to sleep.' She was asleep almost instantly, looking absurdly young, her red hair tumbled across her face, her bruised-looking mouth half-open.

The next day, Copper woke with a hammering headache. She felt hungover and out of sorts all day. Henry came round to see how she was, but she was too listless to respond to him very much. She sat sluggishly staring at the floor during his visit, answering his enquiries in monosyllables.

'What happened between you and Suzy Solidor last night?' he asked in a quiet voice.

'Nothing,' she muttered.

'Then why are you like this?'

'I'm hung-over. I had too much to drink. And . . .'

'And?'

'I smoked some hashish.'

'Who gave you that?' Henry demanded. 'Don't tell me. I can guess.'

'Bully for you.'

His dark eyes surveyed her. 'That woman is not a good friend to you, Copper.'

'You're jealous,' she retorted.

'I'm concerned.'

'Well, don't be. I can run my own life without your help.'

'This isn't going to end well,' he said with a grim note in his voice.

After he left, she struggled to concentrate on her work. Hashish, she decided, did not agree with her; though she forgave Suzy for trying the experiment on her, she would not repeat it.

That other experiment – the feel of Suzy's naked body against her – had left her confused, yet in some way excited. It didn't help that Pearl was sulky with her and lost no opportunity to nag. But her body felt uneasily alive and sensual.

A few days later, Dior came to find Copper at the place Victor Hugo. 'Bébé hasn't come home for days. Not since the party. They're screaming for him at the Pavillon. We must find him. I've borrowed a car. Will you drive?'

'What do you think has happened to him?' she asked as they set off.

'The usual,' Dior said. 'A spree that becomes a binge, and then an orgy. And then he is lost.'

'Where will he be?'

'We'll look under the bridges first. That's where he usually ends up.'

'Are you joking?'

'No,' he said sadly. 'I am not.'

They drove along the banks of the Seine, stopping at each bridge. Under the arches of some were colonies of *clochards*, homeless people, deserters and tramps; most of them alcoholics. The weather was icy, and Copper saw at least one figure lying ominously still at the water's edge. Dior made her wait in the car while he picked his way fastidiously among the huddled groups, peering into the grimy, bearded faces.

'Not there,' he said as he got into the car after the third such visit. 'There are thirty-seven bridges in Paris. This could take a long time, Copper.'

'It doesn't matter,' she said. 'I'm at your disposal.'

'I'm so grateful.' His cheeks were flushed with the cold. As always, no matter how little money he had, he was immaculately dressed. He had on a fine English overcoat and a hat. 'Let's go to the Port de Grenelle. That's one of their favourite places.' As they set off, he huddled into his overcoat like a bird fluffing up its feathers. 'How are things with your Henry?'

'I haven't heard from him.'

'I hear there was an incident at the party,' he said delicately.

'I made myself sick on crème de menthe,' she replied lightly. 'Nothing more.'

'Don't lose him,' Dior said.

'Tian—'

'I say nothing more than that.' He exclaimed suddenly, 'Look out, *ma petite*!' She braked hard. A crowd of men had blocked the street, forcing her to stop. They were marching purposefully towards the river carrying placards. There had been political turmoil in France for several weeks now, marked by regular strikes that often brought Paris to a standstill for several hours at a time. This, however, was the biggest demonstration she had seen.

'I'm going to take some photographs,' she said, reaching for her camera, which went with her everywhere.

'Be careful,' Dior said anxiously. 'They may be dangerous. They are wearing the most dreadful clothes.'

Storing up this bon mot for an after-dinner story, Copper got out of the car and walked towards the strikers, already focusing her viewfinder. The men were sullen-faced, chanting ragged slogans. Copper saw that many of the placards bore the hammer and sickle. As Dior had remarked, they were working men wearing overalls and caps. The crash of their wooden clogs grew deafening as more of them poured out of the side street on to the main road. For a while, they ignored her as she photographed them; but then one or two began shouting at her angrily.

'Copper,' Dior called from the car, his voice quavering. 'Let's go!'

A large banner was being carried along in the crowd, flapping between two poles. She wanted to get a shot of it as it passed. 'Just a moment,' she called back to Dior.

'Copper!'

She was aware of something whizzing past her. It was not until she heard it smash on the cobbles behind her that she realised it was a bottle. Startled, she looked up from her viewfinder, just in time to see a man throw something else at her – a large stone. She skipped nimbly aside and it rattled past her without doing any damage.

'Hey,' she yelled. 'What's the big idea, lunkheads? I'm on your side.'

A shower of abuse came back at her. Other men had their arms cocked back now, ready to hurl missiles at her.

She turned and bolted back to the car where Dior was in a state of panic. 'Are you mad?' he gasped. 'We have to get out of here.'

She grabbed the wheel and turned the car around as fast as she could, riding up on to the kerb in her anxiety to get away. More missiles were flying towards them, bouncing off the bodywork. 'They're a little jumpy, aren't they?' she panted, wrestling with the gear lever. 'I don't mind being cussed out in French, but I draw the line at brickbats.'

'Just go!'

As they sped away, something smashed loudly into the rear window, starring it like a spider's web.

'Holy Moses,' Copper said, examining the damage in the rear-view mirror. 'What did we do wrong?'

'It's the car,' Dior said, still quivering. 'They're communists. They think anyone with a car must be rich. For God's sake, don't do that again. Let's look under the pont de Passy.'

They drove there without further incident and walked under the arches of the great bridge together searching among the rubbish. A stray dog snarled at them before running off and a few *clochards*, huddled against the wind, watched them with bleary, suspicious eyes. Some had lit smouldering fires and were already, at this hour of the morning, clutching bottles of cheap wine. Overhead, a Metro train rumbled slowly towards Passy, showering them with black dust. Dirt, cold and desolation marked the place.

Suddenly, Dior gave a cry and hurried forward to a pile of refuse that lay against one of the iron pillars holding up the bridge. Shivering with the cold, Copper followed him. The pile of refuse turned out to be a man, and the man turned out to be Bérard.

There were tears on Dior's cheeks as he helped Bérard to sit up. '*Mon pauvre ami,*' he said in a choked voice. 'Bébé! *Tu m'entends?* My God. He's half-dead with the cold, Copper. Help me.'

Copper knelt down beside Bérard and stared at him in horror. He was barely recognisable. His bloated face was heavily bruised down one side from a blow or a fall. His beard, always tangled, was matted and filthy; he stank of alcohol – and worse. His swollen eyes half-opened as they tried to rouse him, but he seemed unresponsive.

'Bébé!' Dior said, his voice cracking. '*Peux-tu m'entendre?*' Bérard merely groaned. He was unable to walk and he was a heavy man, so getting him to the car was an exhausting process. 'I have never seen him as bad as this,' Dior gasped, shouldering the burden of his friend. 'My poor friend. I blame myself. I've been so busy with the wretched dolls. I neglected him.'

'It's not your fault,' Copper replied. 'Why does he do this to himself?'

'He's worked himself into nervous exhaustion with this damned *Théâtre de la Mode*. This is his way of escaping.' They hauled Bérard on to the back seat of the car. Dior, weeping quietly, went through the pockets of his greasy coat and came up with a handful of blackened opium pipes, a syringe and a bottle of something that looked like paint thinner. '*Merde*,' he said, tossing everything away.

Copper saw that Bérard's small, dirty hands were still stained with the sky-blue paint he'd been using days earlier. For some reason, this detail made her start crying, too. 'Where are we going to take him?' she asked.

'To the Pitié-Salpêtrière. There's a doctor there who knows how to treat Bébé's problems.'

'What do they do with him?'

'What none of us can bear to do,' Dior said grimly. 'Lock him up and let him scream.'

She found Henry waiting for her at the apartment.

'I hate being at odds with you,' he said. 'I'm sorry if I upset you. I'm just anxious about you. Can we make it up?'

'You are a bully sometimes, you know.'

'I know, and I apologise.' He kissed her cheek. 'You've been crying. What has happened?'

'I went with Tian to find Bébé Bérard.' Copper described the morning's events. 'It was terrible when we got to the Pitié-Salpêtrière. He started to wake up as they carried him in. When he realised what was happening, he started to plead with us. Begging us not to leave him there. He was crying. So was Christian. When they locked Bébé in the room, he started to scream like a child. I couldn't bear it. I had to cover my ears and run away.'

'He does it to himself,' Henry said curtly.

'Henry, it was pitiful.'

'You should save your pity. If he makes himself a beast, he must suffer as the beasts suffer.'

'You're cruel,' she exclaimed.

'No, I'm disciplined. I don't admire the lack of discipline in anybody, no matter how clever they are.'

'While we were searching for him, we had a brush with some strikers. I stopped to take photographs, but they threw bottles and stones at us. They actually broke a window in the car.'

His face was serious. 'These people are dangerous, Copper. Don't go near them.'

'I'm a journalist,' she reminded him. 'I'm supposed to photograph this stuff.'

'They don't know that. They see a camera and they think you're from the secret police.'

'Do I look like I'm from the secret police?' she demanded, raising one eyebrow.

He shook his head gravely. 'Not exactly. You've heard nothing from your husband?'

'I had one letter, but that was weeks ago. All he said was that he'd reached a Nazi concentration camp and that it was shocking. I have no idea where he is now, or what he's doing. I wrote back to him, but he didn't reply.'

'Do you miss him?'

She couldn't lie to Henry. They had always told each other the truth about everything. 'Sometimes I convince myself that the pain has gone. At other times, I feel absolutely wretched. We had happy times together.'

'Of course.'

'Why didn't he respect that happiness more?' she asked. 'Couldn't he have learned to be faithful? Wasn't I enough for him?'

'I don't think he knew what he had, or how lucky he was.'

'Do you miss your wife?'

'Of course. Sometimes I think it is better to be taken swiftly, unexpectedly, than to have to waste away. I wish I could remember her as she was – glowing and vibrant – and not as the suffering invalid she became.'

'You went through a lot together. Do you think that anyone could ever really take her place?'

'Nobody can take another's place. Love doesn't work like that. One can love more than once, but each love is glorious in its own way.'

'I agree.'

'What would you do if your husband wanted to come back to you?'

'It's over,' she said firmly. 'There's no going back.' She looked up into Henry's dim face. 'If I don't say yes to your offer right away, it's not because of Amory.'

'You don't have to say anything yet, my dear. I am a patient man.'

Nine

The next day, Paris woke up to find its streets plastered with posters calling for a general strike.

The posters, blotchily printed on cheap paper, bore the hammer and sickle of the Communist Party. Copper's interest quickened. They reminded her of the handbills she'd seen distributed in New York during the Depression.

And a few days later, an even more lurid poster appeared. This one read *TOUS AUX BARRICADES* – 'Everyone to the barricades!'

This slogan hadn't been heard since the Nazis had left. No barricades appeared in the stately streets where Copper lived, but she heard that on the Left Bank of the city, traditionally the most revolutionary part of Paris, citizens were obeying the age-old call to arms. This was certainly something she had to cover. Taking her camera, her oldest coat and a stout pair of walking shoes (the taxis and buses were obeying the strike call), she set off for the *Quartier latin*.

Near the place Saint-Michel she did indeed come across a barricade. It was made from a *pissoir*. Copper had never got used to the presence of these cast-iron urinals that were placed even in the smartest streets of Paris and were designed so that one saw the legs of the (male-only) users. This one had been wrenched off the pavement and dragged into the middle of the road where it made a very substantial, one-ton obstacle to traffic, and was manned by some twenty or thirty men and women. Copper took a couple of photographs, but she doubted whether any editor would print a photo of a public toilet being used as a political statement.

'You can't go through,' one of the women manning the barricade told Copper, throwing back her press card. 'We're here to block all fascist bastards.'

'But I'm not a fascist bastard,' she protested.

A man wearing a Resistance-style white armband and an army helmet sauntered up to Copper. He had a Gauloise dangling from his unshaven lower lip.

'*Salut*, comrade. Remember me?'

She recognised the seamed face and insouciant manner of Francois Giroux, the self-proclaimed Maquis leader who had taken her to meet Christian Dior. 'Monsieur Giroux! How are you?'

He shrugged. '*Comme ci, comme ça*. Working for the Revolution, as always.' He pulled his jacket aside to show her the black-and-red ribbon pinned to his blouson. 'They gave me the *médaille de la Résistance*.'

Copper noted the revolver stuck in his belt. 'Congratulations.'

'It should have been the *Légion d'honneur*,' he said sourly. 'But they know I'm a communist. Where are you trotting off to?'

'I heard there was going to be a big demonstration today.'

'And you think it's a spectator sport?'

'I'm a journalist,' she replied with dignity.

Giroux puffed on his Gauloise, showering her with sparks. 'A journalist? You write about those bastards who charge twenty thousand francs for a dress. Enough to feed a working-class family for a year. You call that journalism?'

'Well, if you let me through, I'll write about something else today.'

'How do I know you're not a spy?'

'You know very well that I'm not a spy,' she said indignantly.

He showed no inclination to budge. 'I hear your husband ran away from you. And you're very friendly with *la Comtesse* Dior. How is the old pansy?'

'Don't call him that.'

The man showed pointed teeth. 'You like these degenerate types, it seems. Now why would that be?'

'I like him because he's talented, kind and generous,' she replied staunchly. 'Are you going to let me pass?'

He squinted against the smoke of his cigarette. 'What's it worth to you?'

He was plainly angling for a bribe. She produced a couple of hundred-franc notes and passed them to him. 'To help with the Revolution.'

He pocketed the money, tossed his cigarette into the gutter and gave her a helmet. 'Wear this,' he said with a malicious wink. 'There will be fun and games this morning, mark my words.'

'Thank you.'

'Down there,' he said, jerking his thumb over his shoulder. 'But watch your head, comrade. The capitalist thugs don't play games.'

'And neither do we,' a woman shouted after Copper.

The helmet was heavier than it looked, pressing down on her brows. Copper made her way through the roadblock and walked further into the Latin Quarter. As always, the streets were vibrant here, despite the light rain that had begun to fall. Not for the first time, she rather regretted having allowed Dior to settle her in the fashionable part of the city. It would probably be a lot more fun to live here among the artists and the revolutionaries. She might not be an artist or a revolutionary, but she sure as hell wasn't a fascist bastard, either.

A few streets further on, she started to encounter less art and more revolution. Groups of men and women were marching, carrying banners and chanting slogans. They all seemed to be making towards a common point. Copper joined in. She could hear massed singing from up ahead. She felt her heart start to speed up. She recalled marching with her father and brothers on the Lower East Side.

The gathering point was a large square lined with spindly plane trees. There were already several thousand people crammed into the area, singing 'The Internationale' and waving banners. A platform had been set up, decked with red flags, where speeches were evidently going to be made. The needling rain seemed to deter no one.

Wanting to get a shot of the whole, tumultuous scene, Copper asked some men nearby to give her a boost up into one of the trees. Grinning, they obliged, not reluctant to grab handfuls of her buttocks. She scrambled along a somewhat slender branch and got the photographs she needed. It was a good vantage point, but she wanted to get back among the crowd. However, before she could ask her posse of young men for a lift down, the atmosphere in the square changed abruptly.

The crowd had fallen silent, allowing the battering of hoof beats on cobbles to be heard. It grew louder. At the far end of the square, mounted gendarmes emerged from side streets. There were dozens of them. Behind them marched a phalanx of police on foot. Their black capes were slick with rain and they swung long batons, their faces shadowed by the heavy helmets they wore.

A rumble of fear and anger went through the crowd. These were the hated CRS, the security police used to break up riots. They had filtered through the back streets, avoiding the barricades. Resuming 'The Internationale', the mass of people pressed forward to confront the police. A senior police officer began bawling at them through a megaphone, telling the crowd to disperse, but he was barely audible over the roar of the communist anthem.

Feeling as though she were in the grip of an electric current, Copper watched as the first line of demonstrators reached the police. A vehement argument was going on. But then the first police baton was swung. A man fell, clutching his head. A roar went up from the crowd.

It was the signal for a full-scale assault on the CRS. Demonstrators surged forward, swinging weapons of their own – the wooden poles of placards had evidently been chosen to serve two purposes – and clashed with the police lines. A horse reared, its flailing hooves scattering the unfortunates beneath. Men and women were floundering, stumbling, screaming.

Suddenly, the square was full of violence and danger. People surged to and fro, clubbing at each other, retreating, then turning to face the fray again. Copper realised that she was well and truly stuck up her tree, like a lookout up the mast of a ship in a storm. There was nothing to do but try to record the scene. Her heart was racing and her hands shook so much that she knew half of her shots would be blurry. She fumbled for her notebook and pencil, trying not to drop her camera as she shakily scribbled notes. The fighting, which had been taking place at the far end of the square, now spread as the CRS forged a path through the middle of the crowd, effectively cutting it in two.

But the gendarmes were not having it all their own way. Horses were rearing and screaming as a hail of half-bricks and cobblestones showered on them. Copper saw that figures lined the rooftops, prepared with missiles for exactly this moment. Several police were knocked down, and riderless animals were panicking, causing as much chaos among the police as among the demonstrators.

Then, shockingly, there was a shot. Someone had fired a pistol at the police. It was answered by a fusillade of shotgun fire from the CRS. Pellets rattled through the leaves around Copper, making her retreat along her branch in terror.

A second wave of police now poured into the square from a different direction, swinging clubs in disciplined savagery. There was the rattle of a sub-machine gun from the rooftops. This was getting serious. She clung to the trunk of the tree, praying not to be struck by either gunfire or rocks.

After a pitched battle of some fifteen minutes, the crowd began to yield. With faces covered in blood, some hobbling, people supporting each other as best they could, the demonstrators fled from the square, hotly pursued by the CRS, who were wielding their batons to deadly effect. It was a rout. As the crowd streamed away in all directions, figures were left lying on the ground among the discarded red flags, at the mercy of the horses' hooves. Several were too badly injured to get up. Others were immobile. These were all dragged, along with the dozens who had been arrested already, to the police vans that were now careering into the area. The gendarmes were left in possession of the square.

Hanging on to her branch for dear life, Copper hoped to avoid detection. But other people had climbed into other trees and the police were rousting them out, one by one. It soon came to her turn.

'Come down, you,' a gendarme commanded, swinging his truncheon threateningly.

'I'm a journalist,' Copper said, waving her card shakily.

'I don't care if you're Marcel Proust,' the man retorted. 'Come down.'

'I won't!'

The gendarme called over a colleague and by the humiliatingly simple expedient of shaking the little tree, they soon dislodged Copper from her perch. Furious, she was forced to clamber down before she fell. She was immediately grabbed by the two policemen, her helmet yanked off and her camera taken away.

'Don't you dare damage my camera,' she said, grabbing the man's arm. 'I'm an American citizen.'

'So much the worse for you,' the first gendarme said contemptuously. He opened the camera and pulled out the spool, destroying the morning's work.

'You bastard,' Copper flung at him, outraged.

He tossed the camera to his colleague. 'Throw her in the van with the others.'

Twenty-eight hideously uncomfortable hours later, the door of her cell opened, framing a burly gendarme. 'Where's the American woman?'

'Here,' she said.

He jerked his head. 'Come.'

Bidding farewell to her cellmates, with whom she'd been swapping tales of struggle all night, Copper allowed herself to be hustled down the stinking corridor.

'Long live the Revolution!' one of her cellmates called after her.

'Where are you taking me?' Copper demanded, trying to sound brave.

'You've been discharged,' the gendarme replied. 'You've got friends.'

Her rescuer was waiting at the front desk wearing an impeccable camel-hair overcoat and a trilby.

'Henry!'

'Are you all right?' Henry asked anxiously, examining her.

'They took my camera.'

He held up the Rolleiflex. 'I've got it back, don't worry.'

'And they destroyed all my photographs! I had pictures of police brutality in there. The world had a right to see them.'

Henry sighed. 'Any injuries? Physical ones, I mean.'

'Just a few bruises.'

'Then let's get out of here.'

'Hold on a moment,' Copper protested as he started ushering her out. 'I'm not leaving everybody else behind.'

'You can't do anything for them,' Henry replied. 'They're going to be charged tomorrow morning and they'll probably all get six months in jail. Unless you want the same?'

'I've done nothing wrong. Neither have they.'

'I can't help the others. But you – participating in civil unrest, refusing to obey police orders, resisting arrest, assaulting a police officer – it's taken me two hours to talk you out of here,' he said in a low voice. 'They say you were armed.'

'I was wearing a helmet. That's not being armed.'

'You really can be astonishingly naïve,' he snorted.

'I didn't want my brains knocked out by those bastards.'

'Let's go before they change their minds.'

'I'm going to make an official complaint about them destroying my photographs.'

He shook his head. 'I wouldn't. They're already talking about impounding your camera.'

Reluctantly, Copper allowed herself to be hustled out of the police station by Henry. In his car, she was ill-tempered, partly through lack of sleep.

'I didn't need you to come and rescue me,' she said ungraciously.

'Has it occurred to you that if you were convicted, you'd be deported?' he enquired.

'The police behaved disgustingly,' she said, evading the question. 'I saw women being beaten with clubs.'

'A policeman was shot yesterday in that demonstration. And there are half a dozen more in hospital.'

'They had it coming,' she said grimly. 'They attacked the crowd without provocation. They're nothing more than paid thugs.'

'They're doing their job – trying to protect France.'

'From people who speak their mind about injustice?' she asked scornfully. 'Is that this communist revolution you keep talking about, Henry? You told me the world needs freshness and youth; a new start. That's exactly what the communists are promising.'

He was infuriatingly unmoved. 'What they promise and what they deliver are two different things, Copper. You're not too young to remember that when the fascists came along, they were also promising freshness, youth and a new start. They and the communists deliver the same horrors.'

'As a capitalist, you would say that.'

'You may find this hard to believe, but there was a time when I called myself a communist.'

'I do find that hard to believe.'

'Well, it's true. When one first heard of the communists in Russia, one was excited, inspired even, by the ideal of universal brotherhood. But then they started to murder one's relatives, not to mention their own followers, and one realised that the ideal had merely cloaked a darker and more hideous form of tyranny, and that the extended hand of universal brotherhood was a bloodstained claw intent on grasping complete power.'

'France isn't Russia.'

'It may soon become Russia. The communists are buying lock-ups and storing trucks and cars. They've set up printing presses so they can issue leaflets – as well as print false passports and ration books. They've dug up the radio transmitters, machine guns and grenades that they hid after the Germans left. They're well-armed – and they're organising nationwide strikes that will paralyse France and throw the country into chaos.'

'How do you know all this?'

'It's my job.'

'Spying?'

He laughed. 'Gathering intelligence is the preferred term. I saw what the communists did to my country,' he said, his tone light but his words serious. 'I would not like to see the same fate befall *la belle France* – or the rest of Europe.'

'Sorry,' she said, rubbing her eyes tiredly. 'I'm just tired.'

'Is there anything else bothering you?' he asked delicately.

Copper sighed, running her fingers through her knotted red hair. 'When you proposed to me, you said you didn't want to change me, or tell me how to run my life.'

'And I meant every word.'

'Well – and I'm grateful to you for getting me out of the cooler and all – if you meant it, you shouldn't have come galloping into the gendarmerie on your white horse.'

'You were enjoying it in there?'

'I was gathering material for a great story. Until you came along.'

'Are you serious?'

'Yes!'

'Very well,' he said after a pause. 'Next time you are arrested, I will content myself with bringing you a stale crust.'

'That's more like it, buster,' she said. She laughed a little and then cried a little. Wisely, he said nothing. After a while, she dried her eyes with the hanky he passed her and took a shuddering breath.

'I apologise for galloping in,' Henry said at last. 'Having lost one wife, I'm not at all anxious to lose another before she's even mine.' They were driving through the 7th arrondissement, the wealthiest and most privileged part of Paris. Now he pulled up in front of an elaborate wrought-iron gate. 'Here we are.'

'What is this place?' she asked.

'It's my home.'

The house was half-hidden behind a stone wall. They opened the abundantly curlicued gate, entering the overgrown garden. The house itself was stately and serene, its façade clad in ivy.

'It's like Madeline's house,' Copper exclaimed. 'An old house in Paris all covered with vines.'

'Yes,' he agreed. 'But instead of twelve little girls in two straight lines, it has until lately been tenanted by several dozen Gestapo officers. It was one of the first houses requisitioned by the Germans, of course, knowing as they did who I was.' He unlocked the door and they went in. The grand old place was silent, the rooms still in the disorder left by the hastily departing Germans. Fine furniture, some of it broken, was scattered around. The walls were bare. 'They took my collection of Impressionists with them,' he said dryly. 'But left me this.'

On the wall of an imposing dining room was a large oil painting of Adolf Hitler in his brown uniform, glowering at them from under his forelock. 'Now there's an ugly sight,' Copper said.

'I never cared for it, myself.'

'Why don't you take it down?'

'I leave it there to remind me what we're fighting,' he replied. 'And because, if they took van Gogh and left Hitler, they know they're beaten.'

Despite the ill treatment the house had sustained, it remained beautiful. He led her from room to room, explaining that it had been built in the time of Napoleon III in the full Romantic style. The ceilings and mouldings were exquisite. From the upstairs windows, there were views of the golden dome of the Hôtel des Invalides.

'When will you open it again?' Copper asked.

'When the war is over. Until then, I prefer a room at the Ritz. Do you like it?'

'I love it. It's gorgeous. If it were mine, I wouldn't be able to wait.'

'My darling, it *is* yours,' he said gently. 'Yours to do with as you please. When we're married and the war is over, we'll bring this place to life again.'

She looked around her, seeing the place as it would be once restored: one of the most beautiful houses in Paris. She tried to imagine herself, Oona Reilly from Brooklyn, as the mistress here; having the arrangement of the décor, hosting dinners, becoming a leading member of the *belle monde*. Parisian society would be at her feet. 'Somehow, I just can't see it.'

'I can.' He caressed the flowing auburn of her hair. 'Don't be angry with me. But I will have to be away for some time.'

She looked into his face. 'What do you mean, "away"? Where are you going?'

'I told you that the communists are planning a revolt. Well, it has already begun.'

'You mean the strikes?'

'The strikes are just the beginning. They hope to bring France to her knees over the next few weeks. I have things to do.'

'Will you be in danger?'

'Of course not.' He took her arm. 'Look. This would be our bedroom.'

It was an airy, charming room with a large, arched window that framed a perfect view of the Eiffel Tower. Unlike the rest of the rooms in the house, this one was clean and in perfect order. There were fresh flowers on the table and the huge, four-poster bed had been made up, the spotless linen inviting.

'What's all this?' she asked. 'Did you have this room got ready especially?'

'I wanted it to look pretty for you.'

'So that I would fall into bed with you?' she demanded, half angry and half amused.

'One may always hope.'

Copper didn't know whether to be shocked or flattered. 'Henry! And here I was, thinking you were a perfect gentleman.'

'I believe you Americans have a saying: nice guys finish last.'

'I didn't know it was a race.'

'Nor did I. But now I see that there *is* a race – and the first past the post will be the winner.'

She stared at him for a moment. 'You think you're competing with Suzy.'

'I know I'm competing with her.'

'I don't like being thought of in that way,' she said slowly. 'I'm not some kind of prize to be won.'

'Copper,' he replied, his voice quiet. 'I love you. It's not a question of winning you. It's that losing you would destroy my happiness.'

'You're putting too much pressure on me,' she said, turning away from him restlessly. 'You promised you would give me time. You said you were patient.'

'But my rival is not patient. My rival is pressing hard. If I'm patient, I will lose you to her.'

'She's not your rival.'

'It seems that way to me.'

'That isn't fair.' Copper lifted her face to his. She had intended to give him a rebuke, but somehow it didn't work out that way. Her lips brushed his mouth, hesitated there, as though ready to flee – and then decided to remain. His answering kiss was warm, possessive. It deepened, and in a fraction of a second, she remembered everything that she had missed – the strength of a man's kiss, the joy of being held in a man's arms.

Her physical reaction was instantaneous. She felt her head swimming and for a moment she leaned against him, as though drawn in by the force of his gravity. For that moment, it was as though nothing were more logical than yielding to Henry, letting him take over her life. Shuddering, she buried her face against his chest. He held her tight, kissing the side of her neck, inhaling the scent of her skin, the perfume of her hair. Copper felt her breasts and thighs tense with desire. Her fingers dug into the muscular shape of his body under his clothes. She hadn't felt like this since Amory. She hadn't known that she could feel it any longer.

'I feel dizzy.'

'A night in the cells will do that.' She could hear the smile in his voice.

'You know perfectly well what's making my head spin.'

'Perhaps I do. Lie with me on our bed. Just for a moment.' Reluctantly, she allowed Henry to draw her down on to the bed beside him. 'Aren't you happy with me?' he asked, cradling her in his arms.

'Everything's beautiful,' she replied quietly. 'This room is beautiful, the house is beautiful, you're beautiful. But my freedom is precious to me.'

'I know that. And I don't want to take it away.'

'But you do. Isn't marriage a loss of freedom?'

He smiled with a touch of sadness. 'My view of marriage is perhaps a little different, my darling. I believe that marriage means voluntarily giving up certain freedoms – not having them forcibly taken away. If you marry me, you'll be free to choose what you wish to renounce.'

'Even if I want to keep on seeing Suzy?'

'Even that.'

'I don't believe you. You hate each other. Each of you wants me for yourself.' She caressed his cheek. 'Admit it, Henry – you'd go crazy if I stayed friends with Suzy.'

'Friends? No.' He trapped her hand and kissed the palm. 'Are you *more* than friends?'

Copper sealed his lips with her hand. 'Don't ask. If you start asking questions like that, you're already taking away my freedom.'

He took her hand gently away from his mouth. 'Suzy is a madness in your life,' he said. 'The madness will pass and then you'll come to me. Until then, I'll try to be patient.'

His warm hand cupped the back of her neck and drew her face to his gently. Copper felt everything she had just said start to sink into treacherous quicksand as her mouth approached his. She felt his breath on her lips and closed her eyes as he kissed her.

They kissed gently at first, then with growing urgency. As always when he kissed her like this, she felt her resolve and her ideals start to melt away. She needed him to love her, even though she couldn't give herself to him in the way he demanded. There had to be release in her life, some discharge of tension. For a moment, it was as though she were drowning. It had been so long. Yearning rose in her with a force that could not be denied. She lifted her arms around his strong neck and kissed him back, her body pressing against his.

Henry knew exactly what he wanted to do to her and she understood. It was not a complete possession, but a partial yielding. He slid between her thighs, his kisses searching for her. Copper arched her back as his hands cupped her breasts greedily, his mouth bathing her.

'Henry!' she whispered, her fingers knotting in his hair. The pleasure he gave her was like the rush of some drug. She had never felt this intensity before. She had never known that sex could be this tender assault on the senses, this ruthless desire, this cannibal love.

His mouth understood everything about her, knew her every secret wish, gratified it as soon as it was formed. There were no more thoughts of pain or failure, no thoughts of anything beyond this. Only Henry mattered. She called out his name, her voice husky, lifting to a cry. Tension drained out of her in a long shudder of ecstasy. Reality rippled up from the depths of a dark sea, settling around her. Slowly, the drugged ecstasy of gratification filled her veins, relaxing every inch of her, setting the universe in motion again.

She took him in her arms, holding him tight. 'Let me do something for you, now.'

'There's only one thing I want. I want all of you, Copper. You're right. I'll never be content with anything less than all of you. And I'm prepared to wait.' He drew back. 'But I want you to see me.'

He rose and began to undress, his eyes never leaving hers. She lay back on the bed, her hair spread like a pool of flame. One of her thighs was lifted to expose the triangle of hair. She left it like that, wanting her abandon to excite him.

He laid his clothes on the chair and turned to her, naked and unashamed. His body was beautiful, darker-skinned than her own and very strong, with sinews that rippled and tightened as he moved. He was powerfully built, with muscles developed and hardened by exercise, black hair at his chest, armpits and loins. There were scars, too: the marks of bullets and bayonets that had almost taken his life. 'You can see that I am not old.'

'I can see that.' Copper knew she would never forget this moment. She reached out to him. 'Come to me.'

He shook his head, his mouth serious, his eyes smiling. 'On our wedding night I will come to you. Here, in this bed. I have waited for all my life. I can wait a little longer.'

Copper watched him as he dressed again. His self-control was greater than hers and that frightened her a little. He was so certain that she would be his one day. And then what would be left of the freedom she cherished so much? Would she have entered another servitude? Or would it be the beginning of a new life?

Ten

What had happened between them at Henry's house had altered their relationship in more than one way. It had brought them closer and had deepened Copper's feelings for him; but it had also alarmed her. She had made love with a man – albeit in a limited way – for the first time since leaving Amory. She had also committed herself to Henry physically, despite all her resolutions to the contrary. She felt as though she were running away from a remarriage, but losing ground constantly. His absence gave her some time to reflect and think.

Knowing that Henry was away, Suzy had invited Copper to have afternoon tea with her. She asked her to come to her apartment, which was on the Faubourg Saint-Honoré, and Copper duly arrived mid-afternoon. Suzy, however, was still in bed.

She opened the door for Copper rather grumpily. 'Why have you come so early, for God's sake?'

'It's three thirty,' Copper pointed out.

'Well, I didn't get to sleep until nine this morning. I'm going to have a bath. Come.'

Copper sat on the edge of Suzy's bath while it was filling. It was huge, but Suzy was extravagant with hot water – to Copper, the greatest of luxuries – and when she got into it, the water came up to her chin.

'I think we'll go to Maxim's for afternoon tea,' Suzy decided. She gave Copper the soap. 'Will you wash my back, *chérie*?'

'Of course.' She began to lather Suzy's smooth shoulders.

'That Russian of yours. They tell me he has left you.'

'He's away from Paris on business, that's all.'

'Business with some other fool of a woman.'

'I don't believe that. He loves me.'

'And you? Do you love him?'

'Of course.'

Suzy splashed foam at Copper. 'You traitor!'

'I love you, too. Don't splash me.'

'What do you love about him? That thing which he sticks in you?'

'He hasn't done that yet,' Copper said with a smile. 'But he has a rather nice thing.'

'You've seen it?'

'Just a glimpse.'

Suzy frowned. 'I have a number of things in my drawer that are even better. If you like it so much, I will use them on you.'

'I don't want anything like that.' Copper shuddered. 'In any case, it isn't just sex. I like his companionship. I miss being with a man. I like men. Don't you? You've had male lovers.'

'I will tell you something strange. I've been with many men, but never with one who was only a man. You understand? Cocteau, for example. He has shared my bed, but the love of his life is his handsome boyfriend, Jean Marais. There have been others, the same. You see how I live? In a twilight world where people shift from one sex to the other. You cannot tell the men from the women, or the women from the men. One gets so tired of it.'

'I thought—'

'What did you think?'

'I thought that was how you liked things.'

'Perhaps it is,' Suzy said. Her long face was melancholy for a moment. 'Perhaps I am corrupt. But you are a juicy, fresh pear.' She lifted her soapy face to Copper for a kiss. 'And I cannot get my fill of you.'

Copper wiped soap bubbles off her cheek. 'Henry says you are cruel.'

'Oh, so you have been gossiping about me?'

'He told me that you had a mentor. She gave you everything and you threw her aside like an old glove.'

Suzy's eyes widened for a moment. In the cool light, they were almost golden. Then she threw her head back and laughed. Copper watched the smooth column of her throat pulsing. 'Like an old glove! *Chérie*, where do you get such phrases? I thought they had gone out with Sarah Bernhardt.'

'But it's true, isn't it?'

Suzy was still smiling. 'What if it is?'

'Henry said it was almost as though you hated her. Did you?'

'If you had been a little brown beetle and then you became a golden butterfly – wouldn't you hate those who'd known you as a little brown beetle?'

'I think I'd be grateful to the person who guided me,' Copper said. She'd learned that Suzy's intense gaze was due in part to her short-sightedness. She hated to be seen wearing glasses and her struggle to focus gave her a disconcertingly direct stare.

'Like pity, gratitude is an emotion I do not know,' Suzy replied. 'Besides, she had come to believe she owned me. And nobody can own me. What else did your Henry say about me?'

'That you broke her heart.'

'He had quite a lot to say, it seems. Do you believe him?'

'I don't want my heart broken.'

'Don't you trust me?'

'I wouldn't be here if I didn't trust you.'

'Yet you listen to Henry? Why? Because he's a man?'

'Because he's kind and sincere.'

'*Chérie*, people will tell you all sorts of things about me. The little that they know, and the much that they don't. If you listen to any of it, you are a fool.'

'I hear everything and listen to nothing.'

'Good.'

Suzy emerged from her bath like Aphrodite rising from the foam and dried herself. Copper felt no shame in watching her; Suzy was like a supple animal, unaware of its own nudity and therefore evoking no shame in the observer. The curls of tawny hair in the hollow of her armpits and between her legs caught the wintry light and glowed warmly. Catching Copper's eyes on her, Suzy paused, and spread her arms wide. 'Do you like me?'

'You're beautiful. You know you are.'

Pleased, Suzy turned slowly, showing off her lithe waist, the swelling fullness of her buttocks. 'I'm not so young anymore, you know. Yet I have kept my figure. I can still show it in public. Not bad, eh?'

'Not bad,' Copper agreed. 'Why don't you shave your armpits?'

'Shaving one's armpits is so bourgeois.' She lifted her arms to show the tufts on either side. 'Isn't it pretty?'

'To you French, yes. To us Americans, it's anathema to have even a shadow. But if you insist . . .'

Suzy touched the triangle between her thighs. 'And here?' she asked mischievously. 'Would you like me to shave here, too – so you can see everything?'

'No.'

'Why not, if you are so keen to shave my armpits?'

'Because that part doesn't appear in public. The armpits do.'

'How earnest you are.' Suzy laughed. 'You are blushing like a rose, my dear.'

'I've never known anybody like you,' Copper said crossly, aware of the heat in her cheeks.

She watched Suzy as she dressed. Her underwear was enviable, all made for her by a *corsetière* on the rue Cambon from silk and lace in diaphanous pinks. Her smooth, white-gold body disappeared into it, and then into a dark wool suit. She surveyed Copper thoughtfully. 'Today calls for something special. Take off your clothes.'

'I'm quite happy the way I am.'

Suzy made an irritated noise. 'I am not happy. Undress.'

This was a ritual that Suzy insisted upon from time to time. The best thing was simply to obey. Copper took off her dress. Suzy hunted in her closet. They were almost the same size, and most of Suzy's clothes fitted Copper well. On this occasion, Suzy picked out a silk outfit, deep black with delicate, emerald-green stripes. She also insisted on doing Copper's make-up, squinting with concentration as she painted Copper's lips and shaded her eyelids.

'Put your glasses on,' Copper said, 'or you'll have my eye out with that brush.'

'I hate my spectacles,' Suzy muttered, but put them on neverthe-less. They were round with tortoiseshell rims and had a slightly comical appearance on Suzy's narrow face. Yet it was when Suzy showed these rare signs of weakness, Copper felt, that she loved her most.

The make-up completed to her satisfaction, Suzy found her a pair of Chanel shoes with little gold bows and finished her off with a dainty hat and a scrap of black veil that enhanced, rather than concealed, Copper's large, grey eyes.

'I feel like a Christmas present,' Copper commented, examining her gleaming reflection in the cheval mirror.

'Which is exactly what you are,' Suzy said, pulling on a pair of fawn kid gloves. 'And you may keep the clothes if you like them.'

They went out together. The afternoon threatened rain, so they walked quickly, arm in arm, laughing like old friends.

Afternoon tea at Maxim's was one of Suzy's favourite treats. It was an especially feminine ritual. There were red hothouse roses in Chinese vases on the tables, and the tea was served on delicate art-nouveau crockery that was surely as old as the restaurant itself. The rose-scented macarons, a speciality of the house, melted in the mouth. There were cream cakes and Florentines, and vol-au-vents that arrived crisp, hot and light as a feather, and even Darjeeling tea; in short, it was as though the war were already over. It was as though there had never been a war at all.

The tables around them were almost all occupied by smartly dressed women, some in groups, but many in couples, their heads close together in murmured confabulation. Copper wondered how many of these female pairs were lovers. She caught many glances coming her way, some of them unabashedly admiring. One woman, thin and dark, stared at her with an intensity that was positively disturbing; and a square, red-cheeked woman with large green eyes smiled at her constantly, like the Cheshire cat. She responded to none of these advances.

But how different the friendships of women were to those of men. How much more elastic, more nuanced, encompassing an intimacy than men seemed incapable of. Copper had grown up with four brothers and their friends. Her sister had been older, married and working as a nurse by the time Copper was ten. With no mother, she'd had few female contacts.

She had learned a great deal from Suzy in these past weeks about what the friendship of a woman could offer. Her relationship with Suzy included shades of almost every sensation; not just wit, excitement, the unfettered enjoyment of whatever life had to give – but also something romantic.

After the tea, they walked together down the rue du Faubourg Saint-Honoré, looking in the windows of the expensive salons, which were now being lit up as the evening closed in. The rain had held off and crowds of prosperous Parisians were taking the same promenade.

Again, Copper had the sensation that Paris was an island where the war had ceased, floating in the calm eye of a vast cyclone that was circling them, shattering everything in its path but leaving the centre eerily undisturbed.

They went into Lanvin, one of the oldest fashion houses in Paris and Suzy's personal favourite couturier. The clothes were charming, but with her newly educated eye, Copper could see that they already felt outdated, with their intricate embroidery work and beading. Even the delicate, flowery colours seemed to hark back to a simpler and more innocent age. As she wandered among the models, she inhaled the scent that hung in the air.

'My God. That's divine.'

'It's "My Sin" – Jeanne Lanvin's own perfume. Do you like it?'

'I adore it.'

'It's heliotrope and musk.'

'I've never smelled anything like it.'

Suzy went to the counter where she was greeted with the deference due to a valued client. 'Give me a flacon of My Sin, please.'

'Is that for me?' Copper asked, surprised.

'Of course.'

'But you hate perfume.'

'You shall wear it when I'm not there.'

Copper was enchanted by the little, round, black bottle with the golden cap, and by the box it came in with its wicked black cat. 'You're so kind to me,' she murmured to Suzy.

'Really? And just this morning I was so unkind.'

'You can be both.'

'Indeed.' Suzy had taken her compact from her bag and was carefully reapplying her lipstick. She examined herself intently in the little mirror and then snapped it shut decisively. 'Come.'

Carrying their purchase, they crossed the street, where Suzy paused in front of an antiques salon. In the window, a collection of exquisitely inlaid furniture gleamed under soft lamps. 'What lovely things,' Copper said.

'Ah, yes. This is a person who understands lovely things. Come.' Suzy pushed open the door and went in. Copper followed, finding herself in an Aladdin's cave of marble statues, oil paintings and furniture. There was antique jewellery, too, and glass cases full of heavy silverware. A woman dressed in a dark-blue suit came to meet them. It was only when she saw the expression on her face that Copper realised where they were.

'Good evening, Suzanne,' the woman said in a slightly breathless voice, as though she'd been struck a blow in the stomach.

'Good evening, Yvonne,' Suzy replied easily. 'We had tea at Maxim's and since we were passing by, I thought we'd drop in. I hope you don't mind?'

'Of course not,' the other woman said. 'Why should I mind? Welcome to my little shop.'

'This is my dear friend, Copper Heathcote. Copper, this is Yvonne de Bremond d'Ars.'

Presented so formally, Copper held out her hand. '*Enchantée*, Madame de Bremond.'

The hand that took hers was cool, the pressure brief. If Copper had known that this was the shop of Suzy's former patroness and lover, she would never have entered it. But now it was too late to flee. Yvonne de Bremond was past fifty years old with short, dark hair. Her suit was mannish but impeccably chic in its simplicity. At the back of the shop, a large Alsatian reclined regally on a rug, his intelligent eyes observing them closely. Suzy seemed to be the only one at ease here. 'You're looking well, Yvonne,' she said, coolly examining the other woman's face, hands and clothes.

'And so are you, my dear Suzanne.'

'Ah, I'm always haggard, while you are serene as ever. Affairs and intrigues take too much out of one. You're so clever to escape the stresses of human relationships.'

'I have no shortage of relationships,' Yvonne retorted to this sally. 'Though perhaps I am not as promiscuous as you.'

'Really? I hear that you live like a nun these days.'

'Nonsense.'

'You've excelled yourself,' Suzy went on, looking around the shop. 'An excellent haul. So many people in need of money these days and willing to part with an heirloom or two for very little.'

'I pay the highest prices,' the other woman replied stiffly. 'You know that.'

'But everyone likes a bargain, don't they?' Suzy insisted. 'Buy cheap, sell dear – that's the soul of business, not so?' Her smile was silky and ironic.

'If you insist,' Yvonne replied thinly. 'But, in my experience, there is no such thing as a bargain. If you pay little, you get rubbish.'

'Ah, you protest too much, Yvonne. You like to pick things up for nothing. Be honest.'

The older woman's cheeks had turned an angry brick red. 'I am being honest. The cheapest things are also often rotten inside and cause the most trouble to make presentable.'

Suzy seemed amused. 'If you say so.'

Watching the two of them in some trepidation, Copper was reminded of Dior's comment that they could be sisters. He was right. They had the same statuesque bearing, the same athleticism. Even their faces were alike, narrow and handsome, with perfect white teeth. The difference was that where Suzy was on the right side of that invisible line that marks a woman's youth, Yvonne was clearly on the wrong side.

'And how was your tea?' Yvonne asked, turning to Copper. 'Did you have the rose-scented macarons? And the vol-au-vents? They say they're chicken, but alas, they are rabbit.'

'I like rabbit,' Copper replied.

Yvonne inspected her disdainfully. 'And someone has doused you in My Sin, it seems.'

'She has that flawless Irish complexion and hair.' Suzy took Copper's arm and turned her to the light. 'That bloom of youth. Look at her. There's really nothing to match it, is there? The skin of a young woman is the most exquisite fabric there is.'

'And the most short-lived,' Yvonne retorted. 'It doesn't last long.'

'Oh, quite. And once it is lost, it is gone forever.' Suzy touched the other woman's face with gloved fingers in a gesture that would have been compassionate, but for Suzy's cruel smile. 'Although, of course, you don't mind that, being an antiquarian. The older things are, the better you like them, *n'est-ce pas?*' She laughed merrily. 'If it doesn't have cobwebs in every nook and cranny, you turn up your nose in disgust.'

Yvonne forced a laugh. 'How witty you are. Are you still performing in that club of yours?'

'Of course.'

'I do hope you can win the *épuration* round. One hears that they take a dim view of those who were too friendly with the Germans.'

'I will take my chances with the *épuration*. In my experience, all men in uniform are much the same, whatever language they speak.'

'I would hate to hear of you going to prison,' Yvonne shot back, her eyes gleaming. 'You wouldn't enjoy it, despite your fondness for men in uniform. And you would miss your treats. Your little rabbit vol-au-vents, and so forth.'

'Don't worry about me. I have always made my own way in life.'

'Not always,' Yvonne said quietly.

'Well, I do so now.' A well-dressed couple had come into the shop and were inspecting an Empire chaise longue. 'Don't neglect your customers, Yvonne. *A bientôt*, my dear.'

'Do drop in again, any time you have nothing better to do.'

'You may count on it.'

The two women kissed, careful not to actually touch rouged mouths to each other's cheeks. Suzy put her arm through Copper's possessively as they walked out.

On the pavement outside, Copper pulled away from her angrily. 'So that's why you dressed me up so carefully today. To show me off like a pet poodle.'

'Perhaps there was some such thought in my mind,' Suzy said tranquilly. She was looking pleased with herself. 'But you are hardly a poodle, *chérie*.'

'Whatever I am, I'm not your possession. I was absolutely mortified in there.'

'Why should you be mortified?'

'Because you only took me in there to discomfort that woman.'

'You asked to meet her.'

'I didn't!'

'I must have mistaken your curiosity, then.'

'You were horrible to her.'

'Was I?'

'At your worst.'

'I think you exaggerate. Yvonne and I understand one another very well.'

'You were practically at each other's throats.'

'Perhaps. But were we to forgive one another, we might both find life somewhat duller.'

'So you take all your conquests in there to show them off?'

'Don't be silly.'

'You do. I can see it in your face.'

Suzy was laughing at her. 'Of course I want to show you off. You are beautiful. And you are mine.'

'I'm not yours,' Copper snapped. 'I'm going home.'

'Copper, don't go.'

'Don't call me again.'

Copper was deeply offended. The episode had left her feeling used and acutely embarrassed. On her way home, she tried to work out why it had been quite so distasteful. It wasn't just the mortification of being paraded like some creature on a leash; it was the feeling that she had been no more than a dart hurled in a battle between two middle-aged women. It was all very well to be Suzy's friend, but not if that meant she became a pet – with a pet's loss of dignity. There was something suffocating, too, about her pampering. She couldn't wait to get Suzy's clothes off.

She reached the apartment in a temper, to find Pearl nursing a spectacular black eye.

'What the hell happened to you?' Copper demanded.

'I walked into a door.'

'Walked into a fist, you mean. And I know whose.' She examined Pearl's face angrily. The bruise extended from the swollen eye right across Pearl's cheek, fading from violet to yellow. 'How can you keep going back to that bastard?'

'What about you, Copper Pot?' Pearl said wearily. 'She's got you dressed up in her cast-offs. And drenched in her perfume. What's that for – to cover the smell of cat?'

Copper escaped to her room and changed out of Suzy's silk outfit. Her wardrobe was starting to fill with Suzy's gifts. One couldn't really call them cast-offs – most were fine Lanvin designs no more than a few months old – but they all carried something of Suzy on them. Where another woman's dresses might have smelled of her favourite perfume, Suzy's clothes had a hint of her body. Under the arms, they smelled of Suzy's musk, bringing emotions flooding back into Copper's mind. She wondered whether Pearl wasn't right in her dire warnings that this relationship with Suzy would change her forever. It probably would. But perhaps she *wanted* to change. What else was life all about?

She was in her shabby old dressing gown when the knock came. It was Christian Dior, carrying a little white dog under one arm.

'It's Jacinthe,' he said apologetically when he'd been admitted and was settled in front of the stove with a glass of red wine. 'Bébé's dog. She's been locked in his studio all this time. Poor little thing, she's almost starved to death. He'd left food and water, but it obviously ran out. I wondered whether you could look after her? Until Bébé is back with us?'

Copper took the trembling little animal, feeling the fragile, birdlike bones under the matted curls. 'Of course I'll take her.'

Copper took Jacinthe to the bathroom to wash her. She was in a pathetic state, her fur knotted and filthy, and her eyes rolling in distress. She also smelled awful. Dior came to sit with Copper and observed as she gently lathered the small dog.

'How is Bébé?' she asked.

He sighed. 'They won't let me see him yet. But I've been through these cures before with him and it's terribly hard. He gets very ill. Last time, he almost died.'

'Oh, Tian! What a tragedy.'

'Yes. He is the most brilliant person I know. But with Bébé, there are no half-measures. He can't stop until he's completely shattered, whether it's work or play. He simply pours himself out. The rest of us eke out our talents in a miserly fashion because we know how limited they are.' Dior leaned on the edge of the tub. His face, shiny with steam from Jacinthe's bath, was melancholy. 'I don't think he can last much longer.'

'Don't say that.'

'I can't lose any more people I love, Copper. It's too much.' He wiped his tears and swallowed a gulp of his wine. 'Thank you for taking Jacinthe. You're so kind. I would take her myself, but every time I see her, I start crying.'

'It's no problem,' she replied gently. She understood Dior's sensitivity much more now.

Jacinthe appeared to have rolled in linseed oil which had dried, and she had to concentrate on disentangling the fine fur.

'May I ask,' Dior enquired carefully, 'where your Russian gentleman has gone?'

'He's away on business.'

'One hears that his business is somewhat delicate, yes? You must be worried about him.'

'I'm worried to death,' she confessed, 'but it doesn't do me any good.'

'How are things with Suzy?'

'Sometimes she's delightful, other times I feel like strangling her. Today I felt like strangling her.' She gave Dior a brief résumé of the Yvonne episode.

Dior grimaced. 'I'm afraid that Suzy is not discreet.'

'She treated me like a possession. But I don't belong to her. I'm not even a lesbian.' Seeing Dior's raised eyebrows, she exclaimed, 'I hate the word, to be honest with you. Why does it have to be used at all? Why should we be put into boxes in this way?'

'Because for one thing, as we have already discussed, being a lesbian is Suzy's profession. And for another, if we are not put into boxes, the rest of the world does not know what to do with us. Besides, the very fact that you claim not to be a lesbian means that there must surely be such a category for you not to belong to.'

'I thought you were supposed to be bad at logic,' she replied dryly.

'I never made such a claim. I am a logical man.' Jacinthe was now as clean as could be achieved without drowning her, and he helped Copper lift the trembling animal out of the water and wrap her in a towel. 'I have spent most of my life being acutely ashamed of what I am,' he said in a low voice. 'I have endured agonies, as many men like me must. I would not wish you to endure the same agonies.'

'Pearl says men will always be disgusted by me if they know what I've done.'

'I think men are far more likely to accept a woman who loves women than a man who loves men. In fact, it's exciting to many men, which is how Suzy makes her living.'

'I don't understand that.'

Dior was drying the little dog's ears and muzzle with the care of a mother. 'You women can do as you please with each other and it's charming and inconsequential.'

'Inconsequential!'

'It's simply beauty seeking a reflection. There's an innocence about it. Like children at play.'

'Tian,' she exclaimed. 'In some ways you understand women very well. But in others – well!'

He raised his hands in mock surrender. 'You're right, you're right. I'll stick to my dresses.'

Not hearing anything from Henry was very difficult. Though Henry refused to talk about his work, Copper was certain that he was in danger. As he had predicted, newly liberated France was being ravaged by strikes and sabotage. Rioting broke out almost every week as the police attempted to get strike-breaking workers past the picket lines. Communist saboteurs, apparently under the impression that the Lille–Paris Express was being used to carry troops, derailed the train at Arras. In the horrendous crash that followed, dozens were seriously hurt and sixteen were killed. The streets of Paris filled with armed police. The government assured the country that the situation was being contained. But nobody knew what was really going on beneath the surface.

As the violence intensified – and harsh weather returned, with blizzards and a coal shortage – Copper's worries about Henry grew darker.

His silence turned from a relief into a daily, hourly worry that gnawed at her. She was constantly aware of mingled anger and anxiety churning in her stomach. How could he just vanish like this? If he loved her as he said he did, how could he treat her this way?

Unless – and this thought terrified her – he'd been captured or killed. The more she tried to push the idea away, the more it pressed in on her. He'd told her he was gathering intelligence about the communists, but the truth was that she had no real idea what he did, or who he was fighting. Had he been captured? Or had he been put up against a wall and shot?

Or was she wasting her sympathy and had he simply tired of her and found a less troublesome, more compliant playmate? That thought was excruciating in a different way.

He didn't strike her as the sort of man who would propose marriage when all he wanted was a roll in the hay. But then, she'd been desperately wrong about a man before, hadn't she?

Some people might say she'd played hard-to-get with Henry. Perhaps he'd felt she was being false. Perhaps he'd grown disgusted with her.

On a Sunday morning, while the church bells of Paris were still ringing, Copper was roused from her bed by a trembling Dior, his eyes staring from a white face.

'I've had a call. It's my sister. She's alive.' He clutched at her. 'She's coming home.'

The news had come from the Red Cross. The prison where Catherine had been held had been liberated by the Russians. A pitiful handful of survivors had been found. The rest had been massacred by the SS, starved or frozen to death. But Catherine, as Madame Delahaye had always predicted, had survived. She was one of the first to be sent home. She would be on a refugee train arriving the following morning at the Gare de l'Est.

All this Dior told her in a state of trembling excitement as they left the apartment together. 'We must prepare her room,' he said. 'And eggs. We need eggs!'

'Why eggs?' Copper asked, half-laughing at his earnestness.

'To make her a cheese soufflé. It's her favourite dish; she will expect it. And they say she is thin. We'll need to feed her up. A cheese soufflé is the most nourishing of dishes, you know. We always had it when we were sick as children.'

'All right, we'll find some eggs.'

'And flowers. We need flowers!'

They raced around Paris. Eggs, butter and milk were still scarce in the city. Only a few shops could obtain them, and there were long queues at all of these. They waited in line at two, Dior beside himself with anxiety and frustration, only to be told after an interminable procession to the counter that none were available.

At the third, however, they struck lucky, and were able to buy six precious eggs and a pat of butter; and at the fourth, a small jug of milk and a piece of cheese just big enough to make a soufflé.

'She was right,' Dior kept repeating. 'Delahaye was right. They all tried to tell me Catherine was dead. But Delahaye knew. She knew. I'm going to cover that woman with gold.'

At the market on the Île de la Cité, under the shadow of Notre-Dame, they found spring flowers for sale.

'Those won't all fit in her room,' Copper warned Dior, who had gathered armfuls.

'Then we'll put them all around the apartment,' he replied, barely visible behind the bouquets. She was half-expecting him to buy one of the little birds that were also on sale, hopping and chirping anxiously in tiny cages.

Together, they prepared Catherine's room. Dior lit the stove to start warming up the air. Copper prepared the bed, making it as pretty and warm as she could. There were not enough vases for all the flowers Dior had bought, so he had to run downstairs to his neighbour to borrow a couple more. He kept bursting out laughing with sheer joy, or exclaiming aloud. It was indeed a miracle. As the full horror of the Nazi extermination machine had been revealed to the world, it had seemed less and less likely that Catherine could possibly have survived. After all, millions, as they now knew, had died, either killed out of hand or worked to death in the appalling conditions of the camps.

'I am trying to find Hervé, her fiancé. He must be told she's coming back. Oh, I won't be able to sleep tonight,' Dior said, when the place was finally to his satisfaction. 'How will I close my eyes?'

'You must try,' Copper said gently.

In the event, it was she who could not sleep, imagining the joy of the reunion to come the next day. Dior had passed a year of the utmost anxiety since Catherine's arrest; and what Catherine had passed through, God alone knew. The little clairvoyant had been right, after all, however. Catherine Dior was alive. And that was all that mattered.

Eleven

The Red Cross train was due in at nine in the morning, having set off from Germany the previous day. The Gare de l'Est, like all Paris stations these days, was crowded with troops and civilians passing through Paris from all parts of Europe. It was a rainy day and a dim light filtered through the vast barrel roof of steel girders and dirty glass, barely reaching the depths of the echoing station below, where crowds heaved to and fro in abysmal confusion.

Dior was in a pitiable state, trembling with nerves and filled with apprehensions. 'What if she has missed her train?' he kept asking. 'What if she was taken ill? What if we miss her in this dreadful mob?' He was carrying a bouquet of roses, which in his agitation he was almost crushing against his chest. 'What if—'

'None of those things will happen,' Copper said, determinedly steering him towards the right platform. 'Look where you are going, Tian!' He had almost been run down by a porter pushing a trolley piled six feet high with trunks.

The train was late. They waited among a group of people in a similar state of anxiety to their own, seething around the group of Red Cross officials who were obliged to keep repeating that yes, the train was coming, that yes, delays were normal in these times, and that no, nobody had been left behind. Now and then, someone would dart to the very edge of the platform in order to peer down the line and be chased back by an elderly stationmaster.

At last, approaching mid-morning, a singing of the steel tracks announced that a train was coming. A cheer went up. The train trudged with painful slowness into the station, as though the journey had been too much for it and its wheels were hurting. It came to a halt at last. Clouds of steam, released from the boiler, poured from the locomotive, condensing on everything. Dior was clutching Copper's hand as the doors began to clatter open and figures, dimly visible in the billowing steam, emerged from the compartments.

The Red Cross officials had erected a barrier to keep the crowds away from the passengers. This arrangement was causing much anger. People were calling to their relatives and trying to reach those they could recognise. The officials were steadfast. The refugees were to be released to their families one by one, their names ticked off on lists.

'I don't see her,' Dior said wretchedly, trying to peer through the fog. 'She's not there!'

'She must be,' Copper said, squeezing his hand. In his agitation, he had crushed the roses. She had brought her camera to record the great moment. She checked it now, making sure the film had been advanced and the shutter cocked.

After a wretched hour, the first arrivals had been processed and had started to make their way along the platform with their relatives. The crowd, which had been noisy, even belligerent, fell silent now, staring at the revenants. Who were these phantoms who shuffled in scarecrow clothes many sizes too big for them, and stared ahead with unseeing eyes set in dark hollows? Who did not speak, or who croaked with voices like rusty tin? A man uttered an exclamation of pity and disgust, and a woman burst into loud sobs.

There was not a sound on the platform now apart from the steady hissing of steam and the clank of cooling metal. The voices of the Red Cross officers could be heard calling out names.

'Dior! Mademoiselle Catherine Dior!'

'Here! I am her brother.' Dior ran forward. But the figure that waited for him between two helpers hardly seemed like a woman at all. The gaunt skull was hairless; the body, like a winter tree, thin and frail. She held a little suitcase in one hand. With the other, she reached out to her brother, her lips stretching in the caricature of a smile.

'Christian!'

Dior was weeping helplessly. He had dropped the bouquet of roses. They were trampled underfoot, unnoticed. Copper had forgotten to use her camera; it swung uselessly as they took charge of Catherine. Copper reached to take Catherine's little suitcase.

'Oh, thank you. But I am stronger than I look.' A label with her name written on it had been fastened to Catherine's coat. The photographs Copper had seen had shown a fresh-faced, pretty woman with a mass of curly hair. Nothing remained of that prettiness now; and only the beaky nose that was so like Dior's bore out the name on the label. 'Don't worry about me, Tian. I'm sorry I'm so ugly. My hair will grow again.'

'You are beautiful,' Dior sobbed.

'I told them nothing, you know,' Catherine said, as they made their way through the staring crowd. Like the other survivors, she walked in a slow shuffle, her legs apparently barely able to support her. She was in her twenties but she seemed like an old woman. 'They hurt me, but I told them nothing. You must tell everybody that. Even if they don't ask you. Tell them I remained silent. I betrayed no one.'

'Don't worry about such things now,' Dior replied. 'Nobody will dare accuse you.'

Copper could feel that Catherine's cardboard suitcase was very light. There obviously wasn't much in it. 'Do you have clothes?' she asked.

'Only what the Red Cross gave me. Nothing fits, but at least I was warm. They told me to bring my clothes to Ravensbrück when I was arrested, but they took everything away from us the day we arrived. And the Russians burned our prison clothes because they were full of lice. I would like to have kept them. I grew attached to them.'

Why hadn't it occurred to either of them that Catherine would have nothing to wear? 'I'll bring you some of mine,' Copper promised. 'I'm about the same height as you.' She forbore to add that Catherine was several sizes thinner.

'Well,' Catherine said, perhaps catching Copper's thought. 'This is what a year as the guest of the Germans did to me. Don't cry, Tian. I'm much stronger than I look, I promise you.'

She kept repeating this phrase during the drive to the rue Royale. Dior had himself under control now and was kissing his sister's hand again and again on the back seat. She stared out of the window with hollow eyes. 'My God. How wonderful to see Paris again. It's like a dream.' She gave a little, uncertain laugh. 'I'm not dreaming, am I?'

'No, *chérie*, you're not dreaming.'

She saw a kiosk. 'Oh, can we buy a newspaper? We heard nothing about the war for months, only what people whispered.'

They stopped to buy a copy of *Le Monde* for Catherine. She did not try to read it, but pressed the newspaper to her face, inhaling the scent of newsprint and ink luxuriously. 'This is what freedom smells like.'

Dior was talking cheerfully. But because she knew him so well by now, Copper could see how shocked he was by Catherine's appearance. It wasn't only her emaciated state; there was something brittle about her. She was trying hard to be bright, but beneath that was exhaustion and desolation. She was struggling to hold herself together, as though she didn't know what would happen if she allowed herself to relax; as though she didn't know how to be herself anymore.

Copper rushed home and selected some of her clothes for Catherine. Her wardrobe had swelled with Suzy's generosity and she had spares. Some pretty underthings might be welcomed, she thought, and jerseys for that wasted frame, which must surely feel the chill. And a hat for that poor, naked head.

When she returned, Dior was in the kitchen, busy with the soufflé. Catherine sat at the window in a shawl, looking out over the rooftops. She turned with that crippled smile to look at Copper. 'It's so good to see the rooftops of Paris again. One grew so weary of the barbed wire and the distant trees one could never reach.'

'I brought you some clothes.' Copper held out the offerings. 'Please help yourself to whatever you think you can use.'

'Ah, Copper. You are as kind as my brother says you are.'

'It's the other way around. He has been kindness itself to me.'

'Kindness is the currency of humanity. Even in the camps one found it. Debased and broken, but one found it.' She leaned forward to look at the clothes. 'You have lovely things.' But she made no effort to touch anything.

'I thought you might like this cardigan. It's very warm – lamb's wool. And this beret, until your hair grows.' Copper held the garments out in an effort to get Catherine interested.

'So pretty.' At last, Catherine reached out hesitantly and stroked the pale-blue wool. With a shock, Copper saw for the first time that on Catherine's left wrist a number had been crudely tattooed, indigo against the white flesh: 57813. 'Ah, yes. My number. I hate to see it.'

Copper tried to hold back her emotions. She had heard of these things being done, but it was the first time she had seen them. 'Perhaps it can be removed.'

'Perhaps.'

'I'll get you some gloves, if you want them.'

'A pair of cotton gloves? That would be most kind. I'm so ashamed for Hervé to see me like this. He won't recognise me.'

'He will understand. Won't you try the cardigan on? You must feel the cold.'

Stiffly, Catherine pulled on the soft wool garment. 'It does feel very nice,' she sighed, hugging herself. 'Thank you.'

'Please keep it. I don't need it.'

'That I find hard to believe. But you are most kind,' she repeated.

Dior emerged from the kitchen, drying his hands on his apron. 'We are nearly ready. To the table, please, ladies.'

They sat at the little dining table. Dior brought in the food, which let off a mouth-watering aroma. He had baked the soufflés in individual ramekins, and they were perfect, each with a fluffy, golden cloud of crust. He opened a bottle of Chablis and filled their glasses. 'To Catherine.'

Catherine laughed, but Copper noticed she barely tasted the wine. She put down her glass and sat looking at the soufflé before her, in much the same way as she had looked at Copper's clothes.

'Eat,' Dior coaxed. 'I've made it just the way you like it. Like at Granville. And we have to feed you up.'

'Yes,' Catherine said. But it seemed to be an effort for her to pick up her fork. She took a mouthful and closed her eyes. Dior was watching her expectantly.

'Is it good?' he asked.

She swallowed. 'It's a masterpiece.'

He beamed. 'Go on. You know a soufflé doesn't last forever.'

Catherine took a few more mouthfuls. Suddenly, she pushed her chair back and stood up. 'I'm sorry,' she gasped. She ran to the toilet, where they could hear her being painfully sick. Dior looked appalled.

'What is wrong with her?' he whispered to Copper.

'I think it's too rich for her,' she whispered back.

He struck his own forehead. 'My God. What a fool I am.'

Catherine came back to the table. 'I'm so sorry, Tian. Your soufflé is delicious. But my stupid stomach doesn't know how to behave anymore.'

'Oh, *chérie*, I am so sorry.'

'What can you eat?' Copper asked.

'In the prison, they gave us potato soup every day. It was really just dirty water. If one found a scrap of potato, one hoarded it all day. We were lucky. We worked in the factories, so they kept us alive. The others often got nothing at all . . .' Her voice trailed off, her eyes growing absent, looking into another world.

Copper went quietly to the kitchen. There were a few potatoes, some carrots and leeks, and a bunch of parsley. She chopped them finely and put them on to boil. She could hear Dior and Catherine talking in low voices.

When the vegetables were tender, she took them in to Catherine. 'I feel I'm being a dreadful nuisance,' Catherine said. 'I'm not really a fit companion for decent people anymore. I'm so sorry about the soufflé, Tian.' She began to eat the soup slowly and carefully, while Copper and Dior watched in silence. Neither of them had any appetite now, and the soufflés deflated slowly in their ramekins, untasted.

Catherine wasn't sick again, but after a while, her eyes began to close, and her shaven head drooped on its slender stalk. She dipped her spoon into the dish one last time, and then seemed unable to lift it out again.

'You must sleep,' Dior said.

Catherine raised her head wearily. 'I'm sorry. I couldn't sleep on the train. I was so excited to see you again, Tian. And now that I'm here, I'm such poor company . . .'

Between them, they helped her into her bed and tucked her in like a child. She was asleep before they closed the door.

In the sitting room, Dior whispered, white-faced, 'She's dying.'

'Don't even think that. She's come so far.'

Dior covered his face with his hands. 'I never thought I could hurt anyone. But I could kill the people who did this to her.'

'So could I,' Copper said quietly.

Over the next days, Copper learned something of Catherine's history. She had fallen in love with a dashing young man in the Resistance, Hervé des Charbonneries. Before long, she was involved in the secret struggle against the Nazis. It was her task to memorise critical information about German troop movements and weapons production and relay them to General de Gaulle's Free French. They'd hoped that a pretty young woman on a bicycle would escape the attention of the Gestapo, but they were wrong. She had been betrayed. A message to meet an agent at the Trocadéro had turned out to be a Gestapo trap. She had been arrested and tortured in the notorious dungeons of La Santé prison.

'The most terrible thing,' Catherine told her, 'was that we were tortured not by Germans, but by Frenchmen. Our own compatriots.'

Christian had tried frantically to get her released, begging his wealthy clients to intercede on Catherine's behalf. None of them had been willing. Christian himself had been lucky not to be arrested, too.

Now he was overjoyed at Catherine's return, but her weakened state terrified him. He talked of sending her to the country for the clean air and healthy food that were so hard to find in Paris, but he could not bear to be away from her, and in any case, she was exhausted and in no condition to travel any further.

'She was always my pet,' Dior whispered to Copper as Catherine lay sleeping, bundled up in blankets. 'When we were children, I seldom played with my brothers. But Catherine—' He smiled tenderly. 'Catherine was special. I wasn't allowed to have dolls, of course, so she became my doll. I would do her hair in ribbons and bows. I loved to make outfits for her, dress her up and take her out to show her off. With her, I could indulge all my secret passions for lace and frills.'

'She was your first muse, in fact.'

'Yes, she was. And such a sweet-tempered little muse she was; always smiling, always serene. My childhood would have been wretched without her. One of my brothers was insane and had to be put in an institution. My poor mother died soon after. I was never close to my father or my other brother, Raymond. I was a dreamer, living in my own world. Catherine was the only one who could enter that world with me. I really think that losing her would kill me.'

'You haven't lost her,' Copper pointed out gently.

Dior laid his hand over Copper's. 'She needs a woman's touch.'

'I'm not much of a nurse, but of course I'll do whatever I can, Tian.'

Copper took Catherine to see a doctor. The doctor, Séverine Lefebvre, was middle-aged and kindly, which was why Copper had chosen her. Catherine asked Copper to be with her for the examination. Standing on the doctor's scales in her underwear, Catherine was even thinner than Copper had realised, her legs and arms stick-like, her ribs and hip bones prominent under the pale skin, which bore so many discolorations and bruises. The examination was very thorough and included an eyesight test.

At length, Dr Lefebvre invited them to sit at her desk while she wrote out, in her old-fashioned hand, a diet for Catherine to follow.

'You are severely malnourished,' she said as her pen scratched away. 'And it's essential that you receive the correct vitamins and minerals to make a recovery. It will not be easy for you, Mademoiselle Dior, but you must follow my diet to the letter.'

'I will try.'

Before they left the surgery, the doctor embraced Catherine, and kissed her three times on the cheeks. 'You are an example to all of France, Mam'selle,' she said quietly.

Getting Catherine to eat was the greatest challenge of all. The doctor's diet, full of nutritious meat dishes, was well-meaning, but Catherine was unable to keep her food down. Overstepping her capacity by even a spoonful would precipitate retching that would leave her exhausted and weaker than before. This occurrence regularly reduced both Dior and Copper to despair.

Nor was food easy to obtain in Paris now that the war was in its final phase. There were no more lobsters from Granville to be had. Even if there had been, the trains were no longer running. Between the strikes and the war, in fact, the shops were empty, and people were reduced to scavenging for scraps, as they had done during the darkest days of the Occupation. The meat and wine that Dr Lefebvre had prescribed were almost unobtainable. It was heartbreaking to see Catherine bring up the beef or chicken that had been bought at such expense and with such difficulty.

Copper was starting to worry. Catherine had not put on an ounce – in fact, she had lost a little every day since her return. Copper had been brought up poor. She knew something about making nutritious dishes, and she told Dior so.

'This is all very well in theory,' she said, indicating the diet sheet the doctor had given them. 'But it's not working in practice. If you let me, I'll try and feed Catherine my own way.'

'Whatever you think best,' Dior agreed with a tremulous sigh. 'We can't go on like this.'

'Right, then.' Copper went to the market and returned with a laden basket.

'What on earth are those things?' Dior asked in horror, as Copper triumphantly unloaded her shopping.

'My mother called this a neat's foot,' Copper said, examining the grisly object with a critical eye. 'It's a cow's shin and hoof.'

'But is it edible?' he demanded.

'Very much so. This is what my mother made us when we were ill.'

'I thought America was such a rich country,' Dior said, backing away from the stove.

'Not my part,' Copper replied. 'We had to feed seven of us on a millhand's wages. And we didn't get lobsters, believe me.'

Several hours' hard work reduced the neat's foot into a wholesome broth and a translucent, amber jelly. To Dior's delight, Catherine partook of the broth – and wasn't sick.

'You're a genius,' he exclaimed, hugging Copper in the kitchen.

From then on, she produced the dishes of her childhood for Catherine. Her mother had died young, but not before passing on the cookery of her native Ireland – meals that were healthy and nutritious but far from rich. In the absence of chicken, she made rabbit pie; with a few beef bones, she made a delicate broth. Above all, she made vegetable dishes. The humble potato was a godsend now, as were barley, cabbage and beans. Her instinct was that before Catherine could digest the protein dishes the doctor had prescribed, she needed bland, starchy foods that would give her energy, allow her stomach to recover and restore her appetite.

She found that Catherine could be tempted with sweet things. Apple jelly and stewed fruit were dishes she could absorb, and though there was no wine to be had, Copper made a syrup from raisins that was pronounced a great success. Tapioca puddings and blancmanges also made a regular appearance, sweetened with jam if sugar could not be found. Catherine's deadly weight-loss slowed, then halted. The triumphant day came when the weight on the scale had to be shifted along the beam a notch, proving that she had started to put on flesh again. They celebrated with a dish her mother had called 'boxty' – potato pancakes made on the griddle. This dish had to be accompanied by a song Copper's mother had taught her:

'Boxty on the griddle,
Boxty in the pan,
If you can't make boxty
Sure you'll never get a man!'

Catherine grew strong enough to take short walks. Because her eyes were weak from malnutrition and suffered in the sunlight, Copper bought her a pair of sunglasses. She often took Catherine, wearing these and a silk scarf to cover her head, to walk slowly through the Tuileries. The burned-out German tank that had sat there had now been removed and the gardens were starting to be gay with flowers.

'Don't you want to see your fiancé?' Copper asked gently. As yet, Hervé had not even been told that Catherine was alive, something Copper had found puzzling.

Catherine grimaced. 'He thinks I'm dead. And perhaps it's better that way.'

'Why do you say that?' Copper exclaimed.

'I don't know if we can continue; if we should continue.'

'Because of what's happened to you? You're beautiful, and you're getting stronger every day. Your hair will grow. He'll be overjoyed to see you.'

'There's more than that,' Catherine replied wryly. Leaning on Copper as they walked, Catherine began to tell her some of the story of her love affair with Hervé des Charbonneries.

She had fallen in love with him in a *coup de foudre*, love at first sight. She'd walked into a shop to buy a radio. Tall, suave and handsome, he had shown her the latest model. Their eyes had met – and her heart had been captured.

'But there was a catch,' Catherine went on. 'Hervé was never my fiancé. That would be impossible. Hervé is married.'

'Oh,' Copper said.

'Yes – *oh*.' Catherine imitated Copper's flat tone. 'And he has three young children. A man can hardly be more married than that. But I was infatuated and so was he. He was a founder member of the Resistance and he enrolled me at once. So we worked in secret and we loved in secret. Our life was full of secrets. I loved him so much; adored him, in fact. If it were not for that, I think I would have broken under the

Gestapo. But I knew that if I gave up Hervé's name, he would be killed. I endured everything they did to me, and thank God, I was able to protect him.'

Copper's eyes filled with tears. 'That's the bravest thing I ever heard.'

'Love makes one brave.' Catherine shrugged. 'Or perhaps foolish. Who can tell the difference?'

'Hervé should hear what you endured for him,' Copper said.

'Do you think so?' Catherine shook her head. 'I think it would put unfair pressure on him. If I asked him to come back to me, I would be asking him to leave his wife and his children. Before all this' – she made a gesture to encompass her frail state – 'it was an adventure, an escapade. Now it is serious. So many have died; so many have suffered. I don't know if I can face any more suffering, or ask others to endure any more for my sake.'

'So long as he thinks you are still imprisoned or even dead, he'll be suffering anyway.'

Catherine smiled crookedly. 'You see things so clearly, my dear Copper.'

'I try to. Not seeing things clearly has led me into a lot of mistakes.' She paused. 'Do you still love him?'

'I've thought of him every hour since the day I was separated from him. Does that answer your question?'

'Yes, I guess it does.'

'And what about you?' Catherine enquired. 'You are waiting for someone, too, aren't you?'

'I suppose your brother has told you about him.'

'He sounds very glamorous.'

'Yes, he is that.'

'He wants to marry you.'

'Yes.'

'And you love him?'

'Yes, I love him. But—'

'But you cherish your freedom,' Catherine said, looking at Copper shrewdly.

'Something like that.'

'You Americans and your freedom. There are more important things, you know.'

Copper laughed. 'Is that the opinion of a heroine of the Resistance?'

'Well, you see where fighting for freedom got me,' Catherine said, pulling off her scarf to show her bald head. 'Freedom is precious, but other things may be even more precious.'

'I'd like to write a story about you, Catherine,' Copper said.

'There is nothing remarkable about me,' Catherine replied.

'Of course there is. Your bravery, what you've been through, how you've survived – all that is deeply inspiring.'

Catherine was cautious. 'Do you mean for the newspapers?'

'Well, I was thinking of a magazine article, with some photographs.'

'Photographs of me? Now? In this condition?'

'Yes, absolutely. You won't always look like this, you know.'

'I don't think I want that,' Catherine replied hesitantly. 'Let me consider it for a week or two.'

But it was only a couple of days later that Catherine came back to Copper with her decision made.

'Yes, I will let you write about me. And photograph me. Not because my story is unique, but because it happened to so many others, and so many others have not survived. People should know what happened to them.'

Catherine agreed to pose for some portraits that would unflinchingly show what the Nazis had done to her. Copper knew that it took courage for her to do this, knowing that she would be seen by thousands of readers; but Catherine Dior certainly did not lack courage.

And she was willing to talk about her experiences.

After her arrest, she had been interrogated with the utmost savagery, beaten with fists and a leather whip, her arms wrenched out of joint, her head held under water until she was drowning. She had said nothing, though she had heard others betraying their comrades.

When they'd accepted that she wouldn't talk, she had been dispatched with two thousand others, packed into cattle trucks, to Ravensbrück. People started to die on the agonisingly slow train journey in the summer heat with no air or water. After a few days, they were jammed in with hundreds of already rotting corpses. Less than half arrived alive at the railway station of Ravensbrück, where women from all over the lands conquered by the Nazis were being shipped.

Ravensbrück had been touted as a 'model camp', a shining example of Nazi social engineering, where firmness and kindness were to heal those infected with diseases like religion or socialism.

In reality, it was a place of unspeakable horrors.

'The women who didn't die of typhus,' Catherine told Copper, 'were worked to death in the factories. They sent the young ones to what they called "the hospital" for medical experiments. They cut them up without anaesthetics, amputated their legs or took out their organs to see if they could survive without them. They injected them with chemicals, tested drugs on them. Every day we carted trucks of corpses and severed limbs to the crematorium.'

Copper could hardly bear to listen to all this. The fate of the children was too terrible for Catherine to talk about.

'After that, they sent me to Buchenwald, to the explosives factory. They were pitiless there. They picked out the weakest ones every day. We could hear the firing squads every morning. Then I was moved again, this time to a potassium mine. It was really an underground slave-labour camp. The air was poisonous and I nearly died. And then they started moving us from place to place as the Allies came closer. To an aircraft factory in Leipzig. And then to Dresden, where the Russians liberated us. I think I was by then a month away from death. Perhaps less. The Russians had liberated other camps, so they knew what to expect. They were so kind – they fed us and clothed us, and handed us to the Red Cross. Do you know what kept me alive all that time?'

'What?'

'The thought of returning to Tian. I used to dream I was back with him in Paris, laughing, eating lobster. I hated to wake from those dreams.'

Copper was deeply moved. 'Tian never stopped believing that you would come back. He consulted an astrologer about you every week.'

Catherine nodded. 'He was forever hunting for four-leaved clovers as a child, collecting charms, dreaming up spells. I remember once, a gypsy at a fair read his palm. She said women would be lucky for him, and he would make a fortune out of them. He was so excited. How our parents laughed. The idea of Tian making money out of women – well, you know how he is.'

'Yes, I know how he is.'

'If he hasn't exactly made a fortune out of women, he at least makes a living out of them.'

'If he were to break away from Lelong and open his own house, he might make that fortune yet.'

'He was the kindest and most loving of brothers to me, Copper. He made my childhood so happy when it might have been miserable.'

'Why do you say that?'

To Copper's surprise, Catherine portrayed her mother as a disciplinarian who was cold and remote with her children.

'I am sure she loved us. But she was very strict. She was always busy. She didn't encourage displays of affection. We weren't allowed to just run up to her and hug her. If you dared crease her clothes, you would get a stern rebuke. You had to earn her affection, and that wasn't easy. We all learned to tiptoe around her – all of us, except Tian. He followed her everywhere. He learned the names of every flower in her garden, even the Latin ones. Our brothers were cruel to him and called him a mama's boy, but he didn't care. He set out to win her love.'

Copper thought of Dior saying that he lived only to please others. 'And did he win her love in the end?'

Catherine hesitated. 'I think she let him get closer to her than any of the rest of us. He was the only one she took to Paris to see her *modiste*.'

Copper was interested. 'Was that a special privilege?'

'Oh, yes. Not even my sister or I were allowed that. Her name was Rosine Perrault, and she had her atelier right here on the rue Royale, a stone's throw from this apartment.'

'He doesn't move far from his roots,' Copper murmured thoughtfully.

'I think it made a deep impression on him – seeing her fitted, watching the dressmakers at work. It was a mysterious world that he longed to belong to. After those visits, he used to dress me up, playing at being a dressmaker.'

'Yes, he told me that.'

'We had to keep it a secret. Our brothers would have teased the life out of us if they'd found out. Of course, I loved the attention. I worshipped Tian and I adored to be fussed over by him. Oddly, I lost most of my interest in clothes as I grew up.' She ran her hand over the stubble that had started to grow on her scalp. 'Though Tian was the one who worked hardest to please her, Bernard was the one who got the most attention. He grew stranger and stranger, and we could hardly cope with him. And then our father's business collapsed. We lost that lovely house overlooking the sea and the garden that our mother made with so much care. When Bernard finally had to be put in an insane asylum, our mother died of grief. Tian was just a young man and her death shattered him. I saw him turn from a bright, happy person into a shy introvert. I think he felt she was taken away from him before he could win her approval.'

Copper felt a deep sadness for Catherine. She had defended her lover with her life, literally; and yet now she could not claim him as her own. Copper spoke to Dior about this bitter irony.

'I knew there was something going on,' he said. 'But I had no idea she was in the Resistance. No idea at all. She would arrive out of the blue, full of life as always. She would spend the night sometimes, and then pedal away furiously on her bicycle.' He sighed. 'I thought the big mystery was that she was having an affair and sometimes I asked her, but she would never tell me who the man was. Of course, I assumed there was some complication – that he was married, for example – and that there was a need for discretion. I thought the biggest risk was that she would have her heart bruised, and I warned her against that. I didn't know that she was carrying secret information in her head. I only found out about that, and about Hervé, after she was deported.'

'You know she told them nothing, Tian. She endured terrible things to protect Hervé.'

'I know. When she was arrested, I went completely crazy. I rushed around to everybody I knew, begging for help. People just slammed the door in my face. None of them wanted to be in any way associated with the Resistance – though now,' he added bitterly, 'those same people claim they were heroes. The only person willing to help was the Swedish ambassador, and by the time he intervened, it was too late. Catherine was already on the train to Ravensbrück. As for the rest, all those rich people who might have done something to save her, they showed themselves for what they are – miserable creatures hiding behind imposing façades.'

'You said you would find Hervé and tell him she's alive.'

Dior hesitated. 'I have found him. He's here in Paris. I haven't spoken to him yet. Catherine asked me to say nothing.'

'I think she's longing to see him. It's a horribly difficult situation. She's pining for him. And sooner or later he's going to find out that she's alive anyway, isn't he?'

'Yes. But perhaps she wants it to be his decision whether he comes to her or not.'

'It's not your storybook romance, is it? If he comes to her, he'll break up his family. If he doesn't, he'll break her heart.'

'Love is seldom like the storybooks, my dear,' Dior responded. 'Our lives are too tangled for happy endings.'

Twelve

It was a few days after this conversation that Copper opened the door to a knock and found a stranger on the doorstep. He was about forty years old, tall and willowy, wearing a tweed jacket and nervously fiddling with a felt hat. She felt at once that this was Catherine's Hervé. He seemed too emotional to speak, so she spoke for him. 'You're looking for Catherine?' He nodded. 'She's sleeping. Would you like to come in and wait until she wakes up?'

He took a step back. 'I'll come back later. I don't want to disturb her.'

Copper was not about to let him escape. 'Don't go. She always has a half-hour nap at this time of the morning. It won't be long before she wakes up. She'll be so pleased to see you.'

Reluctantly, he allowed himself to be led inside and seated in the plush little salon. Dior was at Maison Lelong and she had been writing an article while Catherine slept. She offered him coffee, but he declined. 'You're working,' he said, gesturing at her papers. 'I've come at a bad time.'

'Don't worry about it.' She decided to be direct. 'When did you find out she was back?' she asked him.

'A friend saw her walking in the Tuileries with someone the other day. That was you, I suppose?'

'Yes. We walk there most days if the weather is good.'

He was fair-haired with a feathery moustache and an aquiline profile. He reminded her of the swashbuckling actor Errol Flynn, and it was easy to see how Catherine had been struck by his athletic good looks. But right now, he was almost painfully edgy, turning his hat round and round in his long fingers, and speaking in a nervous voice.

'How is she?' he asked.

'She's improving. She was very weak when she arrived, but she's started to recover.'

'They say you're working miracles with her. Has she – has she mentioned me?'

'I don't know. You haven't introduced yourself yet.'

'My name is Hervé des Charbonneries.'

'I believe she has mentioned your name,' Copper replied gravely. 'Once or twice.'

'I don't understand why she didn't come to me directly,' he said, getting up restlessly and pacing around the room. 'How could she come back to Paris and not tell me? It's so cruel.'

'She has suffered a great deal,' Copper replied. 'Perhaps more than you realise. It hasn't been easy for her. I don't suppose coming back from the dead is ever easy.'

'I thought she *was* dead. I never expected to see her again. And she has let me continue thinking that. While she was here, alive!'

'Catherine has suffered things that nobody should suffer. She's been in places that you and I can't even imagine, and seen things that would strike us dumb. Nobody can go through that and remain undamaged. But she can be healed. Especially by love. And especially if you can learn to stop thinking of yourself and start thinking of her.'

He was silent for a while. 'I apologise,' he said at last, stiffly. 'But this is hard for me, too.'

'She sacrificed a great deal for your sake. She saved your life.' Copper studied him critically. 'You're what – fifteen years older than she is? And a married man with three children.'

'Well?'

'You got her running errands for the Resistance and you got her into your bed. Which came first?'

The colour was mounting to his angular cheekbones again. 'Madame, you have never known what it is to have an enemy occupying your country. France called for a sacrifice from all of us. But of us all, only a few answered the call. Catherine was one. France will remember that forever.'

'You have quite the gift of the gab.'

'It seems you have appointed yourself Catherine's guardian,' he said shortly. 'But you are not her family. You are not even French.'

'You're right, I'm neither. But I see myself as her friend, not her guardian. She's frail, and if I didn't try to protect her, I wouldn't be much of a friend, would I?'

Copper thought she heard a sound from Catherine's bedroom. 'I'll go and check on her.'

She found Catherine awake and sitting on the edge of her bed. She sat beside her and took a fragile hand in both her own. 'He's here,' she said quietly.

'I know. I heard his voice.' She was trembling.

'Do you want me to go out?'

'No. Please stay in the apartment. But send him in here.'

Copper went to call Hervé. 'She'll see you now.'

Hervé went into Catherine's bedroom, still holding his hat. Copper closed the door on them and went to work at the dining room table. For almost an hour, she heard nothing from Catherine's room except the occasional murmur of voices. At length, Hervé emerged. He said goodbye to Copper curtly, and let himself out. She heard his rapid steps descending the stairs outside.

She went into Catherine's room in some trepidation. Catherine was standing at the window, looking out. To Copper's alarm, she looked feverish, her eyes unnaturally bright and her face flushed.

'There, my dear Copper. He has come and he has gone.'

'What happened between you?' Copper asked.

Catherine's fingers tightened around hers. 'He still loves me. Nothing has changed.'

Copper searched Catherine's face. 'Are you happy?'

'Nothing has changed,' Catherine repeated. 'We had an arrangement before I was arrested, and that arrangement will remain the same – if I choose to accept it.'

'What's the arrangement?'

'He will never divorce his wife. He is a Baron des Charbonneries, and he is a Catholic. Neither circumstance allows him to consider a divorce. It's simply not done. I can be with him. But I can't be his wife. I can't take his name, and I can't have his children.'

'That's hard.'

'But I can have *him*.' Catherine wore her crooked smile. 'What else matters, Copper? So long as I can have *him*, what more can I ask for?'

'She's going to be a Catherine and a Catherinette,' Dior said sadly, when Copper told him of this conversation.

'What's a Catherinette?'

'It's what we call a woman of twenty-five who is still unmarried. After St Catherine who was martyred for refusing to marry a pagan. On her feast day, the Paris spinsters all wear colourful hats. I could have wished a happier fate for her.'

'She has love,' Copper pointed out. 'As she says, she doesn't want anything else.'

'They're two strong people,' Dior agreed. 'They will arrange their lives the way they want to. He says you gave him the third degree. Asked him if his intentions were honourable.'

'I suppose it was none of my business. I just wanted to protect Catherine.'

'He said you were quite stern.'

'I've suffered at the hands of a careless husband,' she pointed out.

Catherine was now strengthening, and a fortnight after this, she announced that she was going to leave Paris and go to the Dior family home in Callian, near Grasse, in the Côte d'Azur. Here, with sunshine and fields of flowers to lift her spirits, her recovery could proceed in peace. Hervé des Charbonneries would go with her and they would map out a life together.

Copper and Dior went to see them off at the Gare de Lyon. Catherine held Copper tight in her arms. 'Thank you, my dear friend,' she said. 'Come to see me.'

'I will,' Copper promised. Though still thin and weak, Catherine was no longer the frighteningly emaciated waif who had arrived at the Gare de l'Est a number of weeks earlier. There was hope in her eyes again. She and Hervé boarded the train, found their compartment, and leaned out of the window to say their last goodbyes.

'Thank you for everything,' Catherine called as the train pulled out of the station. She waved, vanishing as she had arrived, among clouds of steam.

Dior was crying into his handkerchief as they left the platform. Copper put her arm around him. 'We'll see her again soon.'

'My poor little Catherine,' Dior sobbed. 'I should have looked after her better.'

'There was nothing you could have done. We're each on our own tightrope. All we can do is pick one another up after we fall.'

While they were making their way through the crowded station concourse, Copper caught a glimpse of a profile that was painfully familiar.

At first she thought she was dreaming. She stopped in her tracks and called out over the noise.

'Amory? Amory!'

The figure paused, and for a moment she felt he wasn't going to turn. Then he twisted his head to look at her. She found herself looking into the beautiful violet eyes of her ex-husband. Her head swimming, she left Dior's side and pushed her way through the throng of travellers to greet him.

'Hello, Copper.'

'I didn't know you were in Paris.'

'I'm just passing through.' He looked over her shoulder. 'I see you're still hanging around with what's-his-name.'

'Dior. We've just seen his sister off.' She tried to catch her breath. Seeing him again had knocked the wind out of her lungs. He looked leaner than she remembered him, wearing military khaki, his blonde hair tousled, a duffel bag slung over his shoulder. 'Have you got a moment to talk?'

He checked his watch. 'Sure, I have thirty minutes before my train. We can have a glass of wine.'

She explained to Dior, who nodded sadly and went back home to recover himself alone. She and Amory made their way to Le Train Bleu, the heavily gilded and opulently frescoed station buffet. They found a quiet corner in the crowded room. Amory ordered a bottle rather than a glass of wine from a harried waiter.

'You're looking good,' Amory remarked offhandedly, lighting a cigarette. He wasn't showing much interest in her, his eyes roaming around the room. She had never engaged his full attention, she thought bitterly. She never would.

'So are you,' she replied. But it was only a half-truth. Now that she examined him more closely, Amory had lost a lot of weight since she'd seen him last, and while little could diminish his physical beauty, he had a gaunt look. His cheeks hollowed into caverns as he sucked on his cigarette. 'Where have you been?' she asked.

He exhaled. 'I've been at a concentration camp in Germany.'

Copper recalled Catherine's experiences. 'I remember you wrote to me from there. That must have been horrible.'

'As a matter of fact, it's fascinating.' A strange light came into Amory's eyes. 'I'm on my way back there.'

'You're still covering the story?'

'I've been working on it for weeks. It's going to win me that Pulitzer.' The wine arrived, and he filled their balloon glasses. She sipped, but he drank deeply. 'It's a major story. The ramifications are endless. It just goes on and on.'

'What goes on and on?'

'The whole thing. After I left you, I got myself assigned to a forward unit. We saw some heavy fighting. There were casualties every day; a lot of casualties. The officers were pushing us hard. We were trying to beat the Russians to Berlin. I was with the 157th Infantry Regiment when we liberated the place. It's huge. Sprawling. We could smell it from a mile away.' He poured himself another glass of wine. 'The bodies were piled up everywhere: in boxcars, in the huts, in the incinerators. Not bodies – skeletons. Some of the skeletons were even walking around and talking as though nobody had told them they were dead.'

'I don't think I want to hear this,' Copper said quietly.

He gave her a tight smile. 'We didn't want to see it. But we did. We had to. Our boys, battle-hardened veterans, were crying and throwing up. The Germans were still trying to burn the last bodies when we arrived. Know what our sergeants did? They lined the SS guards against a wall and shot them. Prisoners of war, technically. The Nazis were begging for mercy, but our guys kept firing, bringing more cases of ammunition, firing again.'

'Oh God.'

'The German bodies piled up in heaps.' He lit another cigarette from the stub of the first. 'I watched the whole thing, and I was asking myself, are we any better than the Nazis? Is this justice or savagery?'

'And what's the answer?'

'The answer is, it's humanity. Just humanity.' He laughed. His manner was as cool as ever, but his laughter, like his face, was somehow empty, as though he'd lost something. Not just a physical presence, but something internal; something deep inside. 'The inmates took over. We didn't give them any weapons, so they did the job with rocks and iron bars, with their bare hands. They even killed some of the women guards – after they did other things to them.'

'How could you bear to watch any of this?' Copper asked.

'It was like arriving in hell. Our boys were afraid of the inmates – those starved, shattered people, pleading for food, clawing at us for help. Our soldiers shrank away as though they weren't human. Well, you've seen the photographs.'

'Yes, I've seen the photographs.'

'It got into me. Into my soul. I started to understand it. I ended up staying on while the army outfit I was with moved on. I've turned into a concentration camp specialist. I'm writing the definitive account.' He leaned forward suddenly, grasping her forearm with hot fingers. His lilac eyes burned into hers. 'The camps are vast, Copper. They swallow you up. You can walk for days and you're still in them. Still in hell.'

'Amory, this has had a devastating effect on you.'

'No. It's made a man of me.' He let out that brittle laugh again. 'It was the best medicine for what was wrong with me.'

'And what was wrong with you?'

'A lot of things,' he replied succinctly. 'I was drinking too much, falling into bed with every willing girl. You had been the only restraining influence in my life, and without you, I was out of control.'

'Are you in control now?' she asked, watching him anxiously as he yanked the cork out of a fresh bottle.

'Sure. Absolutely.' He poured, his eyes fixed on the glass.

'I don't like what I'm hearing. This isn't you.'

'Oh, it's me, all right.'

'You're drinking too much.'

'As soon as I get back, I'll stop. I don't need alcohol there.'

'You shouldn't be going back. You need a break.'

'I have to keep digging. I have to get to the bottom of it all. What makes us tick. There's always more. We hanged the camp commandant on his own gallows. I photographed that. Isn't that a kick, huh?' He seemed amused by her expression. 'You're shocked. I *need* to be shocked, Copper. I need the jolt it gives me. I'm interviewing a priest at the moment. He spent three years in a camp. Three years! He doesn't want to give it up, but I'm digging it out of him. It's great stuff.' He finished the bottle of wine and reached for his duffel bag. 'My train's leaving. I have to get to my platform.'

They said the briefest of goodbyes. As she watched him make his way out of Le Train Bleu, shouldering through the crowds, it occurred to her that he hadn't asked her a single question about her own life – what she was doing, whether she was happy, if she was okay. She had once loved him madly, but not anymore. Too much water had passed under that particular bridge. She was indeed part of his past now, as he was part of hers. But she was aware of a sinking feeling in the pit of her stomach as he vanished from sight. He had not struck her as a well man. She almost wished that she hadn't seen him, hadn't spoken to him.

Copper had taken the bold step of submitting her story on Catherine Dior to *Life* magazine. She hadn't expected much of a reaction. But to her shock, she received a swift response.

Life would take the story and photographs with a number of cuts; they would also add some file photographs of the camps Catherine had been imprisoned in, and would run the story as part of a group of three 'stories from behind the barbed wire'. She would get credit for her story, and her own byline.

The editor who called her from the States was complimentary.

'It's good work. Do you know what *Life*'s motto is? "To see the world, things dangerous to come to, to see behind walls, draw closer, to find each other and to feel." Well, you've done all that, Miss Reilly – and if you can keep doing it, we'll keep an eye on you.'

The past weeks had precipitated many changes in Copper. Catherine Dior, in particular, had affected her deeply. Through Catherine, she'd seen how fragile life could be and how short-lived happiness could be.

Seeing Catherine leave Paris with a man she loved but could never marry, Copper had had mixed feelings. Life was not perfect, but everyone deserved a shot at happiness. You had to take your chances. Sometimes you had to accept a compromise. And just because you'd made one mistake didn't mean you were doomed to repeat that mistake, or live with its consequences forever.

Seeing Amory, too, had frightened her. In this world, to be alone was a dreadful thing. It could lead one to the gates of hell.

Copper was in bed one night, with Jacinthe emitting ladylike snores at her feet, when the telephone rang. She answered it, hoping against hope that it was Henry. It was. As soon as she heard his voice, she burst into tears.

'My darling, please don't cry,' he said gently.

'I didn't know whether you were alive or dead.'

'I am very much alive,' he said. 'And longing for you.'

'Are you coming home?'

'Not just yet.'

'When will you come?' she demanded. 'I miss you so terribly. I worry about you. Please come back to me.'

'Nothing will stop me once I am free,' he promised. 'But I still have things to do.'

'Are you in danger?'

'None at all.'

'Don't get killed,' she said, breaking into fresh tears. 'I don't want to be here without you.'

'You won't have to be, I promise.'

'Come back,' she heard herself saying, 'and I'll marry you.'

There was a silence on the line and for a moment she thought they'd been disconnected. Then he said, in an altered voice, 'Do you mean that?'

She swallowed the lump that had formed in her throat. 'Yes.'

'You've made me the happiest man in the world,' he said, and she could hear the joy in his voice. 'I'll be back in Paris in a week. I'll arrange a registry office.'

'Please keep it quick and simple!'

'Don't worry. I'm not going to give you time to change your mind.'

What have I said? she asked herself when the call was over. *What have I done?*

She replaced the receiver with a shaking hand. She'd been missing him so badly that she would have said anything to get him to come home. But hadn't she been telling herself she was not ready for another marriage?

There was no retracting her acceptance now. That would break Henry's heart. She'd said the words – she wouldn't have let them out of her mouth if she hadn't meant them. Would she?

She fought against her second thoughts. It was time. She'd been rattling around Paris alone for far too long, rootless and fancy-free. It was time she settled down before she ended up half-crazy, like Amory. Henry offered her so much – security, devotion, companionship. She lay back in bed, cradling the sleepy dog in her arms. She loved Henry, that much was certain, and in the end, that was all that mattered. Like Catherine Dior, if she could have her man, what more did she need? She was glad she had finally capitulated.

Copper decided that the first person she should tell was Suzy. She went to see her the next day. For once, Suzy was out of bed before mid-afternoon and wrapped in her dressing gown. She opened the door of her apartment. Her face lit up. 'You came, after all.' She held out her hands. 'Forgive me, *chérie*. I behaved badly.'

Copper was moved by the expression in Suzy's dark eyes. 'You're forgiven, of course.'

Suzy kissed her on the lips. 'I was afraid you would never come back to me.'

'Well, here I am,' Copper replied ruefully. 'I wanted to talk.'

'Don't reproach me. I was vulgar and cruel. I showed the nastiest part of myself to you. You were right. At least now you have seen the worst. There it is, my ugly soul bared to you.'

Copper smiled. 'You're never ugly.'

'You're so beautiful when you smile.' Suzy was staring into her face.

There was no point in delaying it any longer. She took a deep breath. 'I've come to tell you that I'm going to marry Henry.'

An icy wind cut down all of Suzy's joy in an instant. '*What?*'

'I've agreed. He's coming back to Paris in a week. We'll just have a quick ceremony.'

'You crush my heart.'

'I don't want to do anything so violent, I promise you.'

'But you do. You can't help it. Is this because of Yvonne?'

'Oh no, of course not.'

'It is. You want to punish me.'

Copper shook her head. 'It's because I love him.'

Suzy buried her face in her hands. 'Damn you. Nobody has ever tortured me as you have.'

'Tortured you? Oh, Suzy!'

'You've made me suffer agonies of waiting.' She raised her face from her hands. Copper saw that Suzy was in earnest. Her face was pale, her

'But that's wonderful,' he exclaimed, putting his hands on her shoulders and kissing her on both cheeks. 'Congratulations. What are you crying about?'

'I've just come from telling Suzy.'

His expression changed. 'Ah. I understand. You'd better have a cup of tea.'

Copper sniffed. 'Thank God I can always rely on you for a little stability.'

'I take it she wasn't exactly delighted,' Dior said as he served the tea in his cosy little parlour.

'She took it hard,' Copper admitted.

'It's all somewhat sudden,' Dior pointed out in his mild way. 'You didn't give anybody much warning, my dearest. Speaking of which – when's the big day?'

'Henry said he's going to arrange a registry office and a special licence, so perhaps Saturday the fifteenth.'

Dior rose to his feet in horror, his hands upraised. '*The fifteenth?* You wretch. How am I going to make you a wedding outfit by the fifteenth?'

Copper shook her head. 'I don't want you to make me a wedding outfit at all,' she said firmly. 'This is going to be a quiet affair.'

'There is no wedding so quiet that a gown can be dispensed with!'

'This one will be. We're having a quick registry office ceremony and the smallest possible reception. It's my second time around, remember? I'm not exactly a blushing virginal bride. And there won't be time for any of my family to get here. I'm not even asking a lot of friends. But there *is* something you can do for me.'

'Yes?'

'Give me away at the ceremony.'

'With the greatest of pleasure,' Dior said, his cheeks going pink. 'Thank you for asking me. You know that I regard you in the light of a daughter.' He seemed to have been diverted from the idea of making a wedding gown for now. A big production was the last thing Copper needed. Getting this over, and getting Henry back by her side to start her new life with him was all she wanted.

In fact, Dior had transferred his attention from her wedding outfit to his own. 'I shall wear the English light-grey morning suit,' he decided happily. 'It's almost brand new. And a blue silk tie from Charvet. And a buttonhole from Lachaume, of course. Lachaume will do your bouquet, too.'

'I don't want a big bouquet.'

'Lilies of the valley,' he said decisively. 'My favourite flower, as you know. Oh, it will be such fun! Bébé will be enchanted. This will really perk him up.'

'I hope he doesn't turn it into a circus, like poor George's funeral. You won't invite a huge crowd, will you, Tian? Promise me.'

'I am always the soul of discretion,' he swore piously, as though he were not the biggest gossip in Paris. 'But you know, my dear, all your friends will be terribly offended if you cut them out.'

'The key word is "friends". I don't want strangers riding unicycles or leading giraffes.'

'Perhaps Suzy will turn up and sing "Chant des adieux",' he tittered. Copper shuddered, still disturbed by Suzy's reaction. 'Don't.'

Henry arrived at the end of a week, refusing to say where he had been or what he had been doing, but overjoyed to see her.

'I could hardly believe my ears,' he said, almost lifting her off her feet as she opened the door to him at place Victor Hugo. 'I thought it was a bad telephone line. You're going to be mine at last!'

She clung to him joyously. His face and frame had lost weight, but he looked magnificent. 'When did you get back?'

'This morning at six. But I had things to do.'

'What things?' she demanded jealously.

'Important things.' He grinned at her. 'I've got us a priest – and a church.'

'A church?'

'I hope you don't object to a Russian Orthodox ceremony?'

'The Catholics wouldn't let me back anyway. How on earth did you get a priest to marry us at such short notice?'

'It took a lot of talking – and a lot of promises,' he said ruefully. 'But you'll love the church. It's the Cathedral of St Alexander Nevsky.'

'Oh, Henry,' she exclaimed in dismay. 'We agreed on a quiet wedding.'

'What have we got to be ashamed of?' he demanded.

'It's not a question of being ashamed. I wanted a small ceremony. You promised!'

'But my darling – it's our wedding. And we can make it as short and quiet as you like.'

'It won't be short *or* quiet. It will be two days of chanting and incense and processions – and – and don't the bride and groom wear crowns?'

'Well,' he admitted, 'crowns used to be worn for a week, but now it's just during part of the ceremony.'

'Cancel it.'

'I can't. It took me all day to talk the priest into it.'

'It's not what I want.' She knew St Alexander Nevsky – a monumental church in the 8th arrondissement, complete with towering spires capped with gold onion domes and plastered with ornate mosaics. All the White Russian exiles worshipped there. 'I want something intimate. Half of Paris will turn up.'

'I'd like to be married in my faith,' he said gently. 'A registry office would be so bare and shabby, my darling. I want to show you off.'

'Oh no, Henry. I refuse.'

He kissed her tenderly. 'Please don't refuse. Do this for me. Just this one thing. After we're married you can have everything you want.'

'I very much doubt *that*.'

'For me, my darling!'

'I've just told Tian that he can't make me a wedding dress. He was extremely upset. I don't have anything suitable for a wedding in the cathedral, Henry.'

'Oh, don't worry about that,' he said airily. 'Any old thing will do.'

She glared at him. The cathedral would be packed. It was the haunt of the ageing émigré counts, dukes and princes who'd fled their estates in 1917, plus their pale and haughty Paris-born offspring, not to mention the Moscow secret police in shabby raincoats, writing names down in greasy notebooks. '*Any old thing?*'

'We can go shopping for an appropriate outfit,' he said soothingly, realising he'd said the wrong thing.

'Where? The war isn't over yet. Wedding gowns with ten-foot trains are in rather short supply. I'll have to go back to Tian and beg for mercy.'

'I'll pay, of course,' he promised.

'Oh, buster, you will,' she said grimly. 'Trust me on that.'

Thirteen

Copper and Dior decided on pale blue as appropriate for a second marriage in a new faith. Besides, as he happily pointed out, that would match his tie. She would wear a small veil attached to a simple hat. The dress itself would be made from ten metres of grey-blue chiffon that Dior had stored away in a closet. It would be elaborately gathered and ruffled, and out of deference to the setting, Copper's arms would be covered in lace sleeves to the mid-forearm. She consented to a small bouquet of white lilies from Lachaume, though since Dior was organising this, she had to rely on his idea of 'small'.

He, of course, was delighted that Copper had changed her mind. He threw himself into the project, trusting nobody to do the pattern or cutting except himself. They had a scant fortnight to get the dress ready. Much of that time was spent in fittings, shopping for accessories, arranging the reception (to be held at Henry's house in the 7th arrondissement, which was being prepared for the occasion by an army of servants who had been marshalled by the master of the house) and getting acquainted with the elaborate Slavonic-rite marriage ceremony that Henry was so set on.

The ceremony was, in its most compact form, an affair many hours long, and the spiritual significance of each phase – the Betrothal, during which candles would be held; the Sacrament itself, during which the couple would be crowned; and the civil ceremony afterwards with bread and salt – were explained to Copper at great length by a solemn, bearded Orthodox priest who smelled of incense and garlic. She found it all a little overwhelming, not least the cathedral itself with its murky interior and towering, prison-like walls, from which gilded icons of saints and angels peered down at her suspiciously.

She tried to get into the spirit of the thing, even learning as many of the Russian phrases as she could remember. But the only part she was really looking forward to was the wineglass-smashing at the very end. By that time, she imagined, she would be in the mood to hurl a wineglass.

She also, with great reluctance, gave notice to the landlady at place Victor Hugo. Pearl would have to find new lodgings since, after the wedding, Copper would take up residence with her new husband.

'I know you won't want me as a bridesmaid?' Pearl said, looking at Copper with heavy eyes. It sounded like a plea.

'They don't have bridesmaids at Russian Orthodox weddings,' Copper replied tactfully, which was at least partly true – the priest had told her it was not traditional but she could have a bridesmaid if she really insisted on one. She just didn't want any further complications in what was already turning into a cumbersome affair. 'But you'll be there to support me.'

'I'll get clean for the ceremony,' Pearl promised; but they'd both heard that promise many times before.

Suzy had made no attempts to contact Copper except for a single bouquet of violets, without a note, which she'd had delivered to the place Victor Hugo. Perhaps it was an apology for the last words she'd thrown after Copper. The sweet scent of the violets faded, and Copper tried not to think about the woman who had sent them to her.

From Henry, there came a more permanent gift.

He presented her with an oblong leather box. 'I hope you like this, my darling. It is my wedding present to you.'

Copper opened the box. Nestling in the velvet interior was an emerald-and-diamond necklace. She was overcome by the size and obvious value of the stones.

'Oh, Henry, these are magnificent.'

'They're from Bucherer. I hoped you would wear them on our wedding day.'

'You're so generous. You overwhelm me.'

He helped her put on the necklace. The vivid green stones blazed against her pale skin. She stared at herself in the mirror; Henry's handsome face was at her shoulder. 'You look doubtful,' he said gently.

'If I do, it's only because my mother always said emeralds were bad luck.' She saw his expression change. 'I'm sorry. That was a stupid thing to say.'

'Not at all,' he replied gravely. 'If you don't wish to wear them, I will understand perfectly.'

'Of course I will wear them,' she said, turning to kiss him. 'I'll be proud to. You make me feel like a queen.'

The next day Copper found time to run to the *Agence France-Presse* newsroom to file a story. She found the clattering telex machines, which ceaselessly spewed out a history of the world, fascinating.

Coming out of AFP, she bumped into a familiar figure coming the other way. It was Hemingway, typically dishevelled and braving the cold in shirtsleeves. He put down the typewriter case he was carrying and hugged Copper tightly enough to leave her breathless. 'How the hell are you?' he demanded.

'I'll be fine when I get over my broken ribs,' she said, smiling at him. It was good to see a fellow American, even if Hemingway was always more than a little overpowering.

'Where can I get my typewriter fixed?' he demanded. 'It's urgent, kid. I'll buy you lunch in return.'

'I don't have time for lunch. I'm in a hurry.'

'Don't you dare brush me off.'

She sighed. 'What make is it?'

'A Remington.'

'I know where the agency is. It's ten minutes' walk from here.'

'Come along, then.'

As they walked towards the boulevard des Capucines, she asked him, 'You're not going to make another pass at me, are you?'

'Not while I'm sober.' He grinned. 'I have too much respect for you. I saw your story in *Life* magazine. Not bad for a kid still wet behind the ears. You're a born journalist.'

She was pleased with the praise. 'I try.'

'I still say it's a whore's trade, but you do your whoring neatly, I'll give you that.'

At the Remington agency, he delivered his battered portable for repair and hired a substitute to use in the meantime, which he hugged to his chest. She was sympathetic; she could imagine what it felt like to be a journalist without a typewriter. Then, as he'd promised, he took her to lunch at a bistro. There, over a bottle of Burgundy and plates of duck confit, they caught up on each other's news.

'I hear you're getting married to that mad Russian, Velikovsky?'

'I guess he has to be mad to take me on.'

'So it's true. Well, you'll never have to worry about money again.'

'I'm not marrying Henry for his money, Ernest.'

'Oh, sure. You just want a fatherly presence around the place.'

She had to point a knife at him to get him to stop teasing her. 'I saw Amory a few weeks ago,' she told him. 'He was on his way back to Germany. I haven't heard from him since.'

He frowned at her. 'Then you don't know?'

'Know what?'

'About his breakdown. He's been shipped back to an army hospital in Belgium.'

Copper was shocked. 'He was very edgy when I saw him. But I didn't expect *that*.'

'Well, they called it nervous exhaustion. He was writing a major article. It was going to win him that Pulitzer, you know? He worked day and night to try and capture the full horror. But he couldn't take it in the end. He was on some pills the army medics gave him. He eventually swallowed the whole bottle. They found him just in time. Pumped his stomach out. Shipped him to Brussels packed in cotton wool.'

'Poor Amory. I feel terrible.'

Hemingway held up his hands. 'Now, look. Don't go thinking this has anything to do with you. It doesn't. Okay? Amory is a guy who always liked to pretend that things didn't get to him. Well, this did. It's not something you can forget, no matter how much war you've seen. They say Patton himself threw up at Ohrdruf.'

'Amory told me he was addicted to horror.'

'That can happen. Terrible events trigger something in certain people. They get a feeling of exhilaration, even euphoria. Like any form of intoxication, it wears off, and then there's a slump – depression, despair. They need to climb back up again. So they go back to what triggered them in the first place. It turns into a vicious cycle of highs and lows, until it sucks you in completely. It absorbs you and everything in your life. The high becomes the only thing that matters. It's a dangerous sickness that ultimately ends by devouring you completely.'

'You sound as though you know what you're talking about.'

'Maybe I do,' he said with a grim smile. 'Maybe it's why I'm a writer. The cruelty in those camps was bestial, Copper. Unbelievable.'

'This war has brought out the worst in people,' Copper said.

'It doesn't take much to bring out the worst in people. You don't need a war,' Hemingway said, picking up his knife and fork again. 'You've got a good brain, kid.'

'For a woman, you mean?' she asked sweetly.

He grinned through his beard. 'For a "women's journalist" who devotes herself to the world of dresses and hats.'

'Well, I cover more than hats. But frankly, I'm glad to be writing about progress, rather than war.'

She was sickened by the news about Amory. But talking to Hemingway was always stimulating, even if his comments about her marriage to Henry had stung a little.

What really made her wince was his parting remark in the street:

'Your roaming days are over, little gypsy.'

The pace of the preparations accelerated until the eve of the wedding was upon Copper. Oddly, she found herself in the same state as she'd been the night she'd parted from Amory: hot and cold shivers running through her body, sleep evading her. She felt quite ill. As on that occasion, she knew she was facing a momentous turning point in her life, and wondered whether she was taking the right path. She had been so independent up to now. Being lonely and vulnerable was part of that independence, though she'd found it hard at times.

Life with Henry was going to be far more comfortable, perhaps, but far less emancipated – whatever promises he made about not cramping her style. Men always imagined they were undemanding and easygoing; but it soon turned out that the going was only easy if it went their way.

She'd done so much. She'd grown and developed as a person. Would that process continue as Henry's wife? Or would she end up, somewhere down the line, wishing she'd stayed single? Perhaps regretting her decision to give up the independence she'd worked so hard to achieve?

She'd expected to feel a lot happier on the eve of her second wedding. Perhaps she would wake tomorrow full of joy?

In the event, she slept little. Dior arrived the next morning at nine to help her dress and then take her to the cathedral. He was wearing his white work coat for the important business of dressing her, his English suit in a carefully zipped bag. For some reason, that sent Copper into fits of nervous giggles.

He fussed over her with deadly seriousness. There were never any jokes or gossip when he was working. The slightest wriggle or sigh would provoke a stern rebuke. Even Pearl was not permitted to assist, but had to sit silently in a corner.

'You look a dream,' he sighed at last, stepping back to admire his handiwork. 'I always said you had the perfect figure.'

'You always said my bust was too small.'

'Tastes change,' he replied with equanimity. 'You have big shadows under your eyes, my dear. But the effect is not displeasing.'

'I'll do something about that.' She did her make-up and inspected herself in the mirror. Dior was right – she did look a dream. The dusty-blue silk set off her hair and complexion extremely well, and of course the design itself was irreproachable. He fitted the little hat on her head carefully and adjusted the scrap of lace veil over her eyes. The bouquet he'd picked out was, predictably, huge and baroque. She clutched it like a shield. 'It's going to be hard to give you away,' he said, his hazel eyes moist. 'But it's time to go, my dear.'

He'd hired a Daimler-Benz, said to be formerly the property of General Dietrich von Choltitz, the last Nazi commandant of Paris, to take her to the cathedral. Pearl was to follow in a taxi. Copper felt numb as she got into the huge, gleaming black car that still had a German eagle screwed on to the dashboard. 'This thing is like a hearse,' she said.

'I went to Venice before the war in the company of a young man I was very much in love with. We took a gondola ride down the Grand Canal. They told us that the same artisans who made coffins also made the gondolas. That was why they were so glossy and black.'

'Was it an omen?' she asked.

'Unfortunately, yes. I adored him, but he swiftly got bored with me, and left me in my coffin to go and chase a Venetian faun.'

'Poor Tian!'

'How do you feel, *petite*?'

She fiddled with the heavy emerald necklace at her throat. 'Very anxious.'

'They'll guide you through the ceremony.'

'I'm not nervous about the ceremony. I'm nervous about what comes after.'

'You mean – the *nuit de noces*?' he enquired delicately.

'No, silly. I mean the next fifty years.'

'Ah.' Wisely, he refrained from comment. Indeed, her heart was pounding in her chest and she was struggling to keep her breathing slow and steady. She stared out at the grey streets of Paris, passing her by irrevocably. It was a somewhat rainy morning and the cobbles were shining wet, the girls on their bicycles huddled under capes that billowed behind them as they sped. How free they looked, pedalling along with their trim, stockinged legs.

She recalled Hemingway's valediction: *Your roaming days are over, little gypsy.*

The part of Paris around the cathedral was something of a Little Moscow, with many Russian restaurants and streets named after Russian subjects. They approached the cathedral up the rue Pierre-le-Grand. It came into sight at the end of the street, its domes like golden bubbles bobbing up against a grey sky. Dior instructed the chauffeur to drive to the front of the church. He proceeded with slow majesty.

'It's wet,' Dior reminded her. 'Gather up your hem, my dear, or it will trail in the mud.'

The Daimler stopped at the portico of the church. A crowd was waiting outside to see the bride. Among them she made out Bébé Bérard, released from the Pitié-Salpêtrière, but still weak, leaning on the shoulder of Cocteau. Bébé's beard was wild and his face was a ghastly fish-belly white. When he saw her, he called out her name, pretending a gaiety he clearly did not feel. His shriek of welcome sounded, to Copper, too close to the screams of pain he'd uttered when they'd left him in the hospital.

The outré outfits of the bohemians mingled oddly with the austere fustiness of the Russian *émigrés*. The great church doors were thrown open and she could see into the sombre, crowded interior, right through to the altar where their wedding rings were lying, and where sacramental objects gleamed dully in the light of candles. She could hear the droning of the male choir. A commotion of panic rose in her breast.

She gathered her gown and her bouquet as Dior got out and went round the car to open her door. A blast of cold, damp air rushed into the warm, leather interior. It carried with it a whiff of frankincense and myrrh from the incense burners. It was the scent of the myrrh that did it. Something clicked inside her. She felt it, like a broken bone setting itself.

'I can't do this,' she said, looking Dior in the eyes.

Dior blinked at her, his kid-gloved hand extended. 'What?'

'I can't. I've changed my mind.'

'Copper! What do you mean?'

'You'll have to go and explain to Henry.'

His eyes were so wide that she could see the whites all around the irises. 'Explain? Explain what, if you please?'

'That I'm not getting married today.'

'You're joking?' But what he saw in her face left him in no doubt that she wasn't joking. He clapped his hands over his cheeks. '*Oh, mon Dieu.*'

Pearl, who had got out of the taxi behind, peered over Dior's shoulder. 'What's going on?'

Copper felt strangely calm now, almost disconnected from herself. She was no longer panicky. All that had passed. Her heart was aching, but she was utterly certain of what she was doing. 'Henry will come out and try to talk to me,' she said. 'So I'm going to go back to your place in the Daimler now. You'll get Pearl's taxi when you've told them.' She held out her hand. 'Give me your key.'

Dumbly, Dior fished in his pocket and produced his apartment key. 'What am I supposed to say to Henry?' he asked miserably.

'Say I've changed my mind,' she replied.

'He'll want to know why.'

'Yes, I suppose he will.'

'And I will tell him—?'

'Tell him they burned myrrh at my father's funeral.'

'My dear,' Dior said faintly. 'That is hardly going to soothe a bridegroom who has been jilted at the altar.'

'I suppose you're right. Tell him I'm sorry. And that if he ever decides to speak to me again, I'll try to explain.'

'Don't do this, Copper,' Pearl said quietly.

Copper just shook her head. Pulling her magnificent dusk-blue dress out of the way, she shut the door of the Daimler. 'Rue Royale, please.' Expressionlessly, the man put the car in gear and it glided forward. Copper had an afterthought. 'Wait.'

She took the weighty emerald necklace off and leaned out of the window to hand it to Dior, who took it, open-mouthed. 'Please give him this, with my love.'

Dior turned without a word and made his way into the cathedral, his balding head bowed. And Copper drove away through the rain.

She was alone in Dior's apartment for the best part of two hours. After she had taken off the wedding dress Dior had made her, she spent the time sitting at the window and looking out at the street, thinking.

Why hadn't Henry listened to her about the wedding? If they had arranged a nice, drab registry office, she would probably have walked in without qualms, and walked out again as the Countess Velikovsky half an hour later. But it hadn't been only the cathedral. It had been everything that the cathedral symbolised – the vast edifice of expectation and commitment that a marriage would pile on her.

She'd gone into her first marriage gaily, almost without a second thought. This time, her feelings were different. The burned child had learned to dread the fire. She was still calm, because she knew she had done the right thing for herself. But that didn't stop her feeling terrible about Henry. She had humiliated him in the most public way possible. The waspish White Russian community would be gossiping about it for years. He would be furious with her. Worse, he would be deeply, bitterly hurt. His disappointment would probably keep him away from her forever.

She had not the slightest vestige of an excuse, except that she'd changed her mind – that feeble prerogative of women that went with being frivolous and capricious and all the qualities she most despised.

Dior returned at last, looking rather flushed and smelling of alcohol. She helped him off with his overcoat.

243

'How was Henry?' she asked apprehensively.

'He was magnificent,' Dior replied. 'He made a short speech at the altar, and thanked everyone for coming. Then he invited everybody to the reception. Nearly everybody came. The house is still full of countesses in nineteenth-century clothes, eating and drinking and looking down their noses. And my dear' – he patted her shoulder – 'Henry uttered not a word of reproach about you. Not one word.'

That made her burst into tears. 'I've broken his heart.'

'Yes, I think you have,' Dior said. 'You have to know him well to see it, but it's there. In his eyes.'

'Oh, God.'

'He sent you this.' He presented her with a little beribboned box. In gilt writing on it were her name and Henry's in Cyrillic script, and inside was a slice of wedding cake, all marzipan and pink sugar roses. 'He said you'd be hungry.'

'He cut the cake?' she exclaimed through her tears.

'Well, yes. It wouldn't keep for the next countess, you know. And it's wartime. One can't throw away a three-tier wedding cake from Ladurée.'

'Will he ever speak to me again?'

'As to that, I can't say,' Dior replied. 'But it's very doubtful. You've made rather a fool of him, you know.'

'To put it mildly.'

'A proud man like Henry doesn't take these things lightly.'

'He must hate me now.'

'He will quite possibly arrange to have you garrotted,' Dior replied. 'I believe that's how they handle these affairs in Moscow. The good thing is that I get to keep you for a while longer. You'll have to stay here with me. I'll get your room ready.'

The era of place Victor Hugo was at an end. Pearl had moved into digs in Montmartre. She didn't say where, but Copper knew she must be back with Petrus. All Copper's superfluous things – she hadn't bought much in the way of furniture – were put in storage. She moved back into Dior's apartment with just a suitcase of clothes, her typewriter and her camera equipment, the way she had first arrived. There was no word from Henry.

Le Théâtre de la Mode opened with a fanfare of publicity, providing an immediate distraction. Tens of thousands of visitors trooped through the exhibition in the first days, thronging the hall until it closed each night at nine. Somehow, all the scenes had been completed on time, the last stitches put into the last outfit, the final touches applied to the last piece of gilding, before the doors had opened to an expectant public.

Moving through the crowded halls, Copper could sense that all of Paris was agog. The ingenuity of the idea; the titanic effort put into such Lilliputian resources; the sheer beauty of what had been achieved; all this was dazzling. More than that, the promise of a resurgent Paris, and a resurgent France, brought people out in wide-eyed throngs to gawp and to celebrate. Copper saw people weeping with emotion in the crowds. Since the departure of the Nazis, it was the greatest single statement of joy the country had made.

The exhibition was a personal triumph for Christian Bérard, who had superintended the overall décor – or it would have been a triumph had he not presented such a pathetic spectacle. He leaned on a stick, or on Dior's shoulder, looking exhausted. It was typical of the kindness of Dior that he cared for his friend with the gentleness of a mother nursing a sickly child, shepherding him through public appearances, steering him away from anywhere he might be exposed to alcohol or opium, making him rest when his system seemed in danger of a relapse.

It added poignancy that Paris was entering her luminous spring. The cherries were in blossom, the skies were blue. Life was burgeoning everywhere; while Bébé Bérard had the appearance of a dying man.

For Copper herself, the opening of the exhibition provided a welcome distraction from the debacle of her wedding-that-wasn't, and the thought of the pain and humiliation she must have caused Henry. It also marked the end of her most ambitious journalistic project to date. She was able to take her final photographs of the masses of visitors passing through the hall, and write her final paragraphs.

By far the most spectacular of the scenes was an extraordinary tableau of a burning tenement with silk-clad figures flying through the air. This was the brainchild of Jean Cocteau.

'My set is a tribute to the film *I Married a Witch* with Veronica Lake,' he told her. 'You've seen it, of course?'

'Of course,' Copper said animatedly. 'What a charming idea.'

'This is the scene where the hotel burns down. Very dramatic, don't you think?'

'Oh yes. And what extraordinary gowns.'

'Oh, the gowns? The gowns are nothing to me,' he said loftily. 'To me, fashion is of no interest whatsoever. I am merely supporting my friends.' He waved a long cigarette holder to take in the whole enterprise. 'The idea is absurd, and it is the absurdity that calls to me.'

'Well, perhaps we won't tell the readers that,' Copper said, scribbling in her notebook.

Everywhere she looked, little miracles had been wrought. Tiny handmade buttons had been sewn on to jackets; miniature leather shoes, made by some cobbler goblin, had been fitted on to miniature feet; and the hats! Hats as extravagant as the imagination could make them, with flowers and veils and ribbons.

Elaborate coiffures had been made for the *poupées*, cascades of curls or towering bouffants. Their china faces had been carefully painted to look alive. Tiny tassels swung from exquisite capes; shimmering silks of every imaginable colour swathed miniature bosoms. The smell of sericin was intoxicating. Bows, feathers, frills and swags described lavish curls. Sumptuous flounces disguised the bare wire frames beneath.

The wire hands wore diminutive gloves, miraculously stitched, and the wire wrists dripped bracelets made by Cartier or Van Cleef & Arpels, and carried fairy bags by Hermès and Louis Vuitton. Skilled fingers had sewn tiny beads, pearls and sequins on to the fabrics, and experienced eyes had seen to it that every design carried the sense of something much larger; something important.

From the debris of a world devastated by war and plundered by the conqueror, a vision was being created – the vision of a new world where beauty and style once again reigned supreme. It was as though a company of elves had crept out after the horror and had begun to stitch the torn pieces together. It was a fairy-tale story, Copper thought, and it touched her heart and filled her with admiration.

With Henry still silent, Copper had re-entered the world of Dior and Bérard. When Dior himself was too wearied to nursemaid Bérard, Copper nursemaided Dior. Copper, as the only one who could drive, was in charge of transport, and took the two men around during the exhibition. Much of her own magazine article had centred on the genius of Bérard, without whose presiding artistic authority the *Théâtre de la Mode* would have been unthinkable. As Dior put it: 'Marshalling dozens of Paris fashion houses was not a job for a mere mortal.'

A week after the opening, however, while she was working at her typewriter in her room, the doorbell chimed and, shortly afterwards, Dior poked his head round her door.

'It's Henry,' he said, his eyebrows perched on the top of his head. 'He's asking to speak to you. Shall I send him away?'

'No,' Copper said. It was time for her to face the music. 'I'll see him.' Girding her metaphorical loins, Copper rose from the little bed-side table that served her as a desk, and went out to confront Henry.

He was standing at the window looking out over the rue Royale, immaculately dressed as always. He turned to her, his face grave.

'I'm going out for a walk,' Dior said nervously, snatching up his overcoat and hat and making a diplomatic exit.

When Dior had gone, Copper opened her mouth to start on the speech she'd rehearsed so many times.

'Henry, my marriage to Amory ended so painfully—'

But he held up his hand to stop her. 'I've come to apologise.'

She was taken aback. She stammered awkwardly. 'What for?'

'For everything. For insisting on the cathedral when it was the last thing you wanted. For those unlucky emeralds. But not just for that. For pushing you to marry me when you weren't ready. For trying to override your doubts and make you ignore your misgivings. For forgetting that you've already had one awful experience and haven't yet healed from that. For being so desperate to make you my wife that I accepted an offer you made when you were afraid and alone. I should have known better, and I'm ashamed of myself. For all that, I apologise. I just hope that you will be able to forgive me. And that this won't be the end of us.'

'Oh, Henry!'

She could now see in his face the hurt she'd caused him. He looked like a man who hadn't eaten or slept in days. 'You don't have to say anything now. I'm leaving Paris for a while on business. But I'll be back, and if I'm far luckier than I deserve, perhaps we can be friends again.'

Copper swallowed the lump in her throat. 'We'll always be friends.'

He nodded. 'If there's one thing my life has taught me, it's to never give up hope.' He put his hand on her shoulder and kissed her cheek lightly. 'Goodbye, Copper.'

After the door had closed, she went to the window and watched his tall figure walk down the street. Long before he mingled with the drab crowds, her eyes were blurred with tears.

By the second week, almost 200,000 visitors had been to see the *Théâtre de la Mode*. The profits went to the Entraide Française, the national relief organisation that had been instituted during the Occupation; but the real beneficiaries were the fashion houses, whose triumphant displays made such a powerful impact. The great French designers, who had been compelled to serve the Nazis for four years, were finally making clothes for the French again – albeit in miniature.

Dior himself was not one of those whose names were being celebrated. It didn't even appear in the catalogue. His employer, Lelong, took the praise for the adorable little creations.

'That's just the way it is,' he said, when Copper expressed her chagrin at the Pavillon. 'Don't worry about me, *ma petite*. I'm not one for the limelight, you know that.'

'I wish you were one for the limelight. Why should Monsieur Lelong get all the glory?'

'Because he's my employer,' Dior said. 'And I'm deeply indebted to him.'

'One day,' Copper vowed, 'your name will be in lights.'

Dior shuddered. 'How my mother would hate that. She always forbade me to put my name up over a doorway like a common shopkeeper.'

Copper was amused. 'Wouldn't she be proud of you?'

'You didn't know her,' he replied darkly. 'It was bad enough that I tried to run an art gallery. Becoming a dressmaker would have been too much for her.'

They returned to the rue Royale to see an extraordinary sight: a huge cloud of yellow butterflies had filled the street.

Dior was enraptured. They parked the car and walked along the street among the fluttering, buttery clouds. The butterflies were everywhere, filling the shops and the cafés, making women scream, half in alarm, half in delight; while the waiters rushed to and fro, attempting to flap the insects away with tablecloths. More hordes simply swirled in to take their place. Restaurants were being evacuated, diners hurrying out on to the pavement still clutching their napkins. The powdery yellow wings almost blotted out the spring sky at times.

Rising and falling in their millions, the butterflies had taken over the street. It was impossible at first to tell where they were coming from, and where they were going; then, gradually, it became evident that the butterflies were making their way, with countless pauses and detours, from the place de la Concorde, up the rue Royale, to the Church of the Madeleine. Copper and Dior followed the drifting multitudes to the place de la Madeleine, the huge, neoclassical church which seemed to be their destination. And as they watched, bemused, the butterflies began to settle on the towering stone pillars, thronging in ever-greater numbers, more and more, until each pillar was clad in a shimmering yellow gown pieced out of millions of beating wings.

'They're making a pilgrimage,' Dior said, examining a specimen that had landed on his finger. 'What can it mean?'

'It's a prophecy.' Copper pointed at the bright clouds of wings. 'These are all the women who're going to wear your clothes one day and be made beautiful by you.'

'You don't give up, do you?' Dior replied.

'No. And nor should you.'

They found a café in the square and sat drinking coffee and watching the astonishing spectacle, lulled by the narcotic scent of the lime trees, until the sun slipped down behind the Madeleine, leaving the twilight suddenly chilly. They went to have an early dinner together.

The next morning, the butterflies had gone. They had flown away to wherever they were going. A street sweeper was using his broom to gather the ones that had not survived and that lined the cobbled street in golden seams.

Within a few days, Copper heard from *Harper's* that the editorial staff had loved her *Théâtre de la Mode* story, and that it would be printed in the next edition. This excellent news was accompanied by a substantial cheque – in dollars – that Copper picked up at Henry's 'dusty little bureau' on the Champs-Élysées. The dusty little bureau was actually a smart office in a smart block, with 'Velikovsky et Cie' in gilt letters on the door and a smart secretary at the desk. Henry himself had not yet returned to Paris and his secretary was tight-lipped as to his whereabouts. Copper had had dealings with her before, and while she was unfailingly pleasant, Copper had the strong feeling that she'd been instructed to fend off all curious enquiries about her employer, even from her. Perhaps especially from her.

Copper was missing Henry and felt she had still not been able to explain why she had done what she had done. Even though he seemed to understand, she felt they needed to talk.

The new edition of *Harper's Bazaar* reached Paris and Copper's article was in pride of place. She had been given a four-page spread, and the bracketing of strategically placed ads from some of the biggest American fashion names showed the importance that had been assigned to her work. She was given a sparkling byline – 'Oona Reilly, Our Special Correspondent in Paris'.

This most recent accolade really put her in the public eye. The telephone began to ring with offers of work. A number of newspapers in the States and Britain were eager for short pieces about the renaissance of French fashion. These were short opinion pieces that she could knock out in a day or so, and that brought in decent money. She was also approached by *Picture Post* to cover Pierre Balmain's opening with an article and photos. With the war still raging, no American staff were being sent to Europe. She was perfectly placed to do the work, and she accepted the offer with alacrity. Her career as a journalist had well and truly taken off.

The war news now was exhilarating and terrible. The German Eastern and Western Fronts had crumbled. A million and a half German prisoners of war had been taken by the Allies; tens of thousands were still being killed on both sides. Berlin had been reached, and a vast battle was raging, with Hitler beleaguered in his bunker. The Nazi state was in its terrifying death throes. In Italy, Mussolini had been shot by partisans, his body strung up like a butchered pig's beside that of his lover, Clara Petacci. After six years of bloodshed such as the world had never seen, it seemed that the war was finally approaching an end.

And then, one morning, the bells of Paris began to chime, first in isolation, then in a universal clangour.

'Something has happened,' Copper said.

'Something terrible, perhaps,' Dior said in alarm.

They hurried out into the street. The bells were tolling across the city, louder and louder. People were cheering, laughing and hugging one another. They were confronted by a newspaper kiosk. A man was pasting up a placard with a headline in huge black letters. It said simply, *HITLER EST MORT*.

Copper and Dior clasped each other's hands, hardly able to believe it. But there it was, in black and white. They bought a newspaper and read the front page together. Doenitz had announced Adolf Hitler's death and proclaimed himself the Führer's successor. The monster was dead. The end of the war was surely imminent. Throwing the paper into the air, they grabbed each other's hands and began to dance in the street along with thousands of others.

Fourteen

The real party started a few days later with the announcement that the Nazis had surrendered unconditionally and war had ended – in Europe at least. The whole of Paris erupted in communal celebration even wilder than the Liberation. The Tuileries and every other public space filled with multitudes of Parisians in their gayest clothes. It was typical of the times that even in this joyous moment, the political divisions cut deep. While a huge crowd gathered in place de la Concorde to hear Charles de Gaulle make a victory proclamation, the communists held their own triumphs and speeches, waving the red flag. There were inevitable fights, clashes with the police, arrests.

For Copper, it was a strange moment. The war had brought her to France, and now it was over. Perhaps she should go home?

Getting riotously drunk in a bar with a motley collection of communists, American GIs and journalists, she wondered where *home* was. Had Paris become her home? Was her American life over? It was easy, borne along on the river of champagne, singing 'La Marseillaise' at the top of her voice, to feel a deep and abiding love for France. For France and for Henry Velikovsky. She danced in the street, kissed every man in uniform, climbed up monuments and on to café tables, gulped champagne straight from the bottle until the bubbles and the alcohol made her vomit in the gutter.

After twenty-four straight hours of celebration, she dragged herself away from the party, wrapped in a French flag like something out of a Delacroix painting, to sleep it off. On the way back, she found herself in front of Henry's house in the 7th arrondissement.

She had heard nothing from Henry since that sombre visit after the wedding-that-wasn't. She had deliberately pushed him to the back of her mind. But he wouldn't stay there.

Knowing she was terribly drunk, she rang the bell. If he answered, she would throw her arms around him and beg him to forgive her. Tell him that she'd been a terrible fool at the cathedral, that if the past weeks had shown her one thing, if they'd shown her anything at all, it was that she loved him more than she'd known. That she'd grown to love him almost without realising it. That she didn't want to keep living without him.

But there was no answer. The old house covered in vines was silent as the grave. There was no Henry to whom to blurt out her words of remorse.

She hoisted herself unsteadily up on the cast-iron railings to peer in. The place appeared deserted, the windows shuttered – even the window of the bedroom where they'd lain together. She'd remembered that afternoon in all its sweetness and joy, the aperitif to a feast that would never materialise.

Was it just the drink and the weariness that made her burst into tears in the street now? Sitting in the gutter, huddled in her flag, she'd never felt lonelier. Welling up in her was a deep yearning for stability. A life of adventure was all very well, but she wanted a home. She wanted a family. That was something she'd never considered with Amory. Married couples had children as a general rule; but she'd never felt the rule applied to her and Amory.

There was only one man she loved, and she didn't even know whether he was dead or alive.

The day after the party, her head aching and her bleary eyes shielded with sunglasses, she called the Ritz, but he wasn't currently occupying his room. He hadn't been heard from in some time, and no, they were not expecting him at present. His room, of course, remained at his disposal.

She went round to his 'dusty little bureau' on the Champs-Élysées to speak to his secretary, determined to get some answers.

She greeted Copper with a pleasant smile.

'*Bonjour*, Madame. Isn't the news wonderful? Is there something I can do for you?'

'I wondered whether you'd heard from Henry – Monsieur Velikovsky – lately?'

The secretary, a well-dressed, middle-aged woman, shook her head. '*Désolée*, Madame. I have heard nothing from my chief.'

'But – he's all right?'

The answer was bland. 'I have no reason to think otherwise.'

'You're not expecting him back in Paris, then? Now that the war is over, I mean?'

The woman shrugged slightly. 'As you know, Monsieur Velikovsky is a busy man. He comes when he comes. I can take any message you care to leave.' She picked up her pencil and pad, ready to write down anything Copper might say.

'Just ask him to call me,' Copper said, after considering and rejecting various alternatives.

'*Bien sûr*, Madame.'

Copper walked away feeling empty. At the cathedral, marriage had seemed impossible. She couldn't have gone through with it, even with a pistol to her head. Now, the prospect of marriage to a man she was sure she loved was possible. More than possible – it was essential to her happiness.

255

Copper arrived back at the apartment a few days later to find a note from Suzy Solidor on the hall table. Written in violet ink, it read simply, 'I am leaving Paris. Will you come to say goodbye?'

It was not an invitation she could refuse. She went to see Suzy straight away. Suzy's eyes widened as she opened her door to Copper.

'You came,' she said. 'I was afraid you wouldn't.'

Copper entered the apartment to find it greatly altered. It was almost empty. The paintings had all been taken down from the walls. Only the largest pieces of furniture remained; the rest had been removed.

So it was true, then. Suzy was going. Copper felt a sharp pang pass through her heart. She gazed around the deserted rooms where half-filled packing crates stood with their lids propped against them.

'Where are you going?'

'To America. They tell me they like blondes there.'

'Oh, Suzy! But why?'

'You haven't heard? They have tried me and found me guilty of collaboration. I am forbidden to perform in France for five years.'

'The hypocrites,' Copper burst out. 'How dare they?'

'This is the France of the post-war,' Suzy said with a little shrug of one shoulder, as though it meant nothing to her. 'Everybody wants to proclaim himself a hero of the Resistance, and shave his neighbour's head.'

'I can't believe this has happened.'

'I am a public figure. I am to be made an example of. The future belongs to such as your Catherine Dior – not to such as me.'

'I'm so sorry.'

'Five years.' Suzy's face, as always, was mask-like. She was wearing nothing but a white chemise. Beneath it, she was naked. Her sculpted body was summer-golden; she looked like an ancient Greek goddess as she packed. 'At my age, it is a sentence of death. Who will remember me in five years?'

'Nobody can forget you,' Copper said in a low voice. 'It's not possible.'

'You seem to have had no difficulty accomplishing this supposedly impossible feat,' Suzy replied dryly.

'I haven't forgotten you.'

Suzy replied with one of her enigmatic smiles. 'Well, I am going into exile. And all for "Lili Marlène". She made my fortune, the whore, and now she has ruined me.' She pushed the lid of a trunk down and turned to Copper. 'I'm so glad to see you, *chérie*. Will you have a vermouth with me?'

She opened the doors to the terrace, but they did not go out. They sat on the sofa in the cool breeze that blew the curtains in graceful arabesques. Suzy had produced a bottle of Lillet. The resinous, citrusy drink was one of her favourites. 'And so you are becoming famous,' she said to Copper in her husky voice. 'I cannot open a magazine these days without reading your name.'

'That's an exaggeration. It took me some time to find out what I wanted to do with my life, but now that I've found it, I'm happy.'

'I am happy for you, *chérie*. You are doing well.'

'I'm all right. I have plenty of work. And I'm saving to buy a new camera, a thirty-five millimetre Leica. Lighter and more practical.'

'Lighter and more practical,' Suzy repeated. 'You are a young woman on the move, my dear. You make me feel so old.'

'You look magnificent as always, Suzy.'

'Thank you.' In truth, Suzy did not seem to age. Her face remained flawless, and her body was that of a woman of half her years. 'I might say the same about you. I heard that you abandoned your Russian count at the altar.'

'Yes. But I know now that it was a mistake.'

Suzy grimaced. 'I see. So you have decided to become a Russian countess after all?'

'If he will have me. I haven't heard from him in weeks.'

'Has he turned his back on you? Or have the communists strung him up?'

'I ask myself the same question,' Copper said, trying to sound light, though she felt far from it.

'I am sorry,' Suzy said. 'I wish you the best of luck.'

She lifted her glass and Copper's eye was caught by the smooth hollow of Suzy's armpit. 'You've shaved under your arms.'

'They tell me the Americans insist on it.' She lifted the hem of her chemise. 'Here, too. Just in case anyone wants to look. Are you blushing, *chérie*?' she asked, catching Copper's expression.

'You always take me by surprise.'

'Do I? I am at ease with my body, you see. I like it. I'm not in the least ashamed of it.' Her long fingers stayed between her thighs. 'You're afraid of this, I think. Yet you have one just the same. We could have pressed them together, kissed one another, given each other heaven. I was dripping for you. Only for you. But you ran like a rabbit. Why did you run?'

'There was a gate that I couldn't pass through. Don't reproach me.'

'You found me disgusting?'

'No. Just the opposite. I had to run because I found you all too alluring.'

'I suppose that is a compliment.' Suzy emptied her glass and reached for the bottle again. 'You know, I sang in the girls' choir in the church at Saint-Malo,' she said as she poured for them both. 'Can you imagine that? A skinny gamine with pigtails and a flat chest?'

Copper smiled. 'It's hard to imagine.'

'Well, that was me. Nobody noticed me, although I always thought I had a good voice. Then one day, the priest stopped the choir and asked, "Who is the boy who is singing with the girls?" They found it was me. *La fille qui chante comme un garçon.* They all turned to stare at me. I was excited. Excited and ashamed at the same time. I felt my power from that moment. They called me *la garçonne*, and so I became that creature. The mermaid, never quite one thing or the other. For ten years, there was Yvonne. Then others. Some men, some women. I have spent my life living out the fantasies and desires of others. But I regret none of it. It has been a good life, all in all. I only wanted to make others happy. You think I am as much a *putain* as Lili Marlène, I am sure?'

Copper watched Suzy's face. Under the strength and the beauty, there was something cold, a pain that would never be confessed. 'No, I don't think that. You made me very happy.'

'I could have made you much happier.'

'I don't think so. But I know I could have made you much happier. You've been so kind, so generous. I didn't deserve any of it.'

'Of course you deserved it.' Suzy leaned over and kissed Copper on the lips.

Copper closed her eyes with sadness for this girl who sang like a boy, this woman who desired her like a man. She put her arms around Suzy's strong neck and pulled her tight. 'I'm sorry. Forgive me for hurting you.'

'Can't you love me, even now?' Suzy demanded, her mouth pressed hotly against Copper's throat.

'I do love you,' Copper whispered. She found she was crying. 'I'm going to miss you so terribly, Suzy. I want to thank you – for everything you've done for me, everything you've given to me, the love you've shown me.' She rose to leave. 'I can never forget you.'

The sight of a horse-drawn carriage waiting outside 10 rue Royale was not altogether unusual, although now that petrol was more readily available in France, thanks to the United States Army, the horse-drawn hackney carriages were disappearing from the streets again. They had come out of retirement during the hard years of the Occupation, like the ghosts of a past glory. But now there were fewer to be seen every day, as they drifted back to whatever tumbledown stables they'd come from.

Thinking Dior might be in it, Copper went up to the fiacre and peered inside curiously. The door swung open. Seated on the red leather, holding the door open, was Henry. He was wearing a beard now.

For a moment, she felt that her heart had stopped, robbing her of breath. Then it started beating again, unsteadily. 'That beard will have to go,' she heard herself say.

'I thought you could help me get rid of it.'

'The sooner the better, I should say.'

'Then get on board.'

She got in and climbed on to his lap like a child. 'I thought you would never come back,' she said in a choked voice.

'At times, nor did I.' He crushed her in his arms. 'My secretary called me to say you were looking for me. I dared hope. Forgive me. I have had to be away from you and remain silent.'

They held each other tightly for a long while, rocking to and fro. At last, she drew back and took a shuddering breath. Her heart was still pounding so hard that she found it difficult to talk coherently. 'You look like a stranger!'

He touched his bushy, dark beard. 'I've had to become one of the proletariat to get into the right places. If they'd had any inkling of who I really was, I assure you I would now be more dead than alive.'

'Henry!'

'Dinner at the Ritz?'

'I'm hardly dressed for the Ritz.'

'You look magnificent, as always.'

'So long as I can powder my nose when we get there.' The fiacre set off with a lurch. Rattling along in the smell of horse and harness leather, she tried to catch her breath. 'How long are you in Paris for?'

'I'm back for good.'

She turned away, not wanting him to see her tears. 'Is that a promise?' she asked in a choked voice.

'Yes. I've come for you – if you want me.'

Copper accepted the handkerchief he offered her. 'I'll let you know when I make up my mind. What's with the horse and cart?'

He smiled. 'There are not many cities left where you can still get a carriage to pick up the love of your life. I couldn't resist it.'

'You always were an incurable romantic,' she said.

'I suppose you're right.'

'I've been sick with worry about you,' she said. 'Are you smiling? I can't see your expressions under all that face-fungus.'

'My expression is a happy one, I assure you.'

'Do you forgive me for leaving you at the altar?'

'If you forgive me for being a Bluebeard.'

'Done. Speaking of beards, I really need to remove yours. Can we stop at your house on the way?'

'Of course.'

They reached Henry's house and went in. Everything was bright and clean, and the air smelled of polish and fresh paint.

'It looks wonderful.'

'It's coming back to life,' he agreed. 'It's waiting for a new mistress.'

The bedroom was full of flowers, as before. In the white marble bathroom, he gave her scissors, a razor and the other materials necessary for removing his beard. He stripped to his waist so she could get to work. She made him sit on the edge of the bathtub and began by trimming his beard close to his jawline with the scissors.

'I read your article in *Picture Post*,' he said. 'Balmain must be grateful to you. You gave him an excellent launch.'

'He's brilliantly talented.'

'And when will you be doing the same for your friend Dior?'

She concentrated on cutting the thick curls without damaging his skin. 'One of these days, I suppose. I keep urging him to do something about leaving Lelong. But he can be disgustingly timid. Or disgustingly lazy. Or both.' She lathered his stubbly face abundantly with shaving soap and then set to work with the razor.

'You've done this before?'

'Twice a week until I left home. I was the one who shaved my father, Mondays and Wednesdays. Stop trying to kiss me or I won't be responsible for any cuts.' In fact, her hands were trembling in a way that threatened Henry's life, but she managed to get them under control. It helped if she didn't meet his eyes but focused on shearing away the foam to reveal the familiar contours of his face. 'Where have you been? Tell me the truth.'

'There has been a war for the soul of France. The communists have been doing everything in their power to destabilise the country and annex it for Soviet Russia. But at last the tide is turning and their strength is starting to fade a little. And strangely, that has less to do with me and my beard than with Stalin's own brutality.'

'What do you mean?'

'The glorious Red Army has been the communists' chief propaganda weapon. For years, they've been telling French workers tales of how the Red Army are coming to liberate them from slavery. But now we can all see what liberation by the Red Army really means. We saw the rape and looting which followed them at every step. We've seen them turn Poland, Hungary, Czechoslovakia and the rest into prison nations. Now we see them turning Berlin into a prison city. And Berlin, my dear, is not so far from Paris. My task, in the end, lay merely in pointing out these details in the right company and allowing them to draw their own conclusions.'

'There must have been more than that. You said you would tell me the truth.'

'Well, it was not always easy to get into the right company. And playing one side against the other is always difficult. The Reds would like to take sole credit for defeating the Nazis. According to them, every Resistance hero was a Stalinist. Dispelling that myth was vital.' His dark, slanted eyes took her in hungrily. 'You are so beautiful. I've dreamed of you. But my dreams always fall short of the reality.'

'You've lost weight,' she said, taking in his lean torso.

'I haven't been eating very much. I'm looking forward to our dinner at the Ritz grill.'

'You can't keep living at the Ritz,' Copper heard herself saying. 'Not with this magnificent home standing empty. It's an unnecessary expense.' She scraped off the last patch of foam. 'And we can't keep eating restaurant food, either. It's not good for us. We need healthy, home-cooked meals.'

'I couldn't agree more.' He caught her wrist. 'Copper – how long are you going to keep me waiting?'

She was silent for a moment. Then she freed herself gently and rinsed the razor under the silver tap. 'If you really want me, I'm yours.'

'My beloved!' He put his arms around her. 'I thank God for you.'

She laughed a little unsteadily. 'Henry, you're the only man I know who actually says things like that.'

'I say them because I mean them.'

'I know you do.' She put down the implements and turned in his arms, looking up into his freshly shaven face. 'There, that's better. Now you look like you again.'

'I will try to make you a better husband than the previous incumbent,' he said, gazing down at her adoringly. 'You are not going to run away again?'

'No. I promise. And I will try to be a good wife to you, my darling,' she replied. 'And I promise—'

But she had to leave the rest of the promise unspoken, because his warm lips sealed hers.

The second ceremony, as she had requested, was held at the *office des mariages* in the local *mairie*. It was very quiet. No Russian duchesses were present, nor any Parisian bohemians. Only Christian, Pierre Balmain, Hervé and Catherine came, serving as witnesses.

The room was not a very glamorous one, lined with filing cabinets on one side, but the other side had large windows with a fine view of the Arc de Triomphe, and the public notary was a charming woman who kissed them all roundly after the ceremony. Copper wore a sheer pink dress with a turn-down collar made for her by Tian, and carried a small bouquet of rosebuds, as she had wanted. The men all wore morning suits and coats with top hats. They exchanged plain gold rings, and were filled with quiet joy.

After the ceremony, the wedding party went for lunch in a private suite at the Ritz. The table was decked with cream lilies and the meal was equally elegant and beautiful, beginning with oysters and continuing with lobster and salmon, accompanied by vintage champagne.

Hervé and Tian both proposed toasts. Hervé's was very dignified, but Tian choked up during his and had to be given a handkerchief to dry his eyes before he was able to continue.

Catherine was now on the road to recovering her strength. She and Hervé were living near Grasse, in the south of France. It was she who had supplied the bouquet of rosebuds, gathered from her own garden. Copper could see curves in her figure that hadn't been there before, and her hair had grown; but nothing, Copper suspected, would take the haunted look from her eyes. Several times during the course of the lunch, she caught Catherine staring into nothing, her hands clenched. A touch on her arm was enough to break the spell of what were almost certainly terrible memories, but Copper knew there was a long way to go yet. Catherine still found it difficult to eat more than a few mouthfuls, even though Copper coaxed her.

'When we first got to Ravensbrück,' she said, 'our stomachs used to rumble so loudly in the hut at night that they made us laugh. Really, it was comical. We had competitions to see who could make the loudest gurgles. But after a while, our stomachs shrank and they stopped making any noises at all.' In the silence that followed, she looked apologetic. 'I shouldn't talk about these things.'

'Of course you should,' Copper said.

'I'm sorry,' she murmured to Copper as conversation resumed. 'I don't want to spoil your special day.'

'You're making it beautiful. But I can see that you're still in pain.'

Catherine shook her head. 'When I was in the camps, I could think of nothing but France. And now that I am home, my thoughts return constantly to the camps. My mind is like a monkey that never does what I tell it to do.'

'I know the problem,' Copper said ruefully.

Catherine pressed her hand. 'I'm well. Enjoy your day. It gives me such joy to see you married.'

'She deserves to be happy,' Copper said that evening, as she nestled in Henry's arms in the old house covered in vines.

'Yes, she does. And so do you.'

'I couldn't be happier,' she replied, stroking his cheek.

'Nor could I. I can still hardly believe that you are my wife.'

'You were right about one thing, though,' she said.

'What's that?'

'The registry office ceremony was awfully drab. The cathedral would have been much nicer.'

He stifled a groan, rolling his eyes. 'You will drive me mad.'

'Probably,' she admitted.

'We can still arrange the cathedral, if you want.'

'No, thank you. I've been married quite enough times.' She kissed him on the lips. 'And now I think it's time you made me yours.'

Fifteen

'You're going to be my wife,' Dior told Copper.

'I have a perfectly serviceable husband,' she pointed out. 'You may have noticed that we've already had our first wedding anniversary.'

'He won't mind. I'm just borrowing you for the afternoon.'

'What for?'

'We're going to go shopping for an outfit for you.'

'That sounds fun. Chanel? Schiaparelli?'

'Somewhere much more discreet – Maison Gaston. After all, we're a staid old couple, not young gadabouts.'

'Speak for yourself,' Copper snorted.

Dior had asked her to meet him on the rue Saint-Florentin, but would not explain why. He led her into Maison Gaston now, arm in arm like a respectable married pair.

The shop was redolent of old-fashioned Parisian charm. The bustle of the rue Saint-Florentin seemed to fade behind them. The clothes were somewhat severe. Almost every garment was trimmed with sable or mink, unappealing for the summer, but as Tian pointed out, autumn would soon be here. Middle-aged, black-clad *vendeuses* glided around them, combining icy politeness with an impression of unassailable superiority.

'What do you think of the designs?' Dior asked her.

'Quite sombre,' Copper murmured. 'And awfully conservative.' Even if she had really been shopping for herself, she would have found it difficult to choose a garment she didn't consider old-fashioned.

Oddly, however, Tian was interested in everything. He asked to be shown the latest models, the old stock, the accessories; in short, everything. He gazed around at the fittings, nosed behind the counters, and interrogated the *vendeuses*. There seemed to be no aspect of the establishment that he didn't have an insatiable curiosity about. He even peered in while she was trying on a dress.

'A lovely place to be embalmed,' was his verdict on the changing room.

As always, where his own profession was concerned, he changed subtly; the shy and retiring Christian Dior became someone authoritative. His normally mild expression turned into a frown of concentration, and his tone became peremptory. By the time they left the shop – having bought nothing – the *vendeuses* were practically ready to throw them out physically.

They had spent almost two hours in Gaston, and it was now early evening, the air warm and balmy. One of the last remaining horse-drawn carriages clopped down the street, scattering a group of young novice nuns.

'What did you think?' Dior asked.

'It's a lovely shop, Tian. Why did you take me there?'

'I wanted your opinion.'

'Why does my opinion matter?'

'Because, *ma petite*,' he said, slipping his arm through hers, 'Marcel Boussac has offered to make me the new director.'

'And who is Marcel Boussac?'

'He's the Cotton King. When the First World War ended, he bought up all the linen which was used to make the aircraft in those days. He turned it into shirts and made a fortune. People used to say "as rich as Midas". Now they say "as rich as Boussac".'

'And he owns Gaston?'

'Yes. I trust you to be discreet, *ma petite*. This isn't for public consumption.'

Copper hugged his arm excitedly. 'Tian! You'll be your own man at last!'

He disengaged himself from her, laughing. 'Let's pick up your husband and I'll cook you both supper at my place. I've got a lovely big crab from Granville and a nice Muscadet to go with it.'

The three of them convened at Dior's apartment, which was just around the corner from Gaston – an advantage that Henry pointed out. 'You'll be able to stroll to work every morning, swinging your gold-topped cane and tipping your top hat to your clients on the street. It could hardly be better.'

'When I was a young man, Gaston was as famous as Chanel,' Dior said, as he tied on a snowy apron and got to work in his little kitchen. 'But it's been in decline for years. And the war administered the *coup de grâce*. As you saw, it's old-fashioned and gloomy now. Boussac wants me to restore it to its former glory.'

'It's the opportunity of a lifetime!'

'Hardly that, my dear.'

'Tian, don't tell me you're going to look this gift horse in the mouth?'

'It's always important to look any horse in the mouth, *mes amis*. Marcel Boussac didn't become the richest man in France by giving his money away.' He plunged the crab carefully into the boiling water. 'It may be flattering to be put in a museum, but I'm not sure I'm ready to be stuffed and mounted just yet.'

'You mean – you're going to say no?'

'Yes, I'm going to decline.'

Copper threw up her hands. 'Tian. For heaven's sake!'

He was concentrating on his cooking now. She knew better than to interrupt him when he was playing chef; he took food preparation seriously. But she knew that Balmain was already preparing for his second collection. Tian was being left further and further behind by his contemporaries.

'You can't turn this down,' she said when they were finally seated at the table.

'Gaston is a mausoleum,' he said, portioning out the crab. 'And it smells like one. Mothballs and cobwebs and dust. I may be absurdly superstitious, but I'm not in the business of raising the dead.'

'Gaston isn't dead yet,' Henry pointed out.

'It's dying, which is the same thing. Can you imagine trying to tell those old witches what to do? And as for the atelier – I would have to start by sacking the entire staff, and I can't face that. I have a good job with Lelong, and it would be madness to leave it for something so uncertain. Better to be first mate on a luxury liner than captain of a sinking ship.'

'You can always find an excuse not to do something,' Copper said sharply. 'You just don't want to tell Lelong that you're leaving.'

'It's true I wasn't looking forward to that particular interview.'

'I knew it!'

Infuriatingly, he was adamant. 'Maison Gaston is moribund, and Boussac was misguided, even perhaps *méchant*, to have made the proposal. I have an appointment to see him tomorrow, and I will deliver a polite refusal.'

Saying goodbye to him after midnight, she grasped his lapel. 'I hope you wake up tomorrow and change your mind, you obstinate man.'

'Trust me. I won't.'

'He just won't push himself forward,' she said to Henry as they walked home. 'Sometimes I think Tian will never get out of his rut. Perhaps he doesn't even *want* to get out of his rut. He's happy to be stuck in it forever, growing old in Lucien Lelong's back rooms, happy with his life of parties and dinners, never taking a risk.'

'You've just described a contented man.'

'You are the last person to condone laziness, dear Henry.'

Copper's husband of twelve months had made her happier than she had believed possible. There seemed to be no man kinder or more loving than Henry Velikovsky, and no house more lovely than the home they had made together. Unlike her marriage to Amory, which had begun with a rush of passion and had soon cooled off into apathy and then disillusionment, her marriage to Henry just kept getting better.

She loved his company, hurried back to him each time she was away, and found that despite herself, she pined for him when he had to travel. As for the passion, that had grown steadily. She felt loved and desired, and she loved and desired him in turn. That her husband was crazy about her was evident in everything he did. To be supported and appreciated, to be cherished and adored, these were the sexiest feelings she knew.

It was a life filled with romance and beauty. The old house covered in vines required a staff of five persons to maintain it, including a lady's maid, that most indispensable adjunct to a fashionable Parisienne – even one who had once been arrested for trying to overthrow the state. But Henry's fortune covered all that amply, and it was surprising how quickly one grew accustomed to such a life. There had been a wonderful surprise – the collection of antique furniture and Impressionist paintings stolen by the Nazis had been located and returned from Germany, and now graced the house again.

Copper looked back now on her tough upbringing in Brooklyn and her bohemian existence with Amory with nostalgia. Was that Copper really the same woman as the Countess Velikovsky, who now had a front-row seat at all the *défilés de mode haute couture*, who knew every designer in Paris, whose judgments were published in the great fashion magazines?

She had kept her byline, Oona Reilly. Being a countess was a kind of play-acting, which people demanded of her even though she (and Henry) were amused by it. As Henry had said on the night they'd met, people were snobs and loved to be associated with aristocracy, even one which no longer existed outside of the history books.

'My darling, I've had a communication about your ex-husband.'

She felt an unpleasant shock pass through her heart. 'Nothing bad, I hope?'

'I'm not sure. He's here in Paris. He's asked to see you.'

'When you say, here in Paris . . . ?'

'He's in a sanatorium. The director passed the message on to me.'

'A sanatorium? So he's still sick?'

'They didn't say anything about his state of health, but presumably he isn't well.'

'I see,' Copper replied heavily.

'My dear,' Henry said. 'I want you to know that this is your decision. If you decide not to see him, I will not reproach you. And if you decide to see him, I will not be discomposed.'

'You're sure?'

He pressed her arm firmly. 'Quite sure. It's up to you completely.'

'Thank you, Henry. I'll think about it.'

Copper's decision to see Amory was not an easy one to reach, but she felt a sense of obligation. She had, after all, been his wife for eighteen months, and she ought not turn her back on him now, even though that time had not been a very happy one.

The Marie-Thérèse Sanatorium was set in a leafy park on the banks of the Seine. Americans who fell ill in Paris went there; and indeed, the robust nursing sister who met her, wearing a blue-striped uniform, spoke in the clear tones of the American Midwest.

'My name is Sister Gibson. I've been engaged by Mr Heathcote's family to provide additional care. Thank you for coming to see him.'

'What's wrong with him?'

'He was admitted after he tried to kill himself.'

'Again?' Copper felt cold all over. 'When was this?'

'A month ago. He's still recovering from the wounds he inflicted on himself, but he's not in danger anymore. Not from the wounds, at any rate. The danger is inside him, which is why his family suggested I contact you. He's in the day room.'

The day room was sunny and almost over-warm, its rows of tall windows giving expansive views of the river through the trees. There were patients and visitors seated in groups here and there. Amory was alone at a table at the far end of the room scribbling in a notebook, around which he had thrown his free arm, as though shielding what he was writing from all eyes.

Copper had somehow got it into her mind that Amory had cut his wrists, but she saw with a shock that there was a large dressing on the side of his head. As he raised his head to look at her, she saw the dark bruising that extended over the right half of his face. The eye on that side appeared to have somehow moved position, as though he had developed a squint, and the white was flooded with crimson.

It was all she could do to greet him with something like a composed expression.

'Hello, Amory.'

'Hello, Copper.' He closed the notebook. 'I guess it's too much to hope that you've smuggled in a bottle of rye,' he said when the nurse had left.

'Only this.' She handed him the book she had bought him at Shakespeare and Company, the English bookstore in Paris. 'It's the latest Steinbeck.'

'*Cannery Row*. Another saga of hobos and idiots?'

'I thought it was very good.'

He laid it aside. 'I'll give it a try.'

'Amory, what have you done to yourself?'

'I tried to blow my brains out, but I guess my hand was shaking too much. I removed the top of my skull instead. They've patched me up with a metal plate.'

'Oh, God.'

'You might think the operation would have let a little light in,' he went on, 'but that doesn't seem to have been the case. Which is why they've dragged you here. You're supposed to talk some sense into me. Please accept my apologies for spoiling your Saturday morning.'

'Don't say that. I wish I could help.'

They looked at one another. The gaze of those violet eyes was disconcerting rather than intoxicating now, the clear left one fixed on her intently, the bloodshot right eye wandering into the distance. She wondered if he had lost the sight in it.

'I should never have married you,' he said.

She grimaced. 'Are you blaming me for this?'

'Ultimately, yes.'

'And you don't think any of it is your fault?'

'Oh, I do. And I've tried to administer a suitable punishment. It hasn't worked very well. But don't worry, I'll do better next time. Third time lucky, they say.'

Copper rose to her feet. 'If you've asked me here just to tell me you intend to kill yourself, I have better things to do.'

Unexpectedly, he gave her a lopsided smile. 'See, now, that's what I'm talking about. You always do that to me.'

'What do I do to you, Amory?'

'Make me feel foolish. Like a silly little boy throwing a tantrum. Sit down, honey.'

'I never wanted to make you feel foolish,' Copper said, sitting back down again.

'But you did, right from the start. You were always more grown-up than me. More of an adult. Better at everything.'

'I never said I was better.'

'You didn't have to. It was painfully obvious. I was pretending, but you were the real deal. Hell, you're even a better writer than I am.'

'That's not true.'

He drummed his fingers on the notebook. 'Know what used to burn me up? The way you took over from George. He'd just hand everything to you, and you'd do it effortlessly, like it was nothing. With your high school education.'

'You know I had to save his bacon.'

'You didn't have to do it so damned well. I couldn't stand you constantly showing me you were better than me.'

'I didn't know it was a competition.'

'It wasn't. You were way ahead of me from the start.'

'Why are you telling me all this now?'

'Because I've decided to be honest, if nothing else in my life. You made me see that I was a fraud. That's why I had to hurt you.'

'Are you still making excuses for your infidelities? You don't have to anymore. They're irrelevant.'

'I'm not making excuses. It's the truth. I tried to break your spirit.'

'Well, you almost succeeded,' she said.

'You flatter me,' he said dryly. 'I never came close. I slept with every woman who came near me. It made you stop loving me, but it didn't break you. You know what the problem was? I loved you.' He paused. 'I still do.'

This was a line of talk that she emphatically did not want to pursue. 'A long time has passed, Amory.'

'A long time,' he agreed, nodding his bandaged head slowly. 'After Brussels, I started work on my article again. I still thought the reason I had the breakdown was the horror I was witnessing. It wasn't. It was the realisation that I wasn't good enough. I wasn't up to the job. It was too big for me. I didn't have the strength and I didn't have the talent.'

'I always had faith in your talent.'

'Ah, the burden of that faith,' he replied ironically. 'We should never have come to France. My father offered me a job in the bank. But I wanted to spread my wings. All the way through college, they all told me how wonderful I was. The girls, the professors, you. It took marriage to you to show me that I wasn't a genius.'

'Because you claim I made you feel inferior?'

'The term the shrinks use is "emasculated".'

Despite her compassion for him, she felt anger burn inside her. 'I never tried to emasculate you. I did everything I could to support you and encourage you.'

Amory's gaunt face twisted in that crooked grin again. 'You always had a temper to go with that flaming red hair.'

'And you always had an excuse for everything you did wrong,' she said bluntly. 'I'm not going to sit here and listen to you put the blame on me for everything that's gone wrong in your life. You made me very unhappy. The fact that you made yourself miserable in the process isn't my fault. You want my advice, Amory? Go back to the States and take that job in the bank. It's not too late.'

He pointed to his bandage. 'You think the investors will be impressed by a guy with a hole in his head?'

'Get a wig,' she said shortly. 'Wear a hat. Use your imagination.'

He nodded slowly. 'Tell me about this husband of yours.'

Copper felt the cogs of her mind engage against the idea of exposing her happiness with Henry to Amory's nihilist scorn. 'I don't want to talk about him.'

'He's that good, huh? Or is he that bad?'

Copper gathered her things. 'I'd better go.'

His laughter dried up. 'Don't leave. I'll stop being a jerk.'

'I don't think you will.'

'Maybe you're right. I should get back to my novel anyhow.' He opened the notebook and flipped through the pages. Copper saw that they were covered with doodles in red ink. There were no lines of text, only staring faces and meaningless scribbles. 'This is my best work yet,' he said with a skewed smile.

As she left the day room, Copper reflected that Amory was right in one thing he had said, at least. He was still essentially a child, while she was an adult. If she had felt that way two years ago, she felt it even more now. She had grown up, and she was married to another grown-up, who behaved like an adult and treated her like an adult.

'How was your visit?' Sister Gibson asked Copper at the door.

'I don't know whether it had the effect you wanted,' Copper replied.

'Maybe it did. There was a lot he needed to get off his chest.'

'I hope he recovers from the wound.'

'Wouldn't you say he has more than the one wound?' Copper looked into the nurse's china-blue eyes, wondering what tales Amory had told of her cruelty. Sister Gibson smiled. 'I'll let you know how it goes. I'll tell the family you came. They'll be pleased, I'm sure. Good day, Mrs Velikovsky.'

Sixteen

'I've done something stupid,' Dior said.

Henry poured him a glass of wine. 'What's the matter?'

Dior took the glass, but he was too agitated to drink it. He paced the carpet in distress, his face pale. 'I went to see Boussac. About Gaston, you know. I went in there determined to refuse his offer. But—'

'You said yes instead!' Copper exclaimed.

'I did something far worse. I told him I wanted my own couture house, under my own name.'

'Tian!'

'It all just burst out of me. I told him it was time for a change, that the old fashions were as dead as the dodo. I said there was no use trying to breathe life into a corpse, and that we had to go back to the highest traditions of French couture or go under forever.'

'What did he say?'

'He asked what else I wanted, in a very ironic tone. I told him I wanted the best workers in Paris, making the most luxurious clothes for the best-dressed women in France.'

Copper was listening with bated breath. 'And then?'

'He told me that this wasn't what he had been thinking of at all. He said my plan was overambitious. And then he showed me out.'

Henry refilled his glass. 'At least you told him what you wanted.'

'What if he thinks it over – and agrees?'

'Then you'll be made.'

'Oh, my God. Then I'll be finished, you mean.'

'He must have finally snapped after all the years under Lucien Lelong,' Copper said to Henry when Dior had left.

They were in their bedroom and she was rolling her stockings down her slim legs. Henry had been watching her with smoky eyes while he undressed. 'Stop.'

She looked up. 'Stop what?'

'Just don't move. You're so beautiful.'

'With my stockings half off?'

'I want to remember this moment for ever.'

Copper smiled, pausing in her undressing. 'What's so special about this moment?'

'Every moment with you is special. But sometimes it strikes me—'

'What strikes you, my dear?'

'How very beautiful you are. That you are here with me. That you are mine at last. The miracle of you. All that is astonishing to me. And when that thought strikes me, I want to take a moment out of time and hold it forever, so it can never be lost.' He came to kneel in front of her. 'I can still hardly believe that you're my wife.'

'Well, I am. I promised never to run away again.'

'Are you happy with me?' he asked as he slipped her stockings all the way down to her ankles with deft fingers.

'I'm blissfully happy, Henry. You must know that.'

He took the diaphanous nylons off her slender feet. 'There is nothing that I could improve on?'

'You exceed all my expectations constantly.' She ran her fingers through his hair. 'You're not worrying about anything – anybody – are you?'

He kissed the delicate veins of her ankles with warm lips. 'I want to make you happy.'

'No man – or woman – has ever made me feel the way you do,' she said tenderly. 'If you're worrying about Suzy, she never gave me the happiness you do. You give me heaven. If I'd known how happy you would make me, I would never have left you at the altar like that. I'd have shouted "*Yes, yes, yes*" and dragged you home to bed.'

'That would have been a happier end to the day,' he admitted.

'You've never told me how you felt after I left you standing in the cathedral.'

His eyes darkened. 'I felt like a man who'd had the gates of paradise shut in his face.'

She groaned. 'Did you hate me very much?'

'Not for one moment. I hated myself. I knew the fault was mine. And I knew I had to get you back somehow – or never be happy again.'

'I'm so sorry I hurt you. I was very frightened.'

'And I was too sure of myself. I'll never make that mistake again.'

'Do you understand why I ran?'

'You thought I would take away your freedom.'

'Yes. I didn't realise that you were giving me freedom – the freedom to live my life the way I wanted to; the freedom to express myself. Henry, I can't think when you're doing that,' she whispered.

'You don't need to think,' he said, kissing her thighs. 'This is a moment we're stealing from time. It's ours forever.'

'But you'll have to stop if you want to finish this conversation.'

He smiled up at her. 'What else is there to say?'

'I want to know that you really forgive me.'

'Would I be here – doing this – if I hadn't forgiven you?'

'Come to me.' She lay back on the bed as he slid on top of her. 'I love you, Henry.'

'And I love you,' he replied, taking her in his arms. 'Always and forever.' They gazed into each other's eyes in the magical moment that he entered her. And then there were no more words or thoughts.

When Copper next saw Dior, he was in a panic.

'Boussac has consulted his board, and they're interested. They want to know details of my proposal.'

'Then tell them at once,' Copper said.

'Why did I ever open my mouth? I never meant this to happen.'

'Henry will help you draw up a business plan,' Copper promised. And, indeed, Henry dropped his own work to spend much of each day sitting with Dior in his study, working out figures and projections to show Boussac's people.

'Tian knows the fashion business intimately,' Henry told Copper after one of these brainstorming sessions. 'The problem is one of temperament. He's highly strung, and his self-confidence is fragile. He'll be in the middle of some grandiose scheme and suddenly he'll be crushed by self-doubt. He'll bury his head in his hands and cry, and say it's impossible, it'll never work. I have to cajole him back to the desk like a child.'

'He is a child in some ways,' Copper replied, putting her arm around her husband's neck. 'A talented, delicate child. Be gentle with him, darling.'

'I am being as gentle as I can. But Boussac won't be.'

But within a few days, Tian had given up.

'I couldn't take it anymore,' he said. 'I've sent Boussac a telegram, calling everything off.'

Copper gasped. 'Tian, you haven't.'

'I have. I've told him that it's impossible; quite impossible. I'm going to stay with Lelong.' He buried his face in his hands. 'I was mad to even begin this. Thank God it's over.'

'Tian,' Henry said brusquely. 'This was most unwise. If you reject this opportunity, it will never come again. And worse than that, you'll have given yourself a reputation for flightiness that you will never shake off. Nobody else will approach you. You'll stay in a backwater for the rest of your days.'

But Copper knew that this kind of talk wouldn't work with Tian. 'We're going to see Madame Delahaye,' she said decisively.

Copper hurried into the hallway to make the call. 'Madame Delahaye,' she said in a low voice. 'I'm going to bring Monsieur Christian to you for a reading. He's at a critical point in his career. Not to put too fine a point on it, he's about to throw away the greatest chance he'll ever have of success. I hope you understand what I'm getting at.'

'Bring him to me immediately,' came the response. 'You may be sure that I will give him the correct advice.'

That afternoon, Copper found herself once again in Madame Delahaye's neat little apartment with the potted plants and the lace doilies. The fortune teller laid out the rows of cards in a deathly silence. Dior sat gloomily fidgeting, his eyes following her movements.

'The Four of Cups,' Madame Delahaye exclaimed suddenly. She held up the card for Dior to see. 'Look! He sits with his arms folded, refusing the great gift that is being offered to him.'

'Is that me?' Dior asked doubtfully.

'Of course. The cards show that you are dreaming while your great opportunity passes you by.'

Dior inspected the card anxiously, tugging at his ear. 'Are you sure that's what it means?'

'Have I ever been wrong?'

'Never,' Dior admitted.

'You must accept the offer, whatever the conditions. Nobody will ever make you a better one,' she ordered sternly. 'You must create Maison Christian Dior no matter what your fears. It is your destiny.'

'You are sure?'

'Monsieur Dior, your future is glorious! It's in your name – "Di-Or", the Golden God.'

As they were leaving the apartment, Madame Delahaye put a plump hand on Copper's arm. 'And tell me,' she said gently, 'the golden-haired woman I saw in your last reading – did she cast her shadow over you, as I predicted?'

Copper was struck. 'Oh, I'd forgotten about that. You were right, I think. She did.'

'As for the hand from the east which places a coronet on your head – I think we know what that meant, Countess.' Madame Delahaye laughed with a touch of glee. 'I never forget my readings. And I remember how your hands were black with soot that day, Mademoiselle. Now they are clean. You didn't need to tell me what to say today. It was all in the cards.'

The word of the woman who had predicted his beloved sister's safe return was holy writ to Dior. As soon as they were home, he made a nervous call to Boussac gabbling explanations and apologies. He listened to the answer and then came back to Copper. He seemed calmer. 'There. That's done.'

'What did he say?' she asked.

'Someone intercepted my telegram, so Boussac never received it.'

'Wonderful. What else?'

Dior sat down, looking thoughtful. 'They're prepared to offer me the directorship of my own establishment, Christian Dior Limited. With a starting capital of six million francs, and unlimited credit.'

Copper was flabbergasted. 'Balmain started with a tenth of that.'

Now that his mind was made up, Dior had changed. The breathless, palpitating butterfly was gone. 'It will do to get started,' he said. 'What date are we now?'

'The middle of May,' she replied, awed by his sudden sangfroid.

'Come with me. I want to show you something.'

She accompanied his sober, sleek figure down the avenue Montaigne. 'You know, *petite*, there was something I loved about you the moment we met.'

'My foie gras?'

'Your innocence.'

'Well, thanks to you and your friends, I've lost that.'

'You'll never lose it,' he replied gently.

'You were so kind to me, Tian. I will never forget the way you helped me.'

'What you have given me in return for a little help is very precious to me.' He stopped. 'Many years ago, I dreamed of having my own couture house. I knew exactly what I wanted. I even saw the exact place. I would walk past it often, very often, and be filled with yearning. But of course, I had no way to acquire it. It wasn't even for sale. Just yesterday, I heard that it is now empty and that the lease is available.' He turned her to look at the building behind them. 'Here it is.'

It was a large house, built out of stone the colour of pale honey. A neoclassical archway carved with the head of a goddess sheltered the entrance, and stone corbels supported a balcony. The whole impression was of compactness and restrained grace.

'It's lovely,' she exclaimed.

He pointed to the *bel étage*. 'The salon will be there, with those large windows for illumination. The studios will go on the floor up above.

And you see those windows, up in the roof? We'll put workrooms there, in the attics. It's simple and elegant, just the way I like things.'

She got her camera ready. 'We need a photograph.'

'Mightn't that bring bad luck?'

'Nothing can jinx you now,' she promised. 'Take that frown off your face.'

She bullied him into posing at the entrance of 30 avenue Montaigne. He managed a smile, but his eyes were somehow melancholy. As she pressed the shutter release, she thought of the changes that he was going to face. The carefree frequenter of disreputable clubs, boiler of lobsters, thrower of bohemian parties, rescuer of waifs and strays, was at the threshold of another world.

She lowered the camera, stricken. 'Oh, Tian. I don't want to lose you.'

'Nor I you. But weren't you and your husband the ones pushing me forward?'

'Yes, and we still are. But your life is going to change.'

He put his arm around her. 'We will always be friends.'

With a last, lingering look at the classical, golden house, they walked away together.

During the excitement surrounding Dior's negotiations with Marcel Boussac, other things had been happening in the old house covered in vines. To be more accurate, certain familiar things had stopped happening, while other, newer things had been observed. To get an authoritative opinion on these phenomena, Copper and Henry paid a visit to the family doctor. He made an examination of Copper while Henry waited rather anxiously on the other side of the screen.

'Congratulations, Madame la Comtesse,' he said, shaking Copper's hand once she was decently dressed again. 'You are expecting a baby.

You are in excellent health, I am glad to report. However, I should like to see you each month from now, so that we can monitor your progress.'

Henry appeared dazed by the news. Copper had been certain in her own heart that she was expecting, but had wanted it confirmed. However, Henry was so silent on the drive home that Copper began to fear he was not pleased by the news. She stopped talking about nurseries and cots and fell into a silence as profound as his.

But once they were in their home, with their door closed, he took her in his arms and covered her face with kisses. 'My darling,' he said, with tears in his eyes. 'Once again you have made me the happiest man in the world.'

'Thank goodness,' she sighed. 'I thought you were upset.'

'I was overcome by emotion. I never dared hope that I would be a father.'

'You have to admit that you've been doing everything in your power to become one,' she replied gravely.

He burst out laughing. 'And you have played your part, my beloved.'

'Of course. I've wanted nothing more than to have our first child. I'm not as young as I was, you know. I'll be twenty-eight by the time our baby comes.'

'The most perfect of ages. God has truly blessed us.'

In that same week, the news came that Henry was to be awarded the *Legion d'honneur* for his services to France. The honour would be conferred on him by the provisional president, Charles de Gaulle – and by a happy coincidence, others to be decorated on the same day included Catherine Dior and Hervé des Charbonneries. There was to be a reunion of friends and relatives.

The ceremony took place at the Élysée Palace. Christian Dior was one of the guests, with his father and his brother Raymond. General de

Gaulle, an enormously tall figure in full uniform, towered over the occasion. He had aged visibly over the past two years of political struggle. His short speech expressed the hope that France was entering a period of stability and progress in the Fourth Republic. After he had pinned the medals on to the lapels of the awardees, there was a pleasant surprise: Copper was presented with a box of exquisite silk scarves from eight of the most famous Paris fashion houses.

Drinking champagne in the gilded splendour of the president's salon after the ceremony, they caught up with each other's news. Copper was delighted to see Catherine again, her skin summer-tanned. She was now an official *mandataire en fleurs coupées*, sending bouquets of freshly cut French flowers all over the world. 'The authorities gave us the work as a reward for our war service,' she told Copper. 'They asked us what we would like to do, and that was my choice. We have to start work every morning at four a.m. to get our blooms to the market of Les Halles, but what better career than to be surrounded by flowers?'

'So you have followed your mother, after all,' Copper said.

'You are right. I think of her every day.' She studied Copper, her expression changing subtly. 'Forgive me for asking – are you expecting a baby?'

Copper laid her hand instinctively over her womb. 'I didn't think it showed yet.'

'It doesn't. Not there, anyway. It's in your eyes.'

'You're very perceptive, Catherine.'

'You and I are friends,' Catherine replied. 'And we understand one another well. There's a special light about you, Copper. You're luminous. You must be very happy.'

'I am happier than I deserve to be.'

'So I am right?'

'Yes, you're right.'

'Congratulations, my dear.' She kissed Copper on both cheeks. But as she drew back, her expression was wistful, her eyes sad. 'You are lucky. I wonder if you know how lucky you are.'

'Oh, Catherine. What's to stop you having a child?'

'Hervé has three children already. He doesn't want any more, especially not illegitimate ones. And after what I saw at Ravensbrück, I don't think I would make a good mother, anyway. It changes one's perspective.'

Copper touched the little enamel cross on Catherine's lapel. 'We're so proud of you; of how you endured.'

Catherine grimaced. 'It's a fine thing to be a *chevalière de la Legion d'honneur*, isn't it? They're arresting the people who betrayed me and tortured me, and killed my friends. There'll be a court case, and those men will all appear with their lawyers, defending themselves, explaining that they were only following orders; doing the best thing for France. I'll be interrogated all over again, asked to justify my evidence, humiliated and made to look dishonest. I'm not looking forward to *that*, I can tell you.'

'That's so unfair,' Copper exclaimed.

Catherine shrugged. 'We have to play by the rules, even if they didn't.'

There was a gala dinner that evening attended by the American and British ambassadors. It was a glittering occasion: the men in white tie wearing all their decorations, and the women dressed by the great designers – Rochas, Schiaparelli, Balmain. Copper herself was in a spectacular crimson gown designed and made for her by Dior, which attracted a great number of compliments. She in her turn was bursting with pride over her husband, who looked so magnificent in his black tailcoat, wearing the *Legion d'honneur* and all his other decorations.

At dinner, Copper was seated next to Gertrude McCarthy Caffery, the American ambassador's wife. A woman in her fifties, she was soberly, rather than fashionably, dressed; but she had caught the rumours that Marcel Boussac was about to invest in an unknown fashion designer, and questioned Copper with skilled diplomacy.

'Is he as good as Molyneux, Rochas and the rest?' she enquired. 'He seems such a shy little man.'

Copper looked across the scintillating banquet table to where Dior was sitting, pink-faced and beaming. 'He doesn't just copy what the others are doing. He starts with something fresh and new every time. And the result is different from anyone else's work.'

The ambassador's wife examined Copper's gown carefully. 'I take it this is an example of his work?'

'Yes.'

'It's certainly highly original. And if I can say so, it's perfectly suited to you.' Gertrude Caffery put her glasses on and looked meaningfully at Copper's midriff. 'After so many years of sacrifice and horror, isn't it wonderful to have *all sorts of things* to celebrate?'

Copper blushed. The intelligence service at the American embassy was obviously immaculate.

Seventeen

In a few months, the austere calm of 30 avenue Montaigne had given way to something very different.

Workmen jostled one another through the doorway, carrying pipes, ladders, boards, bags of tools, buckets of paint, coils of electrical cable, sacks of plaster and planks of wood. As Copper tried to get into the building, she was brought up short by four men carrying a huge crystal chandelier bundled into a white sheet. She had to back away, clutching her bump. She followed their progress into the house and up the sweeping staircase. With shouts and grunts, the heavy thing was manoeuvred around the curve, under the great window, and up to the *bel étage*, where the salon was being set up.

Dior was staring anxiously up at the high ceiling. He was wearing a white coat and a worried expression.

'What if the ceiling's not strong enough?' he greeted Copper, who was herself puffing somewhat after the climb.

'It'll make a magnificent crash if it comes down.'

'That's not funny.'

'They know what they're doing, Tian. You don't need to worry about things like that.'

'I worry about everything,' he said gloomily. 'Especially *you*. When is this baby of yours coming?'

'A few more weeks.'

'Well, I wish it would hurry up,' he said, pulling up a chair for her. 'You're fraying my nerves terribly. I've had to advertise for mannequins. I don't have nearly enough. We're having a parade tomorrow to choose. Will you come and help?'

'Of course.'

A towering stepladder was brought in and set up. Dior had already gathered an impressive workforce around himself. He'd shown especial kindness to those who'd lost their places during the war and who were currently unemployed. Many of his *vendeuses* had come from this group. They were all distinguished by their loyalty to him and their belief in his genius.

The chandelier was hoisted into place and with the ladder creaking and swaying, was attached on to its hook. The men gingerly let it hang free. Dior grabbed Copper's hand, but contrary to his fears, the ceiling did not come down. One of the men began fitting the lightbulbs into their sockets while another, clinging to his mate's waist, attached the crystal drops. Finally, the last parchment shade was in place and the last glass ball – a copy of Madame Delahaye's crystal gazing ball – had been fitted on the very bottom. The electrician switched it on. The winter gloom fled. Golden light poured from the chandelier, eliciting admiring *oohs* and *aahs*. Applause broke out.

'Before they take the ladder away, can I get some photos?' she asked Dior.

'Of the ladder?'

'Of you, with one foot on the first rung, looking up.'

Dior, always sensitive to symbolism, was delighted. 'Excellent.' Normally shy about being photographed, he posed happily for her, while she clicked off several shots with the Leica. The golden light of the chandelier shone down auspiciously on his upturned face.

The grimy streets of Montmartre were grudgingly taking on a Christmas sparkle. Fairy lights glimmered in the windows of dilapidated apartments; mistletoe wreaths were being sold on the street corners. Legless war veterans sold roasted chestnuts and sweet potatoes. Braving the dirty snow, a brass band played in the place Pigalle. A small crowd listened dourly, shuffling to keep warm, tossing a few centimes into the bandleader's hat between numbers.

Close by, in a wine bar, Copper found Pearl already waiting in a dark corner.

'Hullo, Copper Pot. Bloody hell, you're *huge*,' Pearl greeted her. 'Just how many have you got in there?'

'Only the one, according to the doctor,' Copper assured her. They kissed. Pearl had already ordered – and started on – a bottle of wine. She poured a slug for Copper and they clinked glasses. 'How are you, darling?'

'Never better.'

Copper peered at Pearl. In the gloom of the crowded little bar, she could make out that Pearl was pasty-looking with dark smudges around her eyes. 'Has Petrus been beating you up again?' she demanded.

Pearl drained her glass and poured another. 'Petrus won't be beating anyone up anymore.'

'Is he dead?'

'Next best thing. He's been sent back to Africa.'

'Oh, Pearl.'

'The police picked him up. He didn't have any papers, not proper ones. He's been here illegally for years. They deported him. He'll never be back.'

'I can't say I'm sorry for him,' Copper commented. 'But I know it must be hard for you. What are you going to do?'

'I've taken over the business,' Pearl said succinctly.

'What business?'

'You know. The girls. The postcards. Everything.'

'You're kidding.'

'Funny, isn't it? I'm doing just fine. Got a stable of my own now.'

'A stable?'

'Stupid tarts, like I used to be. They think it's fun. I don't disillusion them.'

'Where do they come from?'

'London East Enders like me, most of them. Longing for the bright lights and the high life. They haven't had a bar of chocolate or a glass of champagne in their lives. I bring them over on the ferry. Juicy and fresh, and they don't speak a word of French.'

Copper exclaimed in dismay, 'Darling, how can you do that to other women?'

'Easy. I know the ropes, don't I?' The door of the bar swung open, letting in a shaft of wintry light. It illuminated Pearl for a moment, showing Copper that Pearl's face, once so pretty, had taken on a tough, hard look. The pasty sheen came from heavy make-up. But her clothes were showy and smart, and there were flashy rings on her fingers. The door slammed shut again, and the vision retreated into shadow. 'They're suckers. Why should I feel sorry for them?'

'Because they're innocent, the way you were.'

'Nobody's innocent,' Pearl retorted. 'They're here for a good time, and I make sure they get it.'

'But that's cruel. You know what's going to happen to them.'

'They could end up like me, running their own business, if they've got the brains.'

'Or end up dead in the gutter.'

'Can't you be happy for me? At least I'm off the cocaine.'

'Really?' Copper asked sceptically.

'Well, at least I can afford my own stuff now. I don't have to go on my knees to Petrus anymore.'

'No, you get other women to do that for you.'

'Don't lecture me, Copper. You live your life and I'll live mine, okay?'

'Okay,' Copper said sadly.

'So tell me, how's your Monsieur Dior?'

'Spending money like water. Crystal chandeliers, mirrors ten feet high. It's a palace.'

'Is he going to sell some frocks after all that?'

'He's astonishingly extravagant. I get quite frightened sometimes. He was always so frugal, but now nothing's too much.'

'Having someone else's six million francs in your pocket will do that,' Pearl commented dryly. 'I hope Boussac keeps signing the cheques.'

'I have faith in Tian, of course. But when I say he's extravagant, I don't just mean what he's doing at avenue Montaigne. I mean the clothes he's designing. Some of the designs use twenty or thirty yards of silk. They have to have hundreds of pleats, just to make them wearable. It's wonderfully romantic – but who's going to pay those prices? And with everything still rationed!'

Pearl shook her head. 'You can keep a bunny in a cage, but when you let it out, it'll hop, hop, hop. Maybe that's why Lelong kept him locked up all those years. How's married life with Henry?'

'He's an angel. I couldn't be happier.'

'Does that mean you're not bored yet?'

'I'm married, not dead.'

'Hold on to him.' Pearl's eyes gleamed in the dark for a moment. 'He's a handy fellow to have around.'

'I intend to.'

Pearl dug in her handbag and started applying lipstick heavily to her mouth. 'Can't sit here all day chatting,' she said, snapping her bag shut. 'Much as I'd love to. I've got a business to run. Ta-ra, Copper Pot.'

They parted in the cold square. Copper watched Pearl walk away. She had the confident swagger of a woman of means. She'd landed on her feet, Copper supposed, but not in the way Copper had expected.

She began to feel really tired and sore on the walk home. She reached the house to be faced by an agitated Henry.

'I've been worried sick about you,' he exclaimed, helping her off with her coat. 'Walking around the streets in this weather – and in your condition.'

'Perhaps I did overdo it on this occasion,' she sighed, allowing herself to be propelled to the sofa in front of the fire. 'I'm a bit tired. Would you rub my back, darling?'

He obeyed solicitously, firm hands gently soothing away the aches. 'Where have you been?'

'I went to see Pearl in place Pigalle. You'll never guess – Petrus has been deported and she's taken over the business.'

For a moment, his hands paused. 'Really?'

'She's covered in diamonds. Mistress of her own destiny. Did you ever?'

'Life is full of surprises,' he said, resuming the massage.

Something in his voice made her suspicious. 'You're not surprised at all.' She turned to face him. 'You knew!'

'Well, one keeps one's ear to the ground,' he said blandly.

'Why didn't you tell me?'

He raised his exotic eyebrows. 'I would have done, by and by. When I heard the end of the story. But you've just told me it.'

'The end of the story?' she repeated. 'Wait a moment. Did you have something to do with all this?'

'I may have dropped a word here or there,' he replied smoothly.

'Henry!'

'You said yourself he was Pearl's *bête noir*.'

'So you played St George.'

'Pearl came to me for help,' he said, spreading his hands. 'Petrus was becoming more and more violent. There's a psychosis that comes from cocaine abuse. She was afraid he would kill her. I still have friends in certain places. I made sure he was – ah – removed from the picture.'

'You're so devious,' she said, not sure whether she was amused or appalled.

'Not at all. I'm as straight as a die.' He took the gold cufflinks out of the cuffs of his silk shirt and rolled up his sleeves to expose strong brown forearms. 'Now turn around, so I can continue to rub your delicious back.'

'My God,' she said, turning around again. 'I'm married to an ogre.'

'Kind of you to say so. And what is happening in the avenue Montaigne?'

She allowed him to dodge the subject. 'You can't imagine the commotion. I don't think Monsieur Boussac's six million francs are going to last long. Tian certainly knows how to spend money.'

'Do you think it's all a terrible mistake?'

'Time will tell. Oh gee,' she exclaimed, 'he recognises your touch.' She guided Henry's hand on to her belly so he could feel the vigorous kicking that was going on within. She loved the expression that came over her husband's face at these moments. 'Feel that?'

'Yes,' Henry murmured. 'Our little ogre baby.'

'Do you think he has fangs and claws, like his father?'

'I hope so.'

She winced. 'Ouch. I can feel them. I think he's starting to feel cramped in there.'

'That does it. You're not leaving the house again.'

'I can't stay cooped up,' Copper said, laughing. 'It might be weeks longer.'

'I ought to lock you up and keep the key in my vest pocket,' he said sternly.

'My beautiful Bluebeard,' Copper smiled, nestling into his arms. 'You would never be so cruel.'

'Don't count on it. What if you went into labour in the street?'

'So long as it was a smart street with lots of nice clothes shops, I wouldn't mind at all.'

'You're impossible,' he said, kissing her tenderly.

'But I have to be with Tian tomorrow. He wants me to help him choose the mannequins for the fashion parade.'

'That's all very well, but what if you slip in the snow? What if you catch cold?'

'No more scolding.'

'As if I could ever scold you,' he sighed. He cradled her in his arms and looked down adoringly into her face. 'I know you're the chronicler of the age, but the age is a slippery one. I won't have you trudging through the snow like Orphan Annie any longer. Please promise me you won't go anywhere without the car from now on.'

'All right,' she said, kissing his lips. 'That's a deal.'

It seemed that there had been a good response to Dior's advertisement for models. Several dozen women had already arrived and were queuing on the pavement outside number 30. Copper slipped past them and went to find Dior.

She was ushered carefully to the largest chair and given a notebook and a pencil to write down her observations. A runway had been cleared for the candidates to walk along.

The first hopeful was called in. '*Numéro un! Entrez, s'il vous plaît.*'

The woman entered the salon, swinging a parasol insouciantly. She was heavily made-up – much too heavily for daytime. As she made her circuit, she stared boldly at her audience. One of Dior's entourage clicked her tongue disapprovingly. For a model to make eye contact with the viewers was anathema; a haughty indifference was the correct form. Copper wrote down a single word – 'unsuitable'.

'That will do, Mademoiselle,' Dior called. 'Next!'

The next was extremely buxom. That alone would have disqualified her, let alone her flaming red hair and rouged face; but in addition to that, she walked with a provocative, hip-rolling gait that was all too familiar from the pavements of Paris. There were whispers of dismay.

The third was of the same type; a handsome, confident woman, though not in the first flush of youth, who tossed her hair and sashayed with one hand on her hip.

'My God,' someone said when she'd left. 'They're prostitutes. What on earth are they doing here?'

'They can't all be prostitutes,' Dior said. 'Let's see the next one.'

But the next was clearly in the same category. Dior threw up his hands and called a halt to proceedings. 'We need an explanation for this.'

One of the *vendeuses* was sent to get the explanation. She returned, appalled. 'The police have closed down all the brothels. The ladies are out of business, and they saw Monsieur Dior's advertisement, so . . .'

One of the hopefuls was brought in to corroborate the story. She told them proudly that she was from Le Chabanais, the most famous and luxurious brothel in Paris, once patronised by Edward VII and Henri de Toulouse-Lautrec.

'The hypocritical bastards have shut us down because we screwed the Germans. As if they weren't in the same queue.'

'We have to cancel this charade at once,' someone said.

'We can't,' Dior replied. 'These people are without work. And they've all come in response to my advertisement. We have to be courteous, at least. We'll see them.'

'All of them?'

'Yes, all of them.'

'But, Monsieur Dior—'

'Proceed, please.'

The pageant went on. Dior was courtesy itself, though the faces of the women in his entourage were stiff with affront. He had a kind word for all the applicants, but the task appeared hopeless. Every prostitute in Paris seemed to have read the unfortunately timed advertisement. More kept arriving at the sober portals of 30 avenue Montaigne. Copper, behind the sofa, took several photographs, trying to capture the contrast between the opulent surroundings and the raw vitality of the streetwalkers. Some of them were very pretty indeed, but none were remotely suitable for Dior's purposes – except for a single 'respectable' applicant, a shy young secretary called Marie-Thérèse, whose name was taken, and who was asked to come back at a more opportune time.

'I'll never advertise for models again,' Dior said wearily after a long morning with the streetwalkers of the city. 'What a debacle.'

But Copper had been fascinated by this absurd intersection between two of Paris's strata: one public and the other hidden. Her journalistic antennae were twitching. There was an article to be written here, possibly a daring and interesting article. She hurried out to interview some of the disappointed prostitutes before they dispersed back into the streets of Paris.

Anticipating an imminent confinement, Copper decided to gather some reading material. She'd been working hard, and the idea of leafing through an amusing book, plumped up with pillows, was very attractive.

Her waters broke while she was halfway through this errand in Shakespeare and Company. There was a hot gush and she found herself with drenched stockings and buckle shoes, holding a copy of *Lady*

Chatterley's Lover (which was currently banned everywhere except in France) standing at the centre of a spreading puddle of amniotic fluid.

'May I help you, Madame?' a male assistant enquired discreetly.

'Oh, dear. I'm terribly sorry. I seem to have—'

'Not at all, Madame. Allow me.'

The charming young man rescued her from behind the polished wooden shelves, mopped up, called her husband and got her into her car. The embarrassment soon gave way to alarm. She was going into labour. These birth pangs were nothing like the twinges she'd had hitherto. They were terrifying. She clutched her swollen self, feeling the muscles of her womb contracting in a businesslike way. Her chauffeur hunched over his wheel, driving as fast as he dared through the morning traffic. She prayed she wasn't going to give birth on the gleaming leather seat. The contractions were coming at regular intervals, and they were getting perceptibly stronger.

Henry was waiting for her at the hospital. She was by now sweating and frightened. 'Wonderful, wonderful,' he said, holding her hand as they wheeled her along the corridors. 'The great day has arrived.'

'Nobody told me it was going to be like this.'

'Don't worry, you're in the best hands.'

Copper clambered on to the bed as instructed. Her body had grown so unwieldy in these last weeks, her breasts and belly getting in the way of everything she tried to do. 'Where's the midwife?'

'She's on her way,' Henry assured her, heading for the door. 'I called her as soon as the bookshop called me. Oh, and they say you owe them thirty francs for the book.' She was still clutching *Lady Chatterley's Lover*.

The nurses got her ready. Her contractions were now coming fewer than five minutes apart and were lasting an agonising minute each, by the large watch pinned on to the matron's uniform. Every time her womb clenched, she curled up, clutching herself. Each time, the nurses pushed her back down on to the pillows.

Hazily, she was aware of Henry coming back into the room, accompanied by the obstetrician who was wearing his gloves and surgical apron, and Angelique, the midwife. They all were remarkably calm given the dire state she was in; they did not seem to appreciate just how awful this was becoming. The obstetrician examined her. 'Dilating nicely,' he said.

'Henry, I'm scared,' she gasped, clutching at his hand.

'There's nothing to worry about,' he said. He, who had been so solicitous, so anxious about her safety during the pregnancy, was now as cool as a cucumber. 'Just concentrate on what Angelique tells you to do, my beloved.'

Copper cried out as her womb convulsed. 'I want gas and air!'

'They say you don't need it yet.'

'How would they know? It's me having the goddamned baby!'

None of this was as she had expected. Nobody had told her it was going to be like this – frightening. She didn't want to be screaming in front of everyone. But the process was starting to take her over. All self-consciousness was fading away. She just had to get through this, as all mothers did. Panting and pushing as instructed by Angelique, she clung to the iron rails of the bed and heaved at this being inside her who was so determined to get its very large self out of her very small door. It didn't feel possible that she could give birth without some major and irreparable injury to her insides. And all around her was a general air of business in the room: people chatting to each other, going in and out, generally behaving like the spectators at a prize fight.

Things got better for a while, as the obdurate thing seemed to settle down for a rest; and then they got far worse again when it woke up refreshed. At last, by dint of screaming the worst words she knew at her husband, she succeeded in getting the gas-and-air machine. It was wheeled in and set up beside her. She grabbed the mask in both hands and sucked the mixture into her lungs. A woozy, floaty feeling flooded her. The contractions were still there, but she found she didn't care about them so much. The more she breathed the mixture, the further away she floated. But the mask was taken away from her, and awful reality came rushing back. She raged at them, but nobody seemed to understand.

She lost track of the passing of time. The afternoon seemed to be getting on. How long had she been in this condition? An hour? Six hours? She registered that Pearl was now in the room.

'Pearl,' she begged. 'Tell them – to give me – back – the gas.'

'They say they will in a minute, Copper Pot.'

'I haven't got – a minute. I need it – now!'

'You're nearly there. They say they can see the baby's head.'

It was the moment of truth. All her work and suffering had led up to this. With a last huge effort, she pushed the baby into life. Then she heard the unmistakable cry. Her eyes flew open. She pushed herself up on her elbows to see. Henry was holding out a little creature wrapped in a shawl. Its face had a troubled, crumpled look, as though it had found the past hours as wearisome as Copper herself had done. But those weary hours were as nothing now. A huge surge of joy filled her. The weight of labour rolled away like a stone. She reached out for her baby, tears of happiness sliding down her cheeks.

'It's a boy,' Henry said, sitting beside her and stroking her sweaty hair. 'All fingers and toes accounted for. Perfect in every respect.'

Copper stared down at the furrowed little face. The bleary eyes blinked up at her. The small mouth opened as if to cry again, but ended up giving an outsize yawn, showing pink gums. 'Henry, he's so beautiful,' she whispered to her husband, unable to take her eyes off her baby.

'Yes, he is. Well done, my beloved.' He was wiping his own eyes surreptitiously.

Pearl sat on the other side of her, inspecting the baby. 'Nice going, kid. All over now. They say the first one is always the worst.'

The room was bustling with staff, wheeling away machines and clearing up. There was even a young nurse starting to change the wet sheets from beneath her. None of it mattered. None of it touched her. Nothing could come through the walls of the golden Fabergé egg into which she was locked with her baby and her husband.

Copper drifted out of sleep and into a great happiness and a great peace. She opened her eyes. Christian Dior was at her bedside.

'Tian! Have you seen the baby?'

He stooped to kiss her brow. 'Yes, *ma petite*. He's exquisite.'

She passed him the tiny baby to hold. He was sleeping. Dior kissed the child tenderly. 'He's a masterpiece. They told me it was a difficult birth.'

'I don't remember much about it. Thank you for coming, Tian. I know how busy you are.'

'I've brought you something.' He handed her a parcel done up in gold paper with a satin bow. Inside was a delicate lace christening shawl. 'I was baptised in that. It's for your little boy.'

'Oh, Tian. It's so beautiful.' She held it up to the light. The delicate Chantilly lace was embroidered with rosebuds. 'I can't take this – it's a family heirloom.'

'I will never have a child of my own to pass it on to. It makes me happy to think that it's yours now.'

'I'm so touched.'

'My dear,' he said, stroking her brow. 'The nurses can hardly get down the corridor for the bouquets. Shall we distribute them to some of the other mothers?'

The next time she woke, it was late at night. The room was dark except for a pool of light where Pearl was sitting in a corner, reading a book.

'Pearl?'

'You're awake at last.' Pearl came to her bedside. 'How do you feel?'

'Tired but happy.'

Pearl took a silver hip flask out of her purse. 'Have some cognac.'

'No, thank you. I'm so happy you're here. Where's the baby?'

Pearl swigged from the flask. 'They'll bring him shortly. He's been asleep, just like you. He's gorgeous. What are you going to call him?'

'We're thinking of Pierre Henri.'

'Couldn't be better.'

The door opened and a young nurse in a starched white uniform appeared, wheeling in a cot. It contained a very wide-awake baby who was already starting to lose his crumpled look. There was nothing like this flooding, warm joy that filled Copper when she saw him. It was the purest emotion she had ever felt. The nurse put the baby in her arms. 'I think he's hungry.'

Copper opened her gown to reveal one of her swollen breasts, which had started to respond at the first sight of her baby. She put her large, brown nipple in his mouth. After a moment's hesitation, he latched on eagerly and began to suck. She winced.

Pearl was watching with a curious expression on her painted face. 'What does it feel like?'

'Heavenly. I don't know how to explain it.'

'Well, I'll never know, will I?' she said dryly. 'I'll leave you to it.'

'Don't go,' Copper said as Pearl rose to her feet.

'I don't belong here,' she replied, straightening her dress with fingers that sparkled with diamonds.

'Yes, you do.'

Pearl shook her head. 'I'm not a fit person to be around babies. I spend most of my time getting rid of them.' She gave Copper a bittersweet smile. 'Speaking of which, I have to go and look after my girls. Ta-ra, Copper Pot.'

Henry arrived a few minutes later and sat on the bed to watch, his dark eyes gleaming. 'The entire corridor is full of flowers. It looks like a jungle by Rousseau. Every couturier in Paris has sent a bouquet!'

The days after Pierre Henri's birth passed in an ever-faster whirl. Far from reclining on pillows and reading an amusing book, Copper had never been so busy in her life. Dior's call was followed by visits from Balenciaga and Pierre Balmain, and then by several others. Within two or three days, almost every couturier in Paris had called on her, or sent flowers or gifts. She was deeply touched. She hadn't realised how connected she was to this strange world she had decided to enter.

An even more welcome visit came from her family – or part of it. Her brother Mike and her sister Rosie flew from America for the christening. They were her favourite siblings. She hadn't seen either of them for three years, and it was a reunion that lasted over Christmas and New Year.

She was back at her typewriter early in 1947, much to the horror and dismay of many people who urged her to consider her baby and herself.

'I don't think it's going to hurt my baby if I keep writing articles,' she replied. 'And it certainly won't hurt me.'

What was harder, however, was going out and leaving baby Pierre in the care of a nurse. The first time she tried it, she rushed back home again after twenty minutes in a complete panic. But in the same way that she wanted a marriage *and* a profession, she was determined that motherhood would not be the end of her career. She did not see why she should not structure her working life around being a wife and mother. After all, she was not tied to locations or schedules; she did not work in an office or a factory. She disciplined herself to make trips out of the house and resumed her work as much as possible.

Her first port of call was avenue Montaigne.

Eighteen

She was admitted by a doorman and entered a world of organised chaos. Workmen were still everywhere, hammering and painting. Dior himself was not hard to find; he was sitting on a step halfway up the staircase, rivers of silk tumbling around him like a multicoloured waterfall, cursing volubly.

'Tian,' she called, 'what on earth are you doing?'

'This place is too damned small!' he shouted back. 'I'm going to have to build another wing. I need another three floors, at least.'

Copper climbed up to him, carefully avoiding the tumbling bolts of fabric. 'Will Boussac's six million stretch to that?'

'Six million?' He stared, hollow-eyed. 'The six million was spent long ago. We are nearly at the end of the second six million.'

Copper was shocked. Money had flowed through Dior's hands like water. This was a huge gamble, even for France's richest man. She went up the stairs to the *bel étage*, which was still unfinished. A dozen workmen were on their hands and knees, blue-serge bottoms upraised as they laid a pale-grey carpet. She carried on up.

The third floor was a war zone of rattling sewing machines and elbowing seamstresses. The heat up there was intense, the air heavy with the smell of twenty girls who were working (as one of the *premières* complained to Copper) eighteen hours a day, and didn't even have time to eat, let alone wash.

This was something few followers of fashion ever saw – the long hours of hard, highly skilled labour that went into the production of each item of haute couture. Beauty came at the cost of tired eyes, aching shoulders and worn fingers.

'Our manager has had a nervous breakdown,' one of the girls told Copper. 'The pressure drove her out of her wits.'

The others chimed in with a chorus of grievances.

'Monsieur Dior used to be so gentle.'

'Not anymore!'

'Nobody can keep up with his demands. He flies into a rage at the slightest thing.'

The *premières* were all agreed. Christian Dior, turned from shy little man into Napoleonic tyrant, was giving his troops orders they sometimes barely understood because he was resurrecting long-forgotten techniques of dressmaking not seen since the eighteenth century, and demanding levels of perfection that exceeded anything known in this modern era.

Copper made her way back down, jostled by workmen, *premières* and models. Dior's office had been planned originally as a commodious space where he could work on a large Empire desk. This room had long since been invaded by the cutters, who had pushed the desk into a corner to make room for the long table where they pieced out the patterns with battle-scarred scissors. Dior himself had taken up his quarters in a tiny, windowless closet known as 'the cubbyhole'. There was barely room for the piles of sketches he was feverishly producing, drawing and redrawing designs dozens of times, sometimes only to discard the entire project. She found him here in the darkness, wrestling to replace the bulb that had gone out in his desk lamp. '*Merde.* There's something wrong with this lamp.'

'Let me try.' She took over the job, and he collapsed back in his chair, panting.

'Too many hopes are being pinned on me, *ma petite*. How can I possibly live up to their expectations?'

'You'll exceed them,' she assured him. 'Believe in yourself.'

He clasped his forehead. 'If I'd known what this would turn into, I would never have begun it.'

'The girls say you've become a tyrant,' she said. The new bulb clicked into life, and light flooded his desk. 'They say you're driving them to despair.'

Not deigning to answer, he grabbed a sheaf of drawings and began shuffling through them. 'Where is "Bourbon"? Someone has been confusing all my designs!'

She helped him locate the drawings he was looking for and then followed him into the next room. In here stood a patient group of tailor's dummies, armless wooden figures known as Stockman mannequins, upon which the garments were tacked before they were finally sewn up. Dior shooed one of the *premières* away and examined the dress with a critical eye. It was in the toile stage, made of a white linen for testing the pattern. 'This is "Bourbon", but it's all wrong,' he groaned. 'It should be much fuller in the hips. You've ruined it!'

'They cut it exactly as you designed it, Monsieur Dior.'

'Don't contradict me! It's an abomination. I want volume.'

'But Monsieur Dior,' the seamstress ventured timidly, 'the mannequin's proportions will not allow—'

'Allow? *Allow?* Dior's normally pink complexion had grown dangerously red. 'Who tells me what I am *allowed* to do?'

'Nobody, Monsieur,' the girl whispered.

'Get it off,' Dior commanded in a terrible voice.

'Y-yes, Monsieur.'

With shaking hands, the *première* unpinned the toile, revealing the naked wooden torso of the dummy. Dior glared at it for a moment. 'Here is the error. The proportions are completely wrong.' The Stockmans were all adjustable. Dior set to work, wrestling with the system of screws and levers that altered the vital statistics. But this particular dummy was old and stiff, and was not responding to the master's ministrations. Dior's colour grew even darker. He reached into the tool box and pulled out a large wooden mallet. All work ceased and a shocked silence fell over the crowded room as Dior pounded the dummy furiously, knocking the plates in here, knocking them out there. Unnoticed, Copper photographed the extraordinary performance.

Finally, panting, Dior threw the hammer down and studied the dummy with a critical eye. 'There,' he said triumphantly. '*That* is the perfect woman.' He turned to the *première*, who was still clutching the toile to her breast, wide-eyed. '*Now* you may proceed.'

He bustled off, leaving everyone staring at the altered Stockman, with its wasp-waist, expansive hips and deep bust.

'*Mon Dieu*,' someone muttered. 'He's gone mad.'

'No woman ever looked like that.'

'We're going to have to put the girls back in corsets.'

'That won't be enough,' someone else pointed out. 'They'll need padding top and bottom as well.'

Copper watched these experts at their trade, the finest in Paris, as they struggled to solve the conundrum their master had posed them. Dior had taken a hammer and literally knocked womanhood into the hourglass shape that pleased him.

Copper followed Dior back to his cubbyhole. 'How many outfits are you going to present?' she asked him.

'A hundred.'

She was appalled. No wonder there was such a tumult in Maison Dior. 'That's a huge amount for a first collection,' she ventured. Jacques Fath had launched his collection the year before with twenty garments.

'A hundred,' he repeated firmly. 'I cannot achieve my vision with less. I have to make an impact.' She was alarmed to see that he looked slightly wild. 'With a dozen dresses, two dozen dresses, nobody will get the point. They'll say, "It's just Christian and his manias." But with a hundred outfits, people's eyes will open wide. Nobody will be able to ignore a hundred outfits.'

'But the expense—'

'Boussac will have to give me more money,' he said flatly. 'And I will need the fabrics, the accessories, the shoes.'

Her heart sank. 'But – how will you get buyers for so many models?'

He stared at her as though she were mad. 'They'll be queuing all the way down avenue Montaigne. They'll be on their knees, begging for my outfits.' He spread his arms wide. 'This will be the age of Dior, *ma petite.*'

Ten minutes ago, he had been wondering how he could possibly live up to everyone's expectations, and regretting that he had ever begun this. Now he was declaring the age of Dior. He seemed to veer from crippling self-doubt to megalomania, and back again.

Copper had now to prepare for the imminent arrival of Carmel Snow. The editor-in-chief of *Harper's Bazaar*, and the woman who had published many of her stories over the past two years, was coming to France for her first tour since the start of the war in 1939. In fashion terms, it was as important as any state visit. Her report on the new collections of 1947 would be eagerly read from coast to coast. Her approval or disapproval could make or break a designer.

She had made it clear that she expected to do and see as much as possible in the ten days that were all she could spare from running *Harper's.*

On the eve of Mrs Snow's arrival, Copper received a telephone call from Sister Gibson at the Marie-Thérèse Sanatorium. It was about Amory.

'I thought you would want to know that Mr Heathcote made a good recovery. I think your visit was really the turning point.'

'I'm glad to hear it. Is he still in Paris?'

'He sailed back to New York on the SS *America*. He will be joining the family banking firm on his arrival.'

'That sounds like a good decision.'

'He said he was following your advice.'

'Yes, I suppose I did advise him to do that.'

'There was one thing I wanted to bring up. The injury he sustained. The surgeons fitted a steel plate over the hole in the skull, but of course the hair does not grow there any longer. There will always be a visible scar. And despite your suggestion,' Sister Gibson added dryly, 'he will not be able to wear a hat indoors.'

So Amory had relayed that little comment, too. 'What are you getting at, Sister?'

'We all agreed that it would be wise for Mr Heathcote to gloss over the cause of the injury.'

'Gloss over?'

'There are so many young men returning from Europe with wounds sustained in the war. In the light of his future dealings with clients of the firm, and to ease the progress of his career, we believe it's best if Mr Heathcote lets out that the wound was caused by shrapnel, rather than self-inflicted.'

'A war wound?'

'Exactly. As Mr Heathcote's ex-wife, we wanted to be sure that you would—'

'Back up the lie?' Copper asked, as Sister Gibson hesitated.

'Support him in his new career.'

'He could have asked me this himself.'

'He thought it might be better coming from a neutral party. He should not have to bear the burden of a moment's folly for the rest of his life.'

'Don't worry,' Copper said dryly. 'I won't spill the beans. If he wants to play the war hero, I have no intention of spoiling the illusion.'

'Thank you. I will write to the family to confirm what you've told me. I'm sure they will be happy to hear it. I bid you a very good day, Mrs Velikovsky.'

'What was that all about?' Henry asked, as Copper replaced the receiver, laughing a little.

'Vanity and make-believe, my darling. Amory wants it given out that he was wounded in combat.'

'I suppose,' Henry said, rocking their baby in his arms, 'that in the larger sense of life's struggle, most of us are wounded in combat.'

'I hope he never is,' she said, putting her arms around them both and looking down at Pierre-Henri's sleepy face. 'I hope he'll be as lucky as I've been. There's been so much destruction and unhappiness around me – and my life has been a fairy tale.'

Carmel Snow was nothing like Copper's expectations. She turned out to be a small, spry sixty-year-old with a blue rinse and pearls. She had a narrow, lined, Irish face with an upturned nose, and there remained a trace of Dalkey brogue in her voice, despite having left Ireland long ago as a small child.

However, as Copper swiftly discovered, this was no sweet little old lady.

Carmel Snow was determined not to miss a second. She seemed not to need sleep at all, and was as lively at four a.m. as she was at noon. Nor did she appear to suffer from hunger or tiredness. Keeping up with her was a constant scramble. The only thing she demanded – and never missed – was lunch. And as Copper learned to her cost, lunch for Mrs Snow meant several large martinis.

'You know what I'm like with alcohol,' Copper sighed to Henry, rubbing her aching temples. 'One martini, and I'm fried to the eyeballs. At three, I'm comatose. You should have warned me.'

'Pour them into a potted plant when she's not looking,' Henry advised. 'That's what I do. I've known Carmel for twenty years and I've never been able to keep up with the three-martini lunch.'

Carmel had all the energy of a woman who had turned *Harper's Bazaar* from a dowdy periodical for the middle-aged into the most stimulating women's magazine of the era in just ten years. And she was determined to sign Copper up as a staff correspondent.

'Your story about the prostitutes was magnificent,' she told Copper.

'You read it?'

'It's funny yet it's hard-hitting. You're asking some fascinating questions. Whether the profession of offering sexual services is so distant from the profession of being fashionable; the profession of being a woman in a world which doesn't give us a fair break. That's groundbreaking journalism.'

'I'm glad you liked it.'

'It has one glaring fault.'

'What's that?'

'It was written for *Vogue*. I don't want you writing for *Vogue* any longer,' she declared briskly. She herself had started out working at *Vogue*, but had quit the magazine, leaving bad blood behind, which had never been forgotten on either side. 'I need a well-placed Paris staffer. I'll pay well.'

'I'm flattered that you want me, Mrs Snow,' Copper said cautiously. They were lunching together at Harry's Bar – a *croque monsieur* and a dewy pitcher of martinis – prior to visiting Balenciaga, one of Mrs Snow's favourite designers. 'But I value my freedom.'

'Oh, I know all about freedom. But there's more to life. There's being part of a movement. *Harper's* isn't just for well-dressed women, it's for women with well-dressed minds. And that's you, my dear. You've got something to say, and I want you to be saying it for *Harper's*, not for the opposition.'

'Let me think about it.'

'You can achieve far more as part of a team – the best team in the business – than as an individual.' She poured them the third martini of the lunch. Copper's head was already swimming, and there was no handy pot plant at Harry's to transfer it into. 'I want my readers to learn how to live, not just be fashionable. I want them to take chances. Do things they've never done before. Expand their horizons. You belong with us.' She nodded, her pale eyes as bright and cool as the icy cocktail. 'Now. Tell me about Christian Dior. I wouldn't be here if it wasn't for the fact that you've been raving about him. I saw a suit of his I liked before the war, when he was with Piguet in 1937, I think. But I don't believe that he's capable of designing a whole collection.'

'I think he's the most brilliant designer in Paris right now.'

'Better than Balenciaga?' Mrs Snow scoffed.

'Different. More spontaneous, more pizzazz.'

The word 'pizzazz', coined by Mrs Snow herself in an earlier issue of *Harper's*, got a smile. 'So what am I going to see on Wednesday?' Dior had somehow kept the tight blanket of secrecy intact over 30 avenue Montaigne, and very few outsiders had any idea of the designs that were being so feverishly assembled within.

'I can't give you any details. Tian would kill me.'

'What's the big secret?' Carmel, a neat little figure in an immaculately cut Balenciaga suit, crossed her bony legs with a swish of nylon stockings. 'Believe me, I've seen it all. Hemlines to the thigh? Necklines to the navel?'

'It's more than a question of hemlines or necklines.' Copper hesitated. 'It's a whole new look.'

Carmel carried her 'bag of scraps' everywhere with her: a folder of magazine clippings, fabric swatches and notes to herself. She uncapped her pen now and wrote: 'A whole new look. That's a big promise. I hope I'm not going to be disappointed.'

Nineteen

And, at last, the day of days had come – Wednesday, 12 February 1947. Copper arrived at avenue Montaigne just after dawn to find the place already seething. There was a crowd of curious spectators in the street outside the shop who had heard that something special was happening today, and who were hoping for a glimpse through the windows of the activity within. That the whole of Paris seemed to know about the Dior show was a tribute to word-of-mouth publicity, since the Paris newspapers had been on strike for over a month. Some of the crowd were clamouring for tickets from the doormen; but every seat had long since been sold, and without a ticket, nobody would be admitted.

Copper slipped inside. The flowery scent of the new perfume Tian had designed – to be called 'Miss Dior' after Catherine – hung in the air, as a girl with an atomiser scuttled up and down the stairs, squirting extravagantly. Dior had entrusted the great florists of rue Royale – Lachaume – with the floral arrangements. Their men were now bringing in huge bouquets of hothouse flowers and arranging them in sheaves wherever there was space. There wasn't much: little, hard, white chairs were being crowded together cheek by jowl, each one numbered. Pillar ashtrays had been laid out between them, an essential measure since everyone in the fashion industry chain-smoked. The last inch of space had been utilised. The walkway that the models would use had been reduced to a tight circuit with a space no more than a few feet in diameter in which to make

the turn. The dresses were going to be fluttering in the faces of the spectators. Compared to the quiet dignity of most Paris fashion shows, this was
already turning into a circus. As Dior had predicted, workmen were still
busy here and there, hammering in the last carpet tack and fitting the last
moulding in place. The whole place breathed excitement, money, glamour and – despite Dior's predilection for exclusivity – a certain vulgarity.

Dior himself, in a morning coat and with a lily of the valley in his
buttonhole, was pale with nerves. Copper found him in the fitting room
administering some final touches to the ninety-four outfits that were
hanging there: evening gowns, dresses and suits, in groups.

'I'm terrified,' he greeted Copper with something like despair.

'You don't need to be. It's going to be a huge success, Tian. They're
already gathering in the street, trying to look in the windows.'

He clapped his hands over his ears. 'Don't tell me. I don't want to
hear.' He clearly hadn't slept and his nerves were ragged.

Copper went over to the models, who were crowded into a corner of the *cabine*, two to a dressing table, putting the final touches to
their make-up. There were only six of them. It was a small number to
show such a large quantity of outfits. They would be working fast. But
Dior had been unable to find any more with the qualities of grace and
vivacity he had been searching for. Copper watched them craning their
long necks as they thickened eyelashes with mascara, outlined pouting
lips with lipstick and dusted their amazing cheekbones with rouge.
The hairdresser fluttered behind them, combs of various kinds stuffed
between her teeth, putting the final touches to their coiffures. All had
their hair in curls, piled on the top of their heads.

Having been used as no more than dummies over the past weeks,
patiently enduring the hours of fittings, they were now the most important members of the team. How the clothes were viewed would depend
on their charisma and exuberance. They had to show off – but not dominate – the qualities of each garment. They had to enchant the viewers, yet
remain neutral, so as not to distract from the outfits they were modelling.

The hands of the clock were sweeping inexorably around. A large queue of eager ticket holders had formed at the door, waiting impatiently. It was almost nine thirty, and the opening could no longer be delayed. The final workman was whisked away, a broom hastily swept up the last scattering of sawdust. The doors of 30 avenue Montaigne opened, and the guests poured in. Instantly, the atmosphere became even more highly charged. The building filled with a hubbub of shrill voices and excited laughter. After greeting the first few arrivals, Dior fled upstairs and refused to appear again.

Squabbling over seat numbers began almost immediately. It was astonishing how ruthless civilised women could become, pushing themselves shamelessly forward into seats allocated to others, and objecting loudly when asked to return to their own places.

Carmel Snow was an early arrival. Copper greeted her in the foyer.

'The hour of judgment has come,' Mrs Snow said. She raised her retroussé Irish nose and sniffed the air like a connoisseur. 'Hmmm. I smell panic. Where's your Monsieur Dior?'

'He'll be along in a minute,' Copper lied. She knew that he had retired to his cubbyhole to hide, his nerves shattered with the effort of the past few days. 'Let me show you to your seat.'

The flood grew. By ten thirty, the salons were full to bursting. People were even squashed three abreast all the way up the stairs. The *premières* and other members of staff hung over the balustrades above, peering down at the crowd. The smoke from dozens of cigarettes hazed the air.

Famous faces graced the front rows: Carmel Snow was seated next to Bettina Ballard of *Vogue*, who had long been predicting that French fashion was dead and who was wearing an expression of amused disdain. Marlene Dietrich was next to Jean Cocteau. Christian Bérard, his bushy beard wild as usual, sprawled in his chair, his pinpoint pupils indicating that he'd already had his morning opium. Jacinthe, as ever, was in his arms. Close to him sat the Comtesse de La Rochefoucauld, known as the smartest woman in Paris. Lady Diana Duff Cooper, the British ambassador's wife, was there – as was (Copper was surprised and pleased to see) Mrs Caffery, the American ambassador's wife. Actresses, society hostesses, women who were familiar from the newspapers and the newsreels were all jammed together, and apparently happy to be there.

Copper, with her camera slung around her neck, had been given a place next to the door of the main salon from which she could photograph both the models entering and leaving, and the audience. Dior was obsessed with the fear of having his designs stolen and had forbidden any camera other than Copper's on the premises. The Leica was proving invaluable now, light and quick as she snapped off the shots. She herself was wearing the first outfit Dior had ever made for her, hoping it would bring luck. The purse slung over her shoulder was stuffed with spare reels of 35mm film. And the parade was about to begin.

The first model, as luck would have it, was the inexperienced young secretary, Marie-Thérèse. She was dressed and ready to go in. But she was in a trembling state of nerves, tearfully whispering, 'I can't do it,' to the director as the announcer was calling, '*Numéro un!* Number one!'

'You can do it. And you will.'

The director gave Marie-Thérèse the sort of push given by master sergeants to unwilling parachutists. Marie-Thérèse shot forward into the room, white-faced. Copper followed her with the camera. Marie-Thérèse made her way down the narrow aisle somehow – and then, on the turn, disastrously stumbled and sprawled headlong into the audience with a crash. Copper's heart sank. What an awful beginning! Thank God Tian had not witnessed it. There were exclamations and giggles as she recovered and groped her way back out again, sobbing. Nobody had even noticed the outfit, which now had a cigarette burn in it. She was plainly incapable of showing another dress that morning.

But her place was taken by Tania, whose sweet, open face belied her experience. With supreme confidence, she stalked past the crowd, stepping high like a doe. There was an exclamation of outrage from someone in the audience. The deep red dress she wore, with its double-flared skirt, was not like anything that had been seen before, at least not since ration books and clothes coupons and mannish uniforms and khaki serge had come to dominate the clothes women wore. This was a living, walking fuchsia flower, wasp-waisted, full in the bust. The two layers of the spreading skirt made the waist even narrower.

Tania paused, looking around the room. All eyes were upon her. Then, smiling slightly, she pirouetted. As she did so, the skirt began to lift. Its multitude of exquisitely pressed pleats had disguised the fact that it had been made with a full twenty-five yards of crimson fabric. Before the disbelieving eyes of the audience, the red dress burgeoned, blossomed, filled the room with life and colour, expanding and billowing in astonishing lavishness, sweeping away the years of privation and gloom.

There were gasps. Then the audience burst into spontaneous and excited applause. Copper saw that notebooks were being produced and scribbled in, meaningful whispers were being exchanged. Something remarkable was about to happen. The atmosphere, already charged with expectation, had become electric. The air had begun to crackle.

The next model was already coming out, sleek and feline in an evening dress called 'Jungle', a bold leopard print, the waist cinched with a broad leather belt, and a wide-brimmed hat perched on the model's head. The daring, the effrontery of the look produced more gasps. Was this a slap in the face for restraint and economy?

The fourth outfit was one of the stars of the collection, the 'Suit Bar', a Dior classic that Carmel Snow had seen a version of in 1937. The severe, cream shantung jacket was tailored closely around the bust and hips, producing an impression of almost oriental sexiness; the heavy black skirt swung boldly with the model's gait. Indeed, the models – whether on Dior's instructions, or by mutual agreement – had all adopted a swift, pirouetting walk that was quite different from the stately progress that was customary. These girls pranced and danced. They looked lively; more than lively, they looked *alive*. They looked modern. They looked like women who were going places. Their walk was so swift that there was almost no time to take in the design; one had to be quick-eyed and alert.

And they pranced in the daintiest, lightest shoes anyone had seen for years, with pointed toes, thin straps and spike heels. Copper saw with amusement that the women in the front row were glancing ruefully at their own durable, heavy shoes, and trying to tuck them out of sight.

Three evening gowns in shimmering shades of blue followed, the models making miraculously swift changes in the *cabine*. And there were only five to carry the show now: the unfortunate Marie-Thérèse was *hors de combat*. Her outfits were already being distributed among the survivors.

Rapturous applause now greeted each new model. Pencils were racing over notebooks. The faces of the buyers were intent. There were whispered confabulations. To her joy, Copper saw assistants already sliding out of their seats and hurrying to the *cabine*. There could be only one explanation: the chequebooks were opening to secure early orders and cut out the opposition. Behind the scenes, the *vendeuses* would be busy. The occasional sound of raised voices from that direction indicated that buyers were already squabbling over the outfits.

The designs flew past with such panache that occasionally a flounce would sweep over an ashtray, or slap an incautious observer on the cheek. The announcer intoned the deliberately provocative names – *Soirée, Amoureuse, Pompon, Caprice, Amour* – with a tone of increasing excitement.

Copper overheard one of the Bloomingdale's women say, 'God help the buyers who bought before they saw this. This changes everything.'

And in French, she heard a man say, 'Dior has saved the season!'

She glanced across the room at Carmel Snow, and their eyes met for a moment. Mrs Snow nodded her blue-rinsed curls and mouthed the words, 'You were right.'

By eleven thirty, the first four dozen outfits had been shown, each one greeted more euphorically than the last. Dior's vision had stunned the room. Not a single corner had been cut. After the years of rationing, top-class traditional fabrics were almost impossible to obtain; but he had somehow obtained them. He had wanted silks dyed in the yarn, a process almost nobody bothered with any longer. Nowadays the fabric was dyed once it was woven. But this meant a loss of colour intensity, and Dior would not put up with that.

He had demanded real taffeta, faille and duchesse satin. These refined and expensive materials had long since stopped being made, and had been replaced by cheaper and coarser substitutes. Buyers had scoured the length and breadth of France to find the real thing.

He had insisted on twenty-four-carat gilding for accessories. Gold-tone was not acceptable. With gold almost unobtainable, this alone had meant a vast expenditure. The softest leather, the laciest lace, the work of the most skilled hands – all these had been sourced so that there should be no fault found in the smallest detail.

And now it had all paid off dazzlingly. The eye could hardly take in such a rainbow of colours: from rich, sulphurous yellows to deep crimson; from shimmering ultramarine to the palest pearl. Colours such as nobody had seen since the first shot was fired in 1939.

And the quantity of fabric – the sheer, extravagant, glorious abundance of it in each garment – was enough to make one faint. With their nipped-in waists and bell-like skirts, which imitated flowers, the outfits emphasised everything that was feminine and womanly. After almost a decade of tight, straight, drab little garments that skimped on everything, this was a feast beyond any anticipation. For fashionable women, it was coming from starvation to a banquet; and Copper knew that Christian Dior had planned exactly that effect. His genius was undeniable. He had dared to declare that the war was over. Rationing might exist, but in the magical kingdom of Christian Dior, it no longer applied.

Certain people in high positions were going to have a collective heart attack. It was unlikely that the established designers would be very pleased at the bursting of this new rival upon the scene. There might even be legal repercussions from the powers that be; after all, Dior was breaking every tenet of Utility, which was still in force. Copper had a dizzy vision of Tian being marched off by fashion police and locked in some grey dungeon to repent his crimes of extravagance. But that didn't matter. Nothing mattered beside the outpouring of colour, shape and sheer invention that he had unleashed on the world.

But Tian was missing his triumph. Copper slipped away through the crowd and made her way to the *cabine*. It was congested with buyers commanding, demanding, imploring. Tempers were flaring.

'Where's *Soirée*? I had it in my hands a moment ago, and now someone's stolen it!'

'I need *Corolle*! I have to have *Corolle*!'

'What do you mean, delivery in three months? I need four dozen now!'

She saw two smartly dressed women actually having a tug of war with a dress, the pleated silk in imminent danger of tearing as they dragged on each end.

'We can't keep up,' one of the *vendeuses* told Copper breathlessly. 'They've gone insane.'

Copper retreated and climbed up the crowded stairs to Dior's cubbyhole. She knocked on the door, but there was no answer. She opened it and peered in. Dior was hunched over on his chair with his eyes tight shut and his fingers stuffed in his ears like a frightened child.

She laid her hand gently on his shoulder. He looked up at her in alarm.

'Listen, Tian.' She gestured for him to remove his hands. Shakily, he pulled his fingers out of his ears.

'They're booing me,' he said in a tremulous voice, his eyes full of tears.

'No, Tian. Listen.'

From the salon downstairs came the sound of clapping and cheering. It died down as they listened, and in a short while, broke out again as the next model went in. 'They're cheering you. They're saying it's the most important collection since before the war,' she told him. 'Perhaps the most important collection ever. They're saying that you've changed everything, that you've created a new look, that nothing will ever be the same again. You don't need to block your ears anymore, my dear. You've done it. You've arrived.'

'What are you talking about?' he stammered, seeming dazed.

'You can come out of the closet now.'

She led him out on to the landing. They peered down at the excited crowd below and heard the applause. He squeezed her hand, his cheeks wet.

'Is it real?' he whispered.

'It's a triumph, Tian.'

Someone down below looked up and shouted, 'There's Dior!' A sea of faces turned his way. He tried to dart back out of sight, but Copper coaxed him into the light again. He looked down, dazed, at the crowd that was applauding him with *bravos* and blown kisses. A hot wave of cheering and love billowed up the staircase, redolent of cigarette smoke, Miss Dior and the scent of silk.

'My God. What have I done?' he asked.

'Can't you tell?' she replied. 'You've conquered the world.'

AUTHOR'S NOTE

A world may be conquered, but worlds come to an end. And a world – Dior's world – was already fading away.

A few days after that tumultuous first show, a photo shoot of Dior outfits was arranged by Marcel Boussac's newspaper *L'Aurore* to show off the New Look designs that everyone was clamouring to see. Ironically, the scarcity of fabric and the newness of the Dior collection meant that the outfits that had been shown were still the only ones in existence. They had already led a very exciting life – travelling incognito to smart hotels by night to be photographed by fashion editors or inspected by American store buyers, and then rushed back to avenue Montaigne early in the morning to the *vendeuses*, who needed them in the salon. This was the first occasion the outfits had been seen in the light of day, outside of Maison Dior.

The clothes were to be shown against the backdrop of the rue Lepic street market in Montmartre. The colourful, not to say somewhat squalid, background of the market, with its streets strewn with bruised cabbage leaves, was going to provide an interesting contrast to Monsieur Dior's exquisite (and very expensive) creations.

The outfits arrived in a large wooden crate on the back of a *camionette*. They, and the young models who were to wear them, were discreetly ferried into a bar at the end of the street. The market was bustling. Jugs of cheap wine from Beaujolais had arrived and were proving popular with the crowd. After the privations of the war years, food was still a subject of intense interest. This was Montmartre, where for four years people had picked up those trodden cabbage leaves to eat, while the Nazis took the rest.

The first model emerged and strutted past the stalls for the benefit of *L'Aurore*'s photographers. People stopped shouting and haggling to stare. A silence fell. Then a scream of insults came from a woman in the doorway of the tripe butcher. She was shaking her fist, her face furious. The model paused, her smile fading.

Another woman ran across the street with a basin of dirty water. She hurled it all over the model. Shocked, the wretched girl scuttled into the shelter of a shop doorway, trying to brush the muck off her outfit. But two more women were waiting for her there. Shrieking abuse, one grabbed a handful of her hair, while the other set about stripping the clothes off her back.

Other women – mostly middle-aged and shabby – had entered the fray. A burly matron with a towering *zazou* hairdo ripped the bodice out of the yellow gown, leaving the poor model clutching her skimpily clad breasts as she fled. Vile epithets cascaded on her.

The second model, who had unwisely tried to come to the aid of her colleague, was suffering the same fate. The women of the market had hard fists, and they were using them to belabour the envoys from the 7th arrondissement.

'*Salaude! Putain!*'

'Get out of here, whores!'

'Look at this bitch. She pays forty thousand francs for a dress, and my kids go without milk!'

The men were laughing, but the women meant business. They chased the girls, tearing at their hair and clothes, throwing tomatoes, right up to the door of the bar, where a large, white-aproned waiter fended them off. The models, tattered and spattered with filth, disappeared inside. The doors were locked in the face of the howling pursuers.

'And don't come back,' one screamed, throwing her missile, a rotten potato, at the door of the bar. 'Next time it will be Molotov cocktails.'

The battle between Left and Right was to mark France for several more decades. Names like Dior's, though they were synonymous with French culture, were also symbols of excess, and became targets of class hatred.

A success as swift and great as Dior's could hardly be free of controversy. Hostility had arisen in all sorts of quarters, far from the streets of Montmartre. The couturiers who had struggled – and failed – to win back a share of the United States' market were especially bitter about Dior's overnight conquest of the American buyers. Their animosity was expressed in sharp accusations that Dior's designs were wasteful of precious fabrics, were out of the reach of ordinary women, and were horribly retrograde at a time when women's fashions needed to move forward. Dior had cheated. He had seduced everybody using the unfair advantage of Boussac's money. He had broken the rules and was being richly rewarded for it.

On the other side of the Atlantic, there were also American detractors, chagrined to find that French fashion, despite all predictions, was not after all dead. To the disappointment of domestic couturiers, who had hoped that the capital of fashion had moved to New York, it was evident that American women were still eager for Parisian style, and that US dollars were pouring into the pockets of a man who fitted every preconception of what a Frenchman was like: smirking, devious, unmanly.

(Despite all that, copies of 'the New Look' had already been rushed into the windows of every main-street shop, costing a fraction of real Dior, made with inferior materials, cutting every corner, but aping the extravagant lines of the avenue Montaigne, and spreading the gospel of a return to luxurious femininity.)

These jealousies and rivalries had little effect on the Dior juggernaut, which was rolling on regardless. The part that couture was to play in the revival of the French economy was starkly evident. A bottle of perfume brought in more foreign revenue than a barrel of petroleum. A Paris frock was worth more than ten tons of coal. These very equations were evidence, in the eyes of some people, of the indefensible extravagance of haute couture.

Dior alone accounted for three-quarters of all fashion exports in 1947. He was a phenomenon. He might not have won the *Croix de guerre* or the *Légion d'honneur*, but he was a saviour of France nonetheless. More – he was a saviour of fashion itself, because he had single-handedly made being fashionable fashionable again. Ironically, he was already abandoning the extravagant designs that had brought him overnight fame in favour of more restrained and modern lines.

It seems easy to understand how and why Dior achieved this amazing success; and yet the reasons are elusive. There will always be an element of mystery. In a life that had been largely filled with sorrow and failure, the clouds had parted for a while, and some golden god had smiled down on him.

His lucky star had truly risen. The self-effacing back-room dweller was gone. In his place was Christian Dior, couturier: a man whose face was never out of the newspapers, whose name was spoken with awe, whose words took on the weight of law, and whose genius had become abundantly clear to his friends and detractors alike.

As with many of my novels, this one contains characters who were historical figures. I have tried, with careful research, to draw portraits of them. But this is a work of fiction, not a biography, and even the 'real' people in it are as much a product of my imagination as the ones

I made up. The thoughts, words and actions of all the characters in this book were invented by the author.

As sharp-eyed readers will spot, I have taken some liberties with the historical sequence of events; some of the happenings of 1944–1947 have been conflated and condensed in the timeline of the book to make them easier to follow. I beg the indulgence of true historians and repeat that this is entertainment, not history.

The opening of *Le Théâtre de la Mode* took place on 28 March 1945. The exhibition subsequently travelled to several countries, ending up in San Francisco, where the dolls, in poor condition, were abandoned. They and the original costumes have been restored, and are now exhibited at the Maryhill Museum of Art in Washington State.

Christian Bérard died in 1949 at the age of forty-seven, killed by drugs, alcohol, overwork and obesity.

After her ban, Suzy Solidor opened another club, far from Paris, in Cagnes-sur-Mer on the Côte d'Azur, where she continued to perform for many years. She made a partial return to grace in later life, appearing on television, and was hailed by a new generation as a gay icon. She died in 1983 at the age of eighty-two.

Catherine Dior received many awards for her bravery, including the *Légion d'honneur*. Hervé des Charbonneries was similarly decorated. He never divorced his wife, but lived and worked with Catherine until his death in 1989 at the age of eighty-four. She died in 2008 at the age of ninety-one. They are buried together in Callian.

Marcel Boussac made an immense fortune from the Dior fashion house. However, his grip on his businesses weakened, and he began to lose money. He was declared bankrupt shortly before his death in 1980. Maison Dior passed into new hands.

Carmel Snow was pushed out of *Harper's Bazaar* in 1958, and went into semi-retirement. She was succeeded by her charismatic protégée, Diana Vreeland.

Christian Dior was to enjoy his phenomenal success for only ten years. He had his first heart attack just weeks after his debut show.

He continued to consult Madame Delahaye regularly, and to this day, his lucky charms are part of the Dior mystique. The shy man who wanted an exclusive shop in a quiet street became one of the giants of the fashion industry. He enjoyed his wealth, buying a fifteenth-century mill near Fontainebleau and then a chateau in Grasse, and lavishly restoring both.

But travel, work and overeating took their toll on his constitution. He had another heart attack a few years later, and then a third, which killed him in 1957 at the age of fifty-two. He died at the card table at the Grand Hotel in the glamorous spa town of Montecatini Terme in Tuscany, in the company of a handsome young man whom he had described to friends as the love of his life. It was a death he might have designed for himself.

His funeral in Paris was attended by multitudes, and his coffin was covered with 30,000 bunches of lilies, his favourite flower. He was succeeded by his young protégé, Yves Saint Laurent. Along with Chanel and Fath, Dior is regarded as one of the most important influences on modern fashion.

Readers who would like some insights into the personality of Christian Dior can do no better than look for copies of his own books: *The Little Dictionary of Fashion* (1954), *Talking About Fashion* (1954) and *Christian Dior and I* (1957).

My heartfelt thanks go to the many people who made this novel possible, especially to Sammia Hamer; also to Emilie Marneur and Sana Chebaro, who were so inspirational from the outset, and to Mike Jones, Gillian Holmes and Gemma Wain, who worked so hard on the manuscript.

ABOUT THE AUTHOR

Photo © 2015 Marius Gabriel

Marius Gabriel has been accused by *Cosmopolitan* magazine of 'keeping you reading while your dinner burns'. He served his author apprenticeship as a student at Newcastle University, where, to finance his postgraduate research, he wrote thirty-three steamy romances under a pseudonym. Gabriel is the author of several historical novels, including the bestsellers *The Seventh Moon, The Original Sin* and the Redcliffe Sisters series, *Wish Me Luck As You Wave Me Goodbye* and *Take Me To Your Heart Again*. Born in South Africa, he has lived and worked in many countries, and now divides his time between London and Cairo. He has three grown-up children.